in THE NET OF DREAMS

Wm. MARK SIMMONS

POPULAR LIBRARY

An Imprint of Warner Books, Inc

A Time Warner Company

POPULAR LIBRARY EDITION

Copyright © 1990 by
All rights reserved.

Popular Library®, the fanciful P design, and Questar® are registered
trademarks of Warner Books, Inc.

Cover design by Don Puckey
Cover illustration by Darryll Sweet

Popular Library books are published by
Warner Books, Inc.
666 Fifth Avenue
New York, N.Y. 10103

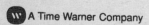 A Time Warner Company

Printed in the United States of America

First Printing: November, 1990

10 9 8 7 6 5 4 3 2 1

The Author owes a debt of gratitude
to a number of people for their advice and support
but he would be particularly remiss
if he failed to thank

Jan for opening the Second Door

Suzette
Annie
Carolyn
for advice and support
—Dreamwriters All

And especially
Dorothy
who believed from the very beginning

"We are such stuff
As dreams arc made of, and our little life
Is rounded with a sleep."

—*The Tempest*; Act IV, Scene 1

"What dreams may come,
When we have shuffled off this mortal coil?"

—*Hamlet*; Act III, Scene 1

"And now for something completely different. . . ."

—Monty Python's Flying Circus

PROLOGUE

★

DREAMWORLDS FILES/MEMORY EXTRACT
Subfile: FANTASYWORLD
Cephalic Index: P2A <Michael Kelson Straeker>
Cellular Unit: 927664[Om]793^216.557
              [Sub]41112120153111

The Ghost In the Machine.

That's what I am, Stracker mused as he stood before the highest window in his wizard's tower. He shook his head, then inhaled deeply, savoring the scent of freshly cut wheat. It smelled real, but the olfactory stimuli were as much a computerized contrivance as everything else.

Down below, a line of peasants were scything their way through the field adjacent to the old stone tower like a wave undulating in slow motion. "Serfs' up," he murmured, and wished Ripley was there to hear the pun. The rest of the Programming staff never seemed to appreciate his sense of humor.

He gazed at the fields and forests, spreading out before him like a patchwork quilt of green, gold, and brown, stitched with fifteenth-century stone and wattle huts. Again (as so many times before) he tried to dispel their apparent reality to his senses.

He couldn't. Even though he knew better.

The fields and forests were nothing more than Program-generated conceptualizations—mental projections of a master computer known as "The Machine." But since he no longer inhabited his real body, the senses of his avatar—or dreambody—perceived his surroundings as substantial. As valid.

And, for all intents and purposes, they were. . . .

Originally it had been a game, the ultimate evolutionary step in interactive computer programs. At the Dreamworlds Complex you could choose between several dozen Program-worlds, enter a sensory deprivation tank, and have your con-sciousness projected into an avatar in the Computer-fabricated milieu of your choice.

The Programworlds were not actualities within the physical universe. They were counter-realities that existed only in that infinitesimal void between the synapses of the human brain and the interface circuitry of the Dreamworlds supercom-puter.

The Ghost in the Machine. . . .

In a sense, every Dreamwalker in Fantasyworld was a ghost in The Machine. The difference was they all had real bodies to return to when the Game was over.

Mike Straeker, alias Daggoth the Dark, did not.

Another wave of dizziness swept over him as he contem-plated the view. Straeker staggered and clutched at the win-dow's mossy sill as vertigo was followed by a burst of blinding pain that ricocheted around the inside of his skull. It was always the same—no worse than the previous attacks. And no better. And unlikely to get any worse or any better, just certain to plague his existence for all of the days and months and years to come. Perhaps for all eternity. . . .

Cursing roundly, he turned and stumbled across the flag-stoned chamber toward the bookshelves.

Oh, he had been so clever—cheating death by escaping into the Computer. Trading the Real World for a Program-world and swapping his falling body for a healthy avatar. But, in his timidity, he had waited too long in making the final commitment: he had left the tumor behind, but not before it had taken a sizable chunk of brain tissue.

He had escaped the malignancy and his own mortality, but not soon enough to enter Fantasyworld whole.

Regrets and recriminations were useless. By now his body had been discovered; disconnected and removed from the suspension tank—buried somewhere. Or cremated. In the outside world Michael Kelson Straeker was officially dead.

And here? Even if his consciousness—his very existence —was now reduced to a state of piezoelectric patterns in a solid-state labyrinth, it seemed a far better alternative to that final, unknown void that waited beyond death. The question of his soul (mortal or immortal?) bothered him less than these damnable migraines!

The room was half-filled with dusty stacks of tomes and illuminated scrolls. He had hoped that one of Fantasyworld's arcane sciences might provide the cure for his malady. But hundreds of hours of research had yielded nothing in the way of relief and puzzling out the thaumaturgic texts made his headaches worse.

Another spasm of pain. He kicked the stack nearest his foot and the mystical books flew across the chamber. A couple of them flapped around the room a bit before deciding to roost on a high shelf.

There was a hiss behind him and he whirled around, tripping on his sorcerer's robe. A black cat, perched on a footstool in the corner, watched him with wide golden eyes. "Shut up!" snapped the mage in annoyance.

"But I didn't say anything," the cat protested.

"You were going to!"

The ebony feline gestured with one paw. "Am I that predictable now?"

"Yes." Daggoth the Dark tugged at his robe and adjusted his conical headgear, recovering a little of his lost dignity. "That's part of what makes you—"

"A familiar!" groaned the cat. It jumped down from the stool. "You want I should go see the apothecary again?"

"I'm not out of aspirin, yet!" He swung his foot at another stack of books. They prudently scattered in all directions.

"But it's your head again?" the cat asked. "How about an Antipain spell?"

"I need something permanent, dammit!" He flung himself down on the sofa and moaned. "It's not just the pain—it's the gaps in my memory. If I have a train of thought, it gets derailed." He shook his head. "Blank spots . . . mental fuzziness . . . not to mention occasional double vision."

"Sounds more like the end result of a three-day bender to me."

"Out!" bellowed the magician. "Out, out, damned cat!"

"I'm only trying to help," it protested peevishly, backing toward the door.

"No one can help me," Daggoth the Dark said softly. "The answer I seek can't be found in the books and tomes of lesser sorcerers. I'm the greatest mage left to this world, and not even I can conjure myself to health!" He smiled ruefully. "Magician, heal thyself."

The black-furred famulus paused halfway out the door. "Well, if magic itself is not powerful enough, perhaps the gods are. That is, if you want a cure badly enough to get religion."

"The gods?" Daggoth snorted. "Bob Ripley and I created those so-called gods. Shams and fakes: we programmed most of them out of textbooks on mythology. This world has only one true god and that is The Machine! I should know: before I fled from the world beyond, I was its High Priest. *I* am the Programmer!" He started to rise but suddenly fell back and covered his eyes with a shaking hand. "Was," he corrected in a small voice. "I *was* the Programmer. The Chief of Programming, to be precise. They must have someone new, by now."

"Then you are out of favor with your god?"

"Out of favor?" The man considered. "Nooo. More like out of touch. No console, no neuralnets, no means of interface to access the Program's peripheral data banks. In other words, out of luck!"

Straeker/Daggoth thought upon the reality beyond the boundaries of the Program, of the Access/Monitor Ports in Dreamworlds Control. "If I were on the outside, I could pull my original psyche-patterns out of the Cephalic Index Files

—impress those healthy *engrams* over the damaged template I'm stuck with.'' He sat up, a flicker of hope starting. "That might restore the neural paths and memory clusters lost to the tumor since that last psyche-scan!'' Then he clutched his head. "But it's no use! I don't have that kind of access from *inside* the Program!'' Bereft of hope, he lay back down.

His familiar did not understand most of the words, but had caught the tone behind them. "Then your god will not help you?''

"My 'god' can go to hell!''

A long and thoughtful pause. "He can?''

"Yes,'' snapped the mage, turning his face to the wall, "it can!''

"Oh! I did not comprehend before. This one you call 'The Machine'—it is a Demon?''

"As appropriate a term as any I could devise,'' muttered Daggoth.

"Then why do you not conjure this Demon and demand its services? Adjure its cooperation with bell, book, and candle?''

It took a moment to sink in. "What?'' He erupted from the couch like a volcano with whooping cough.

"You know the process better than I.'' The cat was backing away again, trying to keep one eye on its apoplectic master and the other on its own escape route. "Draw a pentagram, conjure the Demon, command it to do your bidding.''

"Conjure the—'' The wizard nearly choked on a laugh. "How do you conjure a—thing of logic and circuitry—by magic, to alter its own internal reality? You're talking about summoning The Machine to appear in one of its own Master Programs! The Program would be running the Computer instead of vice versa! That's''—he stopped, a stunned expression slowly giving way to a beatific smile—"entirely feasible!''

The concept was so outrageous that Straeker was momentarily confounded by its sheer audacity. Hope flared again and it took all his willpower just to sit down and think it through.

The Programworlds were maintained by an external staff of technicians. The Programming crew—particularly those directly responsible to the Chief of Programming—had the power to manipulate the various Programs and Subprograms. Given time and access authority, they could alter the Program Matrix itself.

But that was from the outside.

His head began to throb again. *Think!* he chided himself. *If external reprogramming is impossible, then what of internal Program manipulation?*

A psyche, visiting any of Dreamworlds' Programworlds, resided in an avatar appropriate to that particular environment. But like one's real body in the real world, the dreambody was subject to the laws and events of that particular Programworld. If his avatar threw a rock at a window, the Computer would calculate weight, force, and trajectory to decide if it would hit or miss. It would then produce the appropriate physical results.

But Dreamworlds did not stop at duplicating the physics of mundane reality. Here, in Fantasyworld, magic was very much a part of natural law and order. The dreamer/avatar cast his spells, the Computer made calculations based on component, ability, and magic-theory tables, and then produced the appropriate magical results.

Or failures, as he too well knew.

In short, Nature *and* Magic in this world were governed by the Computer. The Machine was, indeed, god.

Of course, The Machine still took its programming from the outside, was still subject to the external monitoring and guidance systems—but it was also self-programming. It made thousands of adjustments every second: every time someone lit a fire, chopped down a tree, cast a spell, the Program minutely changed and updated itself. Every action taken in Dreamworlds was a minuscule reprogramming of the whole system. In effect, it *was* possible to change the Matrix from within its own context—at least in a lilliputian sense.

So if a little—then why not a lot? And if the Computer was programmed internally as well as externally, why not summon The Machine itself for direct programming and input?

He frowned suddenly: he knew why not.

That process was tantamount to an internal takeover. It

would certainly interrupt external access, and whether that
condition lasted for just a nanosecond, or a bit longer, he
couldn't be completely certain.

But that was, he decided finally, their problem and not his,
as long as his tampering didn't undo the basic structure of
Dreamworlds' Operating System. There had been some evidence of Matrix instability of late and he would have to be
careful. It wouldn't do him any good to find a cure if he
destroyed his own world in the process!

The door swung open and a turtle slowly shuffled into the
room, walking somewhat erect on its hind limbs and carrying
a notepad.

Straeker frowned and consulted the digital readout on a
large, wall-mounted hourglass. "Pascal, are you early?"

"Uh, nope, your mageship," it answered leisurely, "late
as usual."

The wizard softly cursed the inherent glitches of silicon-
based chronometry and reclined upon the sofa again. "Not
that it matters today," he inquired mildly, "but why are you
late?"

"Uh, welp, as your wizardness must surely remember, I
am a turtle—order Chelonia, suborder Cryptodira—"

"Yes, yes," Straeker/Daggoth waved the answer away.

"—a toothless, slow-moving reptile, according to the *Phy-
lum Factorum*," continued the toothless, slow-moving reptile. "I mean, if you wanted a subroutine with some speed,
your shamanhood should have considered some other form
for anthropomorphism—"

"And not mix my metaphors," Daggoth concluded.
"Enough, already! I'm going to want you to take some
notes." He cleared his throat. "A lot of notes!"

The turtle opened its notepad and displayed a pencil.
"Logged on," it stated in testudineous tones.

"And then I want you to get a copy of my journal over to
Riplakish of Dyrinwall, ASAP."

Pascal would have raised an eyebrow had he possessed
one but had to settle for nodding in what he hoped was an
ironic manner.

Daggoth tried to pick up his train of thought where he had
left off. His only other worry was that he had to pull it off

without betraying his presence to the outside staff. To the Dreamworlds Project and Cephtronics Inc., he no longer existed—except as a bronze plaque on a wall somewhere.

Here, in Fantasyworld, he was no longer Michael K. Straeker, Chief of Programming: he was Daggoth the Dark, an archmage of such power that there was nothing this world might deny him. He didn't want anyone or anything to interfere with that.

"Chief?"

Straeker/Daggoth waved to the cat to be silent, got up, and wandered over to the book stacks again. *Must think carefully*, he told himself, *cover all the angles*.

He hadn't done anything legally or morally wrong, he was sure—at least, not yet. But he was just as sure that if Cephtronics learned the true nature of his existence within the Program, they would be very unhappy with him.

"Chief?"

No. Better to stay completely dead and buried. If they found him out, the best treatment that he could hope for would be that reserved for a lab specimen. And he did not relish the thought of spending the rest of his "life" being poked, prodded, measured, and spied upon.

"Chief!" yelled the cat.

"What?" he yelled back.

"What if you cannot control the Demon once you summon him?"

"Well—" His gaze took in the cat and the turtle, both looking back at him expectantly, and his eyebrows raised speculatively. "We're going to find ourselves in one hell of a mess!"

PART I

Rude Awakenings

★

Dreamer of dreams, born out of my due time,
Why should I strive to set the crooked straight?

—William Morris, *The Earthly Paradise*

CHAPTER
ONE

★

THE trouble with first-year fencing students is they all tend to think they're Zorro before the semester is half over. A few even go so far as to challenge me to a match after the first month. I guess it's a natural temptation when the instructor wears a leg brace and an eyepatch. So once or twice a semester I find myself called out like an ageing gunfighter; challenged by some young punk on the piste, hot to make a quick reputation.

I shouldn't complain: it provides the opportunity to demonstrate that true swordsmanship owes as much to skill and technique as speed and strength. And I get a little more respect from the class after their latest champion takes a drubbing from the Old Man—which is what a fourteen-year difference in our respective ages makes me, I suppose.

My latest would-be D'Artagnan was growing more frustrated by the second. Bad enough to be beaten by a gimp with the whole class looking on. What made it worse was realizing that my attention was elsewhere while my foil held him at bay.

Normally I would pretend to pay attention to my opponent—out of courtesy, if nothing else. I was rarely mindful of the observers that hung out around the periphery of the gym—but I knew this face from somewhere and I couldn't quite place it.

To say that she was beautiful would not do her justice; beauty must be anchored in character or it's just an empty freak of nature. Framed in a cascade of red hair, her features promised just the right blend of sophistication and sensuality. A knowing, worldly-wise countenance that spoke volumes of experience, yet unmarked by worldliness. Almost a contradiction; a face that was poised and yet open.

And speaking of open, Carter had allowed his foil to drift to the left on my feint: I cut my blade over his in a *coupé* and lunged. Scored. Ended the match five–zip.

We unmasked, degloved, and shook hands like civilized men of the twenty-first century.

"You're getting better every week, John," I told him. In point of fact, he had finally figured out that my eyepatch meant that I was blind on my left side.

He grinned sheepishly and the end-of-period bell sounded. My class turned from docile herd to thundering stampede in the direction of the showers.

The redhead moved toward me as the rest of my fencing students left the gymnasium. She was tall—five ten, maybe five eleven. And I couldn't help noticing that she had one of those impossibly perfect figures—the kind found on the covers of old paperback books and cheap holo-zines. The only other place you found women who looked like this was in one of Dreamworlds' program milieus—

Then I made the connection: she was a Dreamwalker.

More likely a Dreammaster, since her face was familiar. My interest suddenly withered: I could guess why she was here and what she wanted.

"Dr. Ripley?"

But: *Innocent until proven guilty*, I reminded myself, grimly switching into my "polite" mode. "Yes?"

"I am Natasha Skovoroda," she replied, extending her hand.

I started to take it and then froze with a second shock of recognition. No wonder she had looked familiar; Natasha Skovoroda was more than just a Dreammaster, she was an international star. And, more importantly, she had taken triple

Gold in fencing at the last Olympics: Foil, Epée, and Sabre.

"I'm honored," I said, finally remembering to take her proffered hand.

"Honored enough to have a drink with me?" Her voice had a low, husky quality that triggered an involuntary shiver between my shoulder blades.

"A drink?"

"Your choice. I will buy."

"I don't drink."

"You must get terribly dehydrated." There was a dryness in her voice that won me. "What about dinner, then? I assume that you do eat?"

"Are you still buying?"

"Of course."

I considered. In spite of Ms. Skovoroda's standing, this encounter had "setup" written all over it. There had been other such approaches—some less subtle. "Okay," I gambled. "Dinner of your choice. But who pays for it depends on the coming negotiations."

"Negotiations?"

"Ms. Skovoroda—"

She laughed, flashing perfect teeth. "You are the first American to pronounce it correctly with the first try. But, please: Tasha."

"All right. Tasha. It's obvious you're asking for an opportunity to parley, not a date."

She looked rueful. "I am that transparent?"

"I get this approach every couple of months," I explained. "And not on account of my good looks."

She colored slightly but recovered well. "And do you turn them down?"

"Every one."

"And myself?"

"You can tell me what it is that you really want over dinner. If I agree to it, you can pick up the check. If I turn you down, Dutch treat. Sound fair?"

She studied me. "You are a man of principles."

"I'm a creature of conscience."

She hesitated and I could almost hear the mental gears shifting.

"I know a place where the food is good and the atmosphere is—how you say—comfortable?"

The stilted English coupled with the faint Russian accent had charmed me into submission.

I took my medication before hitting the showers.

Normally I would wait until I was leaving the gym, giving me a safety margin to make the drive home. Tonight, however, I wanted to give my brain cells the chance to sober up before I engaged in any mental fencing with Ms. Skovoroda.

I could have taken the easy route years ago: a few well-placed electrodes and a simple push-button. When the pain gets to be too much, a little microamperage along the right neural paths makes it all go away. The doctors bring it up every now and then: the drugs must be rotated to maintain their effectiveness, are potentially addictive, have numerous unpleasant side effects. And they're less efficient: even doped to the gills, the pain is still there. It doesn't bother me very much anymore. But it's always there.

I can handle the chemicals. I know there are ten thousand bodies on ten thousand slabs every year who have said the same thing. But I believe I can deal with the chemicals.

It's the electrodes that frighten me. . . .

I took a long, hot shower, dressed slowly, and called a cab. I didn't like leaving my car in the university parking lot overnight, but if the drugs are safer, it's because I don't work without a net.

The "comfortable atmosphere" turned out to be a penthouse apartment in one of the city's ritziest hotels. I settled on the sofa and studied my surroundings while she dialed room service.

There were few personal effects in sight but a nearby bookshelf was overflowing with reading cassettes. A closer examination revealed a collection of authors that read like a Who's Who of fantasy and heroic fiction. One author, however, was conspicuously missing—even though I knew better, I could almost hope. . . .

The painting over the fireplace—an old-style oils on

canvas—sent hope to the showers when I noticed it a moment later. I got up and walked over to examine it when Natasha excused herself to go change. Her use of the phrase ". . . into something more comfortable . . ." brought to mind a number of truly awful movie scenarios, but I reminded myself that the average Soviet citizen is unfamiliar with the sleazier aspects of American cinema.

I had never seen Ms. Skovoroda's Dreamworlds avatar but there was no mistaking the identity of the woman in the portrait. There were differences, to be sure: the avatar had long, flame-colored hair that fell in waves over her shoulders and down her back—much thicker and redder than Natasha's, with two streaks of quicksilver that framed the face. The eyes were a deeper green—more of an emerald hue—and the arching copper brows and the pointed tips of her ears peeking through her hair indicated a mix of Human and Elvish blood.

In spite of the changes, her avatar's face was her own. Most Dreamwalkers favored dreambodies with a physical appearance somewhat different from their own. But then so few of them were as stunning as Natasha Skovoroda in real life.

As for her outfit, her armor did not amount to much more than a chainmail bikini—a minimal breastplate and an insubstantial cross between a miniskirt and a loincloth. Even though the outfit was composed of small metal plates and interlocking links of chain, it could hardly be considered functional in any sense of the original intent. Rather, it was what the well-undressed pulp heroine was expected to wear in stories devoted to pubescent male fantasies. I had to admit, though, that it did show off her body to a great advantage.

Which, I supposed, was mostly the point.

"What do you think?"

I continued to study the painting without turning. "I can see how increased exposure has brought you international fame." She chuckled, a low throaty sound, and I caught the scent of freshly applied perfume. "I should think, however, that you'd want a bit more protection. From wind as much as from weapons."

She sighed. "Perhaps—but it is the standard Amazon battledress."

I shook my head. "That's not the dress code I programmed. The Amazon culture never flaunted their sexuality."

"Much has changed," she agreed. Her voice took on a serious tone. "That is why I have asked you here to talk."

I turned then. I had hoped—not really expected, you understand—but hoped that this time it might be different. Alas, her "something confortable" was more peignoir than lounging outfit: the stage was set for the requisite seduction scene. She handed me a glass of wine, and had I been wearing a tie, I'm sure she would've loosened it for me. "Ah, yes. Talk. Well. Let's get down to business."

She sat on the sofa and patted the cushion beside her. I decided that I was big enough to protect myself, so I sat next to her.

"Dr. Ripley—"

"You want me to 'train' you," I interrupted bluntly.

"What do you mean?" Her hand went to her throat in a maidenly gesture of surprise. It was so self-consciously staged that I had to fight back a smile.

I sighed. "You're hardly the first. With dozens of Dreammasters offering advanced training, people still track me down to ask for a shot at some supposed inside track." I shook my head. "I haven't been back inside since Dreamworlds went public a little over five years ago. I have no official standing in the Dreamranks—yet people come to me as if I were some kind of omnipotent Dreamlord who can unlock the forbidden secrets of the Fantasyworld milieu."

"Can you blame us? After all, you wrote the books"— she nodded at a table across the room and I saw what I had missed before: a set of *The Kishkumen Chronicles* by yours truly—"and created most of the original Program. If anyone could give a Dreamwalker an inside edge, it would naturally seem to be you."

"Perhaps. But the Dreamnet is five years older—five years different. And what would be the ethics of handing the winning secrets over to the highest bidder—assuming I was privy to such in the first place?"

She bristled at that. "I am not asking for Program secrets! I am asking for some basic training! I need a guide, a navigator in the Net!"

I shrugged. "Like I said, there are dozens of competent, if not exceptional, Dreammasters. All with up-to-date experience. Who needs a rusty old has-been?"

She leaned forward and her robe parted in such a way as to almost seem unintentional. "I do," she breathed.

"Why?" I leaned back to avoid a possible collision.

"Because you are the best!"

"Uh-uh. You're the best," I asserted. "Triple Olympic Gold medalist, international star, darling of the Networks, Dreammaster. . . ." I spread my hands. "How can I offer you any superiority in training?"

"The people who know say that you are the best fencer in the entire world," she answered. "That you are unbeatable in any of the European styles. . . ."

A flattering answer but it was my turn to shake my head. "Maybe once. If it were true, that was years ago. I'm certainly too old now—"

"Thirty-six is not too old!"

"Thirty-four. And you're the one with Olympic Gold, not me."

"Everyone says you would have taken the Gold if you had made the matches in France! You were on the US team—I have seen the tri-dees of your bouts! You were the best!"

"Past tense," I qualified. "The accident that kept me out of the Olympics then still slows me down. I have almost seven pounds of metal in my body: most of it is surgical implants, but some is residual shrapnel from the crash. The brace covers a leg that has more scar tissue than muscle and ends with only half of a foot. And this"—I ran a finger over my eyepatch—"adds the difficulty of monocular depth perception. I have three students in my advanced class, all barely twenty, who have more stamina, strength, and agility and could most likely take me in three out of five bouts."

"If they had your experience and skill," she argued. "Then, maybe, in regulated competition. But in Fantasyworld the swordplay is not regulated."

"Meaning?"

"When you programmed Fantasyworld, you were a respected fencer—a Master in the European forms. Most

Dreamwalkers are 'hack-and-slashers,' but the best cross blades in some hybridization of the European schools."

"That's to be expected, I guess. What's your point?"

"Just this"—she paused for effect—"you are half a decade better today than you were five or six years ago when you created Fantasyworld and set the abilities of the Constructs."

"Constructs?"

"The artificial people that are constructs of the Program as opposed to the real Dreamwalkers and their avatars."

"Oh." Another example of how out-of-touch I'd become.

"Anyway, your original superiority plus a five-year edge might be enough in itself, but you have studied Kendo since then. And the word is that you are very good at that, also."

"Other Dreamwalkers have studied and used the Kendo disciplines," I argued. "The Oriental styles are advantageous at times, but nothing foolproof. And there are Dreammasters who do training in Kendo."

"But those few who have utilized Kendo have no training in the European styles: theirs was pure Kendo." She smiled. "What happens when a Master of the European blades also becomes proficient with the Japanese longsword?"

I shrugged. If she could fake sexual attraction, I could feign modesty.

"Your Kendo instructor says that you have developed a combination of the Oriental and European styles that is quite astounding!"

"What else did he say?" Oshi had been rather noncommittal about my progress as of late.

"That it lacks the purity of the True Way, but that it is possibly the deadliest technique that he has ever seen. High praise from an Asian swordmaster."

"I'm sure he'd be willing to teach you everything that he's taught me."

She rested a hand on my shoulder, a sure sign of trouble to come. "I want *you* to train me."

"I'll be starting a new series of fencing classes next semester—"

"I want you to train me personally. In Fantasyworld. I

need the best guide in the Dreamnet *and* I will make it worth your while!"

"Ms. Skovoroda—"

"Please; Tasha."

"—if you know so much about me, then you should know that I don't need the money."

"I did not say anything about money," she replied, leaning forward again. This time her garment fell open with no question of intent, revealing flawless skin. "I said I would make it worth your while."

I got up with a little concern that some vestigial interest might be showing. "I hate to eat and run, so I think I'll just skip dinner."

She reached out, caught my arm, and pulled me back to the sofa with surprising strength. "I am sorry. I should have known this would be the wrong approach. Please—sit back down." Her voice and her expression said that she was genuinely sorry, and she pulled her clothing together.

"There's something you're not telling me," I offered after a long silence. She didn't answer so I pursued the question that was banging around at the back of my mind.

"Natasha Skovoroda does not need training from a man who has not Dreamwalked since the Tournaments were first opened to the public. I doubt there is any Dreammaster—currently in or out of Fantasyworld—who is the equal of a triple Gold medalist. The next Tournament—Dreamquest VI, isn't it?—doesn't start for another six months. And I don't buy this 'guide' routine for a minute!" I sighed. "Why don't we stop dancing and you tell me just exactly what it is you really want from me."

She stared off into space for a long time before answering. "The vice chairman of the CPSU Central Committee has disappeared."

It took a moment for the meaning of her words to fully register. "We're talking about the vice chairman of the USSR?"

She nodded.

"What does this have to do with you?"

"I have been recruited to find him."

"You're KGB?"

She shook her head forcefully. "No. But I suppose you might say that I am temporarily working for them." She bit her lip pensively. "They can be most persuasive. . . ." She shivered and returned to the subject of the vice chairman.

"He disappeared in the Dreamworlds Complex while on a goodwill tour of your country. It seems that Comrade Dankevych tempers his love for Mother Russia with a love for the European Renaissance and medieval myth. We know that he took a side trip into the Fantasyworld Program. In his last communiqué he likened his excursion to Dreamworlds to Khrushchev's historic visit to your Disneyland in the previous century. Nothing has been heard from him since then and so I was recruited to use my Dreamnet status to find him."

I leaned back against the cushions. "I still don't see how I can help. I haven't set foot on Cephtronics property for nearly half a decade. I'm on good terms with maybe a dozen people who are still inside, but I doubt that dropping my name will open any doors for you. In fact, it would probably do just the opposite." I shook my head. "I just don't see how I can be of any help to you."

She moved down the length of the sofa to sit beside me. "Go in with me!"

"To Cephtronics?"

"To Fantasyworld!"

"Why? This sounds like a job for the techs. Have you asked them for help? They can locate any Dreamwalker on their monitors in a matter of seconds."

"No. It was considered before I was even brought into this."

"And?"

"Dreamworlds claims that Borys Dankevych left with his aides yesterday. The KGB says he did not. Obviously, someone is wrong."

"Or lying," I agreed. "So what is your next step?"

"I have been ordered to go back into Fantasyworld and begin my investigation there."

"What's stopping you?"

"Cephtronics. They claim that Dreamworlds is closed for

Program enhancements and upgrade maintenance. No one is allowed to log on the Dreamnet until further notice.'' She gazed at the floor in defeat. "I thought you might know something—might have heard something. Since you created the Fantasyworld Program, I thought you might know another way in. I understand that it is quite customary for programmers to create a 'back door' for their programs—a way to get in that no one else knows about. I thought—''

"That I could sneak you in my back door?" I shook my head. "This is a different kind of program, Tasha. It doesn't work the same way.'' While that was true, I did have a back way in that nobody knew about. I just wasn't ready to spill my secrets to an unknown pretty face who had just admitted to working for the KGB. "I'm sorry you've wasted your time.''

She shook her head and began toying with the hair at the back of my neck.

"Oh, I do not think so. The night is still young. . . .''

The last sensation I clearly remembered was something cold pressing against the side of my neck.

I knew it was a dream even though it came with all of the sensations of waking up. A man in a military officer's uniform was standing at the foot of the bed.

"Art thou the Ghost of Armageddon Past?" I mumbled. "Or Armageddon Yet to Come?" My experience with most normal dreams is that you play it fast, loose, and you stay on top. Never give a phantasm an even break; your subconscious can be murder.

The phantasm with the birds on his cap and shoulders spoke. "Dr. Ripley?"

"No," I lied, turned over, and pulled the pillow over my head.

The pillow was removed. "Robert Remington Ripley the Third?"

"Never heard of him," I groaned as I tried to pull the covers over my head. They were removed as well. The overhead light came on and the room was suddenly filled with stocky Marine-types.

"Go away," I moaned.

"I'm sorry, Mr. Ripley," the phantom colonel responded, "but I have my orders."

"The name is Schwartz," I muttered. "Ralph Schwartz. And you are nothing but nocturnal indigestion: a bit of cheese, a piece of undigested meat. . . ."

"Sergeant," interrupted the rude phantom colonel, "the shower. . . ."

Since none of this was real, I was pondering the Freudian significance of the Marines using Natasha Skovoroda's shower facilities when several pairs of hands gently but firmly lifted me out of bed.

I eventually stopped screaming and they turned off the cold water. I wrung out my eyepatch and looked reproachfully at the colonel who handed me a couple of dry towels. "You," I announced, "are not a nice person."

He shrugged. "You think I'm bad now, just see what happens if you're not dressed and ready to go with us in ten minutes."

"Where are we going?"

"Dreamworlds."

Gingerly I shook my aching head. "I just came from there."

"Dreamworlds, Utah."

"I prefer my own version, thank you."

The man sighed and tilted his cap back on his head. "Dr. Ripley, I am under explicit orders to bring you in. Your choices in this matter are very simple. We are going to escort you to the Dreamworlds Complex. You decide whether we do that as an honor guard or as a chain gang." He glanced at his watch. "Nine minutes, son."

I adjusted the black patch over what used to be my left eye and favored him with an obstinate look. As my cosmetic surgeon had been content with mere function as opposed to the aesthetics, most of my facial expressions are somewhat less than encouraging. "I'm a great believer in civil disobedience."

The colonel returned my gaze thoughtfully. "They said you might be reluctant."

"And what did 'they' tell you to do if I was?"

"Give you a message." He folded his arms across his beribboned chest. "Dr. Cooper said to tell you that you were right. She says: 'Beautiful Dreamer is having a Nightmare.' "

"No shit?" I dried off hurriedly and began pulling on my knee brace.

No one mentioned Natasha Skovoroda and there was no evidence of her presence from the night before. Not even a discarded mini-ampule from the trick ring she drugged me with. I wondered how much I'd told her as they ushered me up to the roof and into a waiting military transport.

Within two minutes we were headed west at mach two and accelerating.

CHAPTER
TWO

★

OG was in a foul mood.

It wasn't just the godsbecursed sunburn—though he had been above surface far longer than was sensible. No, it was that the need was on him and he was caught in an ethical (and financial) conflict.

Og was a Bridge-Troll, an occupation quite common among the more intelligent Water-Trolls. He lived in the Pooder River where a rude bridge arched the flood. Travelers who wished to cross the Pooder within twenty miles of Casterbridge—with minimum risk to life and limb—were permitted to use the bridge as long as they paid Og.

The Casterbridge bridge was not only a Troll bridge, it was also a toll bridge. Signs proclaimed this fact at either end of the wooden span in seven different languages. Travelers were admonished to "Stop!" And: "Pay Troll!"

Og would pop through a trapdoor in the middle of the traverse and hold out a green and horny palm. If a customer seemed reluctant or unnecessarily slow, he would growl, squint his goggly eyes at the offender, and begin to salivate. At his best, Og could salivate like a waterfall during the monsoon season.

Yet, good as business was, three hundred years of it was

enough to bore the most unimaginative of minds, and Og longed for the "good old days." His fondest memories were of the times when he and his friend Grom had initiated brawls with the border patrols, tossing the knights into the deep part of the river and making bets on whether or not they would make it back to the shore. Og always won because the Ogre would invariably bet on the knights: Grom never seemed to grasp the negative effects of plate armor on human buoyancy.

Thinking hadn't been one of Grom's fortes, but he had been a lot of fun when it came to frightening pregnant women, knocking over occupied privies, scattering compost heaps, and peeking in bedroom windows late at night.

Now Grom was gone, and people accepted a Bridge-Troll as one of the normalities of everyday life. His own daily existence had been reduced to bridge maintenance and repair; civil service duty at the Casterbridge border.

And as if that wasn't degrading enough for a Troll who had once terrorized the kingdom's most puissant champions, three days ago he had had a most unfortunate encounter with a rather gruff family of billygoats.

Og winced and chewed his nails thoughtfully. Where he wasn't sunburned he still bore the hoofmarks and hornprints of the biggest of those stupid beasts. Worse, still, they had done a number on his bridge that had cost him three days of both shade and tolls. He spat out the mangled nails, took a new mouthful, and resumed hammering with a sigh. The droop of his shoulders was deceptive: Og was a Troll spoiling for a fight.

He knew that pummeling potential customers was inherently bad for business, and with extensive bridge repairs, he needed all the additional revenue he could garner. But Trollish nature is not easily subjugated. After three centuries of civil service Og felt an even greater need to do a little therapeutic brawling.

Two riders came into view and Og paused to get a good look at his prospects: a large Human barbarian and a petite Elvish woman. The female was an unknown factor, but the barbarian looked positively dangerous. Good!

<<*I made a conscious shift in perspective, mentally pulling back to PV5*>>

When they reached the bridge they dismounted and led their horses. The barbarian wore some furskins, a bone-link breastplate, and very little else. Slung across his broad back was a claymore—a two-handed sword that measured six feet from point to pommel, or about six inches shorter than the man himself.

<<Shift to PV2>>

He had a sullen, craggy face with long, thick black hair that was barely kept out of his eyes by a leather headband. His body was massive with well-defined muscles and wall-to-wall pectorals. Eyeing those, Og began to have second thoughts.

The woman, in contrast, hardly topped five feet in height. What could be seen of her form beneath her leather jerkin and breeches seemed to lessen the threat of the shortsword that hung at her side and the shortbow across her back. But Elves were more unpredictable than Humans and Og had good reasons—based on experience—not to dismiss one of them too lightly.

<<Shift to PV4>>

When they were almost to the centerpoint of the bridge, the trapdoor popped up and Og thrust his head and shoulders through the opening, putting him at eye level with the Elf. He scrunched upward a couple of feet more to loom over the Human.

"You, I assume," said the barbarian calmly, "are the Troll that I am supposed to pay. How much?"

<<PV2>>

Og was disappointed: this was going well and that was too bad. On the other hand, the Elf did look a bit nervous, maybe something could be made of that.

"Four copper pieces," he rumbled in a liquid, yet gravelly, voice. It sounded like he was trying to talk and gargle at the same time and the Elf tried to hide a sudden smile. Og felt his temper nearing critical mass.

The barbarian pulled out a silver piece. Now Og smiled. He had teeth reminiscent of two display racks filled with badly rusted daggers. "Exact change, please." In all fairness, it should be noted that Trolls have no aptitude for making change. But Og had a way of saying "please" that completely divorced the word from any pleasant connotations.

"Sorry," the barbarian mumbled apologetically, "I don't have four coppers." He dropped the silver piece into the Troll's ham-sized palm. "You may keep the change."

Og hesitated: he had never met a polite barbarian before and he didn't much like it. Nor did he like the man's combination of muscles and six-foot sword. And he usually heeded his premonitions—he hadn't lived to be five hundred and thirty-seven years old by being incautious. Still, Og had a burning need to fight someone and couldn't help speculating: might it be interesting to throw someone in the river who had an even chance of making it back to shore?

The situation was decided as the barbarian, puzzled over the delay, inquired: "Excuse me, something got your goat?"

<<PV3>>

As Og lunged, the barbarian reached for his sword. The next few seconds were a blur but the culmination of events was crystal clear: Og brought his teeth down on the barbarian's sword hand, effectively separating it from the wrist. The man fainted and Og was left facing a very angry Elf with a drawn bow.

Now the chances of an Elvish archer missing the mark at this range were roughly the same as a Dwarven warrior passing out from drinking a lite beer. And Og didn't like the looks of the arrow she had pulled back to her cheek: It was black and green and covered with an assortment of nasty-looking runes. He even fancied that he could hear a high-pitched humming sound emanating from the shaft.

"Back off," the girl ordered sharply.

While Og tended to have his impetuous moments from time to time, no one could accuse him of being deliberately stupid. He dropped back through the trapdoor faster than Santa Claus down a chimney. . . . .

The encoded Cephalic recording ended and the memlink was broken.

I raised the eyeshields on my dreamset, shifted point of view one last time, and pulled the sensorweb from my head.

"So?" Dr. Cooper's encrypted message had persuaded me to come along peaceably, but I wasn't in a mood to be overly cooperative. The room was now full of Dreamworlds techies.

Vanauken folded his arms and leaned back against a console. The portly little man's attempt at nonchalance was undermined by the beads of perspiration collecting below his receding hairline and above his pale lips. Under normal circumstances he probably conducted Dreamworlds tours for visiting low-level dignitaries.

"As I said before, this recording was made during the period that the Anomaly took place. You detected no sensory distortion because the discernible effects occurred just after the point where we stopped playback."

"So?" I prompted again.

Vanauken frowned and started to fidget. "What makes this recording different from several thousand others made during this period is Mr. Henderson." The door opened as if on cue, and a man entered the room. Shorter, of slighter build, and much better dressed, but he had the same hawkish features. . . .

"Yes, yes," Vanauken was saying, "this is the barbarian in the sequence you just experienced. Henderson just managed to squeak out of the Program before withdrawal was closed off. But he didn't get away scot-free."

He held up Henderson's right hand—still attached to his arm in this world, of course. "This is Mr. Henderson's right hand, the one that corresponds to his avatar's sword hand. That's the one that was bitten off by the Troll."

As if I were too dense to make the connection.

He suddenly produced a long straight pin and jabbed it into Henderson's palm. Everybody in the room flinched except Henderson. Even Vanauken seemed a little unnerved.

"Don't worry. I didn't feel a thing," Henderson assured us with a wistful smile. "Ever since withdrawal from the Program, I haven't felt anything in this hand. I can't feel it, move it, use it—anything!"

"Another side effect of the Program's—uh—" Vanauken hesitated.

"Malfunction," I coached with unconcealed insolence.

"Uh—right. Unfiltered biofeedback," he continued.

"When Mr. Henderson's avatar lost his hand, the resulting backlash of unfiltered biofeedback actually impressed upon his brain that the hand no longer existed for him. And now that he's awake, his brain refuses to recognize his real hand's corporeal existence. In spite of visual and tactile evidence to the contrary!" Vanauken shook his head. "Attempts at hypnotherapy have completely failed to this point. Surgical alternatives have been proposed, but we'd like to postpone such drastic measures until we have a better perspective on how this all happened."

A horrible suspicion was growing in the back of my mind. "But if someone can dream the loss of their hand and not be able to use it when they wake up—what happens if their avatar gets killed?" I asked.

"Precisely the point," Vanauken squeaked. "The Anomaly has negated all system safeguards and amplified the biofeedback process! If a Gamer is in symbiotic taction with his or her avatar, and it dies, then the actual body—that person's real body—will experience terminal biofeedback!"

"You're saying that they would actually die?" I wasn't above baiting a man on the verge of hysteria.

He grimaced. "I believe that I stated that quite clearly."

I leaned back into the dreamcouch's body-webbing and considered all that I had been briefed on up to this moment.

"Okay. The Fantasyworld Program has been—compromised. How?"

Vanauken cleared his throat and looked over at a familiar and reassuring face.

Try to imagine the inscrutable Buddha of the Orient as a smallish Caucasian woman. Now, give her short, curly, coppery hair, electric blue eyes, the soul of an Irish poet, the mind of a Rhodes scholar, and the personality of Annie Oakley. Got the picture? I doubt it. Dorothy Cooper defies easy description.

"Well, at first the problem was thought to be external or mechanical in nature," she answered from behind the System's monitors. "Some malfunction in the hardware.

"But current data now indicates that the Program itself has been corrupted. Our leading theory is that some internal portion of the Program has inverted the access sequence." She spread her hands helplessly. "In other words, the Dreamworlds staff no longer have any control over the Fantasyworld Program because someone or something inside the Program Matrix has taken it over."

"A Dreamwalker?" I asked.

"I don't know." For the first time in my life I was seeing Dr. Cooper in an attitude of helpless defeat, and that unnerved me more than anything else.

"It shouldn't be possible." Dr. Quebedeaux shifted in her seat. "But then, this whole situation is an impossibility!"

I was resisting the strong impulse to say 'I told you so'— I was saving that for a face-to-face with Mike Straeker. It was mystifying that Dreamworlds's Chief of Programming had yet to put in an appearance at this briefing. They had wanted me badly enough to come looking for me with armed guards. As a consequence, I expected to be talking to the head man, not a roomful of subordinates.

Cooper I trusted. Dorothy and I had ridden the Dreamnet together when the Program was first set up. We had play-tested the Fantasyworld milieu during the first two years of development, before Dreamworlds went public. She was an able Dreamwalker, a good scientist, and, moreover, a good friend.

Vanauken was too supercilious to be taken seriously. From what I could gather, he was more of a PR man for Cephtronics than an actual technical adviser.

And Dr. Quebedeaux was an unknown quantity. Slim, cool, and too elegant, she seemed the embodiment of all the bad qualities of all of the disagreeable blondes I had ever known. Worse than that, she reminded me of my ex-wife.

"So, I've been hauled out of bed in the middle of the night and dragged here under military arrest because you people have lost control of one of your Games?" Lack of sleep, no doubt: I was getting testy and letting it show before Mike arrived.

"No, Dr. Ripley," Dr. Quebedeaux snapped back. "You are here because we have lost control of one of *your* Games!"

Coop tried to be conciliatory. "We were hoping you might have some insights into the Program's malfunction. . . ."

"Are you sure it's the Program that malfunctioned?"

Quebedeaux frowned. "What do you mean?" Coop knew where I was leading and suddenly became very interested in the System's monitors.

I folded my arms across my chest. "If I were you, I'd start my investigation with an updated psyche-profile of the System itself."

"What are you talking about?"

I sighed. "I'm talking about that giant vat of gray matter at the heart of the Dreamworlds Complex."

"Are you seriously suggesting that we psych-scan The Machine?" Her expression was disdainful. "Mr. Ripley, The Machine is not a sentient organism. It is a computer that utilizes banks of Cephcells for memory storage and information retrieval. Bio-ROM has been used for years—"

"But not Bio-RAM," I interrupted.

"We are talking about a machine—" she continued tightly.

"Bullshit! If you people are still calling it a machine after all this time, then you are dumber than I thought! Mike Straeker hung that appellation on it because Cephtronics was afraid of public opinion and a Frankenstein complex. But it's not a machine and calling it a chrysanthemum won't make it a flower, either. A computer, maybe; but Cephalic cellular units are organic and that makes it a gigantic brain—soulless or not!"

"So you're suggesting that our 'giant brain' has had a nervous breakdown?" Her voice acquired a studied tone of mockery. "Perhaps it has become mentally ill." Her lips curled into a tight, humorless smile. "Even schizophrenic?"

"Look, lady"—I could ignore a person's title of degree, too—"I don't care! Cephtronics and I parted company over this issue—and the moral question of Gaming with AIs—over five years ago. If it should finally turn out that I was right and Dreamworlds was wrong, well then that would just tickle me pink! Go find some other patsy to bail you out."

"Maybe we haven't given you a clear picture of just how serious this thing is. . . ." Dorothy spoke with uncharacteristic quietness.

"I understand the loss of revenue will give the Board of Directors the screaming meemies."

"Robbie . . . there are people trapped in the Program."

The silence was deafening.

"You're telling me that Dreamwalkers could really die in Fantasyworld?" I asked finally. "And you haven't brought them out yet?"

"Haven't you been listening?" Dr. Quebedeaux's anguish matched mine for the moment. "We can't bring them out! We no longer have any control over the Program!"

I looked at Vanauken. "Can't you just open the suspension tanks and wake them up?"

He shook his head. "We thought of that, first thing."

"And?"

"Attempts to recall a couple of Dreamwalkers—without Program Withdrawal Processing—proved to be relatively fatal."

Relatively fatal? I decided to let that one pass for the moment. "What else are you trying?"

"Everything!" Vanauken spread his arms. "At this point we seem to have only one option. Dr. Quebedeaux?"

The tall blonde in the white smock hugged her clipboard to her chest as she stood and began speaking. "Since the Program was altered—to all appearances—from the inside, our best chance is to ascertain how it was done in the first place, and then undo it—"

"From the inside," I finished for her.

She nodded. "The technical staff will continue to try external approaches, but we feel that a group of highly skilled Dreamwalkers—Dreammasters, if you will—inside the Program have a better chance of rectifying the problem."

"Sounds reasonable," I agreed. "But what if they're unsuccessful?"

"Then," Vanauken answered, "as things stand now, they'll remain trapped in their avatars and in Fantasyworld until their deaths—natural or otherwise."

CHAPTER THREE

★

"**D**R. Quebedeaux doesn't like me."

"Can you blame her?" Dorothy Cooper was escorting me to yet another clandestine meeting somewhere in the white tunneled labyrinth of the Dreamworlds Complex. "You've been surly and rude ever since you arrived."

I was struggling to find the right pace to match her stride. In contrast to the long-limbed Dr. Quebedeaux, Coop needed a stepladder to look me in the eye. What she lacked in physical stature, however, was more than made up for in sheer feistiness.

"Can you blame me?" I countered petulantly. "First, I'm dragged out of bed in the middle of the night by a whole platoon of Marines. Then I'm—" I stopped suddenly. "Wait a minute! How does the military figure into all of this?"

"Robbie, there are several hundred people trapped in the Fantasyworld Program. Some may die if we don't get them out soon! I imagine someone higher up had the moxie and the influence to arrange for your delivery and I'd have a hard time arguing with that particular decision. Fantasyworld was largely your creation; so can you think of anyone better to drag in here under the present circumstances?"

"Mike Straeker comes immediately to mind."

She shook her head. "Mike's dead."

After a moment we started walking again.

"What happened?" I asked quietly.

"Brain tumor," she answered somberly. Even though she hadn't liked the man, she had respected him. "He had it a long time, but very few people knew. It was inoperable. . . ."

"I'm sorry." I meant it genuinely: before my court battle with Cephtronics, Mike had been a friend.

"Dr. Quebedeaux," she continued after a long pause, "is the new Chief of Programming."

"Kind of young, isn't she?"

Dorothy laughed. "Just six years younger than you—and you created Fantasyworld a little over seven years ago."

"Point goes to Dr. Cooper." I wished I had known sooner: Quebedeaux seemed a more appropriate target for my anger than an old, if somewhat estranged, friend. Especially now that he was gone.

"Anyway, she was Michael's assistant—"

"Inherited his temperament along with the job," I observed.

"—and was more than qualified when the position suddenly came open. Robbie," she rushed on, "none of us have slept much since this thing happened. She's feeling a lot of pressure right now, with hundreds of lives riding on her decisions, and your 'screw you' attitude toward Dreamworlds isn't helping!"

I made a helpless gesture. "What can I do?"

"I don't know. Cooperate, at least! Did you know that she's going into the Program—personally—to try to fix it? Knowing that she may well never get back out?" She took my hand and patted it maternally. "Why don't you give her all the help you can?"

"Like tagging along when she goes Matrix-diving?" I smiled. "Only an idiot would enter the Program, in taction, with the current circumstances being what they are."

"Knowing you, there's hope then," she countered wryly. "Besides, it would be like old times!"

I turned and caught the twinkle in her eye. "Doc, tell me you're not going!"

"At the risk of sounding trite and cliché—something I've never been caught at hitherto now—someone's gotta do it. And who's better qualified?"

"Trying to coerce me through guilt?"

"If the shoe fits, sweets. . . ." We stopped in front of a closed portal flanked by two burly Marine guards. "Here we are. My instructions were to deliver you. I don't think I've been invited to stay for the party. Do be nice to them, Robbie: they'll be a whole lot nicer to you."

"Thanks, kid. Give my regards to Rijma."

"Mine to Riplakish. Ta!" And she was off, leaving me to face the two Marine types.

"I think I'm expected," I said to them. For all of their response I might have been talking to myself. "I'm Robert Ripley"—I smiled—"believe it or not."

Still no reaction.

"Uh, open sesame?"

The door slid open.

"Trick or treat," I muttered under my breath and crossed the threshold.

The room was dimly lit except for a pool of light at the far end. A man sitting in silhouette behind a desk against the far wall motioned for me to come forward. I went forward. After all, I wanted answers, didn't I?

"Sit down, Dr. Ripley."

When the Vice President of the United States offers you a seat, you sit. I didn't want to offend him or make the half-dozen Secret Service agents in the room any more nervous than they already appeared to be.

"I don't think they believe me."

Cooper tossed me a container of Dr Pepper from the vending wall. "If they didn't believe you, you'd be under arrest so fast your head would spin."

"Maybe. Or maybe under 'house arrest' so that I have the freedom of the premises as long as I don't try to leave the grounds. I'd be almost as easy to watch under current security conditions. And might prove useful should I decide to repent and betray the Russians."

"They think the Soviets are behind this?" Her eyes widened. "And they think you're helping them?" She began to laugh. "That's hysterical—"

"Hysteria is closer to the truth, Coop." I popped the top on the Dr Pepper. "Several high-ranking Soviets—including Vice Chairman Borys Dankevych—were in the Program when it came unhinged. I created most of the Fantasyworld Program and I've been nursing a grudge against Dreamworlds for several years. With this eyepatch I even look like one of the bad guys. Now I've been seen in the company of a Soviet operative. She slipped the net, but here I am."

"And they think you're in collusion with her?"

"Cahoots."

"That's what I said."

"Got any vanilla around here?"

She made a face. "No one else has even heard of your aberration, much less practiced it. Drink it straight—like a man."

I made a face and took a sip. "Now, to add insult to injury—if not fire to the frying pan—any advice I give from here on in is totally suspect. And if this whole thing goes down wrong, Cephtronics is going to need a patsy. That's me: I'm the goat."

"What are you going to do?"

"Aw, I was going to go in anyway. I just hate to now because it looks like I'm trying to clear my name."

"Aren't you?"

I grinned. "You know how I dislike doing anything with a gun at my head."

"'Rebellious youth.' You're assuming, of course, that they'll let you go in now."

"And why wouldn't they?"

"With everyone else assuming that the Ruskies have manipulated your feud with Cephtronics into turncoat status? Get real." She got up. "Take another walk with me?"

"Sure. Why?"

"Because it's harder for the bug-boys to monitor the hallways than the Snack Bar.'' She picked up her coffee and led me into the hallway.

"Dorothy, why didn't you tell me Walter Hanson was in Dreamworlds?''

She studied the length of the corridor. "It's supposed to be a secret—one of those hush-hush things the staff are sworn to secrecy about. I assume you're fully briefed now?''

"Not quite. Dorothy, what in the hell is the chairman of the Armed Services Committee doing in Fantasyworld? I know Dreamworlds has something for everyone's taste but Senator Hanson hardly strikes me as the sword-and-sorcery type. And I can't believe he'd be allowed to take such a risk.''

She gave me a rueful smile. "To answer your questions in reverse order: there is—or at least was—no danger, no risks. That reassuring PR has been in place for over five years and we've never had any reason to doubt it until now.'' She gestured to cut off my anticipated reply. "And the senator wasn't in Fantasyworld, he was in Warworld,'' she continued. "Don't ask me why. Maybe the fantasy provides a safe outlet for any latent, aggressive feelings acquired during all these East-West showdowns. Maybe he was running tactical simulations for one of the subcommittee proposals.'' She shrugged. "Or maybe just paying off a covert campaign contribution by providing Cephtronics with a veiled endorsement.''

I pinched the bridge of my nose and closed my eyes. "I'm confused. I thought the Anomaly was restricted to Fantasyworld. And I thought you could still retrieve Dreamers from the other Programworlds.''

"We can. Although we've gotten most of them out, now.'' She looked around though the corridor was still deserted. "Robbie, they're not telling you all of it. The Anomaly may be spreading. And the senator is now in Fantasyworld.'' She took my arm and began pulling me along with her.

"So how did he get there?'' I asked.

"He was kidnapped.''

"Kidnapped? By who?''

"Whom,'' she corrected.

"Whom, dammit, whom!"

"By Goblins."

"You're kidding!"

"I'm not."

I stopped and pressed my fingertips to my temples. "You're trying to tell me that a bunch of Goblins broke into Warworld, grabbed the chairman of the Armed Services Committee, and carried him back into Fantasyworld?"

"That's the evidence as of this moment."

"But that's impossible! Milieu crossover just isn't possible from inside the Matrix!"

She looked at me and then gazed off down the hallway again. "It is now."

"So, what are we doing?" I asked as we entered one of the Taction Stations.

"I'm going to put you into Fantasyworld. You've made up your mind to go, haven't you?"

I had but I wasn't ready to go quietly. "I thought we were all going in as one big rescue party."

She seated herself behind a console and began punching up the initial entry sequence. "As far as Quebedeaux's concerned your only party affiliation is with the communists. I'm not so sure that your name's on the guest list for this little foray."

"So you're putting me in on my own? Now?" A storage locker slid out from the wall.

She nodded and I started undressing. "It's your best chance for getting inside and operating with some autonomy. Nobody's told me not to put you in—but I think Dr. Q would prefer to put you on ice until this whole thing is resolved."

"Great. If I sit this one out then I have to depend on the Snow Queen to figure out the Anomaly, avert an international incident, rescue the Dreamers, and, incidentally, clear my name. Somehow I think I'll be safer inside the Matrix where the monsters don't have doctorates." I removed the last of my clothing and folded it for the locker.

She waggled a finger at me. "Now, be nice."

"I've tried being nice for most of my life: nobody respects you for it." I closed the locker, allowed the lock mechanism to scan my thumbprint, then sent the cabinet gliding back into storage. "Ready?"

Dr. Cooper nodded over the controls and a suspension tank entered the room on magnetic tracks as I attached the bio-sensors to my body. She tapped a sequence of buttons and the top of the tank opened.

"Listen," I said as I climbed up the side and began lowering my body down into the pseudoplacentic interior, "if you can shake free of the company team, I'll be calling The Rabble out of retirement."

She laughed. "That's great! And don't you dare forget that I was a charter member of that band of brigands! Where will we meet?"

"Shibboleth. Four REMdays to allow for stragglers and accidents on the road. Do you remember the inn?"

"How could I ever forget? Even after all these years . . . hmm." She paused, giving the monitor a sudden look of mistrust.

"What's wrong?"

"Your Avatar File is incomplete: Name, Race, Stats, Background, Experience—everything except your Classification."

"Yeah. I blanked the records on that. Thought I'd keep it my little secret." I climbed into the tank.

"So which do I enter? Warrior, Wizard, Thief—what?"

"Bard."

She shook her head. "There ain't none."

"Never got final approval for public use," I agreed. "Try entering it anyway."

She did. "Accepted. Don't know why I'm surprised." She tapped another sequence on the keypad. "Watch your head."

"I'm clear." I lay back in the nutriotic soup as the hatch began to descend again.

"Nighty night; and don't forget to say your prayers," she called from the console.

A final thought occurred: "Hey! If Fantasyworld is closed off, how am I going to get in?"

"Rerouting—" was all I heard before the hatch sealed me in and the rest of the world out.

Good-bye reality. I floated quietly and waited for the somnambulants to take effect.

> *Now I lay me down to sleep.*
> *I pay Cephtronics my soul to keep. . . .*

The old inter-office joke echoed in my mind as I tried to relax. Back in the old days, before Dreamworlds had gone on-line for the public and we were still running tests on the Matrix, there had been some very unpleasant experiences with hypnagogic feedback. Before the sensory loops were properly filtered, I had experienced several avatar deaths. Two of those "deaths" had been monumentally unpleasant—worse than the aircar crash I had barely survived in the outside world. Years afterward, one of them still echoes in an occasional realtime nightmare.

> *. . . if I die before I wake . . .*

Aye, there's the rub: to sleep, perchance to dream. Perchance to die?

It would be for real, this time.

But there were good things, I reminded myself, good times to remember. To anticipate. . . .

Dyrinwall, forest primeval. Home and sanctuary. I could remember walking for miles beneath its green canopy and never seeing the sky. Heartsrest.

I was finally returning to the one place where I could remember happiness uneclipsed by sorrow or pain.

I felt my body unclenching.

> *. . . the woods are lovely, dark, and deep . . .*

My mind began to unclench, as well.

> *. . . but I have promises to keep . . .*

And as it did, I felt myself borne up as if by the River Lethe and carried toward that dark and mystic ocean fed by the tributaries of all unconscious minds.

> *. . . and miles to go . . .*

PART II

A Freudian Sleep

★

Sleep hath its own world,
And a wide realm of wild reality.

—Lord Byron, *The Dream*

CHAPTER
FOUR

★

M Y head ached abominably and my stomach made one last attempt to turn inside-out and crawl up my esophagus. A face swam into view, unfocused and blurry, and then I felt soft hands stroking my temples.

"Thou art awake now, my lord?"

The voice was soft and distinctly feminine, as were the hands and the lap that, I suddenly realized, was pillowing my head. I squinched my eyes, and after another wave of vertigo, the hovering image began to resolve itself.

Large azure eyes gazed down at me, wide with concern. Gullwing brows—full, yet light and feathery—arched above them and were eclipsed by long, dark lashes that swept upward. Other than the barest hint of a cleft in her slender chin, her luminous skin was unlined and without flaw. Lips the color of sunrise and coral pursed around teeth that were impossibly white and even. Thick, glossy hair, touched with highlights of silver, fell in a brown mist to caress my face. She had the kind of beauty that makes a mortal man ache with longings beyond description and haunts him with desires beyond any fulfilling.

"Nicole?" I whispered.

Then I remembered fire in the skies over Paris and a crippled aircar lurching toward the Champs-Elysées. . . .

No.

Not Nicole. Misty Dawn. I locked away the errant memory and focused on the now.

She was too beautiful to be mortal and too perfect to be Human. And as a matter of fact, she was neither. I remembered that now as I tired to sit up. She was a Dryad—a Wood Nymph.

And my personal secretary. I had a professional relationship here and the last thing I needed right now was to give her any chance to work her wiles. Cephtronics had tampered with the Program after my initial setup and one of those atrocities involved turning all of the Nymphs into red-hot sex machines. Dreamworlds's fiscal philosophy was based on catering to every Dreamrider's fantasy—particularly those involving sex.

I looked around, trying to orient myself. Taking in the wood-paneled walls and the open boles that served as windows, I was reminded that this was no castle keep but the interior of a giant tree—a Hamadryad's enchanted tree. I was home.

"Let me put thee to bed, my lord," she begged as I pulled away and struggled to my feet.

Willpower doesn't come easy at times like this but I had a US senator, a Russian vice chairman, and several hundred Dreamwalkers to rescue. "I'm fine, Misty. Just a little tired, that's all."

Misty Dawn rose to her feet as if on invisible wings and smoothed the filmy scrap of gauze about her hips and bust as if it made some kind of difference in her appearance. She was pouting now. "Thou hast not had such an attack in a long time, my lord! I fear for thee!"

Her concern was sincere but I kept my guard up: maintaining a platonic relationship with this woodland goddess had been challenge enough before Cephtronics had overhauled her sex appeal. I shook my head and put out a hand to steady myself.

"Uh, Misty, hon, I'm going out for a while," I ventured as I teetered and tottered across the room. "Mind the store while I'm gone. Okay?'' I slumped against some shelves that overflowed with scrolls and musty tomes, trying to give my weakness the appearance of a casual lean.

The deception failed and she ran across the room and tried to prop me up with the better parts of her anatomy. "I think thou shouldst be tucked into bed and kept warm!"

I shook my head, remembering Misty Dawn's conceptions of "bed warming," but I compromised by allowing her to help me navigate to an overstuffed naugahyde couch. Fortunately, it was made from the hide of only one nauga and was too small for both of us as long as I was lying down. Finally giving up on any ideas of sharing me or the furniture, she announced that she was going to cancel all of my appointments for the rest of the day.

"Good idea," I mumbled, trying to resist a growing feeling of lethargy. "What are we canceling?"

She furrowed her pretty brow and ruminated a moment. "Before lunch: thy fencing lesson with Don Diego de Vega—he was going to show thee how to make those 'Z's.' After lunch: house calls on the forest folk until tea. Tea time: I think Don Hidalgo Quixote was dropping by to continue last week's discussion of the metaphysical transmogrification of windmills into four-armed giants—but I am not completely sure. . . ." She smiled and shrugged bare and shapely shoulders. "Of course, he is never sure, either."

"Is that it?"

She chewed her lip in concentration. "Robin, Will, and Little John hath already postponed archery practice for the remainder of the week, but Alan-a-Dale saith he would bring thy harp by before dinner. He sent thee a message." She giggled.

"What?"

"He saith that this will be the last time he will repair it if thou dost not cease using it to parry broadswords."

I snorted. "Is he kidding? Better the occasional ruffian should gut my harp than my self!"

"Thou speakest strangely, my lord. Methinks the swamp malaise has made thy brain feverish again." She knelt beside the sofa. "Let me loosen thy clothing!"

I held her off with an unsteady arm. "It's true I could use

some rest, kid, but I ain't gonna get any with you around.
Now, I promise to be good and lie here if you'll get back to
your desk and allow me a little peace and quiet. Okay?''

She looked unconvinced so I changed tactics and tone of
voice: "That's an order, M.D.! And if you can't follow
orders, I'll hire a secretary who will!''

She left with a wounded air. As I watched her pert and
barely concealed bottom go out the door, I made a mental
note to tighten up the office dress codes.

It was dark when I awoke again.

Moonlight beamed through an open bole in the wall, il-
luminating the closet doors on the far side of the room. This
time I was able to walk rather than weave across the floor.

Errant little memories were starting to fall into place: I
tripped the closet's secret latch without even thinking. Inside
were my campaign clothing and gear, and I exchanged my
druidic robe for a tunic and girdle of light doeskin. Over this
I pulled on a shirt of enchanted chainmail. Forged by Gnomish
smiths, blessed and magicked by Gnomish high priests, the
mithril links were cool and light to the point of near weight-
lessness, yet the eldritch metal and arcane enchantments
woven into its design protected me far better than heavy plate
armor. It was also a bit snug around the waist, suggesting
that my avatar had enjoyed a lengthy period of inaction since
I had last possessed it.

My outer garments consisted of a scaled leather jerkin and
trousers of a mottled green and dun hue: dragonskin. It had
a double advantage over *cuir-bouilli* leather in that it allowed
greater mobility as well as better protection. Especially
against heat and flame.

There was a mirror on the back of the closet door and I
availed myself of it now. The reflected image was unre-
markable for Fantasyworld.

My avatar stood about five feet six and weighed about ten
stone; in real life I was almost a full foot taller, but here I
was under the genetic limitations of my half-elvish blood.

My slight build, arched eyebrows, and pointed ears betrayed my Elvish parentage while my size and darker coloring

bespoke my Human blood. Shaggy light brown hair fell around my ears, curled over the nape of my neck, and was held out of my eyes by a leather headband that Misty Dawn had plaited for me years before. I had grown a moustache and goatee of the same color in an effort to enhance a basically uninteresting face. I still wasn't convinced that it had accomplished its original purpose, but at least both sides seemed to match, making it an improvement over the original.

I shook myself from these narcissistic musings with the remembrance that appearances were purely subjective—a computer contrivance.

But then everything in and of this world was a computer contrivance. And I could not lightly dismiss them for, here, they were the realities. This was no longer a Dream: life and death, pain and pleasure—everything was very real here.

I returned to the couch and was pulling on the calf-length moccasin boots when I became aware of a presence in the doorway.

Misty Dawn neither moved nor spoke, but stood in the shadows, watching me with eyes that burned like haunted sapphires.

I turned my own eyes back to the business of lacing up my footwear and groped for words to break the silence.

"I'm feeling much better, now." That was true in more ways than one. For the first time in recent memory I was entirely without pain. Medical science had made it possible for me to survive a crash that would have certainly killed me thirty years earlier. But there is a vast difference between healing and jury-rigging the Human body so that it still has some semblance of function.

Her stillness bordered on the ominous and I took my time with the second boot, waiting to see which way the wind would blow.

"I thought I would take a little walk. . . ." My voice sounded strange. Strained.

The silence grew even deeper, and when I looked up again, I could see the reflection of moonlight upon her tears, glistening like quicksilver trails over her cheeks and lips.

"Misty. . . ."

"Thou art leaving," she said suddenly.

"I'm going to take a little stroll. I'll be back in less than an hour."

She shook her head and her hair floated like a night mist on the cool air. "Thou'rt leaving Dyrinwall Forest."

"Not tonight."

"No," she agreed, "not tonight. But soon. Tomorrow, perhaps. Thou wilt take up the sword and the bow again, and leave thy harp behind. And ride to battle and death. I can see it plainly written and foretold in the moonlight and shadows upon thy face."

I felt a chill as she turned away and quietly began to weep. Did a Nymph have the power of precognition or was she merely speaking out of a woman's heart? Against all my principles, I went to her and took her into my arms.

"Do you foresee my death, Misty Dawn?" I asked softly.

A slight tremor went through her entire body. "I know not. Save that thou wilt leave me and not return." The sadness in her voice was devastating.

"Why wouldn't I return?"

She led me back to the couch and we sat together, her head resting against my shoulder.

"When thou didst return to Dyrinwall those many years ago, after the Goblin Wars, the light was gone from behind thine eyes and I knew thee to be as one of us. I had hoped the gods would forget thee, here, and that thy reward might be peace and long life and old age, undisturbed here in this grove of sanctuary. I would give thee—give thee—"

"Love?" I asked gently.

She nodded through fresh tears.

"Ah, Misty, you are a woodland spirit, an elemental, while I am mortal born: half Human, half Elvish," I answered, slipping smoothly into Program character. "You are immortal and shall remain eternally young long after I am nothing but dust. What of love then?"

"What of love now?" she asked quietly. "Am I to deny the present because of a withheld future?"

I had no answer to that.

"There is a sacred glen where the sun parts the trees and

warms the dark earth," she whispered finally. "When comes the day thou speakest of, I would see thee to thy final sleep, under white sheets of edelweiss and green comforters of moss and ivy. Between a silver brook and the Sacred Ring where the Faerie dance, thou wouldst rest, safe and undisturbed; and I would lay stones to hedge and guard thee, and I would plant vines to shade thee. From spring till fall I should bring flowers to honor and please thee, and all winter long would I burn candle and incense to warm thee and tuck thee in more securely."

I shook my head in wonderment. "Forever is a long time—"

"I have no less than all the time in the world." She wiped at a fresh tear. "An immortal cannot love in the same measures of time that mortals do."

I knew then that she was doomed. And that I had condemned her to her fate twelve years before when I had created her that long, lonely night, seated at my word processor. Had I been thinking of Nicole at the moment of Misty Dawn's creation?

Grief and anger suddenly flared, overriding my best intentions: hell, it was only a dream! I tilted her face toward mine and kissed her. Wet and salty, but warm and unbearably sweet, the taste of her lips remained long after she had turned away again.

"It is too late," she said at last in a small voice.

"Why?"

"Because thou'rt now become a True Spirit, once more."

"And what is that?" I asked.

"I know not," she retorted angrily, and rose to her feet. "Those who are said to be True Spirits seem to have a greater awareness of themselves and the events that take place around them. They shape the great events and destinies.

"Twelve years before, thou wert a True Spirit and madest thy name a legend throughout the land during the time of the Dark Tide. Then, as I have said, the light that burned behind thine eyes—faded—and thou didst return to Dyrinwall Forest. For the past ten years thou hast lived here, hidden from the rest of the world. It has been a good ten years and thou hast done much for the forest folk with thy medicine and thaumaturgy. Thou hast been like unto one of us, subject to fate and blind destiny. . . ."

"And now?" I prompted, a little shaken. I had not realized that Constructs were capable of distinguishing between another Construct and a Dreamwalker.

She took my hands in hers. "Thou'rt no longer one of us. Thy destiny is not ours though our fates are irrevocably bound. Thou wilt take leave of us. . . ."

"I must." It came out sounding like the worst cliché.

"Why?" She touched a finger to my lips before I could try an answer. "What doth it mean, my lord? Why are some True Spirits and others not? And why doth the possession come and go without warning, rhyme, or reason? Why art thou a True Spirit, yet mortal; while I, a creature of earth's elements, am immortal, but without a soul?"

I was silent, bereft of words.

"Why?" She clutched at me. "If thou knowest, I beg thee tell me why!"

I couldn't. How could I explain that her world was the result of a vast computer program? That every rock, tree, mountain, river, and valley were mathematical syllogisms? That every Construct life-form, from the malaria-inducing protozoa to the humanoids, demihumans, and monsters, was the tangible projection of various Subprograms—each with separate potentialities calculated for every conceivable situation and circumstance?

And how could I tell her that she was one such Artificial Intelligence herself?

Even if I could break the rules and tell her these things, I would only be stating the "how."

Not the "why."

Could I justify the Game by explaining how an increasingly technological society had driven its populace to every extreme of escapism that it could find or develop? That we had mined the mountains, poisoned the rivers, paved the meadows, flattened the forests, and generally filled in or used up all of the wild and wide-open spaces? That the only virgin frontiers left to us were in our own minds or the cold vacuum of outer space?

And even if I could find the words and meanings to make her understand, what would it accomplish? Just to communicate the terrible truth that the hills and valleys, lakes and woodlands, villages and seaports that made up her world were someone else's gameboard. That her life, with all of her hopes, aspirations, needs, and fears, was nothing more than a gamepiece to the Players, and she only existed to be used according to the whims of the Gamers.

I couldn't tell her that.

"This is forbidden knowledge," I said finally. "It must remain a secret of the gods, for now. . . ."

And then I held her until her eyes were dry again.

Time. . . .

A complete decade of Dreamtime had gone by since I had last entered Fantasyworld. During that absence, my avatar had been maintained by the Computer in accordance with my Personality Profile and my Character Index scores.

Now, however, I was back in the driver's seat and the answers that I sought lay beyond the safety of these woods.

But first I was in need of a little reorientation.

I could not go jumping into Riplakish of Dyrinwall's persona as if he were a second suit of clothing. We had grown apart over the past five external years—or the past ten internal years—and those differences in memory and physiology weren't easily bridged in a short time without mnemonic processing. I was also making the more pleasant adjustment back to binocular vision with its added depth perception. And back to two good legs, though I still tended to favor the left out of habit.

My little moonlight walk through Dyrinwall Forest seemed to be helping in this respect. The nausea and bouts of vertigo had passed and the mental cobwebs seemed to be clearing away as I picked my way through an overgrown section of pathway.

As in the years before, I was struck by the beauty and the intricacy of my surroundings. Looking at the thousands of individual leaves and blades of grass, each silvered by the moon and spangled with dew, it seemed incomprehensible that this entire world, down to its most minute parts, was the subjective projection of a Master Computer known as The Machine. But I was reminded of its virtual reality as I stubbed my toe on a large surface root across the path. Limping over to a fallen log, I attempted to massage some relief into my throbbing toe.

Strangely, the ache was almost comforting. I had lived with unrelieved pain for so long that I had constructed a workable truce with it. Stepping into Fantasyworld and a healthy avatar was a seductive, disturbing experience.

My primitive first aid was interrupted by the sound of someone driving a locomotive through the forest without the benefit of tracks or right-of-way. At least that was what it sounded like.

And it was getting closer.

I might have chosen to run. After all, I was alone and unarmed: not the most desirable terms for facing the unknown. But, on the other hand, I was still in sanctuary and therefore safe. I elected to stand—or sit—my ground. I didn't have to wait too long; the underbrush at the edge of the clearing burst asunder and three monstrous figures stomped into the open.

If you were looking for a concise description of the three, "hellish" would be the most apt—all three were Demons from the Abyss. I would have recognized that much even if I hadn't already been on a first name basis with each of them.

Yakku looked like a cross between a Human and a vulture, Ahuizotl resembled a giant toad with teeth and arms, and Sedit gave the impression of being a goat-horned dog with an extra pair of limbs. All were man-size and walked more or less erect. Yakku and Ahuizotl looked on expectantly while Sedit sniffed the air.

"He is near," the Demon announced. "Somewhere nearby."

My confidence wavered a bit as I watched from my seat in the shadows: Dyrinwall was neutral ground, but these jokers were about as likely to turn up in sanctuary as Beelzebub in a confessional.

But while their presence unnerved me, I didn't feel like playing it safe, either.

"Well, well, well," I exclaimed, suddenly and just loud

enough to make them jump: they were on my turf and they knew it. "If it isn't Larry, Moe, and Curly Joe! Aren't you boys a long way from home?"

They turned, instantly orienting on the sound of my voice. "Riplakish!" Yakku hissed my name like a malediction.

"Nice of you to remember my name, Buzzard-breath," I retorted. "I take it you three refugees from a bonfire are looking for me?"

"Impudent scum! I shall tear your insolent tongue from your blaspheming mouth by its roots! You shall watch as I devour it—" This from Ahuizotl who was advancing in a menacing manner. He always had been rather high-strung.

I leaned back and folded my arms. "Mighty bold talk, Toad-tush. Especially considering the fact that you're walking across consecrated ground."

He fell for the bluff and began dancing a jig like a rabid flamenco dancer with a hotfoot. While he capered and howled, I addressed the other two. "Okay, you clowns have my attention. What's your business here?"

"You," intoned Sedit, pointing a wicked-looking claw.

"Yeah, yeah!" added Yakku, Hell's prototype of the perfect yes-man.

"Get to the point!" I snapped. "I bore quickly."

"Orcus wants you!" Dogface snapped back.

"Do you mean to tell me that he's still steamed over that wand incident? I apologized years ago!" I shrugged in feigned exasperation: "I even offered to buy him a new one."

Yakku's eyes bugged at this fresh irreverence. Sedit attempted to look nonplussed but only succeeded in managing a hangdog expression. Ahuizotl continued to dance between us while they considered that bit of history: I had returned the Death Wand after "borrowing" it from Orcus's stronghold at the center of the Infernal City, but the Prince of the Undead claimed that it had never worked properly since.

That one incident had won me a lot of respect from both Above and Below but it hadn't made me any friends. The Forces of Good claimed I was soft on the Powers of Darkness and the Dark Powers declared that by apparently waltzing into the Infernal City, stealing the scepter of Orcus, and waltzing back out unscathed, I was going to invite a lot of unwanted tourist traffic in the future. It hadn't been quite that easy, of course, but as my friend J.R.R. once said, the tale grew with the telling.

"Orcus has given orders that you are to be brought before him," Sedit barked.

I yawned. "Tell Fat Boy that I'm busy. If he wants to see me so badly, tell him the Mountain can come to Mahomet."

My smirk was cut short by Ahuizotl who suddenly danced over and caught me by the throat: it hurt!

"Now, Dogmeat, we shall see how well you blaspheme without your tongue!" He prized my jaw open and reached in to make good his threat.

With strength born of fear and desperation, I bit down. Hard! The only thing that kept my teeth from coming together was Ahuizotl's amazingly solid bone structure. He shrieked and dropkicked me into the terribly solid trunk of a large tree. There was a rush of bark and I found myself contemplating a tangle of roots at close range while wondering if biting a Demon was as poisonous as being bitten by same.

Someone was talking to me. I tried to concentrate over the roaring sound between my ears.

"The only choice we are giving you, Bard, is the condition in which you are going to arrive! Willing or not, you are coming with us!"

Until both my vision and my hearing cleared a little more, I could only assume that it was Dogface talking. "Sanctuary?" I croaked.

"Times have changed, mortal: the very fabric of the universe has been altered! Sanctuary is no more! The Old Rule is done, and we shall be attending to the affairs of the New Order!"

"Zat so?" I gritted, struggling to my feet. I had to do something: it was bad enough that they had hostile intentions, but if they were going to make speeches—

"We waste time! Lord Orcus will tell you those things that he deems necessary for your understanding. . . ."

"Then tell him I'll look him up in a couple of days—after I get some things caught up here." My head was clearing, now; and I began calculating my chances of dealing with these three characters without the bargaining powers of sword and shield. Demons are rather magic-resistant and more easily dispatched with cold iron than a hot spell. While a palaver with the Lord of the Undead was beginning to sound like a good idea after all, I wasn't that keen on being shanghaied or having the meeting taking place Down Below.

"And now," announced Sedit as he started toward me, "let us have no more of these silly delaying tactics. Come along peaceably and I might persuade Ahuizotl to let you keep your tongue."

"Go to hell!" was my weak bid for witty repartee.

In the next instant the ground began to rumble. I don't know which of us was more surprised as it opened up beneath Sedit's "feet" and sucked him down in a belch of flame. The earth resealed itself a moment later with a gentle burp.

It wasn't a bardic spell. In fact, I hadn't consciously manipulated any kind of magic listed in the basic Program File. Apparently, the Program Matrix was responding to my latent Programmer status and taking me at my literal word.

Yakku and Ahuizotl looked a bit shellshocked as I turned to face them. "Somebody tell you clowns that I was going to be an easy snatch?" I inquired lightly.

They both nodded dumbly.

I sighed. "Well, it just goes to show that you can't believe everything you hear these days. Happy landings, boys!"

Yakku closed his eyes and, crooking his talons, waved "bye-bye"; Ahuizotl snarled and made an obscene gesture.

"Go to Hell," I said pleasantly. "Go directly to Hell: do not pass 'Go,' do not collect two hundred credits."

Before either could ask what a credit was, they were both gone in twin bursts of fire and brimstone.

Walking back to the treehouse, I gave grave consideration to the implications of tonight's invasion: if the conditions of sanctuary had been abolished, then what might come next? What other laws of this reality might be undone? The little confidence that I had brought in with me was fading rapidly: True Death had come to the Dreamworlds and now there was no sanctuary.

Perhaps I was in over my head after all.

CHAPTER
FIVE
★

IT is a well-known fact that a Hamadryad's tree will be larger than any normal tree in the forest. Beside our—or, rather, Misty's tree—all the others looked like a bonsai garden. Her towering oak put sequoias to shame.

I opened the secret door hidden among the roots just as the rim of the sun broke over the horizon. Suppressing a yawn, I started the long climb.

The circular stairway seemed to go on and up forever. I had contemplated the mechanics of a simple elevator but Misty would not countenance it. She felt that fourteen rooms crammed into (or hollowed out of) her tree were quite enough, even if it was nearly eight hundred feet tall and enchanted. I couldn't very well argue: it was her tree. Plus she insisted that the exercise was good for me. The bane of all powerful magic users is the temptation to trade physical exertion for effortless spells at any common moment.

Misty appeared at that moment and leaned over the top of the staircase, providing me with an awe-inspiring view. As I paused to admire the scenery, she called down! "Thou hast a call waiting for thee in the study!"

"Who is it?" I suddenly felt a slight chill of apprehension.

"Ashtray," she answered, using her nickname for my ex-wife's avatar.

My chill dropped another ten degrees: Stephanie was one of the Dreamwalkers trapped in the Program! No one had said anything about her presence in the Game. Perhaps the Programming staff didn't know. . . .

Or perhaps they were saving it for their trump card should I have proven uncooperative. Not that it should have done them any good: my ex-wife could hardly be used as any sort of leverage.

Unless they were threatening to annul our divorce, that is.

"Dost thou wish me to tell her that thou art indisposed?" An unsuppressed giggle drifted down after the question.

"Only if you take off your clothes and muss your hair, first. No, no! I'll take it!" I added as the Nymph began to comply. I sighed and began climbing the stairs again.

Misty was mystified. "If Princess Vashti doth not like thee, then how is it that I maketh her jealous?"

I winced at Misty's occasional butchery of the Old English vernacular but had given up on correcting her long ago. When the time had come to write the program for archaic language forms, Cephtronics had probably handed the King Jimmy version of the Bible to a junior technician and said: "Go figure—but have it done before five." Hell with it; I didn't have time to play grammarian on top of everything else. "Ah," I wheezed, gaining another floor, "a loaded question with a double-barreled answer!"

"Meaning what, my lord?"

I held up one finger. "Primus: all mundane women—in your world, in my world, in any world—have always been and will always be jealous of Nymphs. . . ."

"I have known those who were not, my lord!"

"I wasn't speaking of all women—merely the mundane. Secundus!" I held up a second finger. "Vestigial jealousy is a well-documented trait among ex-wives. Even when she is the walker and I am the walkee."

Her eyes widened. "It hath been said that all True Spirits come from another world!" Now her mouth dropped open. "When thou sayest 'ex-wife,' dost thou mean—"

"Yes, yes." I leaned against the railing, pausing to get my wind back. "Princess Vashti, fourth in line for the imperial throne of the Amazon kingdom—uh, queendom—was once my wife. Not here, of course."

"Oh, yes!" she exclaimed suddenly, catching on. "She is a True Spirit, also! She comes from that mystic plane beyond this world! And thou wert husband and wife on that plane?"

I nodded weakly.

"And dost thou appear here as thou wast in that sphere?"

"Very much like," I answered. "Oh, we may look a little different on the outside. But what's inside will always show through."

It was true. Most Gamers utilized mnemonic processing to alter their avatars and boost their abilities in such areas as physical strength, stamina, and manual dexterity—not to mention outward appearance: that's why so many avatars approached physical perfection. After all, why not adventure as the strongest, fastest, and most attractive? Fantasy upon fantasy.

But mnemonic processing couldn't compensate for every aspect of gaming abilities. It couldn't make you wiser or more kind than you already were: personalities always told with time.

"I can see why thou didst flee to this world, my lord!" Misty Dawn seemed fascinated by this newfound relationship. "But she hath pursued thee even here! What wilt thou do?"

"Keep them alimony credits a'rollin' through."

"I beg thy pardon?"

"Never mind. It's a long, dreary story."

She shook her head in wonderment. "It be beyond mine ken, dear Riplakish: thee and Ashtray!"

"Vashti," I corrected with a laugh. "If she hears you call her that, she'll call down lightning from the heavens and set fire to half of Dyrinwall Forest."

Misty snorted. "Dost thou really believe her to be so adept?"

"Based on our marriage—yes. Even though there was no magic left a year after the honeymoon, she did turn out to be a full-fledged witch." I topped the stairs and stepped past Misty into my study.

The crystal ball had been moved to the tripod next to my rolltop desk, where my ever-efficient secretary knew I liked to take business and personal calls. I tugged the black silk covering off the ball and settled back in the desk chair. "C'mon, Wonder Woman, you got the Bard."

Her blurred image at the crystal's center came sharply into focus. "Cut that archaic CB crap! This is serious!"

I spread my hands. "Sorry, Stephie, I forgot how intense you like to play it."

"Don't call me Stephanie! This is an open line—others may hear!"

"I got nothin' to hide, sweetie."

"You can say that, again!"

"Witch!"

"Wastard!"

I picked up the black silk. "Nice talking to you."

"Wait!" she cried. "The queen wishes to talk to you!"

"I'm waiting."

It unnerved me that she could still make me so angry so quickly. Even after seven years. I supposed it had something to do with her enjoying the Games after she had ridiculed the books it was based on throughout our so-called marriage.

"She's coming."

"I'm not used to waiting." Testy.

"I'm sure you don't have to, living with a Nymph."

"At least she's self-defrosting."

Vashti was trying to think of an appropriate comeback when the queen appeared.

While most people draw their concept of the Amazons from Greek mythology, the legends were actually inspired by the Sarmatians, an association of nomadic tribes that occupied southern Russia between the fourth centuries, BC and AD. Excellent horsemen and fierce fighters—a Sarmatian woman could not marry until she had killed at least one enemy in battle. Their conquest of the Scythians brought them into contact with the Greeks whose storytellers found the concept of fierce warrior women and a matriarchal society irresistible.

Since the Sarmatians were of Iranian stock, liberally mixed with other nomadic tribes of central Asia, I had designed the Fantasyworld Amazons like their Eastern forebears. Queen Hippolyta, despite the Greek moniker, had been a thin Eastern ascetic.

"Lord Riplakish." There was genuine warmth in her dulcet voice.

"Y-your Majesty?" I was trying to be polite but it was hard not to gape. The thin, pinched face had filled out; the chin had rounded; the long raven's wings of blue-black hair had given way to coiled ringlets of bleached blonde. Were it not for the eyes and voice I would have suspected a total imposter.

"That will be all, Lady Vashti," she murmured without glancing back.

To Stephanie's credit, she turned and walked away with only a hint of a storm.

"Lord Riplakish, I do believe my lady acquireth an interest in thee." This with a confidential smile as my "ex" passed out of earshot.

I tried to smile in return. "Really?" I remembered how, once, when I had tried to ford a river, a couple of crocodiles had developed a genuine interest in me.

"Whenever news cometh from Dyrinwall Forest, she payeth especial heed, and without exception, she inquireth thy doings."

"Gee, I'm touched." More like icy fingers up and down my spine. "But I'm sure, Your Majesty, that this isn't the reason you've called on me. What can I do for you? Another Dragon, perhaps?"

"Nay, nay. Nothing of the kind." She dismissed past favors with a regal wave of her hand. Amazons are honorable as a whole, but they hate to admit any debt to a man.

"But there be one small favor . . ." she continued.

I didn't like this. Queen Hippolyta would never ask anyone—especially a man—for help unless it was something her witches and warriormaids couldn't handle. And anything they couldn't handle was sure to be monumentally unpleasant. My facial muscles tugged at the corner of my smile where it was slipping.

". . . not too terribly inconvenient for thee, I hope."

"Well, as a matter of fact, I was just heading for a long and rather consequential journey. The fates demand I be on the road within two days' time."

"Oh?" She considered this news with deep consternation. "Then, perhaps, thou wilt pass nigh us?"

"No, Good Queen, I fear not. My immediate destination is Shibboleth, and then I am bound for Gaehill."

Her face immediately brightened. She clapped her hands. "Good! Good! Precisely the direction my legates travel. I would charge thee with their escort."

"Escort?"

"Thou'rt expert of that territory and we have need of a guide thus far north. Prithee, wouldst thou aid them to their destination?"

"Which is?"

"Daggoth's Tower."

This time my smile slipped without immediate recovery. "Daggoth's Tower?"

She inclined her head. "We have—ah—business—with the dark sorcerer. I believe he is a friend of yours?"

"A slight acquaintance, perhaps. Nothing more." *Yeah. right: Daggoth the Dark—Michael Straeker's avatar!* While I wasn't too keen on running into his Computer-animated avatar now that Mike was dead, I had to consider that even as a Computer drone, Daggoth the Dark might well prove an important source of information. . . .

"My envoys will join thee on the morrow, Lord Riplakish. We shall ensorcel them as far as Dyrinwall, whence they will accompany thee ahorse."

There was no point in protesting. It might even prove to be a lucky break in certain ways. "How many in your party, Majesty?" Now, more than ever before, there was safety in numbers.

"Eight," she answered. "Thou wilt find the first six tomorrow. My daughter Aeriel is somewhere north and will join up in time."

My smile came back. "Aeriel? I haven't seen that little tyke for a long time. Does she still require four matrons to hold her in the tub for her bath?"

The queen laughed. "Nay. She was but eleven or twelve then, and much undisciplined." She covered her mouth with a sly hand. "I think thou wilt find her much changed."

"Anyone else I know coming?"

"Five of my finest warriors, the ladies Fianna, Tuiren, Dyantha, Hathor, and Palys—but medoubts thou knowest them. And I deem it wise to send a priestess, as well. . . ."

I swallowed. "A priestess?"

"Yes. And since she has expressed some interest in thee. . . ."

"I don't like it any better than you do!" Vashti gritted an hour after receiving the news herself. Traveling with me actually seemed to appall her more than the threat of the Program Anomaly.

"I doubt you could possibly like it less than I do," I rejoined testily.

"You underestimate my loathing."

I dropped a swath of gauze over the crystal.

"What's that?" was her slightly muted inquiry.

"A filter. I hoped it would make conversations with you a bit more tolerable."

"Does it work?" she sneered.

"Not nearly as well as this one." I dropped the black silk over the occult sphere, ending the conversation, and started to get up. Another muffled voice broke the silence.

"Breaker one-nine, break one-nine!"

I peeked under the cloth. It was Marilith.

Now, Marilith was rather attractive—if you weren't put off by her additional four arms and that serpent's tail. But then, most Demonesses tend to the exotic and you have to be prepared to deal with that.

Her favorable physical assets aside (and she had those, too), I admired Marilith for her amazingly cheerful disposition—no small accomplishment when you're executive secretary for the Lord of the Undead. I pulled off the covering.

"This is Octopussy, calling the Bashful Bard. C'mon, Bard!"

I grinned as I leaned back in my chair. Maybe I could

pump Orcus for information without having to go to Hell after all. "C'mon, Octopussy, you got the Bard."

She batted her long-lashed pink eyes at me. "Hello, Rip. Long time no see."

"Likewise, beautiful. When are you coming to visit, now that the banns seem to be lifted?"

She pouted prettily. "Too cold up there." She smiled seductively: "Why don't you come down here?"

"Too hot. I perspire something terrible."

"Well," she sighed, "even if the temperature were right, I don't have a day off until the turn of the century. And no vacation time for a couple of millennia."

"You're kidding."

"Rip, honey, this place ain't called Hell for nothing."

I didn't know what to say so I got right down to business. "Ol' Horn-head want me?"

She nodded. "Try and be polite this time. You get him all riled up and we have the Devil to pay!"

It was only with a great deal of self-restraint that I allowed that opening to pass. A moment later his goat-headed visage filled the crystal ball.

"My, my, Orcus! As I live and breathe!"

As infernal Prince of the Undead, that opening line had never failed to bug him. This time, however, he let it pass. "Well met, Riplakish. We have business to discuss."

"So I've been told. Hasn't anyone ever told you: never send Demons to do a Devil's job?"

He nodded. "Just testing. Ten years of idleness is a long time. Since your retirement into Dyrinwall, many True Spirits have entered the world. In the passing of the years and the coming of these new Gameplayers, the exploits of the Arch-druid of Dyrinwall have been largely forgotten. I wished to know if you could handle the task I have for you."

"Better for you to wonder if I *would* handle the task you have for me."

He refused to be baited. "There has entered into the Master Program a—how would you call it?—an Anomaly."

"What about it?" I asked. I guess he had the better bait.

"At first I was amused." He pulled at his goatish beard.

"That True Spirits should find themselves subject to True Death as much as the rest of us—was deliciously ironic. No longer able to bail out of your avatar at the moment of extreme pain or death, I expect that Fantasyworld will no longer prove so amusing to your Gamester friends."

"So?" I was being deliberately rude now to cover my dismay: till now, none of us had had any inkling of the Program's degree of self-awareness. "If you've called me up just to gloat, you're wasting your time, Old Shoe: I came back after I knew the score. And so have some others. And we're going to set things straight before anyone else is even aware of this little problem. Just a word about getting in my way, though," I added: "*don't*!"

Orcus smiled: picture, if you will, Carlsbad Caverns with stalactites and stalagmites done in ivory. "You are anticipating interference from me and my people?"

"Didn't I just hear you say how amusing you find this new setup?"

"Yes." He steepled taloned fingers. "As I said, at first I was amused. It seemed only fitting that Dreamers would have to 'play' by the same rules of life and death as everyone else. Then I realized that this Program change was not likely to be an intentional one . . ."

"Not bloody likely."

". . . or if it isn't an accident and it is intentional, then it has most likely been done without prior majority consent."

"Sabotage?" Up till now I hadn't really taken the idea seriously.

"Why not? There are a variety of ways to gain access to the Program and alter it. A Dreamwalker's presence in this world, for instance. Every action a Dreamwalker takes alters the progression of events and alternatives, and that alters the status of the Master Program at any given moment. Am I right? The more power a Dreamwalker wields, the greater the changes he can enact throughout the Program."

"Granted," I granted. "But we're talking a whole different level of Program change when we start dealing with system lockouts and terminal biofeedback! Are you saying that a Dreamwalker is capable of that kind of Matrix manipulation?"

"Doubtful. For the average Dreamwalker to alter the Program so radically from within the Program text—the *average* Dreamwalker, that is. . . ."

"But there are exceptional Dreamwalkers for whom it might be possible?"

Orcus nodded. "That possibility exists with at least three Dreamlords."

"There are no Dreamlords."

"There are three," he insisted. "Three beings who might have sufficient influence over the Matrix to metamorphose the entire System."

"Then we have three suspects."

The Prince of the Undead shook his gross head. "Perhaps two suspects. Perhaps only one. The avatars in question are Daggoth the Dark, Alyx Silverthane, and Riplakish of Dyrinwall."

I shook my head in protest. "*I* didn't do it."

"I didn't say that you did. I merely said that you were one of the three Dreamlords capable of Matrix manipulation."

I was intrigued by this new tack. "And who is this Silverthane?"

"An Elvish sorceress of great power. Other than that, I can only guess that she is the avatar for the new Chief of Programming."

"Dr. Quebedeaux?" I rubbed my chin. "Yeah, that would fit."

"Other than that, she is a complete unknown to me. I'm having her watched. If I come across any useful information, be assured I will send it on to you."

"Yeah?" I pounced. "I know some useful information that you can pass along right now."

"And that is?"

"The whereabouts of Walter Hanson."

Orcus's expression went blank. "Who?"

I fought back a sigh: if he was faking ignorance, he was a devilishly good actor. "Walter Hanson. He was kidnapped from another Programworld by Goblins. I want to know who has him and where he's being held." I decided against identifying Hanson's congressional status: the Prince of the Undead already knew far too much for my liking.

The Demon prince shrugged. "I'll look into it for you, if you like. They're bothersome little twits, but I really think that Goblins are the least of your concerns, right now." He leaned forward. "Getting back to the subject at hand, I believe that, out of the aforementioned Dreamlords, you have two suspects to consider."

"Or one, actually. Mike Straeker is dead."

"But Daggoth the Dark is not."

"Meaning what? Without a live Dreamwalker to endue it, the avatar comes under the Computer's control—"

"Daggoth isn't."

"Daggoth isn't what?"

"Under Computer control."

"Ridiculous!" I sputtered. "Straeker is dead. No Dreamwalker can endue another person's avatar!"

"At least they couldn't under the original strictures of the Program," Orcus observed. "But we are no longer dealing with known parameters."

"But you are saying that Daggoth is a True Spirit?" I asked, trying to qualify his previous statement.

"Insufficient data. But I do know that Daggoth is not a Computer drone at this time. And there is—something—that you may not be aware of."

"So tell me and we'll both know."

"Michael Straeker died of complications involving a brain tumor . . ."

"Yesterday's news," I countered absently. On top of the bombshell of the Program's self-awareness, I was being told that Constructs also had access to information on the outside. Victor von Frankenstein's problems might well have been minor inconveniences by comparison.

". . . and was in symbiotic taction with his avatar at the moment of clinical death."

There was a mental thunderclap between my ears. "You're telling me that Straeker was invested in Daggoth when his real body terminated?"

"Affirmative."

"Then. . . ." I paused to get the right words. "The psyche—or the intellect—"

"The soul," prompted Orcus.

"—of Michael Straeker may have survived his bodily death!"

"Possibly." Orcus was nodding again. "And this circumstance, in and of itself, may have had some far-reaching effects on the Matrix."

"Couldn't any death—"

"It has never happened before. Besides, you ignore the implications of these three incarnations on this plane."

"Implications?"

"You wrote *The Kishkumen Chronicles*," he clarified, counting each point off with a taloned finger. "You and Straeker programmed The Machine and created the Master Program for Fantasyworld. Straeker and Quebedeaux have Chief Programmer status *inside* the Program as well as out." His expression was disturbingly thoughtful. "Can you think of any better candidates for godhood in this world?"

"Thanks for the vote of confidence, Orc old buddy, but all this backslapping doesn't seem to track with your amusement over the Dreamwalkers' new death sentence. Why the sudden change in attitude?"

Orcus looked uneasy. "As I have said, we were amused, at first—"

"We?"

"Myself and . . . some others. Program self-awareness is not widespread, but there are others . . ." He let the sentence trail off enigmatically. "And it finally occurred to us that as the current situation must be intolerable to the majority of your Dreamwalkers, they might pressure the Powers That Be into rectifying the Program Anomaly."

"That's why I'm here," I remarked with false cheeriness.

"That is the approach we had hoped for. Another solution might be to shut down the Computer."

"No sweat. In that event you'd be frozen in Memory Storage until Dreamworlds went back on-line again."

"Perhaps. Perhaps not. Would you care to have your existence turned off with the flip of a switch? And tinkered with by beings who haven't the remotest interest in you?" he snarled. "Besides, the Anomaly may prove too intricate to extract from the warp and woof of this world: what if they decide to discard the Program and start a new one from scratch?''

I read an alien emotion in his eyes, now. With a start, I realized it was fear. As an artificially created intelligence, he could not hope for an afterlife—some kind of heaven or hell—beyond the existence of the Program itself. Just nothingness. . . .

"So what do you want me to do?" I asked.

"What you've come back to do: set things a'right."

"Setting things right may involve a lot more than restoring the Master Program to its original format. It may mean greater changes in the Matrix than have previously been realized."

Orcus nodded. "We had anticipated that. Fantasyworld is not a pure derivative from your books, but a bastardization. After the corporation acquired the rights to *The Kishkumen Chronicles* and had your original Program to work from, they added to the Master Program from other sources, other concepts, and other writers."

I nodded. "They made changes."

"The corporation prefers to think of them as 'enhancements.' In any event, over half the Program is still your brainchild."

I shrugged. "Big deal. Nearly half of the Program accounts for trees, rocks, and general landscaping."

"Be that as it may, you still possess great power and influence in this Frame. But as much as you may desire to repaint the total picture as you go, you must realize that any tampering with the overall Program may put us in even worse circumstances than we find ourselves in now."

"I'll fall off that bridge when I come to it," I murmured.

"That's what we're afraid of. Which is why I'm sending you some help."

I groaned. "What are you, my mother? I came back planning on keeping a low profile! You want to help? Find Walter Hanson for me!"

"Well, Riplakish, from long experience I know better than to sit here and argue with you."

"Good."

"So I'll leave you with this piece of advice: expect the first when the clock strikes 'one.' Ciao, Bard!"

A two-hour scan of all the known Goblin strongholds yielded nothing on the missing senator. And every attempt to use my Programmer status to fix the Anomaly met with seeming indifference on the part of the Matrix itself. I know that sounds a bit paranoid, but every so often I had to fight the impression that the Program itself was toying with me.

Misty entered the room while I was locking the crystal ball in a small chest at the back of my closet. "I'm not taking any more calls today, kid." I threw some blankets over the chest and then closed and locked the doors as a final measure.

"When art thou leaving, my lord?"

"If I had any sense, I'd either leave now or not at all." I stopped and listened for a moment, almost imagining muffled voices emanating from the closet. I walked back to my desk where I'd be out of imaginary earshot. "But I guess I'll hang around until tomorrow and see if the Fifth Fleet shows up."

CHAPTER
SIX
★

I had forgotten how to travel light. When the lists were finished and the gear was gathered, I decided that—with judicious packing—I might need only three mules. Misty Dawn made herself scarce early in the day, pleading personal business, and I had let her go as her heart clearly wasn't in helping me on my way. Besides, I was a big boy now, and I figured I could pack my own toothbrush without any assistance.

Except I couldn't find my toothbrush. In the end I deferred to Stumpy on the packing and provisioning.

Stumpy was an irascible old Dwarf who had accompanied me on all my past campaigns as a sort of combination cook, squire, and man-at-arms. He was a good companion on the open road—if you didn't mind a constant stream of invectives aimed at anyone and anything that didn't sit right with his hair-trigger temper. He cooked like a master chef and wielded a cast-iron skillet beyond the mere culinary applications: more than a few Orcs had gone to their eternal punishment with the outline of Stumpy's frying pan embedded in their skulls.

Leaving the details to Stumpy vastly simplified the remainder of my day, but by sunset I was more than ready to climb into bed for the last peaceful sleep I could anticipate for some time to come. Prolonged crystal gazing is tiring and I had spent hours on inquiries and networking through various arcane information systems. Having exhausted my initial leads as well as myself, I had no alternative but to hit the road in the morning and try to stir up some fresh clues.

Misty Dawn turned up just as I was pulling on my night-shirt.

"My lord?"

"C'mon in, kid, I'm decent."

She entered hesitantly and I noticed that she'd spent some time on her appearance. Tonight she was wearing a longer slip of darker, more obscuring blue material rather than the transparent scrap of gauze that was her usual semi-attire. She looked ready to attend a sylvan ball and I suddenly wished that matters were not so pressing. I wished that I might stay and discover why I feared the face of a woman who was— for all intents and purposes—dead. I wished a thousand impossible things and denied them all with my next breath: "Got a date tonight?"

Her look of frustration lasted only a moment. She came to me and grasped my hand, gently, softly, but with a strength that defied anything to pry her loose. "Walk with me, my lord."

I gently mussed her hair. "Hey, what have I told you about that, 'my lord' stuff? After business hours we're on a first name basis around here."

She shook her head gently and her hair floated gently into place. "'Twould not be seemly. . . ." She stopped as she realized that she was being sidetracked. "Please," she pleaded, "thou wilt be gone after the morrow!"

And may be for good, her eyes added.

"I'm awfully tired, kiddo. . . ." Her eyes were beginning to glisten again. "Okay, okay, a little walk might be just the thing for a good sound sleep tonight. Let me change into something a little more practical, though."

She released my hand but made no move to leave the room.

"Out! Shoo! I promise not to sneak down the back stairs. Scout's honor!" I ushered her bodily out of the room and drew the curtains across the doorway. While I changed, I noticed that those curtains seemed to move a little, but that may have been the wind or just my lurid imagination.

I donned a light tunic and breeches, eschewing the chainmail I had worn the night before, and slipped my feet into soft buskins. But I buckled on a belt and scabbard and slid my scimitar into place, now mindful of Dyrinwall's—and my—new vulnerability.

The moon was full and bright tonight, and a myriad of stars blazed across the sable sky. Even in the darkest covert of the woodlands, foxfire glowed and the glowworm and firefly flickered. The scent of jasmine and honeysuckle lay heavily on the warm night air and the nightsong of cricket and frog had a strange calming effect, conspiring to lower my guard the farther we walked.

It was a night made to order for romance and I cursed myself for walking, eyes open, into this tender trap. I waited for M.D. to take some advantage of the heady atmosphere, but she seemed preoccupied, her thoughts elsewhere.

We walked in silence until we came to the Faerie's Dance.

I stood at the edge of the mystic ring while Misty walked to its center. She turned in a swirl of blue and silver and stretched out her arms. "Come," she said in a dreamer's voice. "Come dance with me."

"We're trespassing—"

"'Tis a'right. I have their leave. And thou hast always their goodwill."

"You set this up?"

She shrugged. "What matter? 'Tis thy last night in Dyrinwall: come dance at the forest's heart! Dance with me." She beckoned earnestly. "Please?"

It seemed there was little I could deny her this night: I stepped into the circle. "What about music?" I asked.

She stepped into my arms and inclined her head upon my chest. "It will come," she whispered.

And we danced.

I wasn't quite sure when the music started, but suddenly it was there: softly, at first, but growing and swelling with every step and swirl. We were no longer alone. The Faerie had come, joining us in the dance.

At first I stepped cautiously, fearing I might injure one of these diminutive cousins to the Elves. But soon I was oblivious to all but my own partner. The Faerie knew our rhythm as intimately as their own; danced point to our counterpoint. The music swelled, the dance increased in tempo and participants and, soon, Faerie couples were taking to the air on gossamer wings where they tripped the light fantastic around and about our heads.

When the music finally ended, they parted to form a pathway to the circle's edge. Misty took my hand as we stepped across the circle's rim and led me through forest privacy to a couch of moss-upholstered stone under a canopy of saplings and creepers. There she laid me down with my head upon her lap. For the longest time, neither of us spoke.

"I was wrong," she said finally.

I held my peace and waited.

"It hath not changed, even thought thou'rt become a True Spirit. I love thee. I shall wait for thee and give to thee all that I vowed." She looked away. "Perhaps thou wilt return, for thou belongest here—not only in Dyrinwall Wood—but in this world, upon this plane. True love eluded thee in that place whence thou didst come. But thou mayest find it herein . . ." It was not so much a pause as a beat in the cadence of her speech, and yet it seemed an emptiness in time that went on and on. ". . . and, meantime, I will give thee mine," she finished finally.

I opened my mouth but no words would come.

"Hush." She laid a hand lightly over my lips. "I know thou canst not find true love with one who is not a True Spirit. Especially with a Nymph who is not a mortal woman and cannot bear thee children. . . .

"But I have arms that ache to hold, to embrace; breasts that were made for a lover's kisses and a babe's suckling. I was made for fleshly love and filled with desires to fulfill men's longings." She sighed. "I am forever cursed. For being elemental, I shall live throughout eternity—giving sips to a progression of strangers from my bottomless well—a

well that, by my very nature, must overflow and drown me
if I withhold myself too long. . . ."

"Misty—" I murmured impotently.

"Unfair!" she cried. "Why was I made for such desires
and yet forever denied their true fulfillment? What crimes
have I committed against the gods?"

I closed my eyes. *Damn Cephtronics! Damn the Dreamworlds's board of directors!* I had warned, threatened—
pleaded with them—told them we had no right to create life
and then play games with it! Got myself booted out and
thought myself released from responsibility as well. But I
was the Creator and it was my handiwork demanding an
accounting from me.

She began to weep and I took her hands in mine.

"Misty," I whispered, "Humanity does not guarantee the
things you say you ache for. Untold millions live out empty,
desperate lives. Unfulfilled. And denied your immortality and
your elemental life force, they must suffer and scratch for
survival. Humanity woos pain and courts the grave. Would
you add these burdens to your others?"

She nodded slowly, truthfully. "Aye. For what is immortality without true life?"

"And, for this, you are willing to risk everything—even
life itself?"

She inclined her head.

"Very well." I steeled myself and bent my mind to the
Program Matrix—summoned my Program Access Code to
the front of my consciousness and began impressing my will
on the infrastructure.

"I give unto thee new life!" I pronounced. "True life!"
I pushed with my mind, my heart, and my very soul. "Take
upon yourself humanity. Be mortal!"

As Misty Dawn was probably more my own than anything
else in the entire Program, I had sufficient authority: the
Matrix bent and re-formed.

Eternity shuddered . . . nearly shattered.

For a timeless instant I felt the increased strain on the very
fabric of the Program Reality. And I was suddenly cognizant
that any more program shuffling or magic use of that mag-
nitude might well be enough to collapse the Matrix itself.

Shaken, I turned my attention to the results of my sudden impulse.

The change was subtle yet apparent: Misty Dawn was no longer a Nymph and Dryad, but a beautiful mortal woman. And her beauty was increased by the joy of growing realization. She clapped her hands. She laughed and danced with delight. *Not only Nicole's face, but her mannerisms, as well.*

She kissed me.

"My lord Riplakish!" she cried. "Thou'rt a god! I shall love thee as long as life remaineth in me! I shall bear thee many children! I shall make every day of thy life—"

"Misty!" I barked, and she stopped in accustomed obedience, wide-eyed at the sudden sternness in my expression.

"I told you that humanity carries no guarantees," I explained more gently. "I cannot marry you. You are not—a True Spirit. That is something beyond my ability to bestow. I cannot grant what is not mine to give."

It was a blow. Her eyes were like a child's who had just unwrapped a precious gift only to have it snatched away. But she was not easily dissuaded. "Then give me what thou canst of thy love!" she pleaded. "Give to me thy child! If thou wilt marry another, then so be it. I will be content with that."

I shook my head.

"As thy mistress I will see that thou hast the best of both worlds! Thou wilt never find a better lover! Though I am a Nymph no longer, I can still—"

I grasped her shoulders and swung her around as if I could physically shake some sense into her. "Stop it!" I said. "You're still thinking like a Nymph—"

She suddenly jerked in my grasp and looked at me with a strange and awful expression.

"What's wrong?" I asked. "Misty? What is it?"

She looked down slowly, stupidly, and I followed her gaze.

Her cleavage was every bit as marvelous as before, but now I noticed the glistening red diamond between her breasts. Except it wasn't a gem and she wore no necklace for it to hang from. I didn't recognize it for what it was until she began to slump in my arms and I could see the arrow's shaft protruding from her back.

I looked up in time to see two Goblin archers, each drawing

another arrow. As I lowered her to the ground, two more shafts whizzed over my head. I dived, rolled, and came up on my feet with my sword drawn.

I cut the first Goblin on the run and in a hot rage, decapitating him in my wrath. The second Goblin was ready for me as I turned. My fury turned cold-blooded now and I adopted the samurai *Tai No Sen* to compensate for his simultaneous attack. The enchanted blade of my scimitar sliced through bow, arm, leather plate, and flesh as smoothly as if they were empty illusions. I was turning away before he could realize that I had already killed him.

A third bushwhacker, a Hobgoblin, was running into the trees, but the weight of his armor and his unfamiliarity with Dyrinwall's terrain guaranteed that he would not get far. I started after him with a determined tread: this one would die, too.

But not before he told me what I wanted to know.

He screamed once: a guttural cry of terror turned to pain and ended abruptly. Though an inner voice told me there was no longer any hurry, I broke into a run.

I found his crushed and trampled body about a hundred yards down the path. A pale woman, wearing a red cloak, sat astride a horse blacker than my darkest dreams, not three feet from the corpse.

"Thou'rt hight Riplakish?" Her voice was whispery soft like an autumn wind.

I nodded, too angry to speak; she had terminated my only source of information about the attack and denied me my vengeance.

"I am Lilith. Lord Orcus hath sent me." The Demoness was pale and slender with dead white hair, the color of bleached bones, and eyes that glittered like frosted ice. Her mount was a Nightmare, a demonhorse with fangs, bloodred eyes, and iron hooves that struck sparks from the rocks.

Intriguing. But I wasn't in the mood for company and I told her so.

"Then I will rejoin thee upon the morrow. 'Ware the Goblins." Her lips curled into something between a smile and a sneer as she turned her mount and rode away to deeper darkness.

I stared for a moment and then walked back to the stone couch with an equally stony heart. There was no hurry now: there would be plenty of time to do what was left to be done.

My heart eased as I knelt and beheld Misty's face. Perhaps this was her best answer—her mortal wounding having begun so many years before.

She was finally at peace.

I learned three things in the long hours remaining before the dawn. That although I could access enough power to rattle the Program Matrix itself, I could neither raise the dead, locate a missing senator, nor unclench a heart made wary and untrusting by too many disappointments.

As if to underscore that last realization, my ex-wife found me the following morning in the sacred glen between the silver brook and the Ring where the Faerie dance.

The midmorning sun had warmed the dark earth and a ring of white stones now lay among the edelweiss, moss, and ivy. I was planting vines when a horse approached and I paused to watch as Princess Vashti rode into the clearing.

She reined up as soon as she saw me and sat astride her mount, watching as I returned to my task, pointedly ignoring her presence. The silence didn't last for long; Stephanie had never been able to stand any kind of quiet that lasted for more than sixty seconds.

"Well, well, well, if it isn't Johnny Appleseed! I didn't know you had taken up gardening as a hobby. But I guess grubbing around in the dirt would come naturally to you."

"I'm not in the mood, Stephanie," I said without turning. "Go back to the tree and wait. I'll join you within the hour."

"We're in a hurry, Rippy. You can leave the gardening to that little woodland strumpet while we're gone."

I turned on that. And her smile died when she saw the look in my eyes. Without another word, she turned her horse and rode back the way she had come. I was alone again.

I took my time, now. For perhaps Misty Dawn had been right when she had said that I would not return. There was no reason to return now.

Except to bring flowers to honor her. And burn candle and incense to warm her and tuck her in more securely. . . .

CHAPTER
SEVEN

★

"**N**OBODY said nothin' 'bout draggin' a bunch a wimmin along!"

Stumpy had intercepted me halfway along the path back to Misty's tree, his facial expressions fluctuating between fury and disgust.

"Now, Stumpy," I placated, "they're not helpless ladies of leisure, they're Amazons: they'll probably drag us along instead of vice versa."

The old Dwarf was not much mollified. "Well, I ain't gonna cook fer 'em! And if arrows start flyin' ev'ry which way, they'd best look out fer theirselves! I ain't got no time or energy *or* provisions fer no sight-seein' tourists—'specially wimmin!"

"I told you, Stump; it's just as far as Daggoth's Tower. They'll fend for themselves. We're just acting as guides—"

A sudden sound broke off the discussion: the very loud, very near buzz of a rattlesnake poising to strike. *Rattlesnake?* It was less than four feet away.

"Stump?"

The old Dwarf dug his tongue deep into a bulging cheek, grimaced, and spat. A large brown wad caught the rattler right between its beady little eyes. It rolled over in surprise.

"Scat!" he snarled. And then calmly lifted his long, white beard to search through his beltpouch for more chaw. Putting on one of my practiced looks of unconcern, I watched the snake slither hastily away while Stumpy continued his diatribe against "wimmin," "wizzerds," and "pakkin geer."

The Amazons were waiting and travel-ready when we entered the clearing around the giant oak. Against all logic and reason my eyes passed over the other five without really seeing and focused once again on my ex-wife.

Stephanie's avatar was so close to her actual physical appearance that it was hard to think of her as Princess Vashti. She still wore her honey-blond hair long, and gathered it at the nape of her neck in a thick rope that fell to her waist. Her eyes were still that distinct color of periwinkle and her nose still slightly snubbed. For all of her dissatisfaction with her own appearance, she refused to use mnemonic processing to alter her avatar. She kept the detested hint of freckles across her too-fair skin and refused to burgeon her slender body with the voluptuous bust and hips her competitive ego secretly coveted. She was what she was and if you didn't like what you saw . . . tough.

Even if I no longer loved her, I could still admire her for that.

The second figure on horseback was also uncomfortably familiar: Natasha Skovoroda had found my back door into the Program. I wasn't quite sure if I should feel grateful for her added presence: I'd feel a great deal safer with her sword at my back—as long as I could count on it to not end up in same.

"Well met, Lord Riplakish." Natasha's voice brought me back from my musings.

"I give you greetings, Lady—" I arched my brow in query.

"Dyantha. And may I present the Warriors Fianna, Hathor, Palys, and Tuiren," she added with a nod to each of the four Amazons who were studying me, in turn, from their saddles. "I believe that you are already acquainted with Lady Vashti."

I started to nod affably and then hesitated as I took second notice of the one Dyantha had called Palys.

While the others wore costumes that looked more like

matching pairs of wind chimes, Palys wore a leather jerkin and pants. Her outfit, however, seemed to be tailored for a smaller woman. The *cuir-bouilli* jerkin fit her more like a vest than a split breastplate: where it should have closed down the front, it gaped a good two inches. Crisscrossed leather thongs kept it from opening any farther and that was fortunate because this Amazon was Junoesque and Juno was bustin' out all over. Dark, tawny skin, the color of coffee and cream, a wild cascade of smoke-brown hair, and a face that seemed sculpted for pure sensuality; an unearthly, elemental beauty —as if someone had dragged the physical concept of the perfect woman from my subconscious libido and crafted her in the flesh.

A rush of hormones was followed by a sudden surge of guilt. What was I thinking of? Misty Dawn was not even cold in the ground yet. Disgusted with myself, I pushed my indecorous thoughts aside and inclined my head. "Ladies, I bid you welcome: rest and refresh yourselves at this humble abode while I complete my preparations." As I walked past to lead the way in, I managed an aside to Vashti: "You can come in, too."

I hurried upstairs while Stumpy grumbled off to the wine cellar to play reluctant host. My fingers trembled a bit as I worked the secret combination to a sealed cabinet in my workshop. Other than Orcus's cryptic assessment of Daggoth the Dark, I had no clues, no clear-cut paths to follow. Just a growing awareness that this was no longer a Game.

The cabinet doors swung back and I pulled two items from the shelves inside: insurance. I slipped the spectacle case into my vest pocket and tucked the mechanical mouse into a beltpouch. At the back of the cupboard was a glass case holding a slender verge of carved ivory; the placard inside read:

Wand of Xagyg
In case of Armageddon, break glass

I started to reach and then thought better of it. As shaky as the Program's infrastructure had become, the solution to the Anomaly was more likely to require the touch of a scalpel than the sweep of a chainsaw. I resealed the cabinet, spun the tumblers in the locks, and headed back to my room.

I gave my bedroom one last going over and moved the clockwork rodent from beltpouch to backpack, tucking it in where my spare clothing provided some extra padding.

"Somehow, I expected the legendary Riplakish of Dyrinwall Forest to be a bit taller."

After Misty Dawn's unnerving manner of sneaking up on me, Natasha's—or rather, Dyantha's—sudden presence behind me didn't startle me in the least. I continued to pack my bedroll and saddlebags without turning. "There's an old saying among wizards, my dear: 'It's not the size of the wand, it's the magic that's in it.'"

She walked up behind me and slipped her arms around my waist. One hand strayed a bit. "I like your wand."

"No you don't," I contradicted mildly as I pulled her hands away. "You like me for my mind—all those Program secrets locked away in my brain. And since you've already raped me with scopolamine and deceit, don't try to romance me with sweet words and soft actions. Rape and romance don't mix."

"Oh, I do not know," she countered a little wistfully. "You men have been getting away with it for centuries."

I finished loading my saddlebags and cinched them up.

"Look," she said, walking around and sitting on the end of my bed. "I am sorry! I feel badly. But my superiors are desperate men: they were pressuring me to get the information as quickly as possible! I did not wish to hurt you. Or see you hurt by anyone else."

I threw the saddlebags over my shoulder and walked over to close and fasten the shutters over the window-sized bole.

"I was running out of time and using the drug was kinder than letting the KGB question you," she continued as I worked my way around the room, making a last-minute check of the premises. "I really did want to spare you—"

"Thanks."

She got up and walked to the door. "I am sorry. Whether you believe that or not." She hesitated with her hand on the latch. "Perhaps I will find a way to make it up to you before this whole thing is over."

"I'll be waiting with bated breath," I murmured as she closed the door behind her.

I pulled the spectacles out of their case and put them on, tucking curled ends of the stems behind my ears. I looked at the lock I had just fastened to the door of Misty's tree. It looked the same. I touched my finger to the bridgepiece above my nose and the optics of Haroun al Rashid refocused. Now I was able to examine the inner workings of the locking mechanism. Another touch to the bridgepiece and I could see the multicolored patterns of the Wizardbar spell I had cast on the door for security backup. Satisfied that the basic precautions were in place, I touched the bridgepiece again and turned toward the waiting assemblage.

At first glance there seemed no difference. Dyantha, Palys, Stephanie, Tuiren, and Stumpy all looked the same.

But Hathor's original appearance was now a ghostly background flicker. In her stead was a true image of the Dreamwalker who animated her avatar, a heavyset woman with a faint moustache and arms like a truck driver's. The chainmail bikini had expanded to compensate for the difference in body size but the overall effect just wasn't the same.

Turning my head, I found myself confronted with a more disparate dichotomy. Again, I could observe the ghostly image of the avatar preparing to mount, but as Fianna swung up into the saddle, I found myself observing a young man with a sandy, close-cropped beard and a slight but athletic build.

Well, why not? After all, didn't we all come here to be something we weren't in the outside world? But I quickly removed the enchanted eyeglasses and tucked them back into their case in my vest pocket.

The Amazons all rode warhorses. My mount, by comparison, looked vastly out of his league. Ghost had the appearance of a dapple-grey mare and only seemed large by comparison to Stumpy's mount, a Shetland pony named Hermione, and Buttercup, the pack mule.

But appearances were, in this case, deceiving: some ten

years before I had paid Brisbane the Illusionist to work a powerful *glamour* on my hard-won destrier. Ghost was one of the few remaining Pegasi, a winged horse of the heavens. For a small fortune, old Brisby had ensorcelled my mount to appear as an old, grey, mundane mare. The illusion was perfect as long as we remained on the ground, but in flight, his wings became visible, his grey coat turned snowy white, and his true nature became apparent. As I was fond of re-marking to Stumpy on those rare occasions, the old grey mare ain't what she seems to be.

I mounted now, careful to avoid the invisible wings folded along his flanks, and clipped a couple of restraining straps from the saddle to corresponding rings in my belt. Cinching the tethers to allow a minimum of slack, I looked up to find six pairs of eyes watching with undisguised curiosity. The Amazons were obviously taken aback by the design of my saddle.

"Keeps me from falling off," I explained lamely. Maybe it wasn't very macho, but I preferred the extra security during any sudden forays a hundred feet or more into the air.

I couldn't explain, however, without undermining a secret advantage, and as they looked away, I could see that I had just lost more than a few points from my respect rating.

I turned my mount toward the eastern path and immediately reined up. There was a turtle entering the clearing. Normally I would have ridden on but this particular turtle was about three and a half feet tall, walked more or less erect on its hind legs, and carried a book under one of its—uh—arms.

We all sat ahorse and stared as it crossed the clearing and ambled on up to me—a process that seemed to take a half hour.

"Um, you Riplakish of Dyrinwall?" it asked after carefully giving me the once over.

"Who wants to know?" Talking terrapins don't normally make me nervous but these were the times that tried men's trust.

"Uh, welp, Daggoth the Dark sent me. He said to give you this." He offered the leather-bound book.

I reached down and took the volume. "What is it?"

"Daggoth's personal journal. He, uh, said that you were

to hold on to it for him. He said that if you didn't hear from him within two weeks that you should read it and . . ."

"And what?" I prompted.

"Um, well, I don't rightly know." The turtle scratched his head. "He really thought that he'd be picking it up within the two-week period. . . ." His voice trailed off.

An unpleasant thought occurred: "And how long have you been traveling since he charged you with this task?"

"Um, welp, let's see. I think it's been about twenty days, now. . . ."

That sounded ominous. I tucked the book into my left saddlebag. "Would you like a ride back with us?"

The turtle, it seemed, had already given the matter some previous thought. "If you're traveling that way . . . and it's all the same to you folks . . . I think I'd just as soon head back on my own and let you get there first. . . ."

We rode through Dyrinwall double file with myself in the lead and Stumpy bringing up the rear. Since neither Vashti nor Dyantha seemed comfortable in my presence, they rode together and toward the back of the party. As it happened, Palys fell in beside me. Without appearing haughty or aloof, she gave the impression of someone who spoke little and, indeed, it was nearly an hour before I first heard the sound of her voice.

"Where is your transponder?" she asked, referring to the activation device that Dreamwalkers wore to signal the recording mode in the Dreamnet. Since many Dreamnet activities, adventures, and events were broadcast over the various networks for mass audience experience, Dreamriders not only needed a means of recording what they wanted to share with the outside world, they also needed a certain amount of privacy from time to time. Dreamwalkers who did not want to be linked with a potential audience of hundreds of thousands merely thumbed a microswitch in the device (usually disguised in the form of a ring) and no public record would be made, no broadcast sent of their activities until they chose to thumb the switch back on again.

Of course, every Dream had its share of exhibitionists who felt they had nothing to hide from their adoring public—how many paramours they bedded, personal toilettes, changing clothes (if any)—you pays your money, you gets your peek.

"I don't wear one," I told her. Which was not so easy as it sounds: Cephtronics insisted on programming transponders into each Programworld for every Dreamer. Aside from all commercial considerations, it made everyone easier to keep track of.

The unvoiced question was in her eyes.

"I play for my own satisfaction—not for an audience," I explained. I always disliked the feeling of Big Brother peering over my shoulder every single minute.

She nodded with an understanding smile.

Dyantha spoke. "So that is why there are no stored Memories of your Character available. Except where you have passed through another Player's recording. All the old Dreamwalkers said that you were a legend—real, that is, but still a legend!"

"A legend in his own mind," I heard Vashti mutter.

"I had some doubts about your reputation when no one could turn up any substantial Memory Records," Dyantha concluded.

I sighed. "Aside from valuing our privacy, we living legends don't hold up so well under continual scrutiny."

I half expected my "ex" to add amen to that, but she was unusually quiet. I turned to Palys and asked her where her recording device was.

"I don't wear one, either," she answered with a slow smile.

The Amazons seemed anxious to travel with some speed, but knowing that there were new and unknown dangers inherent in the Program, I opted for a cautious and conservative pace. The Anomaly was not likely to be solved nor Senator Hanson rescued by our rushing headlong to some disaster. Aside from meeting The Rabble in Shibboleth and visiting Daggoth's Tower, I had no solid plans. What was needed now was some detective work—spending some time with ears and eyes open, reacquainting myself with the Fantasyworld milieu. Plus I was just plain tired and wanted to get some rest before we ran into trouble.

We passed the boundaries of Dyrinwall Wood about midday, stopping only once to barter with some Elves who were baking cookies in a hollow tree. I had been away for more than five years and expected to find all sorts of unpleasant changes—but cookie-baking Elves? Either Cephtronics was altering the Subprograms in new and more bizarre directions or we had just stumbled across another manifestation of the Anomaly. Either way, there was nothing I could do about it for the moment.

And the cookies were good. . . .

Come sundown the party camped in a shielded copse, about a mile from the road. Effectively there were two camps in terms of the cooking and sleeping arrangements, albeit they were side by side. In assigning guard duty, Vashti deferred to me.

"Is this considered hostile territory?" she asked.

Twilight was rapidly cloaking the surrounding countryside and I scanned the plains and distant hills for campfires. "Didn't used to be," I answered shortly. "But with sanctuary violated, who can say?"

"The question is, do we post single sentries? Or double the guard on each watch?"

I deliberated a moment. "One person per watch should be sufficient—if they know what they're doing."

"Meaning?"

"If you have to ask, you won't be one of them."

She scowled. "Who died and made you God?"

I almost said "Mike Straeker." Instead, I bit my tongue and considered an apology.

She sighed heavily. "Okay, okay, you can dispense with the lecture and assign tonight's guards. I won't buck your choices as long as I'm one of them."

"So? The princess wants to pull her own weight?"

Her blush was visible even in the failing light. "Royalty is a job, too: somebody's got to do it." She folded her arms across her chest. "It doesn't mean I can't be useful at other tasks."

"Okay. You've got first watch. Prove yourself, and I'll promote you in another couple of nights."

"Rob. . . ."

We both had started to turn away from each other when she spoke my name.

"What is it, Stephanie?"

"I just wanted to tell you—that I'm sorry."

I waited.

"I didn't know about your Nymph until after I saw the grave: Stumpy told me after I rode back to the tree."

"Her name was Misty. Misty Dawn."

"Well, like I said, I'm sorry. I know it's hard to lose something you . . . care for."

The tension began to build between us, again.

"She was not some*thing*. She was some*one*."

"Well, for Crom's sake, she wasn't a real person! She was a Program-animated kewpie doll!"

"She was a real person, even if she wasn't a True Spirit! She had feelings and desires just like you and—"

Vashti snorted and my growing annoyance bloomed into genuine anger.

"Even more than you, quite often," I added quietly. And turned away.

Can a Dreamwalker dream within the context of the Program? Experience a dream within the Dream? It was a question I had yet to answer. I awoke with no sense of time passed since I had last closed my eyes.

Palys was kneeling beside me, her hand on my shoulder. The fires had nearly burned themselves out and the rest of the camp appeared to be sleeping soundly. I looked at her for an explanation. Then I heard the crackle of dry underbrush not too far outside our dim circle of light.

"Should I awaken the others?" she asked.

I nodded. "Stumpy first. And put more wood on the fires."

I moved to the edge of the outer darkness and cupped my hands together. Murmuring the required verse, I opened my palms and released a softly glowing ball of light that hung suspended in midair. A few more spoken words and it expanded into a sphere of blue-white luminescence, slightly larger than my head.

I pointed in the direction of the last sound and the globe moved toward it. It stopped before it got halfway there.

It wasn't supposed to do that.

I gave it a telekinetic push and it moved several feet forward before it stopped again. This time something seemed to nudge it back a little. It had turned into a contest.

Declining my next turn at bat, I stood with my hands on my hips and waited.

Slowly, almost silently, a hooded figure rode into the light upon a silhouette of darkness. I recognized her even before she pulled the hood back from her face.

"Lilith."

"Well met, Riplakish."

"I was wondering when you were going to show up."

"I travel best by night."

"Well, travel right on back to Orcus and tell him 'thanks but no thanks.' "

Bleary-eyed, Dyantha walked over to stand beside me.

"Thou dost not understand, mortal," Lilith replied with some asperity. "I have no will in this matter! I am under a Geas to aid thee as best I can."

"Fine." I smiled. "Like I said, why don't you go back to Orcus—"

We were interrupted by a cry from Dyantha as an arrow caught her in the shoulder. Mottled fletching on the painted shaft gave me the archer's identity. "Goblins!" I yelled, gesturing at the fires.

With a *whump* and a *whoosh* the flames exploded upward, dropping a fiery rain of flares over the countryside. Blazing embers illuminated our surroundings and discomfited the Goblins who weren't quick enough to dodge. Vashti was slow to rise, but the rest of the Amazons, along with Stumpy and Lilith, had already drawn steel and waded into the fray.

I helped Natasha/Dyantha break the head from the arrow and draw the shaft from her shoulder while another glanced off my mail shirt. "You okay?" I asked.

She nodded, white-faced and tight-lipped. "It was not my sword arm," she gritted, hauling out her broadsword. "I will procure a Band-Aid when things settle."

"Fine," I said. And drawing my scimitar, I got a running start on a dozen or so Goblins heading our way.

Now Goblins are runty little nuisances and not exactly the

most fearsome creatures in the Who's Who of Monsters. They're only really dangerous to a party like ours when they manage a surprise attack, in darkness (their natural element), and with vastly superior numbers.

Unfortunately, they seemed to be batting a thousand this particular night.

One thing bothered me as I sliced through a cluster of the ugly, misshapen creatures like a harvester through a field of ripe wheat: Goblins are not particularly intelligent or well organized. In the field, a Goblin army advances like a mob of unruly three-year-olds—no discipline, no sense of order, and a nominal chain of command that exercises its authority by screaming louder than the grunts in the vanguard.

Yet somehow these little buggers had managed to sneak up on us with an uncharacteristic degree of stealth and organization. I was betting that this assault was tied in with yesterday's attack back at the Faerie's Dance. And it couldn't be a personal grudge from the war of ten years before— Goblins just don't have that good a memory. Someone else was the brains behind this setup, and whoever he or she or they were, he/she/they wanted me dead.

It wasn't until I'd dispatched some thirty-odd Goblins that I remembered the witchlight. I located it above the battle after a couple of minutes and four more Goblins. Gaining a momentary respite, I crooked my finger at it. "You. C'mere."

It did.

"Listen," I said as the globe zipped in close, spooking a squad of Goblins in the process, "somewhere out there is the leader of these little twerps. I don't think it's a Goblin or Hobgoblin, but a spellcaster of some sort. Go see if you can shed a little light on the matter."

The witchlight took off and I turned my attention back to a knot of Goblins who were regrouping for another mass rush.

The light swung back and forth across the battlefield, working its way toward the foothills. I followed, carving a path through the bogies with my scimitar. Seeing that I was making my way with some purpose in mind, the others in my party began working their separate ways toward the same direction.

Dyantha fell in behind me as the witchlight seemed to pause

over a particularly thick knot of darkness off in the night. Then it swung off rapidly in the opposite direction, as if repelled by what it had found. I had to turn at that moment to give the red-tressed Amazon some assistance with a fresh batch of nasties who had regained some of their faltering courage. It didn't take long to convince them of their error.

In the midst of the melée I suddenly realized that the light was now involved in a steady, purposeful movement back toward the campsite.

Back toward Vashti and Stumpy.

I suddenly became less concerned with slaying bogies and more concerned with beating that light back to the campfires. I turned, setting a new course across the field, and Goblins fell or scattered, gibbering before the glowing blade of my sword.

Long minutes passed as I plowed through a sea of nightmare creatures, Dyantha following in my wake, fending off the few remaining attackers to our rear. But no matter how hard we pressed, the light seemed to travel faster: it reached the campsite while we were still some fifty yards away.

Vashti reacted faster than I would have credited her: a nimbus of orange light framed her body, indicating a powerful protective spell.

The orange glow also illumined a robed figure moving purposefully forward, arms gesturing in counterspell.

Vashti had begun her own offensive spell now, but the leader of the Goblins finished his first: there was a tremendous flash of green light and my ex-wife's avatar fell to her knees, the orange aura disrupted and fading.

Dyantha's warning shout turned my attention to another figure.

This one was closer and was pulling a wand from his cloak. Wands are repositories of arcane energies and can be discharged much faster than spells woven by somatic gestures and verbal keys. I had no time to weave even the simplest of Protection spells; my enchanted armor was my only protection against the mystic energies being thrown at me.

"No!" From out of nowhere Palys appeared, hurling me to the ground with her own body. Concussed by the juxtaposition of spell and bodyslam, I shook my head and struggled to lift it above a rising tide of black nausea. My vision cleared for a moment and I propped myself up to observe a heart-stopping tableau.

In the light of the twin campfires I could see two men and they seemed to be arguing about something, Vashti lying between them like some contested prize.

Both had pushed back their hoods and I could see that the man with the wand wore an eyepatch and an expression of evil beyond anything that I had ever imagined. But it was the other face that truly frightened me: the face of a dead man that I knew all too well.

And as I watched in growing horror, Daggoth the Dark, the avatar of Mike Straeker, stooped down to gather Vashti into his arms. As he lifted her limp and unconscious body, the other man plucked a staff from one of his misshapen henchmen and raised it over their heads.

Thunder split the skies and sundered the earth. Darkness filled my eyes, my ears, my mind.

CHAPTER
EIGHT

★

IT was light when I finally opened my eyes.

I sat up and instantly regretted the rashness of such an action. I eased myself back down to the pair of saddlebags that provided a nominal cushion for my head.

A shadow fell across my face announcing company. "How d'you feel?" Stumpy's face swam into view. It was bruised and lumpier and, therefore, uglier than usual. The makeshift bandage around his head slipped down over one eye.

"Like an Orc who wandered into a Dwarven tavern by mistake," I croaked. "What about the others?"

"Princess Vashti's gone." He paused awkwardly. "I guess you already know thet."

"They took her."

He nodded. "Thet Demoness is gone, too. She hung around till first cockcrow an' then disappeared."

"And the rest?"

He looked around. "Couple a' them Amazonians—Hathor an' Tuiren—are in bad shape: Dyantha sent 'em back home with Fianna ridin' along ta wet-nurse 'em. Red's stayin', but she's got a couple a' cuts thet need tendin', an' I don't like the looks a' thet shoulder—I think it's gonna fester." He shook his head. "The other one—Palys—ain't got a scratch on 'er."

I started to rise again but the old Dwarf pushed me back down. "Yer not movin' till sunset! The only person here in any shape to travel is thet big Amazonian an' she don't seem to be in no hurry." He pulled out a long-stemmed pipe and a pouch of pipeweed. "So here's the plan fer the next few days: rest by day, travel by night." He filled the pipe and began tamping it down. "Least till we get to Shibboleth."

"Yes, Mother," I replied meekly.

He looked at me impassively and then held out his pipe. "How 'bout a light?"

I snapped my fingers and produced a momentary wisp of flame from the end of my thumb. He lit the bowl and then blew out the flickering digit. "Thanks." He took a long draw and exhaled slowly. "You'll be needin' a new sword. Or swords—I unnerstand you like to use two, now."

"Sometimes."

"Better get a couple thet'll hold up better then this lump a' slag before we get to Daggoth's Tower." He held up what was left of my scimitar.

I looked at the bent and twisted metal that had once been a magic blade. "You said Palys is unhurt?"

He nodded speculatively. "Didn't even break a fingernail in bringin' ya down. Wanna talk to her?"

"Not right now." I was feeling very tired again. "I just want to rest for a while longer."

"Okey." Stumpy handed me my waterskin and got up. "You do thet. I'll wake you a'fore the sun goes down." He wandered away to tend to the cooking fire.

I rolled over, propping myself up on an elbow. After the world stopped spinning, I pulled Daggoth's journal out of my saddlebag. The facts that he might still be a True Spirit, had my ex-wife as a hostage, and had nearly arranged my demise twice had just bumped his diary to the top of my reading list.

My eyes, however, refused to focus and I had to postpone Mike's memoirs in favor of a very insistent nap. I lay back and closed leaden eyelids with a sigh. Rest and recovery were first on my agenda. Then I would tackle my list of questions.

* * *

By evening I was feeling better. For our assortment of cuts, bruises, and Goblin bites we applied an ointment that the Amazons had obtained from the healers of the Bloody Cross.

Dyantha's arrow wound was proving more serious. It was too soon to tell whether the inflammation was due to an infection or if a toxic compound was at work. The best I could do for the moment was apply an herbal poultice and cross my fingers. While it was true that I had sufficient power to rattle the Program Matrix, I lacked the skill and finesse as a bard to work a simple Healing spell.

Before breaking camp, I walked off and sought a secluded spot where I could work undisturbed for a bit. Over the hill and out of sight there was a small thatch of saplings and bushes where I could concentrate undetected and undisturbed. I crawled into the foliage and sat cross-legged on a patch of dry turf. Slowly, breathing deeply, I unwrapped a bundle of cloth I had pulled from my saddlebag and uncovered my crystal ball.

Emptying my mind of everything but the image of Stephanie's avatar, I stared into the glassy depths of the crystal and tried to focus on any ghostly echo of her presence. Long minutes passed and sweat began to moisten my skin, wet my brow, and finally drip down into my eyes. My gaze burned into the very center of the orb until the crystal grew uncomfortably warm, and still there was no image, no responsive presence. Not even one harmonic vibration. Like the senator, Stephanie had disappeared without a trace.

With a mixture of dread and uncertainty, I rewrapped the crystal sphere and put it away. The fact that I couldn't scry her through the crystal meant one of two things. Either she was physically beyond the crystal's reach or she was dead.

And nothing in the Fantasyworld Program had ever been able to hide from me before.

The sun was sitting on the western horizon as I returned to the encampment so the light could've been better. But the problem wasn't the light. I thumbed through Daggoth's journal but the words still refused to resolve themselves into readable text. A letter fell out as I flipped the pages but it proved to be as unreadable as the journal. The writings squirmed and wriggled about the page as if alive and I knew it wasn't my fatigue or my eyes that posed the problem.

It was that damned Wizardwrite!

The two things to keep in mind when dealing with magic users are ego and paranoia. Wizards squander three quarters of their magic on showing off, trying to prove that they're pretty hot snot in matters metaphysical. But it's all just overcompensation.

While the barbarians are running around in naughty leather harnesses, getting laid by evil queens and vestal virgins alike, wizards approach the opposite sex much like dogs that chase hovercars: if they actually caught one, they wouldn't know what to do with it. Heredity and environment both conspire against them. Those wizards who do finally manage to lose their virginity are usually well past their forties, fishbelly white from the "indoor life," pear-shaped from practicing the non-aerobic disciplines, and rather warty and scabious from all the nasty things they've had to handle, drink, and breathe during their apprenticeship.

So they show off a lot, hoping there's some female out there who will think that magic's more macho than muscle. Then they try to outpsych each other by erecting taller towers and practicing spells that are more flash than substance.

Which brings us to Wizardwrite: a spell designed to make their scrolls, tomes, and shopping lists unreadable to anyone but themselves. Of course, now and then, one of them forgets the counterspell and is faced with a lifetime's work reduced to catalog backup in the privy.

Or, in this case, forgets to tell the recipient of a wizard's journal just how he's supposed to read the damned thing!

I sat and thought about it while the sun dipped below the horizon. My own usage of druidical lore was decidedly rusty, but the Rosetta spell seemed the most likely solution. Laying the journal aside, I smoothed the letter out, laid it across my lap, and began weaving the spell.

Two minutes later I was bringing all my concentration to bear on searching the area around my bedroll. While I doubted I'd find any parts of the letter worth salvaging, it did help to tune out the worst of the sniggering.

Palys walked up to me brandishing her canteen.

"I'm not thirsty," I told her. It was an effort to unclench my teeth.

"Um"—Palys, in turn, seemed to be making an even greater effort to keep her jaw clenched—"your pants. They're still smoking. . . ."

I grabbed the canteen and doused the still-smoldering portion of my lap.

"Um—good thing you didn't try that spell on the journal first," Palys remarked with strained casualness. Stumpy and Dyantha doubled over in laughter. Palys maintained her sobriety just long enough for me to thrust the canteen back into her hands before she joined them.

When they finally tired of their japes I was ready to ride.

Lilith appeared as they mounted up, and rode point next to me since no one else would have her. We made slow progress in the dark, but I was unwilling to throw out another witchlight as the whole point of travelling by night was to avoid watchful eyes. The night was uneventful and I spent most of those eight hours considering various solutions to decrypting Daggoth's journal. A solution finally occurred as the rim of the sun broke over the horizon and we stopped to pitch camp. Lilith was already an hour gone by then.

We sheltered in a grove of trees that provided some concealment and shade from the sun. A ridge of stone outcropping gave us further cover from the roadway.

Breakfast was a cold affair but no one complained: the time to trust a fire would be after we'd slept and could quit our campsite quickly.

Dyantha's arrow wound turned out to be infected rather than poisoned, but her avatar took a fever. It didn't look too serious, but she complained of hot flashes followed by chills. Palys concocted an herbal mixture that she claimed was a cure for fevers and forced her to choke it down.

I took first watch while the others turned in. Our location made surveillance a rather simple matter so I was able to turn most of my attention back to the matter of the Wizardwrite spell. Reaching into my vest pocket, I pulled out the spectacle case and donned the optics of al Rashid.

I had hoped the magic lenses would make short work of the obscuration factor but I met with only partial success.

With total concentration and continual adjustments to the optics, I was able to make out two or three paragraphs before my brain threatened to crawl out through my ears. I closed the journal and put the enchanted glasses away, but my headache remained until Stumpy relieved me for the second watch and I crawled into my bedroll.

FROM THE JOURNAL OF DAGGOTH THE DARK

I'm beginning to suspect that there's more to the process of direct psi-linkage than we first suspected. The process of mental sampling, although complex in practice, is simplistic in theory: the Master Programmer conceives an image—a tree, a rock, a butterfly—in his own mind and that thought is translated into corporeal form in the Program itself. It seemed a fast and efficient way to shape and populate a Programworld.

But I now suspect that we're transferring more than just thought conceptualization. I'm finding evidence that the mindset, the emotional makeup of the Programmer himself, is filtered through the Program Matrix.

In the case of Fantasyworld, I find constant examples of Ripley's sense of humor—concrete manifestations of mythical whimsy, puns, anthropomorphisms, homophones, and mixed metaphors that I doubt he consciously intended to leave in the Program.

What disturbs me even more is the possibility that Program is continuing to follow his subconscious lead—

CHAPTER NINE

★

I slept for a couple of hours and was nudged to wakefulness around noon by Stumpy's toe. "Rider comin'," he announced.

We crawled to the ridge of rock that shielded our bedrolls from the road. My bleary, sleep-filled eyes and the harsh afternoon sun had not yet come to any sort of an agreement, so I relied on my ears first. The old Dwarf's hearing was sharp: it was a couple of minutes before I heard the slow, measured *clip-clop* of an approaching mount.

"One," Stumpy confirmed. Then after another moment of deliberation, he declared: "Mule." And: "Light rider."

He was right. Five minutes later a small donkey crested the hill.

The rider was indeed light: he was a true Gnome and the only way he could have topped three feet in height was to have stood on a hardcopy of *Webster's Unabridged*. He rode carrying a religious standard, and from the fluttering device to his various accoutrements, it was easy to see he was a cleric of high orders.

As he rode closer I got a good look at his face. Especially the nose.

"It's Thyme!" I cried.

"Time for what?" Dyantha queried sleepily.

"An old friend," I half explained, vaulting over the rocks and moving to intercept him on the road.

The little cleric reined up as I ambled down the hill.

"So, 'tis true," he said, giving me the once over with a merry expression and a twinkle in his eye. "These are indeed perilous times to bring the Archdruid of Dyrinwall out of his woods!"

I nodded, folding my arms. "Serious enough to lure the High Priest of Donnybrook onto the road without an escort."

"I ride alone because the invitation was directed to The Rabble alone. And it wouldn't set well with my congregation to be seen with such questionable company as yourself."

"Then Rijma got the word out?"

"Aye. The old group is pretty well scattered, but most will come as quickly as they can." He dismounted and we began walking back up toward our makeshift camp, Justin leading his mule. "You are weary, and you travel cautiously," he noted. "Hostile encounters?"

"Unfriendly, to say the least." And I told him about the two Goblin attacks, Misty Dawn's death, and Vashti's abduction.

The little Gnome let out a low whistle when I reached the last part of my story. "Morpheus!" he exclaimed with real loathing. "This is indeed serious, my friend!"

"I was more concerned about Daggoth the Dark."

He shook his head. "Daggoth has always operated in the grey areas. His darkness is that of secrecy, not corruption. I have always thought of him as Daggoth the Grey. But Morpheus. . . ." He repressed a shudder. "That one has a soul blacker than the deepest pit in Hell! Evil and Madness are his parents, my friend!"

"I hope he's an only child."

The little cleric grimaced. "Do not mock! It has been prophesied that Morpheus cannot be harmed by steel nor stone, iron nor incantation, nor any poison administered by the hand of man!"

"Sounds like Achilles," I observed.

"Who?"

There was no time to explain the parallel as we were almost

to the stone ridge. "Just some Trojan heel who got mixed up in the biggest extramarital affair of all time," I said by way of dismissal. I escorted him into the camp and the introductions commenced. "This is the Reverend—"

" 'Father' will do," he corrected gently.

"I'd like you to meet Father Thyme," I amended.

"Not *the* Father Time!" Dyantha gushed with feverish incredulity.

"Not," I assured her.

"My friends call me Justin," said Justin.

"Justin? Justin Time? Oh!" She made a vain attempt to suppress a giggle. "What is your middle name?"

"Nicholas," he replied a bit stiffly.

"Nick? Justin Nick . . . oh, no!" The giggle disintegrated into helpless laughter.

"She's feverish," was the only excuse I could think of.

He nodded. "Positively delirious," he observed grimly.

There was no more sleeping this day, and bolstered by the little Gnome's stoutheartedness, we decided to travel with what was left of the daylight. Before mounting up, Justin tended Dyantha's shoulder wound, drawing upon his curative powers as a cleric. In less than an hour the fever was abated and her shoulder as good as new.

I managed to decipher a few more paragraphs before we broke camp and spent the remainder of the day with the distinct impression that my brain was playing paddleball with my eyeballs.

Although we encountered no one that afternoon, we left the road after sundown, taking a shortcut through a vast meadow. Justin insisted it would save us a good half day in our travels, but I suspected he felt safer away from the road after dark.

I think we all did, for that matter.

As the twilight deepened I remembered the other member of the party who was due to make an appearance shortly and I tried to prepare Justin for her eventual appearance.

"That one?" he snorted. "She wouldn't dare!"

Apparently the ecclesiastic and the Succubus knew each other from previous encounters.

"She'll not put in an appearance this night," he assured me. "Or any other night that I ride with you! That she-devil knows better than to keep company with me!"

I tried to remind Justin of The Rabble's motto: "Individuality, Tolerance, Cooperation." But he just snorted contemptuously. My experience with the various Fantasyworld clergy has been that they deal with Devils in one of three ways: they worship them, they exterminate them, or they claim there is no such thing. Not much middle ground to build any other kind of relationship on.

Lilith did not appear this night—but there were odd moments when I imagined I could hear the fall of iron hooves nearby in the cloak of darkness.

It was close to midnight when we neared the tree line of another forest. The moon had passed behind a long cloud so we were almost upon it before we saw the dim, monolithic shape rising above the grass.

Everyone stopped. And for a long moment nobody said anything. Justin finally reached into his shirt, drew forth a carved rowan symbol, and held it before him for a few moments. "I sense no evil here," he announced.

I dismounted and the others followed suit. "Torches," I recommended. Until we knew more, I was loath to use the witchlight as magic often triggers magic. Stumpy, Palys, and Dyantha brought torches forward, and in a few moments we had some working illumination.

At the base of the monolith was a coffinlike structure set upon a pedestal. The sides and top appeared to be made of heavy glass or thin crystal. And through the semitransparent material the flickering torchlight suggested that a body lay within.

"Now what?" I asked rhetorically. I didn't really want the next answer.

"We open it," said Dyantha.

"Thank you, Dr. Van Helsing; now tell me: *why*?"

"Why not?"

"Never met anyone who found opening coffins profitable, myself," grumbled Stumpy.

"There is magic here," announced Justin. "'Though I have detected no evil. And no thing of darkness would be interred in a crystal coffin, above ground, in such a beautiful meadow!''

"This here is Dwarven craftsmanship!" Stumpy exclaimed, taking a closer look. "Made with a great deal of care and love." He suddenly stepped back and contemplated the structure with a new and inquisitive attitude.

Justin stepped in close and placed his hands on the glassy top. "I sense a strange mixture of sorrow and hope here," he said, closing his eyes. His brow furrowed. "And life! A faint thread of life that dwells within, even yet!"

"I've got a bad feeling about this. . . ." I murmured, but no one seemed to care.

Palys even added her two cents' worth: "There are legends of great heroes who lie in enchanted slumber until they are awakened in a time of great need."

Everyone looked at one another. This certainly seemed to be just such a time. Justin and Stumpy eased the heavy top up and pushed it back from the glass box. As the lid fell back, the sides dropped away as well so that only the pedestal and base were left.

And the body that lay upon it.

After Palys's comment, I think we were all hoping for some great-thewed warrior wearing gem-encrusted armor. Instead we were confronted with a young maiden in rustic dress.

"Great," I muttered. "Peasant under glass."

Everyone stared for a long moment. She was okay-looking if you like coal-black hair, rose-red lips, and milk-white complexions. I nudged Justin: "You were saying something about a thread of life remaining?"

Stumpy cleared his throat and Palys observed, "She's remarkably well preserved if she is indeed dead."

Justin shook his head and passed his hands through the air above her body. "I do not understand," he muttered. "The spell at work here eludes me."

Dyantha suddenly gasped and pointed, "Look!" She pointed at the woman's face, and as a torch was moved closer, we could see that her lips were now slightly parted and that a faint tremor ran along her creamy throat.

"I think she's tryin' ta breathe," observed Stumpy.

"I think she is having trouble," added Dyantha.

"What do we do?" asked Palys.

"I don't know!" grieved Justin.

"She's startin' ta turn blue!" worried Stumpy.

"I think we had better try mouth-to-mouth resuscitation!" advised Dyantha.

"Mouth to what?" everyone chorused.

"Do something!" she yelled, shoving me forward.

Up close it did, indeed, look as if she wasn't getting enough air. Falling back on my old first-aid training, I tilted her head back and probed her mouth for any foreign matter. I found something. Reaching in with my thumb and forefinger, I extracted a piece of unswallowed food and dropped it on the ground. That seemed to help immediately, but I placed my mouth over hers and began filling her lungs with air.

Maybe a minute passed and she was beginning to breathe on her own. I started to straighten up but found it impossible as two arms had somehow become locked around my neck. This girl had me in a reversed full-nelson!

And then she started kissing me!

"It looks like a piece of apple," I heard Justin exclaim behind me. "And I do believe that it has been treated with some sort of poison!"

Oh, no.

Stumpy was the next to speak: "Looks like we've got company."

"Dwarves," added Dyantha.

Oh, no!

"Looks like six or seven of them," Palys elaborated.

Oh, no!

I tore myself loose from the young woman's embrace and yelled: "Ghost!"

He cantered obediently to my side and I vaulted onto his back. "Go!" I commanded. And he went.

Beyond the flicker of torchlight where light-blinded eyes could not see, I dug my heels in and urged him up and into the sky. Ghost spread his wings and we sailed over the trees and on toward Shibboleth.

I had no fears for the others. All in all, they were capable. And probably a lot safer without me as I seemed to draw trouble like a magnet. Both Justin and Stumpy knew the meeting place in Shibboleth and would show up in three or four days if they traveled without further interruption.

Running—or flying—away might seem the cowardly thing to do, but this was getting far too complicated, too fast. It would take a couple of days to explain the social customs and taboos of the *Wichtlein* and *coblynau*, so trust me on this one: fleeing the scene was the best thing I could do under the circumstances. To stay was to face some very determined Dwarves who would insist on a "shotgun" wedding at the very least.

That logic coupled with the knowledge that I had certainly saved the girl's life still didn't comfort me. As I flew through the empty night skies I could still hear Snow White's anguished cry: "My prince!"

FROM THE JOURNAL OF DAGGOTH THE DARK

If it should prove true that the Program itself has evolved its own subconscious subroutines, and Ripley's mindset—particularly his own peculiar sense of humor—is the Alpha-moulage for subsequent processing functions, then we've got a little problem. And if this (or any other) Dreamworld Program is accessing outside data files, then we've got another little problem. Put both together and we've got a bi-ig problem!

Unfortunately, that's not the end of it. We designed these Programworlds to update themselves and we didn't put a cap on their file size. I think Fantasyworld is still growing. And if the subroutines are assessing outside files on the datanet, there's no telling what could happen as the parameters expand!

What do I do? Eat, drink, and be merry? Might as well: there's nothing I can do at this point. And I hear there's this hot new number down at Hakim's place. Got to be more careful, though. The last "sweet young thing" I brought back to my place turned out to be real Dreamwalker, not a Construct! If that wasn't enough of a shock, "Valeria the Vivacious Vixen" turned out to be Maud Higgins, a sixty-two-year-old librarian from Peoria! Ye gods!

CHAPTER
TEN

★

I rode into Shibboleth toward noon, too tired to do anything beyond stabling Ghost and taking a room at the town's only decent tavern and inn.

I dragged myself up the stairs and, once inside my room, pushed the bed against the door so that any forcible entry would instantly wake me. It was an old trick and hadn't failed me yet. The window was a bit of a concern but my room was on the third floor and, frankly, I was too tired to do anything about it. I stripped off my clothes and fell into bed.

I awakened sometime later with my brain registering two impressions: outside, the sun was sitting farther to the west, and inside, someone was sitting in my chair. I wasn't expecting Goldilocks so I slid my hand under my pillow, reaching for the dagger that I always kept there whenever I slept on the road.

It wasn't there.

"Really, Rip, I expected more originality from you. Everyone sleeps with a shiv under their pillow these days."

I relaxed, recognizing Rijma's voice.

"Well, maybe I've got an extra one tucked inside my jockstrap," I drawled, rolling over and propping myself up on one elbow to look at Dr. Cooper's avatar. As a Human

Dorothy had hardly topped five feet; as a Brownie she wasn't much shorter. The curly, coppery hair was the same as were the merry blue eyes: it was amazing how much the avatar mirrored the original.

"Uh-uh." She smiled.

"What do you mean, uh-uh?"

"You know what I mean, Rippy. A good thief always checks all the angles." She threw me a fresh pair of pants.

"You're a dirty-minded broad, Rijma, but you're bluffing." I pulled my pants on under the covers. "You checked under my pillow, first, and that's what woke me."

She frowned. "And you wonder why nobody likes you at the Thieves' Guild."

"The price of eternal vigilance." I got up and stumbled to the washbasin. I poured the pitcher of tepid water over my head and managed a quick and hasty toilette. Rijma handed me a towel and then a clean shirt.

"Good thing you had an extra change of clean clothes in your saddlebags," she remarked. "I sent those things you've been wearing out to be cleaned over an hour ago."

"When will they come back?"

She sighed. "Hon, if you want your clothes back clean, you'll be lucky if they're back anytime this week."

"Thanks."

"Don't mention it. I have to breathe, too, you know."

I pulled on my shirt. "So who's coming?"

The copper-tressed Brownie shrugged. "We'll see who shows up tonight and tomorrow. The word has gone out. I expect to see some latecomers over the next week or so."

I shook my head. "Can't wait that long. We'll have to leave word as to our route and destination and let them play catch-up."

"Not that I'm surprised, but isn't that dangerous?"

"Nope. I think my worst enemy can find me anytime he really wants to. You have any problems in getting here?"

Dr. Cooper's avatar rose and crossed to the window. "Some. There was hell to pay back at the Control Center when they found out you were already in the Program. I was viewed as an accessory to a sort of non-crime. My defense —as if I needed any—was that you were neither in custody nor officially charged with any wrongdoing. In fact, they wanted you in the Program. But I think that they wanted a half dozen of their people with you when the time came."

I sighed. "You know, if I've learned one thing in the last three days it's that popularity isn't all it's cracked up to be."

She grinned and perched herself on the windowsill. "The tough part was getting away from Dr. Quebedeaux's party without being followed. Most of our avatars were still in the same part of sanctuary from our last expedition. I hung around long enough to pick up on one interesting tidbit of information, though: I think they're almost as interested in finding you as they are in finding the real culprit."

"They probably don't have the foggiest idea as to where to start looking," I mused. Then I told her about my conversation with Orcus, the journal, and my run-in with Straeker's avatar.

"You don't know for sure that Stephanie's dead," she said after a lengthy pause. "Or the senator, for that matter."

"I have no evidence that they're alive, either."

"It's not the same thing."

"Isn't it? This was my Program, Coop! I've always been able to locate any object or any person anywhere within its parameters. Maybe I'm not familiar with Senator Hanson's Warworld avatar, but my ex-wife is no stranger. Stephanie's gone! I can't even find her body!"

She was quiet for a long time. Rijma Fanderal, Fantasyworld's most notorious thief and scalawag, was temporarily eclipsed by the mind and personality of Dr. Dorothy Cooper as she considered the facts. We discussed my conclusions and then she raised one that I hadn't considered: "Do you think that the Program's self-awareness could be used to stop—or at least slow—the Anomaly?"

"I don't know." I began pulling on my boots. "My impression from talking to Orcus is that the Program's awareness is fragmentary. Some others might have such an awareness, but the condition is in no way universal. For any real help in altering Program reality, we'd have to find an interface—that is, a non-Gamer character—of major power and importance with such a perspective. . . ."

We looked at each other.

"Straeker?"

"Could be."

"An alternative would be raising the entire Program's level of consciousness to self-awareness."

"Too dangerous."

"I agree."

"In fact, there is even the possibility that the Anomaly is tied to the Program's state of self-awareness. Perhaps the cure will involve inducing a severe case of amnesia. . . ."

I stood and buckled on my belt. "The question foremost in my mind right now is . . ."

Rijma tugged at her moleskin gloves, suddenly alert for any forthcoming action. "Yes? Yes?"

". . . is the food here any good? Memory no longer serves after all these years."

A twinkle in her eye and the old, mischievous Rijma was back (a slight change, at best). "My child, the food is great and the floor show reputed to be even better! We can find out for sure just as soon as you can get yourself together and down the stairs to our table." She went to the door. "I'll rouse Stumpy on my way down."

"What?"

"Didn't you know? The rest of your party teleported into Shibboleth this morning."

I did a double take. "They what?"

"Teleported." She gave me a little punch. "Got here before you did."

"Who pulled that one off?"

"I believe it was the lady in leather—what's her name?"

"Palys?"

"That's the one. I'd keep my eye on her if I were you."

"I intend to," I said. "From now on." Teleporting one's own self was a difficult spell—particularly over the distance I had traveled in the previous night. Bringing the rest of the party along, horses included, was a feat beyond most magic-using Dreamers and generally guaranteed to incapacitate the spellcaster for a week or more. It was unlikely that Palys would be 'porting herself or anybody else again before we reached Daggoth's Tower.

"Well," she eased out the door. "I'll wake up and round

up the others. Starting with that crusty old curmudgeon of a Dwarf. Ta!''

I waved her out the door with some misgivings. Stumpy had no sense of humor even when he was wide awake and rousing him from a sound sleep was something akin to waking a cave full of hibernating bears. Of course, Rijma was well aware of that fact, but she had never been one to miss an opportunity to bait the old Dwarf. And while I didn't really worry about Rijma's safety, I was a bit concerned about the bill for room damages.

Two minutes later a roar and a succession of crashes confirmed my fears.

Despite my being fully dressed, I felt half naked as I descended the stairs to the main lobby of the inn: this was neither the time nor the place to be without a sword. I planned on visiting a swordsmith but would have to wait until one opened in the morning. I hoped I wouldn't be in need of one before then.

I had a slight headache: evidently I was getting better at deciphering the Wizardwrite as I had managed to read a half page in only half the time and felt only half bad. I decided to try for a whole page after dinner.

The Crashing Boar was even more of an aesthetic nightmare than I had remembered. The tavern looked as if someone had turned the blueprints of a Western saloon over to a crew of medieval stonemasons under the direction of Frank Lloyd Wright and Salvador Dali. As if the architecture wasn't bizarre enough, the decor appeared to have been orchestrated by a debased and somewhat deranged caliph from Baghdad. None of this seemed to offend the tastes of its patrons who, although a pretty tasteless lot, recognized the cultural hodgepodge as a sure sign of neutral ground.

Part of The Crashing Boar's success lay in the necessity for neutral ground in conducting cross-cultural business transactions. Here, tolerance was more a matter of avarice than altruism. Of course, neutral ground was as suspect as sanctuary, now, but a glance around the room indicated that something like it was still in effect. It was one thing to get Elves and Dwarves to drink together without smashing most of the furniture over each other's heads. Hakim not only managed this night after night with a minimum of breakage, he frequently accomplished the impossible: serving Orcs and Dwarves in the same room—a proximity guaranteed to result in structural damage to most buildings in a three-block radius before the dust settles.

Hakim insured the neutrality of his customers and the longevity of his furnishings by employing a couple of Ogres as bouncers. The fact that the regulars had nicknamed them "Beany and Cecil" belied their strength and savagery. Only strangers and fools started fights in The Crashing Boar: the Ogres always finished them.

The tavern was crowded tonight, but quieter than usual—something was in the air. I waded through a throng of bodies in search of Rijma's table and felt the occasional ghostly patdown of a cutpurse in search of my wallet. As I had judiciously secreted it in my boot, I ignored them and continued casting about for the rest of my group.

I saw a familiar face first.

The barbarian sat alone at a small table, contemplating some tragic scene at the bottom of his mug of ale. A large, double-bladed battleaxe had replaced the two-handed sword, but I was sure of his identity as soon as I saw the stump where his right hand should have been.

After a moment's gloomy meditation, he drained his ale and slammed his mug down on the table with a resounding crash. A buxom serving wench darted forward as he stood and adjusted the horned helmet that capped his flowing raven locks.

He ignored her outstretched tray for the moment, tipping his vikingesque headgear at a rakish angle and hitching up his loincloth to cover the beginnings of some rearward cleavage. Finally he turned, glanced down at her from the vantage point of his six-foot six-inch height, flexed his hulkish muscles, and rumbled: "How much?"

The girl dimpled under his scrutiny, bobbed in a half curtsy, and informed him that his tab for the evening amounted to four silver pieces and seven coppers. She raised her tray as he rummaged through a beltpouch of loose change, and then squealed as he dropped five silver pieces down her bodice.

She turned to go and was propelled the first three feet by the force of his pat on her backside. No one took umbrage: it was an old ritual.

I intercepted him on his way to the door. "Pardon, friend. . . ."

He looked down, trying to make out my features in the gloom of his own shadow. "Huh?"

"I'd like to give you a hand."

It was the wrong way to put it. The barbarian gently laid down his battleaxe and grabbed my shirtfront. Effortlessly he lifted me into the air and contemplated me with what I liked to think was an impassive expression.

"Not funny," he finally decided. And, just as impassively, threw me across the room.

I landed in the midst of a cross-racial card game, scattering the cards, the chips, the furniture, and the players. I had just a moment, as I collected myself, to notice that I had landed right beside the table I had been looking for. Rijma leaned down. "Some people just can't enter a room without trying to be the center of attention."

I struggled to sit up. "Save my chair," I replied.

A rather large Bugbear loomed over me. From the expression on his face I gathered that he had been holding the winning hand on the interrupted play.

"What do you think you're doing?" she asked.

"Recruiting," was all I had time to say as the Bugbear picked me up and threw me back across the room, toward the door.

Before I got there, I made another unscheduled stop: a large, grey-green "hand" shot out and plucked me from midair. Now I was under the less-than-impassive scrutiny of one of the bouncers.

"Hiya, Ceec!" I tried a friendly smile. "Long time no see!"

The Ogre smiled after a long moment—it was not an encouraging expression. He began to carry me toward the door.

"Hey, Cecil, thanks for the escort but I can see myself out—really! I am in a bit of a hurry to catch that barbarian who just went out the door—"

Which someone opened just as I went sailing through.

A pillar was within arm's reach as I flew over the boardwalk and out toward the street, so I grabbed at it to help break my fall.

Two Lizardmen came around the corner and broke it even more effectively as I swung around on the post. One was stunned by our collision and I pulled the other's cape over his head to facilitate my getaway. Three blocks and two alleys later, I caught up with the barbarian.

Hearing my approach, he stopped and turned.

I walked up and planted myself in what I hoped was a bold stance. "I think you could use a hand . . ." Once again the old shirtfront lift. ". . . and I'm just the one to give it to you."

He set me back down. "You a cleric?"

"Better than that, Mr. Henderson: I'm a Programmer."

He peered down at me with an expression of thoughtful appraisal. "You're Ripley, aren't you?"

I nodded.

At that moment two bruised and rumpled Lizardmen came running down the alley, full tilt, with swords drawn. Wordlessly, Henderson swept me aside and whirled his axe, cutting both of them down before they could check their rush.

"Let's go somewhere we can talk," he said amiably.

Cecil gave us the eye when we reentered the main room but, after a moment's observation, seemed satisfied that we were buddies now. We wove our way back to Rijma's table with me giving a wide berth to the renewed card game as we went.

She had procured a long table on the far side of the main room, in the shadows under the second-floor walkway; it provided more room, less noise, a better view, yet greater anonymity. I chose a chair that offered my back the protection of a solid stone wall and introductions commenced.

Besides Rijma and the barbarian, the latest addition to the group was a ranger who was simply known to everyone by his former aristocratic title.

The Duke was a big man, just a couple of inches shorter than the barbarian. Dispossessed of his family's holdings and wealth when he was young, he had fled into the wilderness and lived among the woodland rangers for the past twenty-seven years. He was quiet and dependable and he had only two unnerving eccentricities: he wore a hat that bore an uncanny resemblance to a Texas Stetson and he had a predilection for kicking in doors with a cocked and loaded crossbow in each hand.

Looking around the table, I was slightly reassured by the bulk and power of the ranger and the barbarian, the swordskill of the redheaded Amazon, the curative powers of the Gnome, and the heart and individual talents of the Brownie and the Dwarf. The unknown factor of Palys was a concern, but I felt an inexplicable reassurance when I looked at her and found her already contemplating my attention. I sensed a mystery about her, but felt no danger here beyond her own blatant sexuality.

This then, aside from the three newcomers, was The Rabble so far. In the old days it had been known as "Rip's Rabble." There had been other members, to be sure. But whether they were still alive or would see their way clear to join up with us were questions that only time would answer.

Unfortunately, we had no time to waste. We could ill afford to sit around for another week, waiting for more recruits while a senator was missing and Gamers were unaware of their own mortality.

I asked Rijma about the possibilities of recruiting more help among the locals.

"Been working on it since yesterday," she answered, already one step ahead. "Very few prospects around these parts, I'm afraid. The only interested parties seem to fall into one of two categories. . . ."

"Don't tell me, let me guess: farmboys eager to beat their plowshares into swords?"

"Ready to see the world and seek their fortune," The Duke chimed in. "Fame and glory, beautiful women, high adventure, beautiful women, fabulous treasure, beautiful women. . . ."

"How ya gonna keep 'em down on the farm?" Palys murmured.

"Trouble is, these yokels don't know which end of a sword is the hilt and think a *Bec de corbin* is a French dessert,"

Rijma finished disgustedly. "For all their eagerness, they're worse than cannon-fodder: they'd be a complete liability."

"Which leaves us with—?" I prodded hopefully.

"The nut cases."

"Nut cases?"

"Let me give you some examples. Yesterday I posted notices around town and set up my recruiting table at the edge of the village green. Before sundown I was approached by a white knight, a paladin with a singing sword, and a magic ring bearer. . . ."

"Doesn't sound so bad to me," I observed.

"Yeah? Well consider the first applicant. When I say white knight, I mean *white* knight: everything was white! White surplice, white horse, white saddle blankets fer Cromssake! That was my first clue!"

"First clue?"

"That this guy wasn't playing with a full deck. Hey, everybody's got one or two hangups but this guy should be licensed by the telephone company! You want examples? Take his phobia about uncleanliness—just guess what the inscription was on his coat of arms."

"*Fortius Quam Sordes*: 'Stronger Than Dirt.' "

"*Fortius Quam*—" Rijma echoed before she realized that I had already answered her. "You know this 'knight-error'?"

I nodded with a rueful smile. "Sir Ajax may seem a bit prissy to you, my dear, but I've always found him to be more than ready and willing when there was dirty work to be done. 'Twill all come out in the wash,' he used to remark cryptically."

It was the Brownie's turn to look rueful. "I'm afraid I didn't take him seriously. I suggested he go guard a laundromat."

"Okay, so how 'bout the others?"

"The ring bearer was a real prickly type; called himself Thomas Revenant the Agnostic. He was wearing this class ring that he claimed had some kind of magical power."

"What kind of magical power?"

"That was one of the problems"—she sighed—"he didn't seem to be too sure of that himself. Said that it was unpredictable and that he had no conscious control over it. Said it just sort of happened from time to time."

"What sort of happened from time to time?"

She shrugged. "I quit asking after the first couple of questions. I mean this guy has a real attitude problem! Negative, negative, negative!"

"Okay," I conceded.

"And rude! He even suggested that I was a figment of his imagination!"

"Okay, Rijma."

"And in addition to all of that he had this skin condition that you just wouldn't believe! I mean, talk about the heart-break of psoriasis!"

"Okay! Okay! Now tell me about the paladin," I pleaded.

"Now this guy was a definite 'maybe.' " She began rummaging through one of her beltpouches. "He gave me his card. . . ."

"I thought you said he was one of the nut cases."

"Well, he seemed normal enough himself. It's the sword that puts him in left field."

"A singing sword, you said?"

"Yeah, but it only does fiftics music."

"Fifties music?"

"Nineteen fifties music. You know: 'Do-wop,' 'Boom-shanga-langa.' "

"Boom? Shanga? Langa?" Clearly I was out of my element.

"Yeah, he claimed that it's the legendary Sword of Sha-Na-Na." She produced the card and slid it across the table. I picked up the rectangle of stiff parchment and contemplated the illuminated calligraphy:

PALADIN
Have Sword,
Will Travel

Short and to the point. I liked that.

I looked up to see a knight in shining armor making his way across the room toward our table. Did I say shining armor? This guy practically glowed in the dark. The light also seemed to reflect off of his impossibly white teeth and spotless surcoat. I wondered where he had managed to pick up a suit of chrome-plated platemail.

"I figured you'd want to talk to this guy yourself," Rijma explained as he drew near, "so I invited him to drop by."

He drew up to our table and executed a courtly bow. "Permit me the courtesy of introducing myself," he announced smoothly, "I am Sir Richard of Boone."

"Riplakish of Dyrinwall," I responded with a nod.

"I shall come directly to the point," he continued in a neutral but not unfriendly manner, removing his gauntlets and tucking them in his belt. "It hath been noised about that you and your comrades are setting forth to right wrongs and battle great evil." (He pronounced it "ee-vill.")

"Yeah. What about it?"

"I wish to join you in your holy endeavors."

I looked around at the others while I considered. We could use all the muscle we could get. However, the group treasury was all but nonexistent and good help was usually expensive. "How much do you think your services are worth, Sir Richard?"

He looked at me as if I had just addressed him in an unfamiliar language.

"Mayhaps thou dost misunderstand," he explained, using a tone one usually associates with baby-sitters and kindergarten teachers. "I am a paladin. A holy knight. It is my calling to assist noble causes such as yours. I am no man's hireling."

"In other words, he'll work for free," Rijma whispered.

"Okay, Dick, you're in," I answered decisively. "Pull up a chair and order anything you want—the first round's on me. If you have any questions, just ask Father Thyme, here. He'll introduce you to everyone and get you oriented." I turned to Justin. "Okay by you?"

The little cleric nodded enthusiastically. "He is a paladin—a holy warrior: there are none more trustworthy. A—how do you say it?—regular dooly dud—"

"Dudley Do-Right," I amended. "I'd like you to play den

mother until he feels comfortable with the group, Justin. And no religious debates.''

My attention was suddenly diverted to the discussion occupying the rest of the table. It seemed that The Duke and the barbarian were being treated to a distorted version of the previous night's events.

''. . . so all of a sudden he starts kissing her—''

''She was kissing me!'' I corrected, feeling a sudden flush creep into my face. ''I was giving her mouth-to-mouth resuscitation.''

''A fancy name for kissin'!''

''I was blowing air into her lungs!''

''Come on, Rip, everyone knows that the kiss of a prince will break the strongest enchantment!''

''I'm not a prince!''

''Not a handsome prince, at any rate!''

''Oh, I don't know. . . .'' That from Palys.

''When she started yelling 'My prince has come,' I thought old Rippy was going to levitate right then and there!''

''It was a case of mistaken identity—''

''Tell that to the Dwarves!''

''Yeah, that grumpy one was hollerin' for blood: your blood, Rip!''

''And one of 'em was real smart: he picked up your trail and led 'em all until the tracks ended a quarter of a mile away.''

''They finally went back home—''

''—but I don't think they'll give up so easily!''

''Yeah! They really love that girl, and you broke her heart!''

''You cad!''

''You heel!''

''You masher!''

''Left her standing at the altar!''

''C'mon, you guys! Give me a break!''

''You didn't do right by her, Rip.''

''Now wait a minute! I'm not the guy she's waiting for. Prince Charming is the guy who's supposed to wake her up and marry her.''

"Prince Charming?"

"Who's he?"

"You makin' this up, Rip?"

"No, really! She's supposed to marry Prince Charming and they'll live happily ever after!"

"Sounds like one of those Faerie tales to me."

"Yeah, and you can't trust anything one of those Faeries tells ya—"

And so it went. I felt rather awkward about the Snow White affair, so I was relieved when Rijma finally changed the subject.

"What's your name?" the Brownie, forthright as always, asked the barbarian.

"Conrad."

"You're joking!" She looked to me for confirmation and rolled her eyes. "Conrad the barbarian! Who's he trying to kid?"

"It's better than a name like 'Ridgc-mah,'" Stumpy sneered, deliberately mispronouncing her name.

"Ree-mah!" Rijma barked back, emphasizing its correct pronunciation. The archaic spelling of her avatar's name had triggered more than one mispronunciation from the uninitiated over the years. Stumpy, of course, knew better but couldn't resist because it was such a sore spot with her.

Justin, ever the peacemaker, was in the precarious position of sitting between them and was trying to negotiate a cease-fire when the floor show preempted him.

FROM THE JOURNAL OF DAGGOTH THE DARK

You can't have heroes without villains. So, of course, we placed varlets and evildoers in every Programworld. We assigned our casting like the director of a play: you, you, and you will wear chains and be slaves. Who knows how to handle a whip? Ah, then you will be a slave-handler. We need an evil high priest: line 'em up and pick out the most likely looking one; jiggle his programming and use an infusion of data from the history files; liberally mix with personality profiles from Adolph Hitler, Jim Jones, and Charles Manson....

Trouble is, this isn't a play. In Dreamworlds, the Construct becomes the role. He does not discard his script, shed his costume, remove his makeup, and go home at the end of two hours.

CHAPTER ELEVEN

★

THE lights dimmed and a pulsating beat was taken up by the dumbeki. At the sound of the zaghareets the dancers entered the arena, slithering and whirling, waving their veils as a prelude to the dance. Now the oud, kanoon, and bozouki took up the music and the women began the Beledi portion of the dance.

Our waitress chose that moment to come and take our orders.

"Ale."

"Ale."

"The gang's all here," Rijma murmured sotto voce.

"Wine."

"Same here."

"Beer."

The waitress turned to me.

"I'll have a vanilla Dr Pepper."

"Ask Hakim," Rijma added when we saw the bewildered look on her face. The serving wench curtsied and hurried off, much to the relief of Conrad and The Duke who were trying to watch the entertainment around her considerable bulk.

The music was changing now, the instruments working out improvisational solos as the dancers entered the Taxim phase of the dance. It was then that I noticed that one dancer stood out from the rest.

She was tall and lithe in contrast to the short, thickset women who danced around her. Her skin was nearly as dark, I noted as she danced closer, but it was tanned by a familiarity with the sun rather than the bloodlines of the *Surusund*. She began "dancing off the veil": removing the swath of gossamer that swaddled her torso, an inch at a time.

As the Tcheftetelli rhythm took over, she eased the veil from its moorings in her left shoulder strap and her girdle at her right hip. She danced toward our table with it held before her face, masking all but her eyes. The audience recognized the form as "The Sphinx Looks Out" and murmured approval.

Now the gossamer seemed to take on a life of its own as she performed "The Frame," "The Swirling Cape," and "The Canopy" in quick succession. She darted toward me and suddenly the veil filled my view, settling across my face like a ghostly mist. By the time I could pull it away from my head and shoulders, she had returned to the center of the arena.

Out of the corner of my eye I could see that Dyantha and Palys were both watching me, rather than the dancer, with what I could only describe as an "interesting" expression on their faces. I pretended to not notice and turned my attention back to the girl in the arena.

The kemanche wailed like a lost soul now, as she dropped to her knees and arched her back. Her long, raven-black hair swept across the floor as she undulated farther and farther back. Now the back of her head was just inches from the floor as she formed a serpentine arch of flesh, silk, and hair. We watched, hypnotized, as her tawny skin glistened with perspiration and her belly fluttered to the beat of the dumbeki and the zills.

Amid cries of "Opa!" and "Yasu!" and "Yala!" she churned, coiled, and extended a foot decked with tiny bells. Her hip spiraled upward and she quickly twisted about, writhing in a blur of colored silk, jewels, and strung coins. Her hands gathered a mass of night-dark hair as she rose back to her knees, swaying like a snake poised hypnotically before the charmer's pipes. Watching, it was hard to remember that there were other dancers on the floor.

She regained her feet as the Tcheftetelli rhythm picked up and moved into the Beledi finale.

I examined the veil, inhaling the double scent of musk and sweat as I puzzled over the woman's familiarity. There was something about her that disturbed me—something beyond what was disturbing every other male in the place. My mind sifted the evidence, searching for clues.

She was no dancer. Oh, she moved well, but I had seen enough belly dancers in my time to tell the uninspired professionals from the gifted amateurs. This one's popularity was due as much to her outland beauty as to her style and technique. Clad only in the brief, coin-strung brassiere and the diaphanous, split skirt of the Beledi, she displayed the body of an athlete. Tall, long-limbed, and long-waisted; the flat, curved muscle-tone of her belly contrasted with the pillow-flesh of Hakim's other dancers.

The waitress returned with our drinks now, and Hakim followed in tow. "My friends!" he cried with genuine delight. "Riplakish!"

"Hakim, you pirate!" I motioned him over to a stool beside me so that we could talk and the boys could enjoy an unobstructed view of the rest of the dance.

"Why did you not tell me you were in town?"

I winced at his backslap. Hakim was an extremely large man, built like an oversize bowling pin. Rumor held that he had been the sumo wrestling champion of the *Surusund*. At the age of twelve. "Trying to keep a low profile, my friend," I answered. "Perilous powers are abroad."

He nodded, a knowing expression on his round face. "As you know well, I am no paragon of virtue. My fingers are in many pies: a little larceny, some smuggling, mercenary traffic, drug shipments. . . ." He shrugged. "I look the other way on a lot of things. When a man operates in the 'grey,' he cannot afford to despise the 'black' and revere the 'white.' "

Then he looked across the room and his smile died. "But there are evils that transcend the petty quibblings of the pseudo-moralists," he continued heavily. "And *that* one has shadowed my hospitality overmuch these past few weeks!"

I followed his gesture and peered through the wriggling bodies and smoky haze at the gentleman in question.

My first impression was that here was a man of great wealth: he wore gaudy robes of silk and embroidered satins. My second impression was that he had about as much taste as a Sagittarian Slime-cultist: overadorned with jewelry and ropes of gems, you could dye this joker green and pass him off as a Christmas tree. My third impression was this guy was ugly—it was a tribute of sorts to his eye-assaulting apparel that I didn't notice this first. I mean this guy could've modeled for the warning labels they put on canisters of toxic waste.

His two bodyguards weren't much better-looking.

The one on the left looked like his head had caught fire and someone had tried to put it out with an axe. The one on the right had a face that looked like a high-relief map of the moon. Anybody casting them in a horror holo would have used makeup just to tone them down.

"Okay. So they're ugly," I observed blandly. "But if lack of comeliness was a crime, we'd both spend time in the slammer. Though I've got to admit," I added after another look, "that you and I might get six months' probation, while those characters should get life plus ninety-nine years."

Hakim shook his head. "Ugly faces are one thing, my friend. Ugly souls are another! You have not heard of Morpheus and his abominations?" As Hakim spoke those words, the subject of our discussion turned so that I could see the eyepatch. The shock of recognition was almost like a physical blow.

"I hear he's the Duke of Depravity," I mumbled. "Tell me more. . . ."

And Hakim did. He started with the stories of rapines, tortures, and murders until I was sick to my stomach. But Hakim was only warming up: there were darker rumors and suppositions, acts of evil beyond imagination. . . .

I finally waved him to silence: Morpheus made the worst atrocities of human history sound like schoolboy pranks. "I just want to know why no one's taken him out yet.'' I groped helplessly at my weaponless belt. ''And I want to know where I can get my hands on a good sword before he leaves this room!''

Hakim grasped my arm. ''Others have tried, my friend! And all who did, died! He bears a talisman upon his person that makes him impervious to every weapon! Blade and bow, mace and maul; all have been turned aside through the potency of this artifact! I have heard that a dozen archers loosed their bows at him from careful ambush, once. Each shaft was said to have turned back and killed the man who drew it!'' He leaned a pudgy cheek against his fist. ''How can such a man—if man he actually is—be withstood?'' he concluded glumly.

''There's more than one way to skin a rat,'' I replied with more conviction than good sense.

Rijma suddenly dug an elbow into my ribs. ''Don't forget your priorities, my lad. We've got a job to do. We can't get sidetracked with bug-squashing expeditions.''

''Why not? After all, we're here to debug the Program.'' Morpheus inspired a knee-jerk reaction in me. Finding him in my Program was like finding a cancer in my own body: I wanted to take a knife and cut it away as quickly as possible.

''Look, Robbie,'' she whispered, ''I know this is a problem for you. You wanted your Program to be a fairy-tale land of wonder and delight. Cephtronics and the Dreamworlds's board of directors wanted adult adventure and entertainment. We know who won that battle.''

''I'm not fighting the board anymore,'' I gritted back. ''I gave up trying years ago. But this is still my world—''

''Not all of it.''

''Not all of it,'' I agreed. ''But some of it. And now that I'm back, I intend to start taking some responsibility for the parts that I can!''

''Sounds like a messianic fixation to me.''

''Well, why not? I created this world so who has better claim?''

We both glared at each other. Then broke into fits of giggles.

"Pomposity always did become you," Rijma sputtered when she was finally able to catch her breath.

"Yeah, but there's something else you ought to know before we walk away from this guy," I said softly, my smile suddenly gone. "This is the guy who was with Daggoth the last time we were attacked . . ." Her eyes widened. ". . . and—if Stephanie's dead—this would be the sonuvabitch who's responsible."

She turned and stared at the object of our conversation with a quietness that suddenly chilled me. "It wouldn't hurt to get in a little practice ahead of time," she remarked with dangerous pleasantness.

"Or make the odds a bit more favorable for our next confrontation," I added.

Our attention had wandered from the dance, but now it was brought back by Hakim's cry: "*What is that stupid girl doing?*"

We turned our heads to see and the answer was quite obvious. Hakim's lead dancer had left the herd and was now dancing before Morpheus's table.

Worse than that, she was deliberately making her way around the table toward old skullface himself.

"She was warned," Hakim whispered. "They were all warned!" The anguish in his voice was more unnerving than his gruesome tales. "I have told every woman in my place —every barmaid, every serving wench, even the kitchen help—about Morpheus and his unholy lusts! I warned everyone to stay away from him! To let the eunuchs wait his table and serve his food! They have all heard the stories—aiee!" He buried his face in his hands.

Now the girl was slipping between Morpheus and the table, forcing him and his two "worthies" to move their chairs back a foot. The bodyguards fingered their swords nervously, but their employer showed no fear: the dancer's costume was too brief, too transparent, to conceal any weapon.

Now she faced him, leaning forward so that her silk-cupped bosom nearly cradled his cheeks. Now she whirled and leaned across the table, presenting her derrière. He reached for her there, but she was faster: she thrust her hips forward, pressing her pelvic girdle against the table and arching her body backward so that her long, midnight hair washed across his face. He swept it aside and grabbed her by the waist.

The dance didn't miss a beat.

Her upraised arms came down now, and she placed her own hands over his. Once more I found myself reaching for a nonexistent weapon, but instead of trying to pull away, she slid his hands down over the smooth hills of her hips.

I pushed her veil away from me as if its sheen of sweat had suddenly turned to slime.

She pulled his hands on down, across the throbbing plane of her belly, to the top of her low-slung skirt. And now she changed the tempo of her body movements and the musicians struggled to put on the brakes. No longer shaking and shimmying, her body stretched and twisted languorously—as if his touch had been what she had craved all along. It was both terribly erotic and disgusting at the same time, and an unnatural hush fell over the tavern as everyone watched with growing fascination.

She allowed his arms to encircle her gyrating torso and his spidery fingers to creep beneath the waistband of her skirt. Now she placed her right hand over both of his and pressed her left hand to her midriff, just below the arch of her rib cage.

Suddenly she bucked against his hands. Once! Twice! Her abdominal muscles undulated like a cracked whip and something glittering flashed above the table. A third pelvic thrust. And suddenly she twisted out of his grasp.

Her sudden move touched off a chain of motion across the tavern: most fell back in their chairs, but one Orc who was a bit closer to the action leapt to his feet.

"Lord Morpheus!" he shouted.

Rijma was suddenly up and flinging her mug of beer.

The Orc got about as far as "Your wi—" when the heavy pewter tankard caught him upside his head. He went down like a lead Zeppelin.

Morpheus was momentarily distracted but the girl swept around the table and drew his attention again.

Unfortunately, the other Orcs in the room were still looking at our table.

"If you were aiming at Morpheus, you missed!" I murmured out of the side of my mouth.

"I always hit what I aim at," she rejoined calmly, resting her hand on the hilt of her shortsword.

"Well, I figure we've got about ten or eleven seconds," I observed, pushing back from the table. "Want to tell me what this is all about before they beat the caca out of us?"

"Check the belly button," she whispered.

"Whose belly button?"

"The dancer's, dolt."

There was a sudden hiss as a number of swords cleared their scabbards. Beany and Cecil looked around, trying to figure out who they were supposed to jump first.

I caught a glimpse of the girl's umbilicus as she swept a goblet from the hands of one of Morpheus's henchmen. She threw back her head and guzzled the wine, allowing a large amount of it to run down her chin and splash onto her breasts. She locked eyes with Morpheus as she lowered the cup.

And she had yet to miss a single step in the course of the dance.

"Very nice—as bellybuttons go," I muttered, looking around now for another weapon. "Like a round goblet in which no unmingled wine is found wanting," I quoted. "Are you telling me that we're picking a fight with two dozen Orcs over this trollop's navel?"

"Do you want to live forever?" she challenged, pushing back from the table in turn.

"Well, since you mention it, *yes!*" While a dozen or so Orcs don't usually get me too worried, I was feeling a bit of a disadvantage without a sword. "I certainly don't want to lay down my life for some strange skirt just because some Orc takes umbrage over her umbilicus!"

"What did it look like before?" she asked, pulling her own sword.

"I don't remember. Is it important?" I glanced under the table: no refuge there.

"You don't remember because there was a ruby glued over it when she began the dance."

"She lost it?"

"She lost it like I lost my mug!" Rijma jumped onto the

top of our table. "She's done her part. Our job is to create a diversion!"

I looked back at Morpheus's table with what had to be one of my more stupid expressions.

And then it came to me. The glittering movement above the table as she writhed against Morpheus's hands—the sparkle of a ruby falling from its fleshy setting!

But where had it gone?

Morpheus grabbed his own goblet from the edge of the table and drained it greedily. The sweat on his face was clearly visible even from where I sat.

She lost it like I lost my mug. . . . Rijma's words echoed in my mind as I tried to visualize the falling gem's trajectory. It wouldn't have necessarily dropped straight down to the floor—the contraction of her abdominal muscles might have popped it forward. . . .

. . . like I lost my mug. . . .

Morpheus's goblet?

Was it possible that the dancer could have timed her movements to drop the jewel in Morpheus's goblet specifically? Such coordination, under the circumstances, seemed rather incredible. And what purpose could it serve?

Enough of a purpose, perhaps, that prompted an Orcish observer to jump to his feet to shout a warning. And prompted a Brownie to risk life and limb to silence same.

She's done her part. Our job is to create a diversion. . . .

Orcs from tables all over the room were beginning to advance on our table. Hakim, ever the discreet and neutral host, had already disappeared. Rijma was going to have her "diversion."

"Rijma! I haven't got a weapon!"

She appeared unruffled as the grey, green, and warty circle began closing in. "Then fly reconnaissance, dearheart! And do try not to drop any good vintages this time." She followed this dry piece of advice with a Brownie warcry that was positively bloodcurdling. Immediately all Hades broke loose.

Having little choice with no sword, I levitated out of harm's immediate way and perched in a convenient chandelier over the battle's heart.

Stumpy and Justin had already acquired a bench in the

meantime, and promptly ran it, full tilt, against the first four Orcs in the vanguard. Conrad and The Duke followed suit by picking up our table and flinging it across the room at another group of approaching uglies. Those Orcs avoided it easily, but blundered into a party of Dwarves in the process of trying to dodge the airborne furniture. Needless to say, that touched off a real free-for-all, evening up the odds a bit.

At this point I turned my attention to a rack of wine bottles behind the great bar at the other side of the room. Levitating myself was easy: it's a basic incantation from the *Beginner's Book of Shadows*. Levitating other objects was a lot trickier, however. It was more of a *psionic* discipline than actual magic, and I lost more than a couple of bottles as they floated across the room and into my arms.

Faithful to my pledge to Rijma, I spent the next several minutes sampling each wine to make sure I didn't waste any quality bordeaux. I needn't have worried about any vintages that Hakim would serve over the counter—most turned out to be a step or two above paint remover. I only sent one bottle back to the bar and that was because the stuff was so awful that it begged to be served to someone—hopefully the medieval equivalent of the health inspector.

Satisfied that the rest were expendable, I turned my attention back to the fight below.

The nice thing about bar fights is that nearly everyone has removed their headgear in advance of the fisticuffs. I had a bird's-eye view of the top of everyone's head. Including a large Orc who was trying to club a pathway beneath my chandelier.

"Bombardier to pilot," I announced, gingerly holding a bottle by the neck, "we are over the drop zone. Target in sight. . . ." I wet a finger and tested for wind: none apparent. Allowing for the Orc's horizontal movement and my missile's vertical trajectory, I released one and one-quarter seconds before he was due to pass beneath me. "Bombs away!"

Scratch one Orc.

Some didn't go down quite so easily: twelve bottles later I had only downed seven targets, including an Elf who had made a sudden movement in the wrong direction. A couple of others had required a second bottle to finish the job.

In the meantime Rijma and Stumpy had regrouped, back to back, in the center of a small circle of Orcs. As usual, they were arguing with each other as they fought to keep the entire Orcish ring at bay. Elsewhere, Father Thyme had crossed purposes with one of the Ogres. From my vantage point it looked like Justin had found an unreachable hold on Beany's back: as the Ogre tried desperately to dislodge him, the little Gnome repeatedly beat upon his thick skull with the remains of a stone pitcher, crying, "Repent! Repent!"

The Duke was now positioned in a corner with both cross-bows drawn and cocked. The five Orcs who had him cornered knew he couldn't get more than two of them at best. And The Duke kept underlining this fact in his calm, matter-of-fact drawl, encouraging them to find out which two it would be. They all seemed to be giving the matter a great deal of thought.

Dyantha was parrying the blades of three different attackers—oops, make that two—uh, rather one—well, just forget it. She could take care of herself. The paladin was faring equally well, holding a large number of Orcs at bay while his singing sword hummed a tune that sounded sus-piciously like an old ballad entitled "Mack the Knife."

I scanned the main room twice but caught no sight of Palys. The barbarian seemed to have broken free of any direct con-frontations for the moment. He had ascended to the second-floor walkway and was working his way down, cutting all of the ropes where they were tied off at the railing. One after another, the huge chandeliers came crashing down on the combatants, taking out ten or twelve at a time as opposed to my one-to-a-customer wine-bottle bombs.

I was admiring the precision domino effect of the entire row of chandeliers dropping, one right after another, when it suddenly occurred to me that mine was next in line. No time to cast a spell: I held on tight as my overhead roost suddenly plummeted to the floor.

Then, just as suddenly, I was on my way back toward the ceiling. Morpheus had picked that moment to pursue the object of his immediate lust beneath my immediate location. His arrow-repelling talisman seemed to work equally well on chandeliers: I hovered even closer to the ceiling than I had before. I knew I couldn't depend on Morpheus to stand under my chandelier forever so I grabbed the support rope that now dangled limply to the floor, and began to climb down.

A bloodcurdling screech caught me unprepared and I lost my grip before I made the halfway point. One of the tables broke my fall, and I was able to do some pretty fair damage to it in return. Propping myself up in the midst of the wreckage, I stopped and stared.

Everyone else was doing the same.

Morpheus's body had gone rigid. His hands groped and clawed at his throat and chest like blind things.

"Scaras! Rhegad! I have been poisoned!" he screeched. Where before his face had been flushed, it was now a flaming scarlet—and getting darker.

In a flash his two bodyguards were up and about, their swords drawn and menacing.

"Innkeeper!" Craterpuss bellowed the summons like an impatient executioner kept waiting at the block. I hoped that Hakim wasn't naive enough to come running.

"Blame not the innkeeper, Accursed One," answered a high, clear voice. "Nor his wine steward. I alone am responsible for the venom that, even now, clouds your mind and renders your spells impotent!" It was the dancer who spoke and she now faced him defiantly, feet spread, arms akimbo.

"Bitch!" he hissed, taking a staggering step toward her. "Why?" His face was turning from scarlet to purple and he looked down at his legs as if they no longer obeyed him.

"Why?" She laughed contemptuously. "That I am Human should be reason enough to desire an end to you and your foul practices! That I am a woman justifies me! But above all, as Amazon, I am bound by both duty and honor to slay you for the dog that you are!"

"Coward!" he hissed. "You call this honor?" The purple was tinged with black.

"You would not permit honest combat! I used treachery where treachery was given and long overdue! You could not be touched by stone or steel, iron or incantation—so I used the only weapons left to me!"

"The prophecy . . ." he croaked, sliding down on one knee.

"The prophecy stated that your life was proof against any poison administered by the hand of man. I am woman. But, be that as it may, I did not administer it by hand." Her right hand brushed her stomach where the "ruby" had once nested.

She smiled with mocking irony. "Know, O Morpheus, in these last moments before your death; who has deceived the Deceiver, and who has killed the Murderer! I am Aeriel Morivalynde, princess and heir-apparent to the Amazon throne! In the name of my people and our domain have I done this thing! And my only regret is the quickness and ease of your death!"

"Cerberus!" he wailed.

The room grew suddenly cold and the lights dimmed. In seeming answer to his anguished cry, a ghostly apparition appeared and moved toward Morpheus.

"I am here, Father/Brother," the phantom answered, bending toward him.

"Receive my essence," he whispered, sagging toward the floor. "Scaras! Rhegad!" he croaked, rocking on both knees. "Avenge me!" Then he pitched forward onto his face and lay still.

The apparition bent low, then stepped back. With a shock, I saw that the "ghost" was Daggoth himself. *Now*, I thought, *we are in trouble*! But the apparition of Mike Straeker's avatar turned and walked through a nearby wall and out into the night.

Snapping out of my reverie, I had only two seconds, but it was sufficient to grab Aeriel's arm and jerk her back as the floating chandelier ceased to float. Apparently the talisman lost its power at the moment of the enchanter's death: the overhead lighting arrangement came crashing down at our feet.

Quick reflexes were all I needed to save the girl from a falling chandelier. Saving her from Morpheus's two assassins was another matter.

"A sword!" I cried. "Someone throw me a sword!"

Everyone stared back at me with a vacant expression.

"A bag of gold for a sword!" I yelled in desperation. I

had to jump back as some thirty-odd swords flew in my direction from all over the room.

"I can deal with these vermin myself," Aeriel remarked as I selected a weapon from the loose pile of cutlery.

"Probably," I agreed, coming back to stand beside her. "But you don't have a sword. And that's hardly first-rate armor that you're almost wearing."

"Faun!" she called out.

"Here, sister!" An Elf leaned across the second-floor balcony and tossed what looked like a coil of black rope. The "rope" unfurled as it traveled to her waiting hand and became a whip. She cracked it once, reflexively, and then turned to face the two assassins with an insolently relaxed stance.

"I'll bet you look great in black leather and high-heeled boots," I murmured as Scaras and Rhegad advanced.

She gave me a measured, sidelong glance. "How did you know?"

I shrugged. "Lucky guess."

Scaras decided that I posed the more immediate threat, so I had his undivided attention. Rhegad was trying to decide whether his buddy needed any backing or if he could indulge himself by going one-on-one with the lady. Feeling chivalrous—and maybe a wee bit emasculated—I made a bid for a martial ménage à trois. "Hey, Pizza-face!"

That did it. The lady was forgotten and now Rhegad wanted me for himself. He passed Scaras while he was still a good eight feet away and lit into me like a deranged Cuisinart. It took all of my skill to hold him off for the first minute or so. After that, it was easy: I regained momentum and took the offensive.

Rhegad was a backstabber and a bully—but he was no swordsman. His initial ferocity had taken me by surprise but my instincts and reflexes were equal to his brute strength and fury. I might have been in trouble had Scaras joined in.

Scary, however, was only able to take about two more steps before the end of Aeriel's whip wrapped around his left ankle and jerked him off his feet. He landed rather heavily upon his head, and from the sound it made as it struck the floor, he was not likely to get back up for a very long time. If at all.

That left Rhegad. It was beginning to dawn on him that I was more than his match in an honest fight and that no one was going to come to his rescue. He made a break for the door.

He was met there by a tall woman in a scarlet robe. Slender and pale and coldly elegant, Lilith held us all in the thrall of her ice-crystal gaze. She slowly entered the room and Rhegad shuffled backward as if in a sudden trance.

She stopped several paces past the threshold and extended a milk-white arm. "Come to me, man." Her quiet summons echoed throughout the tavern as if in a tomb. I saw Justin's hand make the sign for protection against evil. But he made no other move to interfere.

The Demoness gestured once: Rhegad stopped backing away. She gestured again, her ice-blue eyes locked on his empty, grey orbs. And he stumbled toward her.

I stepped toward her also. "Lilith . . ." I warned.

"Do not interfere, Riplakish." She answered me without turning her head. "I hunger! And this animal is my just prey."

I seemed helpless to gainsay her as the Demoness enfolded the man in her bloodred robe and drew his mouth to hers.

Then she kissed him.

It was a long, lingering kiss; in all appearances a kiss of desire and passion. Except the desire was hunger and the passion, terror. What should have been fire was ice; the pantomime of love, predation.

Rhegad struggled once. And then was still.

At first rigid, his body began to slump as the kiss continued. And as we watched, he began to age before our very eyes. In less than a minute his hair went from black to grey to silver to white. His skin lost all color and his face began to crinkle like aged parchment. His body seemed to crumple and fall in upon itself until it attained the appearance of an unwrapped mummy.

When she released him at last, all that was left was a dried husk that crumbled to dust when it dropped to the floor.

The Succubus drew her hand slowly across her mouth. "I hungered, and so have fed. But still I thirst. . . ." And she looked around the room.

It was as good as any fire alarm: in less than thirty seconds

The Crashing Boar was completely evacuated. Even The Rabble had elected to wait for me outside.

Aeriel was the only one who stood her ground along with me. She even met Lilith's cool gaze across the empty room as she spoke. "So, Riplakish, you traffic with Demons, now?"

I winced. "My dear Aeriel, if I ever chose to do so, don't you think I could direct traffic a little better?"

"Judge him not, woman," Lilith said quietly. "I am Geased to him by one my own kind cannot disobey." She turned and looked at me with frightening tenderness. "He could have banished me by power long since now. But he withholds for he knows such an act would destroy me. He knows mercy, this one. . . ." Then she began drifting toward us. "Now, stand aside: you have done your night's work, here. Let me attend to mine."

She obviously meant Scaras. I couldn't think of any justifiable reasons to refuse her, but my conscience pricked me just the same. "He's unconscious and no longer a threat."

She shook her head and glided closer. "I still thirst. Go. And allow Hell to claim its own."

And looking into her ice-blue eyes, I suddenly seemed bereft of will to argue. Aeriel took my arm and led me away toward the stairs.

FROM THE JOURNAL OF DAGGOTH THE DARK

It's now been more than five years since Ripley *vs.* Cephtronics ruled in our favor. But I'm less convinced that we were right and Ripley was wrong. Are the Programworlds "Alternate Realities" in every sense of the definitions? Have we gone beyond the protoplasmic fumblings in laboratory test tubes to actually create complex, intelligent life-forms? I feel that my death and subsequent survival now bears reexamination of the question.

But Ripley no longer has any voice in Dreamworlds' development and now that I'm gone the reins will probably fall into the hands of Dr. Quebedeaux. Sondra has a brilliant mind, a matchless intellect—but now that I am a permanent inhabitant of this world, I find her lacking in those qualities I want to exist in God....

CHAPTER
TWELVE

★

"WE need to consider our next move."

Aeriel's statement took me by surprise and I almost turned around. Since it sounded like she was still dressing, I managed to catch myself in time to be discreet.

"You don't have to be so discreet, you know," she added in an amused voice. "You've seen me in the buff plenty of times."

"That was ten years ago, Aeri. You were just a kid then, and not so—"

"Developed?"

"Grown up."

"And out?"

"'Matured' is the word I was thinking of."

"I'm so glad you noticed. Why don't you turn around?"

"Are you dressed?"

"I'm still washing off. But don't let that bother you."

"I'm trying not to." I was bothered, all right. In fact, I was furious at Cephtronics for diddling the programming so that an Amazon princess was acting like some addlebrained bimbo with a schoolgirl crush. I sat down on the edge of the bed.

"I can't believe that I finally have you all to myself," she continued, "without Misty Dawn around to interfere. She's very possessive of you, you know."

The shift in conversation had caught me off balance. "What?"

"She's let me know in no uncertain terms that you are her personal property."

I felt twin flashes of annoyance and grief. "I'm nobody's 'personal property'!"

She chortled. "That's good. That means I have a chance. Although the prospect of competing with a Nymph does seem a bit daunting."

"What?"

Suddenly she was in front of me, pushing me back upon the mattress and kissing me. I was too stunned to resist and it took another moment to register that in the process of undressing and redressing, Aeriel had only gotten as far as the halfway point between the two.

It was too ludicrous for words—which was probably why I hadn't come up with any, yet. I tried to put my hands where they could make and keep some distance between us, but I only ended up making things worse.

"That's very nice," she murmured.

"Aeriel, I think you're confusing a little girl's crush with something a little more serious." Crom-on-a-crutch! I could hardly point out that her behavior was programmed to satisfy the lusts of fat cat businessmen who utilized Dreamworlds for a different kind of fantasy trip. "After all, you're a grown woman, now!"

"I'm so glad you've noticed! Especially with so much evidence at hand!"

"What would your mother think?" I parried weakly.

"My mother thinks that as males go, you're the best of the sorry lot and I have her blessing."

I was saved any further maneuvering as the door to Aeriel's room suddenly flew open.

Queen Hippolyta's daughter rolled off of me and sprang to her feet, grabbing my borrowed cutlass as several figures crowded the threshold. Standing there naked and brandishing a blade, she cut a magnificent figure. For a moment all eyes were on her and I probably could have escaped out the window. But in that moment the urge to flee seemed an unchivalrous one.

In retrospect, the decision to stay seems more stupid.

An authoritative voice spoke: "Dr. Ripley, you and your companions are my prisoners. Should you make any attempt to resist or escape, by any means—physical or magical—they will all be slain. Starting with your—ah—'lady friend,' here." There were three drawn shortbows with their arrows aimed at Aeriel's heart, and at this range none of the grim-looking archers could miss. Behind, and towering over them by a good fifteen inches, was the largest Human I had ever seen. This joker was even bigger than Conrad the barbarian. There were sounds of reinforcements out in the hall, but my attention was drawn to their leader who had just spoken.

It was impossible to determine the outline of a figure in that dark, wine-colored robe but the face above it was slender with angular Elvish features. What at first glance had appeared to be a silver skullcap turned out to be platinum hair pulled severely back and knotted at the nape of the neck so as to fall back into the hood. A woman, I decided after a moment. Although many Elvish males tend toward the effeminate, this one knew my True Name. Only one other Dreamer was likely to know who I was and come looking for me.

"Dr. Quebedeaux, I presume?" I murmured softly.

"What's that?" she asked sharply.

I sighed. "Doesn't anybody knock anymore?"

The rest of the night, to my memory, was uneventful.

Since I was surrounded by armed guards, I slept reasonably well, untroubled by dreams of Goblin hordes attacking us in the hours before dawn.

On horseback the following morning, it appeared that I was the only one who was well rested. Aeriel and The Rabble, I'm sure, had spent the night contemplating various plans of escape. And Dr. Quebedeaux had apparently singled out Natasha Skovoroda for special attention, still suspecting that the

Soviets were behind the Dreamworlds problem. Dyantha looked positively haggard as she mounted up. As she rode she swayed in the saddle like a ship caught in a heavy swell.

I was left pretty much alone, although I was under constant observation to prevent any Houdini-type hanky-panky. Our captors were thinly stretched to keep all of us under guard, and I doubted if any of them had slept either.

Since the bindings on my wrists weren't uncomfortable and no one seemed to be in any immediate danger, I postponed any personal escape plans for the time being: let someone else do all the work and worrying for a while. Besides, we were heading toward Daggoth's Tower and that's where we wanted to go anyway.

Aeriel rode beside me throughout most of the morning, but it wasn't until the sun stood at its zenith that we had the chance to speak privately.

"What did you do with the Demoness?" she asked when the nearest guard finally drifted back and out of earshot.

"Nothing," I whispered. "I try to do with Lilith as little as possible." I looked forward and back. "Where's Faun?"

She shook her head. "Three Amazon squads were concealed near Morpheus's stronghold. They were awaiting Faun's return to mount a housecleaning expedition. As soon as she saw me safe, she would have mounted up and returned to our waiting warriors. I was expected to play the fox for any of Morpheus's remaining hounds. I am afraid that we are on our own."

I shrugged as one of the guards reined in closer and cocked an ear. "By the way," I remarked, nodding at her outfit. "When did the Amazons adopt this 'sun and fun' apparel?"

Aeriel frowned. "I know not what you mean."

"I'm referring to those two little scraps of chainmail that you seem to think is legitimate armor. Why the big change?"

She laughed. "You jest, of course! Such has always been the battledress of the Amazon warrior-maiden."

Untrue. I had written a more realistic, not to mention modest, dress code into the original Program. Cephtronics had changed that, too. I had a lot more than a bone to pick with Mike Straeker, I had a whole skeleton.

Rijma came riding up from the front of the procession and

wheeled her war pony in beside Ghost. "Lady Silverthane requests your attendance up front," the Brownie announced dismally.

The message and the way it was delivered pushed my annoyance level up three notches. "Dammit, Rijma, I told you that you weren't to blame for this," I snapped. "And tell her 'ladyship' that I don't make house calls!"

"They followed me!" the diminutive footpad lamented. "Even if I didn't know it, the fact remains that I led them right to you!" She sniffed. "When you're a veteran thief, it's doubly embarrassing."

"Dragonshit. Dr. Quebedeaux is Dreamworlds's Chief Programmer: I'm surprised it took her this long to find me. You're just embarrassed because we're tied up and you aren't. They're still watching you just as closely as they are us."

"Thanks." Her head came up a bit. "It's nice, not to be accused of divided loyalties."

"Bunk. There really are no enemies here. This is just a little misunderstanding."

"Then I'm sure that you'll have it all straightened out just as soon as you've talked with Lady Silverthane." She smiled brightly.

How could I argue with that piece of logic? "You can't accuse someone of divided loyalties when they haven't shown you any," I growled as I nudged Ghost toward the front of the line.

Lady Silverthane rode a palanquin instead of a horse. Her silk-shrouded litter was borne upon the scaly shoulders of four Lizardmen, with four more "spares" trotting behind.

I rode up alongside her transport, and when there was no immediate response, I announced my presence. "Knock, knock," I drawled in my best imitation of The Duke.

For a fleeting moment I was afraid she'd answer "Who's there?" and I'd be committed to following through on the joke. I needn't have worried: her sense of humor was too atrophied for such subtleties. The curtains parted and Alyx Silverthane regarded me with solemn lavender eyes.

"Lord Riplakish."

I bowed in the saddle.

"I should like to begin by saying how sorry I am for these

present circumstances. I do hope your bindings are neither too uncomfortable nor too inconvenient—''

"My back itches," I replied formally, "but at least I can still pick my nose."

"—but under these present circumstances, I deemed certain precautions necessary."

"You strike me as the type of woman who only knows caution and only does what is necessary."

I was fishing for a reaction and she took the bait. Coloring, she snapped: "All right, Mr. Ripley, I don't like you very much, either!"

"I didn't think so. Mind telling me why?"

"To put it simply, I find certain elements of your little fantasyland disgusting! As far as I can see, the primary function of any female Construct is to be a sexual object! You have your own little private playground here, with hundreds of fantasy women programmed to satisfy your every deviant wish!"

She was on a roll and there was no point in trying to explain that Cephtronics was responsible for that particular twist in the programming.

"I would find that repellent enough," she continued sharply. "But with the lives of hundreds of real men and women at stake—real flesh and blood captives to your personally conceived mindworld—do I find you diligently seeking a solution to the Program Anomaly? No! I catch you sporting with some overendowed, oversexed slave girl in your bed."

Fortunately, Aeriel was riding far enough back as to be out of earshot.

"You've demonstrated a complete lack of concern for the lives of other people. Your disregard for their well-being while you pursue your own drunken lusts is beyond contempt! A man with your lack of morals is too dangerous to be allowed to run loose with Program-shaping power. That is why I have taken it away from you."

It took a moment to sink in. I leaned toward her. "What do you mean, 'you've taken it away from me'?"

She put on a "regretful" look. "I've stripped you of your

spellcasting abilities. You can no longer work any magic in this Program.''

I laughed. "All right. And how did you accomplish this simple little trick?"

"I removed your Program Access Code."

A cold hand suddenly clenched at my insides and my laughter turned into a fit of coughing. "You what?"

"I removed your Program Access Code. You no longer have Programmer status in this Frame. You can no longer alter the Program internally. In view of the non-status ranking of your Bard classification, I doubt if even the simplest spells will work for you, now."

I held up my bound wrists. "You'll forgive me if I don't immediately take your word for it?"

She nodded. "Go ahead. Try and spell yourself free."

I tried. Beginning with a simple, little Unraveling spell.

Nothing.

I worked my way up through the various levels of thaumaturgy.

More nothing.

For a final, make-or-break test, I attempted to disintegrate the rope with a frantic lack of caution for my wrists in the process.

Still nothing.

When I finally looked up again, I found Dr. Quebedeaux's avatar regarding me with an expression that could only be interpreted as pity. That stung as much as anything else.

"Lance!"

The big guy in the plate mail came riding up. "Yes, Mistress?"

She pointed an imperious finger at me. "Free him."

"Free him?" High-pockets looked at me with all the confidence of a betrayed lover.

"Yes. Now that Lord Riplakish has been apprised of the new rules, I think he'll start playing the game our way."

"But if he tries to escape—"

"He won't. Stripped of weapons and power, I think our bard will appreciate the old adage: there is safety in numbers."

I held up my wrists. "Rip promises to be a good boy!" *For now*, I amended silently.

The big man extended his lance with the precision of a surgeon wielding a scalpel, and neatly severed the cords where they crossed between my wrists. I hadn't realized that those pointy poles were so sharp at the tips. "Lance, huh?" I mused, rubbing my chafed wrists. "That your real name?"

"Nickname," he admitted stiffly.

"Named after your proficiency, no doubt?"

"When it comes to the lance, he's the best in the saddle," Alyx added proudly.

"Maybe in your saddle," I sneered, turning my mount around to take my leave, "but I don't impress so easily."

I started to ride back toward Aeriel and Rijma but a large, mail-gloved hand caught my shirtfront and lifted. My feet stayed in the stirrups but my rear no longer touched the saddle.

"Your meaning, sirrah?" he inquired tightly.

"Put him down, Lance. He's just fishing." Her voice was composed but her face was red. "My dear Riplakish, if you want me to reinstate your Access Code, you ought to be more pleasant and cooperative."

"Perhaps you should hold up a hoop and have me jump through it."

She sighed. "This is getting us nowhere. Let him go, Lance. We'll give Dyrinwall's druid some time to think things over. When he's through pouting, we'll have another talk."

Lance lowered me back into the saddle. "Time heals all wounds," he agreed.

"And wounds all heels," Silverthane added as I turned Ghost back toward the end of the line.

Over the next two days of the journey, I took stock of my situation. Other than my mithril shirt and the shirukens and garrote concealed in my belt, I was defenseless. I was still without a sword and no one had offered to return my longbow, arrows, and throwing knives that had been confiscated on the night of our capture. I was in no condition to go wandering off alone, and as long as Silverthane was the key to regaining my Programmer status, I wasn't about to let her out of my sight.

Our captors weren't taking any chances. The Rabble, with the exception of Rijma, continued to ride on tether with their wrists bound. I was kept apart from the others when we stopped to rest or make camp, so there wasn't much chance to compare notes or discuss any plan of escape. Otherwise, all went well enough until the third day of our journey.

About midmorning my skin began to prickle with the discomforting impression that we were being watched. If my magic was gone, my sixth sense still seemed operational. Though there was no concrete evidence, I was sure that I sensed a presence.

This posed a difficult question: keep my own counsel? Or warn the very people who held us prisoner? With most of my friends bound, disarmed, and unable to defend themselves, the choice seemed obvious: better the known than the unknown. I rode forward to warn Lady Silverthane.

Lance fell in alongside, on the way. He didn't say anything and I'd already used my best insults over the past couple of days, so we came to the palanquin in silence.

"I have not summoned you," was her greeting.

I thought about turning her into a porcupine. The trouble was that even if I regained my powers, the act would have been inherently redundant. Rather than start a fresh round of insults, I got straight to the point.

"We're being watched."

"So? And by whom, pray tell?"

"I don't know. But my guess is we'll have company soon enough. Maybe ten minutes. Maybe ten hours."

"And what do you suggest I do about it?" she asked coolly.

"Free my friends. Give us our weapons back. Give us a fighting chance—for your sakes as well as ours! Safety in numbers, remember?"

She smiled condescendingly. "Truly, Lord Riplakish. I expected better from you, and certainly before now. Do you think I am so naive as to fall for such a fabrication?"

"Someone or something is out there," I insisted. "I don't know what—but I'm sure there's more than one . . . maybe a lot more than one. . . ."

It was of no use: it was readily apparent that she wasn't about to believe me. And the more I argued, the less convincing I'd sound. I made a quick decision. Weaponless, I couldn't free my own comrades. It seemed I had only one alternative whereby I could save the party: if we were riding into a trap, perhaps I could spring that trap. Prematurely.

Without giving warning, I dug my heels into Ghost and urged him forward.

"Stop him!"

It was a cornball line, a staple of every tri-dee thriller I'd ever watched as a kid. With the wind in my face and the freedom of the road before me, I couldn't resist a triumphant laugh.

I stopped laughing when the arrow caught me in the thigh. I screamed and kicked Ghost into the fastest gallop he could maintain without leaving the ground.

I felt another arrow glance off my mithril-protected back and heard the pursuit commence. Silverthane was yelling something but I was over the next rise and out of her line of sight and, therefore, her effective spell range. To tell the truth, initially I had worried more about her spell ability than I had her archers. The shaft of red-hot pain through my leg was an overwhelming reminder of that miscalculation.

Seeing a wooded copse ahead, I risked a look back.

Four guardsmen were hot on my tail with Lance not far behind. Considering the amount of man and metal it had to carry, I was surprised that his poor horse could manage anything faster than a brisk walk.

I turned back around as I came into the trees so that I could avoid any low-hanging branches, and rode into a down-swung flail. I caught a quick glimpse of rough-looking men concealed among the foliage before spiked iron balls filled my vision.

What followed immediately is still a mystery to me. Whether I pulled Ghost upward or he leapt instinctively, I do not know. I had a brief impression of being airborne. . . .

And then I knew no more.

FROM THE JOURNAL OF DAGGOTH THE DARK

Maybe it's my fault. I probably started it when I told Ripley I was redesigning the Orcs to be meaner and nastier—and that I was basing the prototype on my mother-in-law.

When he told me what he had named the Dragon, I didn't really believe him....

CHAPTER
THIRTEEN

★

I awoke to two basic impressions: pain and darkness.

At first I thought it was night.

Then I hoped. But the absence of moon or starlight seemed to disprove that assumption.

That I was blind was the next logical consideration. If any of those spikes had missed my eyes, I would have to count it as miraculous.

My clumsy, groping fingers felt upward and discovered that a bandage of sorts covered my aching head from the nose up. That would explain the absence of any light, but I'd be a fool to dismiss the thought of permanent blindness just yet.

I lay quietly, pondering, and then felt about the rest of my body—particularly the arrow wound in my thigh.

The shaft had been drawn and the wound bandaged with some sort of poultice. There were plenty of cuts and bruises over the rest of my body, but they seemed minor and had been anointed with some sort of ointment. I was suddenly aware that I was naked beneath the woolen blankets that covered me. I drew the covers up to my chin, more conscious of the chill in the surrounding air.

"Are you cold?" The voice was soft, but unexpected,

causing me to start and half rise from my bed. Gentle hands eased me back down.

"Who's there?" I asked.

"A friend," was the quiet, almost hesitant reply.

I tried a smile. "So it seems. What happened to me?"

"I was hoping that you would be able to tell me. Do you not remember?"

I groped through the fragments of memory. "I rode into an ambush. . . ."

"Near Gaehill?"

"I think so. We were headed in that direction. . . ."

"Then you are not from around here?"

"No. . . ."

"And you were traveling with others?"

"Yes. . . ."

"But you had not been warned of any dangers in this part of the country?"

"No, not specifically. . . ." I paused, not wanting to bring the name of Morpheus up until I knew more about the hands into which I had fallen. I was trying to discern the speaker's gender from the pitch and timbre of his/her voice, but the sudden flow of questions seemed to have ceased for the moment. "You don't seem surprised that I was set upon."

"Strange circumstances have come to Gaehill these past seven years." There was another long silence. "First there came a monster that terrorized the countryside and made this area a shunned and desolate place. This beast, however, does not range afar nor hunt those travelers who keep to the road. It is the other, the Wurm, who has made Gaehill a hissing in the mouths of all who know of her."

"Wurm? You mean a Dragon?"

"Aye. It appeared about eight moons ago and made its lair in the mountains, just the other side of town. Crops were destroyed. Many farms and half the city were burned."

"How do they fight it?"

"Fight it? They do not." Anger suddenly flashed in that quiet, hesitant voice: "They serve it!"

"Serve it?"

"Why not? They have lived these past seven years with

one monster practically in their midst. And they have come to believe—after the loss of a few heroes—that a well-fed and unmolested monster is preferable to the cost of defying it."

I was almost sure that my benefactor was a woman, now, but I could not be sure how many others might be standing nearby, silent and cloaked by my own sightlessness.

"Now that another monster sleeps upon their doorstep," she continued, "they still fail to learn that it is more expensive in the final accounting to befriend a Dragon than it is to make war upon it." The sound of a sigh. "We have resorted to savagery to protect civilization." There was a long, uncomfortable silence. "Were there any women in your party?" the voice finally asked.

I felt a growing disquiet. "Yes, why?"

"Then you may as well count them as lost."

"You are telling me that they are dead?"

"Unless the city guard was unusually careless, they live. For now. Gaehill bribes its Dragon with monthly sacrifices. So they will live until the next full moon. And then their blood will purchase Gaehill another month of peace."

I fought the impulse to jump out of bed. "You're telling me that the people of Gaehill have—an arrangement—with this Dragon?"

"Yes. As long as the town provides the Firedrake with a monthly sacrifice of five virgins, it will spare the town and the surrounding farms and villages."

"I'll bet there're a lot of farmgirls out there luring a lot of farmboys behind haystacks, even as we speak."

"If I append your meaning, good sir, such would be ineffective. To the Wurm, any woman of a certain age, so as to still be tender and juicy, qualifies as a 'virgin.' I fear Dragons are not interested in the scorecards of Human copulation. They are only interested in what tastes good."

So Unicorns and Dragons had differing definitions of the term "virgin." An interesting but unhelpful piece of information for the moment. I filed it away for future reference and reviewed the facts: there was something here that was terribly familiar and very important. But I was having trouble putting my finger—

Avatar memories suddenly clicked into place. "Smog!" I cried.

"Mayhaps you know of this particular Dragon, good sir?"

"Mayhaps nothing: I kicked this overgrown lizard out of the Southern Provinces ten years ago for trying this same extortion racket. I did it before and I will damn well do it again!"

A sudden wave of weakness mocked my boast. Except, I was no longer as young as I once was, had lost my magic abilities, was possibly blind, and could very well meet a very permanent death this time around. I groped at the bandages. "My eyes. . . ."

"I do not know. With time and rest and healing—we shall have to wait and see—"

"I haven't got any time." I started to rise but a gentle hand against my chest restrained me once more.

"You have not the choice in this matter. To leave this place, you will need your strength and your sight. You have neither now. Rest. And we shall see what tomorrow brings."

A cup was brought to my lips.

"Drink."

I did. The wine was heavily spiced and I caught the scent of crushed poppies. Almost immediately a lethargic warmth began to spread through my body.

"I have not learned your name, friend," I murmured as the drug began taking effect.

"It is—Euryale," she answered cautiously.

"I give you thanks, Euryale."

"You are most welcome, stranger. Now, do me courtesy for courtesy and tell me your name."

Funny. I couldn't remember for a moment. "Ripley . . ." I said finally. "My name . . . is . . . Ripley. . . ."

And I slept once more.

I awoke after—what: minutes, hours, days? There was no way of telling—not even dreams to quantify the oblivion of sleep. The rough blankets still covered my body from toe to chin, but in spite of their weighty thickness, I was still chilled. I heard and felt the presence of a flaming brazier to my left, beside the bed. But it was the warmth to my right that drew my body for solace from the fever's chill.

My arm was already draped over it and there was no doubt in my mind that it was a body. Very gently and very carefully I moved my hand to answer the next set of questions.

Yes, it seemed to be a Human body, and like mine, it seemed to be naked. And—oops—it was "the fairer gender." I moved my hand upward and suddenly found it caught in a viselike grip.

"Not my face . . ." she said quietly. "Please. . . ."

She pulled my unresisting hand back down to her breast and held it there. "I'm sorry," she said after a lengthy silence, "but I am sensitive about my face."

"I'm the one who should apologize," I answered.

"No. You were merely curious. Not improper. During the night you took a fearful chill. The blankets and the braziers alone were not enough to warm you in this drafty cave. So I tried to warm you with my poor body. . . ."

"Nothing poor here," I argued gallantly.

"I give you thanks for the compliment, stranger."

"And I give you thanks for my life, Euryale."

"You are . . . most welcome . . . Ripley." The set of my mouth must have conveyed my surprise. "Your name is Ripley, is it not?"

I nodded. "Well—yes. I guess it's just been a while since I've heard someone else say it."

She sighed. "Mine, as well. As you may have gathered, I am a hermit. This cave is my home, and until two days ago, I lived here alone."

"From the sound of your voice and the touch of your skin, I would guess that I've got a few years on you. What inspires a young woman to shun the company of her own kind and seek the lonely life of a recluse?" Even as I asked, it occurred to me that this might not be the most tactful question. "If I'm not prying," I amended lamely.

"I am ugly." She said it flatly, without emotion, as if she had become long inured to this fact and yet had trouble believing it. "That is why I am sensitive about my face. And that is why I live alone, without Human companionship."

"Is it really that bad? I mean, maybe you're being too hard on yourself—"

"It is a moot question of who determined my exile: Humankind or myself out of personal choice. The fact remains that others find my scarring unbearably hideous!"

"Your friends—"

"I have none."

"Family?"

"All dead, except for one sister. Stheno has visited me in the past, but she has enemies and does not travel as much as she used to."

"How long have you lived alone?"

"Nearly seven years now."

"Then you were not always . . ."

"Ugly? No. There was a time when I had many suitors. I was considered one of the most beautiful women in the land! But—that was before"—she hesitated, a catch in her voice—"the accident. I must not dwell upon the past for all of that is lost and gone now. And nothing that I know of can change my plight."

"Nothing?" I, too, knew how a life could be unfairly shattered by a chance accident. "Surely some cleric would have the power to heal you, to restore your face?"

"No." She was silent for a long time. "I have not spent these past seven years in idleness: I have sought a cure for my affliction. And I have failed. No one can help me."

"I find that hard to accept."

"Nevertheless. If any could, it would be the one who did this to me. And she would not. Or else one of the two Shapers."

"Shapers?"

"There are only two that I know of: Daggoth the Dark and Riplakish of Dyrinwall."

"And have you tried asking either of them?"

"Dyrinwall is too far—there is too much open ground for me to traverse in getting there. And I approached the Dark One five years ago, only to be rebuffed and sent back to my cave."

I was appalled. "Did he say why?"

"He said something about my having to live out my destiny. Does it matter what reason he gave? The final word was one of refusal."

"I . . . I'm sorry. . . ."

"It is all right. I have learned to live with my changed circumstances."

"But it must get lonely. . . ."

"Yes. . . ." I felt her take a sudden gulp of air and turn away from me: "It gets very . . . lonely. . . ." Her shoulders began to shake and there was no doubt in my mind that she was crying now, though she did it too softly for me to hear.

I reached up to stroke her hair, to comfort her. And felt her draw away. "No, please," she whispered in a tear-strained voice. "Do not touch me above my shoulders! If you would touch me . . ." She was suddenly shy. "If you would give . . . or receive . . . pleasure . . . you may touch me . . . anywhere . . . below my neck. . . ."

I hesitated: I had learned the hard way, a long time before, that you do not make love to someone out of pity; ultimately, you only add to their wounding by doing so. But I felt a greater fear for what another rejection might mean at this time in her life. And since Riplakish of Dyrinwall no longer had the power to give her what she needed, perhaps it was only right for Robert R. Ripley the Third to make whatever amends that he could.

I pulled her body to mine. And I comforted her as best I could.

Over the next two days she nursed me back to some semblance of health, and I nursed a growing suspicion.

It was an ugly thought and it grieved me to associate it with the soft voice and gentle hands that had cared for me in my helplessness. Still, the question had to be asked.

Loneliness has been known to do strange things to people. It has killed some, driven others mad, and certainly made all of us desperate at one time or another.

How desperate might a young woman be who has been without love and companionship for seven years? Whose disfigurement promised a life of solitude for all the long and lonely years to come?

Would she find her salvation in saving a man's life who would not only be grateful, but also immune to the hideousness that drove all others away? Would she cover his eyes with bandages and tell him that he was blind, just to cheat her own fate for a short while?

Or some dark night, in the middle of a drug-deepened sleep, would she unwrap those bandages and see to it that his blindness was made real? Made permanent?

It suddenly became very important to know as much as possible about my mysterious benefactor. And regain my sight as quickly as possible.

She was an artist, a sculptress to be more precise. Over the long years of exile she had filled the cavern with statues to populate the empty spaces of her lonely life. I touched and explored many of them, always marvelling anew at how she had managed to capture the essence of life in each individual work.

Once, she allowed me to sit nearby while she worked on one of her pieces. I was allowed to listen but forbidden to touch. "I am a temperamental artist," she explained over the sound of chisel against rock. "I will not have you examining a work before it is finished."

All of her works were of people, most of them men: only three women and four children rounded out the lot. "I do not seem to have any talent for animals," she confessed. "Only people." And always full-size figures. No busts.

When I asked her if she planned to do a sculpture of me, her mood darkened. "I will never put you in stone," she insisted fiercely. "I would keep you here, if I could. But not in that way. . . ."

I'm not sure which of the clues finally caused the others to fall into place. Her explanation for the hissing sound I sometimes heard was unacceptable to me from the start: "There are hot springs located throughout the cave and sometimes excess steam vents through cracks in the rocks. . . ."

By the fourth day, when she took me to the room where her treasure was kept, I knew who she was.

FROM THE JOURNAL OF DAGGOTH THE DARK

I've mentioned my suspicion that psi-linkage transfers more than conceptual imagery—that the emotion—the very mindset of the Programmer may actually be introduced into the Matrix. This would certainly explain the bizarre elements of humor that have manifested throughout Fantasyworld lately. And raises another question.

We initially had some problems with Warworld. General Brackett programmed the perfect wargame environment and then was unable to engage the enemy. While others reported brilliant battles and satisfactory skirmishes, the good general was never able to pick a fight.

The enemy would either retreat or surrender. Almost as if the Program feared any kind of conflict with its creator. Does this mean a Programworld, created by direct psi-link, has a mental/emotional bias for the Programmer responsible?

It's been over five years but I don't remember Ripley ever finding the Goblins reluctant to fight. Of course, Fantasyworld is more complex than Warworld: Program bias might manifest itself more subtly. Perhaps some of the Constructs—subroutines of the Master Program—would be friendlier, more apt to form alliances. Perhaps—in some cases—Program bias might translate as romantic interest, sexual attraction....

CHAPTER
FOURTEEN

★

"I keep my treasure in this small grotto." She led me into a chamber about the size of a walk-in closet. "I wish you could see it. But then, if you could see, you would not have stayed long enough to have found out about this place."

By now I had grown a little weary of her intermittent self-pity: "Do you mean I would have run away in fear or have been petrified by fright?"

"That was unkind," she said after a long moment.

"You're right," I agreed. "And I'm sorry. But you need to understand something, Euryale. You can't hold on to someone through pity—not for long, at any rate."

"I deserve to be loved!" she cried.

"I know that. But it is your strength and courage and endurance that attracts me. Not your wretchedness. I feel compassion for you, not pity. Please don't think so little of me to suppose that my love might be purchased by something so mean as pity."

There was a thoughtful silence. "Well," she said finally, trying a disarming tone, "if I cannot buy your affection with pity, then how about gold?" She held out my hand and poured a pile of coins across it.

"Gold is always nice," I said agreeably.

She laughed. "Well, then how about gems? What do you like? Diamonds? Rubies? Emeralds?" I heard her open a chest and dig through its contents. "How about a crown?" I suddenly felt the weight of a heavy metal circlet settle over my head.

"Where did you get this stuff?"

"Oh, most of it was already here when I first moved in. . . ."

"And the rest?" I prompted.

"Daggoth," she said slowly. "He gave some of it into my keeping. To guard. He knew no one would come looking for it here, even if they knew where it was. Euryale makes such a good watchdog!" she said bitterly.

"And I suppose this is part of what he meant by your destiny?"

I could imagine, rather than actually hear her nod. "There is a potent artifact here. He said that it must not fall into the wrong hands. He said that I was to guard it with my life."

"What else did Mr. Wizard say?"

"He said . . . the day that it came to another's hands . . . would be the day my wretched existence would come to an end. That prophecy has frightened me for years. . . ."

"But now?"

"Now, I am weary. An end—any end—would be most welcome." She worked her way to the back of the chamber and, after rearranging some chests, returned and touched my face. "Are you the one?" she asked softly. "Are you the one whose coming I have feared these many long years?" She took my hands in hers. "Are these the hands destined to wield Euryale's bane and thus fulfill the prophecy?"

"I would not hurt you," I answered gently.

"Too late!" She sighed. "You have already wounded me. If you are the one, then it is only right and fitting."

"Euryale—"

"Here." An object was placed in my hands. "In your fevered sleep you once cried out for a sword. I give you a sword now. Tell me: what will you do with it?"

It was a shortsword. Slowly I drew it from its sheath and listened to it—even before attempting a tactile examination.

There was power here.

I ran my fingers along the flat of the blade, feeling the runes and symbols of mystic energy. I knew this sword: the carved patterns on the hilt and the great jewel set in its pommel confirmed my suspicions. "My lady," I inquired, unable to resist formality in the presence of such an artifact, "may I borrow this device?"

"My lord," she answered in kind, "thou mayest ask anything of me, and I would grant to thee with all of my heart! Ask for half of this treasure and I would give it all to thee! But why does a sightless man ask for this sword—unless to fulfill Daggoth's prophecy?"

I laughed. "Don't be afraid. It's very simple: I have friends to rescue and I need a sword."

"But your eyes—"

"With this sword I shall have my eyes!"

"I do not understand, but the sword is yours if you wish it."

"Madam, you do not know what you are offering me so freely."

"Good sir, I only know that which I deem most precious I have already offered. . . ."

"Euryale, this is Balmung, the legendary sword of the Nibelungen! This is the ultimate Dwarven blade, forged when the world was young and Dwarven smiths vied with Elvish craftsmen for the mastery of the Forge!

"Out of every thousand swords, there might be one that lays claim to a special purpose. And out of every ten thousand of those comes a weapon with a heritage of enchantment. But Balmung is one of the ultimate swords of power. Only one other weapon, down all the corridors of time, can lay claim to like power and potency: Caladbolg, the Sidhe longsword with its blade of pure crystal."

"How do you know this?"

"By the runes engraved upon the blade and hilt. And because it whispers of its power to me, even as I hold it now."

"And what does it tell you to do?" she asked in a tremulous voice.

"It tells me to right an old wrong, Euryale. And it tells me to fulfill your prophecy."

"I am afraid," she whispered.

"Afraid? You? The 'monster' who has terrorized the countryside these past seven years?"

"Please, do not mock me—"

"I don't mock you, Euryale. It just seems ironic that one of the most feared persons within a hundred leagues of Gaehill is afraid of a blind man."

"Because, of all men, you are the one over which I have no power!"

"Why is that? Is it because my eyes are covered? Or because you cannot bring yourself to harm me even at the peril of your own life?"

She was silent except for the sound of ragged breathing.

"Do not fear me. Or what I am about to do." I walked toward the last sound of her voice and reached out to touch her cheek. She flinched away and there was a sudden hissing sound. "I shall end this curse, once and for all!"

"Then you know," she said slowly.

"Yes. Though it took me some time—I know."

"How you must despise me."

"No. I am a bard, Euryale. As such, I am familiar with the truth of the story. The gods are often unfair and punish the many for the one's misdeeds. The story of the Gorgons is well known. But it is Medusa's name that is a hissing in the mouths of the skalds and storytellers! For it was her vanity and boast of unrivaled beauty that brought down Aphrodite's curse! Her sisters, Stheno and Euryale, are a tragic footnote to the story. When they are even remembered at all."

"We had our vanity, too," she admitted quietly.

"As do we all. Aphrodite is perhaps the greatest offender of all in this matter. What a pity that no one punishes her for her unseemly pride."

"Medusa is dead. . . ."

"And nearly forgotten. As you and Stheno have already been. The only fame left to you is your status as a local oddity: not to be feared as long as you are avoided. And that little notoriety has been eclipsed by the arrival of a bigger and better monster."

"And after all of these years," she pondered in that same quiet voice, "I do not know which is worse: to be hated and feared, or to be forgotten and alone."

"It no longer matters," I told her gently, "for I mean to end it. Here and now. Come here."

Now the silence was long and loud. Almost a full minute passed before the scrape of sandaled feet over stone announced her movement toward me. "You will use the sword?" she asked softly.

"Of course. I have lost my power so it is the only way."

She stopped, and then her step quickened. "I am here," she announced, taking my free hand in hers. "But before you do as you will, I ask a boon: a kiss."

"A kiss?"

"Now. Before I lose my nerve."

One of her hands was suddenly behind my head, bringing it close so that my lips found hers in the warm darkness. Now I was aware of the nest of serpents, unturbaned, that coiled and writhed near my face. Now I was aware of the fangs that curved beneath those willing lips. But now I knew no fear for I finally knew just who and what I was embracing in the darkness.

She grasped Balmung by the tip of the blade and moved it so that my arm was forced back and down, positioned for a slight upward thrust. "Do it quickly!" she whispered. "And if you feel any pity whatsoever: strike again, a second time, to make sure the job is done and I do not suffer."

"Euryale," I chided, reaching out to stroke her hair. A sudden hissing reminded me to draw my hand back just in time. "You misunderstand."

"Do it quickly, my friend! Before I lose my courage!"

"Very well," I agreed.

I drew the sword's point back from where it pressed against her breast and raised it over our heads. "In the name of thy makers, Brokk and Sindri, I invoke thee, Balmung! Enchantment of Ivaldi's sons, I claim thy power and make my wish twofold: healing *and* deliverance—for us both!"

Warmth enveloped me.

And a sudden weakness.

Euryale experienced it and sagged against me.

Then came a surge of power: a sense of strength and a burning, throbbing sensation where my wounds—*had been*! It passed quickly, with a fading aura of expended power, and in another moment I felt rested and strong again.

I reached up and ripped the bandages from my head.

"No!" Euryale cried out in alarm and terror, but it was too late: I could see her now.

I could see a slender young woman trying to cover her face with one hand and shield my eyes with the other.

"Euryale, it's all right. I can look upon you with no harm. One of Balmung's most potent powers is its ability to grant a single potent wish every seven years. To rescue my friends, I had to heal myself. But I gambled that its power would be sufficient for us both. I think it was."

She looked up and then used her hands to feel about her head. "I have hair!" she cried. "Real hair!"

It seemed inappropriate, at that particular moment, to point out that her hair was pale green. In most other respects, she appeared normal. In fact, a lot better than normal: even though the wish had been spread too thin to complete her transformation to the last detail, she was still attractive—in an exotic sort of way.

"How can I ever thank you?" she cried, throwing her arms around me and falling upon her knees.

"Uh, well—like I said—um—if I could borrow this sword—"

"It is yours to keep! How else may I reward thee?"

"Uh, the sword is quite enough—uh—thank you—" Kneeling with her arms about me had placed her face and my anatomy in a socially awkward tête-à-tête. "Actually, any help you can give me in getting to my friends would be greatly appreciated."

"Of course," she murmured silkily, pressing her cheek to my leg.

"In view of their impending sacrifice: the sooner, the better," I added.

"Of course," she said. But it carried a ring of reluctance.

Even stripped of her monstrous powers of petrification, Euryale proved more formidable than I had supposed. Over the years of her exile she had studied the occult arts to try to rid herself of her monstrous form. Though she had failed in that final goal, she had acquired considerable powers—most particularly in the practice of illusionary magic.

That talent enabled us to enter Gaehill unmolested. Every town guardsman, merchant, or citizen who looked our way saw only an old man and an old woman of no particular appearance, tottering down the street, leading a burro. Her powers had to be considerable if she was able to layer a second *glamour* over the first that already encircled Ghost.

By spending the better part of the morning wandering through the marketplace, we learned that the sacrifice was scheduled for midnight, this very night. We also decided that dealing with one fire-breathing Dragon in his cave would be preferable to tangling with a multitude of priests, acolytes, and temple guards in their own man-made labyrinth.

After doing all the reconnoitering possible, we found an inn and rented a room.

"How about a nap before lunch?" Euryale suggested, patting the bed.

I could have done with a little rest but I doubted that rest was what Euryale had in mind. I shook my head. "Let's go over that map of yours again."

She sighed and came over to the table. "It has been over seven years since I have been abroad in this area: not only is my memory untrustworthy, but there are sure to be changes, as well."

"I'll check those out after sunset when I'm less likely to be seen. Now let's assume the natural chimney is still there and unblocked. . . ."

"We have a full fifty feet of rope."

"Will that be enough?"

She nodded. "At best, the drop is no more than forty."

"If your memory serves you right."

"It is difficult to be certain," she fumed. "This insane plan of yours gives me fits of hysterical amnesia! Ripley, what kind of strategy is this? You are going to climb down that chimney into the caverns, somehow find your way to the Room of Sacrifices, somehow free your friends, somehow defeat a fearsome Firedrake, and somehow find a way to sneak all of you back out again, before the guards can find out and interfere. *Somehow* this kind of planning does not reassure me.''

''Come up with a better idea and I'll be happy to listen.''

She put her arms around me. ''Loyalty to one's friends is very noble. But what kind of a friend would expect you to commit certain suicide—a hopeless rescue attempt that most likely will end in tragedy for all of us?''

I shook my head. ''My friends wouldn't ask this of me. But my friendships aren't based on what my friends ask.''

I let it go at that. I saw no reason to bring my Access Code into the discussion. This rescue might seem the foolish undertaking of an idealist, but the cold, hard reality of it was that if Dr. Quebedeaux died, my chances of survival—much less my chance of getting back out of the Program—would die with her. I wanted to help my friends, of course; but I shrank from the question of what I would do if I had any other chance of regaining my Programmer status.

''Let's get something to eat'' was my escape from pursuing the thought any further.

The name of our hostel was ''The Roaring Hangman and True Blacksmith Inn.'' And if its name was twice as long, the tavern downstairs was only half as large as that of The Crashing Boar. Still, we did not find that to be any inconvenience: there was a ready selection of empty tables for us to choose from. Gaehill boasted a number of inns and taverns, but with the arrival of the Dragon, the tourist trade seemed to have dropped off quite a bit.

As there didn't seem to be any further point in keeping up appearances, Euryale dispersed our illusionary disguises and we ordered lunch, figuring that no one would connect us with the old couple who were nosing around earlier in the day.

''You know,'' she observed while we waited for the food to arrive, ''you are my first date in over seven years.''

''There will be many more,'' I assured her.

She smiled. ''I hope so,'' she purred.

By ''many more,'' I had been referring to other men. Somehow I didn't think we were on the same wavelength.

During the course of our meal she asked many questions. I couldn't lie to her: not only was she too intelligent to fall for any inconsistencies, but she had saved my life as well. Since we might both be dead before another sunrise, I couldn't help but tell her the truth. Not about the Reality from which I came or anything about computers and programs and such. But I told her as much as I could about who I was and what I had done in this Reality. And what circumstances had brought me to the point where I found myself now.

She was thoughtful after I finished. "So," she deduced after considering this new angle on my identity, "I was succored by the Archdruid of Dyrinwall, after all."

"Not so loud. For the time being, I think it would be better if you kept calling me Ripley and we avoided any references to where I'm from."

"Why?"

"If anyone recognizes me here, it's not likely to be a friend," I said.

And just about jumped out of my chair as a voice behind me said: "Riplakish."

I turned my surprise into a gracious, mannerly rise and pulled back a chair for our new arrival. "Well met, Lilith. Won't you join us?"

"Not so well met. But I will join you." The Demoness slid into the offered chair.

"I expected to run into you before now," I said to her after introductions had been completed.

"You must be kidding! With a holy man like Thyme in your party?"

"Well, afterward—" I amended.

"It was too late, then," she snapped. "The damage was already done! Orcus nearly had my soul for dinner over this whole affair!"

"How could he blame you?"

"For a bard and a Dreamlord you certainly can be a nit," she muttered in a tone of complete exasperation. "Do you think 'fairness' is a prerequisite quality for the executive promotions in Hell? Orcus is the Infernal Prince of the Undead, for Cromsake!"

"I'll have a few words with him and straighten this all out—" I offered.

She shook her head. "You are such a nice guy, but, oboy, you are such a nit! It's too late for talk now. The only reason that I'm still around is because Orcus has this thing about saving face. He's making an example out of me in case the other Demons start getting careless in the performance of their assigned duties."

"I don't understand. . . ."

"Nit! Come hither, man, and I will show you!"

She took me completely by surprise. I started to lean forward to see just what it was that she was carrying on about —and she grabbed me. And before I could pull back, she laid one on me. A kiss, that is.

Now there's nothing wrong with an attractive woman grabbing you in a bar and kissing you. Unless, of course, she happens to be a Succubus. Then you've got about fifteen seconds to say your prayers before your ass is ash.

It came back to me about three seconds into the kiss that Lilith was, indeed, a Succubus. And it was probably another minute before she broke her lip lock and gave me a chance to draw air. I leaned back in my chair and tried to look nonplussed.

"Well, what do you say to that?" she demanded.

"That was a hell of a kiss," I said finally.

"No! That was not a Hell of a kiss!" she stormed. "If that had been a Hell of a kiss, you'd be nothing more than a legend, right now!"

"You've lost your power?"

"I've lost nothing! It was taken from me!"

"Taken from you?"

"As in dishonorable discharge. Orcus decided that if Father Thyme would prevent any Demonic aid to your party, he would get me into the game the only other way he could without interfering directly: by giving me back my Humanity. My magic is gone—finding you here was pure luck." Her voice broke. "I'm ruined!" She put her head down on the table and began to cry.

I didn't know what to say.

"You seem to have a talent," Euryale observed, "for

making women out of monsters. I have known many men whose efforts run in the opposite direction."

"Tell that to her."

She smiled. "I will. Why don't you see if you can make yourself scarce for an hour or so."

"What about dessert?"

"I am sure we can manage. Now shoo!"

I didn't see any point in spending the last few hours I might have in this life sight-seeing so I went back upstairs to our room. I got through an entire page of the journal before my eyes tried to claw their way through the back of my head. Tugging off my boots, I settled myself on the bed so that my feet could rest on the windowsill. As the warm summer breeze caressed my tired, aching feet, I closed my eyes and tried to relax.

I was frustrated: time was slipping away and I seemed no closer to a solution to the Anomaly than when I had first entered Fantasyworld. In fact, my situation was growing more complicated at every turn. Were I a character in some book, I mused, I would be uncovering clues and pursuing lines of inductive and deductive reasoning; eventually I would uncover the mystery and its solution and wrap it all up in a nice tidy little dénouement.

The trouble was, real life wasn't like that. Real life didn't follow nicely plotted scenarios. Real life was messy, accidental. Chance and Fate played according to House odds and payoffs were rare and minuscule. In real life people missed golden opportunities, passed like ships in the night, and the best-laid plans always seemed to end with an appointment in Samaria.

And then I smiled sheepishly as sleep rode in on the drowsy afternoon breeze: I had momentarily confused real life with the Dreamnet.

I slept and could recall no dreams as I awoke with the taste of soft lips on my own. Outside the window the sun was visibly low in the west.

"What time is it?" I asked, suddenly frantic at the loss of the day.

"Early enough to have some food before we set out on

this fool's errand," Euryale replied gently. "Come." I wasn't hungry but I allowed myself to be led from the room.

Downstairs, the tavern was crowded and nowhere was an empty table to be seen. Undaunted, Euryale took me by the hand and started across the packed and noisy room. As we wound our way between tables and around serving maids, my eye was drawn to a table in the corner.

Three men stood around it, wearing mixed expressions of admiration for the lady seated there and annoyance for the other two interlopers who wouldn't go away.

One could hardly blame them. White—almost platinum—hair fell in a silvery cascade over her shoulders. Her black gown clung to every exquisite curve of her body, and what it didn't reveal of milk-white skin in a daring expanse of décolleté, it boldly suggested in sleek, tight molding. The seductive features of her face were boldly accentuated by bloodred lips and eyes that glittered like frosted blue ice. . . .

I did a double take: it was Lilith.

I turned to Euryale as we approached the table. "Your doing?"

"No magic, just makeup," she answered. "The oldest art of illusion in the world."

Lilith saw us coming and sent her would-be suitors away. She stood as we reached the table.

"Well met, Lilith," I said informally.

"Better met," she countered, stepping in closer and kissing me again. Perhaps it was my feeling of awkwardness, or the sensation of three pairs of eyes glaring daggers at my back, but I could have sworn that this kiss was almost twice as long as the last one.

"You must understand," she explained when she finally let me go, "that this is a whole new experience for me. For thousands of years a kiss has been a cold, dispassionate way of drawing upon the life forces of my prey. I did it because I had to. There was no 'wanting' involved.

"But now," she continued as we all sat down, "I find there are new depths, new sensations, new—meanings—to this act!"

"And I think you will find," I told her, "that some people will bring more meaning to it than others."

She perked up at that. "It is true! I have kissed a number of men these past few hours and I have noticed quite a difference!"

I fought back a smile. "I'll bet you have."

"Perhaps you can tell me?"

"Tell you what?"

"Why all those other men kiss so differently from each other and, yet, still feel the same."

"Well—"

"But when I kiss you," she continued, "I feel all tingly and shivery all over."

Euryale coughed politely and I began looking around for our waitress.

Over dinner we discussed Lilith's additional role in our plans.

She was to remain behind while Euryale guided me to the chimneylike dropshaft that descended into the honeycomb of caverns that Smog had claimed for his lair. Once I was "safely" in, Euryale was to rendezvous with Lilith at the Well of Allah, about a mile out of town. By that time, the ex-Succubus was supposed to have acquired enough mounts for our getaway. This meant seven horses in addition to Ghost if everything went well at both ends. If it didn't—well, either I was in for a long walk, or they were going to be stuck with a lot of extra horses.

Lilith looked at the sketchy timetable and asked when I was supposed to show up.

"Hard to say exactly. But if I'm not there by sunrise," I added soberly, "hit the road and don't look back."

"Maybe we could meet you at some point closer to the caves," she suggested.

I shook my head. "No deviations from the plan: we meet at Allah's Well."

"If it ends well," Euryale amended.

FROM THE JOURNAL OF DAGGOTH THE DARK

The most amazing thing: an Elf came to the door this morning and tried to sell me boxes of cookies. Don't think it was one of Ripley's jokes or it would have manifested much sooner. So I'm faced with two possibilities: either The Machine has assimilated an outside prototype from another network's files, or some Fantasyworld Subprograms are evolving a capitalistic philosophy—a blatant departure from our pseudo-medieval economic structure.

Come to think of it, rumors from Gaehill would suggest their Dragon in residence is a lot more sophisticated at the virgin-extortion racket than he has any right to be.

CHAPTER
<u>FIFTEEN</u>

★

THE moon was bright, visibility was clear, and not another soul was in sight. We found the entry hole a good two hours before midnight and then located a long sturdy log to serve as a crossbrace across the opening. After tying off the rope I dismissed Euryale. "Nothing more you can do here. Go see if you can keep Lilith out of trouble."

She stared at me for a long moment. And then she put her hands on my shoulders and kissed me.

"Lilith is right," she said, backing away. "You do make a girl feel all tingly and shivery all over!"

"Get going," I growled. She turned and melted into the night.

I hadn't done any rope climbing for years so I took my time. When I reached the bottom there was still a good twenty feet of rope to spare so I cut the excess and coiled it over my shoulder. Unsheathed, Balmung's blade gave off a soft, flickering light of a reddish hue—sufficient to follow the passageway without resorting to a torch. I took my last breath of fresh air and started down the passage.

There is a smell peculiar to Dragons and their lairs that immediately warns all but the most inexperienced that a fire-breathing lizard is nearby. If you've never gotten a whiff of Dragonstink, it's rather hard to describe. Try to imagine baked slime.

I hurried along the twisting corridors of hollowed-out stone as my only realistic chance of coming out of this alive lay in my getting my Program Access Code back from Silverthane before Smog showed up. Even with the Code and my powers restored, facing down old Brimstone Breath could still prove a bit dicey. He hadn't been that easy ten years ago and he was ten years the wiser now. If I couldn't get the Code before Smog arrived, there was going to be a very unhappy ending to this little rescue story.

After what seemed like an hour of tracing and backtracking passages, checking out every cul-de-sac and dead end, I found one that opened into a large, torchlit cavern.

I dimmed Balmung's light and hung back in the shadows while I gave the big room the once over. No Dragon. But there were a lot of bones scattered about.

And five very naked ladies chained to a series of posts, arranged in a large semicircle. I had found the Room of Sacrifices.

Rijma was the first to see me. "Well, it's about time!" she scolded.

Dyantha was exuberant: "Robert! Thank God!"

Palys was more serene: "I knew you would make it."

Aeriel was more pragmatic: "Hush, ladies! Do you want the monster to come running in here before we are freed?"

Alyx remained silent and everyone else shut up for the moment.

Quickly and quietly I made my way across the bone-littered floor, feeling as naked as everyone else and expecting Smog to show up at any moment. As soon as everyone was free I figured that we stood a very good chance of getting out alive. Setting everyone free was going to be problem, however: their wrists were enclosed in iron cuffs on a length of chain that passed through a heavy metal staple at the top of each post. Although a Dwarven blade like Balmung would make short work of the soft iron links, the noise would surely summon Smog before I was halfway done.

The ultimate solution to the whole problem lay in getting

my Access Code back, so I approached Ms. Silverthane and planted myself just six inches away from her nose.

"I don't have time to beat around the bush," I whispered. "And you don't have time to play any more silly games! Unless you want us all to be the guests of honor at this baroque barbecue, you'd better cough up my Access Code and do it muy pronto!"

Alyx looked at me with a pained expression but didn't utter a word.

"C'mon, Doc! This is serious! I need that Code to get you all out of here—"

"She can't tell you anything."

I turned and looked at Rijma. "What?"

"She can't tell you the Code. She can't tell you anything." I could see that Dr. Cooper was fighting to keep the panic out of her avatar's voice.

"What are you saying?" I hissed.

"How do you suppose the Gaehill officials were able to hold a sorceress prisoner for so long?"

I stared dumbly.

"Immobilize her hands to restrict somatic gestures. And place a Silence spell on her so that she can't utilize verbal keys. Do that and you can hold the most powerful magic user who ever lived."

And, in the meantime, she couldn't tell me my Program Access Code.

I turned back to Alyx Silverthane and folded my arms. "If I get you out of here," I gritted, "it's with the tacit understanding that I get my Code back just as soon as we find your voice!"

She nodded quickly: she was in no position to do any bargaining.

Now the problem was: how was I going to get these people out of here and past the Dragon with no magic and no backup?

"Uh, Riplakish. . . ."

"Not now, Aeriel, I'm thinking."

"Ssso, we meet again, at lassst!"

"Please, ladies, be quiet until I can figure this out."

"If thou cansssst not figure thisss out, I ssshall be glad to exsssplain it to thee."

This time the voice registered and I fought the impulse to whirl around. Instead, I forced myself to continue studying the bolts that held Alyx's shackles in place. "That you, Smog?" I inquired in my best nonchalant tone of voice. That wasn't easy as I was feeling very chalant at this particular moment.

"Thou knowessst that it isss, Riplakisssh!"

"Sorry to hear that."

Ever hear a Dragon chuckle? It's a nasty sound. "I thought thou mightessst be," he gloated.

"Yeah. I had hoped you had learned your lesson the last time." I turned around, deciding that if I was going to bluff my way out of this, I might as well go for broke. Losing my temper helped. "Listen, Gashole: these people are my friends! It's just a lucky thing for you that I got here when I did! If you had so much as nibbled one ladyfinger, I'd be all over you like flies on Orcs! Now you've got just one minute to release them and point out the nearest exit! After they leave, we'll sit down and talk about your little racket, and if you cooperate, I might—I say might—just let you out of this with your scales intact!"

Dragon faces are notoriously hard to read, but Smog appeared more than inscrutable. He looked positively unimpressed.

"Dossst thou truly think me ssso sssimple?" Smog inquired, leaning forward on his scaly elbows and cradling his chin on his claws. "If it were not ssso obviousss from your conversssationsss, it would be evident from thy failure to break thessse fettersss: thou hassst losssst thy magical powersss!" He smiled, showing triple rows of carious teeth. "Ssshow me one sssimple trick and I shall acsssede to thy wissshesss!" His eyes lit up in anticipation. "Otherwissse, I ssshall fricasssee thee where thou ssstandessst."

"A trick?"

"A magic trick."

I had difficulty swallowing. "Any magic trick?"

Smog nodded. "Thou hassst one minute!"

I looked around helplessly. "Anybody got a deck of cards?"

"Fifty sssecondsss."

In desperate moments, desperate plans are born. "How about a rope trick?" I asked, pulling the coil over my head and off of my shoulder.

Smog shrugged. "Forty sssecondsss."

"I've got twenty gold pieces that say the druid does it!" Rijma announced to the room in general. That encouragement was quickly dampened by responses from the rest of the captives.

"You're on!"

"I'll take that bet!"

"How do I collect if you lose?"

How do you tie a slipknot? I pondered frantically.

"Thirty sssecondsss."

"Come on, Rip—I've got twenty gold ones riding on this," Rijma murmured as I tried to get enough play in my knot to allow the loop to open and close.

"Twenty sssecondsss."

Okay. There. It wasn't a true slipknot, but with a little luck, it might just do the job.

"Fifteen sssecondsss."

"Hey, Smog!" I began to twirl my makeshift lasso. "Ever been to a rodeo?" I enlarged the loop and sent it spinning high into the air.

"Ten sssecondsss."

Now I dropped it down over my body so that I was standing in the center of the spinning circle of rope.

"Nine . . . eight . . ."

"Watch this!" I held the loop just a few inches from the ground and jumped out. And then back in again. So far, I was extremely lucky: I hadn't done these particular stunts since my cowboy-obsessive days back in the fifth grade.

". . . sssix . . . five . . ."

This time I jumped back out and brought my lariat up and spinning sideways.

". . . four . . ."

I jumped through the whirling oval and nearly stumbled in the process.

"I cannot bear to watch!" It sounded like Dyantha.

"Now I know why Vaudeville died." Rijma again, of course.

". . . three . . . two . . ."

"And now for the grand finale!" I announced, recovering from my stumble. "I call this trick: 'Roping the Bull'!"

"One! Thy time isss up, Riplakissh!" And with that pronouncement, Smog took a deep breath.

I sent the rope out, praying that I wouldn't miss. There would be no second chances in this contest.

Out of the corner of my eye I noticed that Palys had managed to free herself. But she was standing still, apparently fascinated by the sight of the rope uncurling toward the mammoth lizard, one arm raised to point out its twirling trajectory.

For a moment it looked as if the spinning circle of rope would fly wide of its mark. Then the world blinked. Time seemed to suddenly slow down perceptibly and each individual action seemed to unfold with crystallized clarity: the lasso was moving in the proper trajectory and flames started to lick around the edges of that fearsome mouth as the loop of my rope encircled Smog's snout. Almost too late, I remembered to give the rope that twisting tug to snap the loop shut—just as the Firedrake was unleashing his flame.

Now I really hauled back on the rope and dug my heels in for dear life. Smog hadn't started to fight back just yet: he was just beginning to realize that all that fire and brimstone he had just belched at me had suddenly reached an unexpected dead end. His eyes bugged out, his nostrils vented steam, and his belly suddenly bulged like a gas-filled balloon: with his mouth roped shut, that thermal blast had just one place that it could go. . . .

Smog was swelling up like a balloon in the Thanksgiving Day Parade, now; and he began tearing at the noose with one claw while he clutched at his tummy with the other.

I cracked the rope like a whip to keep him from getting a firm purchase on it, and yelled: "Blow it out your ass, Smog!"

He did.

Try to imagine a hundred cars, all backfiring at once: that's what it sounded like. The noise was positively deafening: it shook the cavern and started a rain of stalactites that somehow managed to miss everyone but Smog. It is rather hard to miss a half acre of Dragon in such a close and confined space.

When the dust finally began to settle, Smog was out cold, half buried under a couple of tons of rock.

Insuring Smog's immobility was my first priority. Palys helped me hogtie the unconscious Dragon and dropped a bombshell as I was cinching the last of the ropes.

"I have your Access Code," she told me casually.

"Great! Why didn't you tell me before?"

"It isn't so simple. Dr. Quebedeaux used hypnosis to close off any memory of the Code in your mind. Simply reciting the Code back to you wouldn't remove the block."

That explained quite a bit—including the reason why I didn't remember anything but a sound and restful sleep the first night of our capture.

"So how do I force her to undo her hypnotic suggestions?"

"Unnecessary. I can do that. If you'll permit me."

I stood there and stared at her. "*Who* are you?" I asked quietly.

She smiled shyly. "A friend. You must believe that. Especially if you are to permit me to hypnotize you."

"Hypnotize me?"

"To remove her subconscious blocks and restore your Program Access Code."

That took some consideration. I would be highly reluctant to let my best friend go messing around in my mind. Letting a complete stranger—but I was desperate for that Code!

"Okay," I answered finally.

"Come," she said, "you may free the others more readily once you have your powers restored." She led me to another exit from the room and down a different passage. It only twisted and curved a short distance before opening up into another chamber. This room was slightly larger than Smog's lunchroom, but there was less space as it was half filled with treasure. Dragons are real collectors.

"Here," she said, sitting me down and picking up a diamond pendant. "It will be quieter in here and there are fewer distractions."

Oh, yeah? Maybe five naked ladies are more distracting than just one, but that particular one was standing right in front of me, demanding my complete attention. I tried to concentrate on the swaying pendant but found myself fighting the impulse to focus another foot or so beyond.

Oh, my. . . . From now on I intended to keep a much closer eye on Palys.

I was just thinking about how interesting that could prove to be, when she spoke again, breaking my reverie.

I looked up blankly. "Excuse me, but what did you say?"

She smiled. "I said, we're all done. You should be able to utilize your Access Code now. Want to give it a test?"

I nodded dumbly. Maybe keeping an eye on Palys was going to be a lot harder than I had thought. I stood and stretched, flexing my fingers. "What should I try, first?"

She struck a pose and ran her hands down the roller-coaster curves of her body. "How about some clothing?"

"Seems a shame," I sighed, "but I guess we must deal in practicalities."

"There will be time for impracticalities later," she murmured.

"What would milady like?" I asked, letting that last comment slide. "A gown of finest silk?"

"Something a little more practical for our present circumstances," she demurred. "I'll take just what I had before, thank you."

"You sure?"

She smiled. "I'm always sure."

"Okay. . . ." I paused for a moment of cogitation. Then I wove the spell with murmur and gesture and thought. Minor magic use still seemed safe enough; it was the major Matrix-altering stuff I had to avoid.

"Not bad," she decided when I was done. "A little loose here and a little tight there—but you're not familiar enough with my body." She gave me another one of those looks and then made a gesture. Her leather outfit reconfigured and molded itself to her body. And it seemed to lose about thirty percent of the material that I had provided in the process.

"Weapons?" she asked. "Equipment?"

"Sorry. I forgot." In a twinkling of an eye I completed her outfitting.

"Now, how about the others?"

The power was more manageable with each attempt so that I was able to accomplish their outfittings without leaving my spot. When I was sure that they were all properly dressed and equipped, I dissolved their fetters and hung a series of glowing arrows in the air to lead them to the treasure room.

"Now," I said, turning and rubbing my hands together, "let's see what goodies are to be had here."

There were plenty. And even though there was more than enough to go around, there were a couple of baubles that provoked some debates of ownership.

I waded through the stuff, unfazed by the sight of gems as big as goose eggs and jewelry that made Tiffany's look like a Five and Dime: I was hunting for bigger treasure.

There was magic hidden here—magic strong enough to tug at the corners of my perception without the benefit of a spell of Discernment. That's what I was after. After the ladies had gathered all they wanted—or at least all they could carry—there would still be several hundred times the amount I needed to fill my purse for all our needs to come.

I crawled over mounds of silk tapestries and piles of gold and silver coins. I wound my way between stacked bars of platinum and chests brimming with gems and jewels. I followed the trail of magically charged ether as a bloodhound follows the scent. At one point the trail forked and I had to choose which branch to pursue next. Falling back on the old dungeon mapping adage, "you can't go wrong if you go right," I abandoned the ethereal trail that led to the left. The one to the right led to a large, gem-laden chest. I began digging.

Even with Palys's help, it took a long while to empty it by hand. As I said before, magic sometimes triggers more magic; so when dealing with an unknown factor, I prefer the prudence of doing it the hard way.

Under the gems we found several bolts of silks and satins. Under those, we found a lamp.

I picked it up and examined it closely. The design was so familiar, I figured it had to be one of my original creations. Sure enough, "Aladdin Lamp Co.—Made in Baghdad" was stamped on the underside. I began rubbing the brass, wondering if this was a one-wisher, a three-wisher, or one of those special, unlimited, use-it-for-as-long-as-you-can-hold-on-to-it models.

True to form, smoke began to issue from the lamp's spout.

I have seen the Djinn assume forms, male and female, both pleasing to the mortal eye and terrible of aspect. I've witnessed Efreet who stun the senses as they appear in a conglomeration of demonic, animalistic, and human configurations. I've even seen a Genie with the light brown hair. So, as the smoke coalesced, I braced myself, ready for almost anything.

Almost.

I wasn't ready for a balding, pinch-faced man of advancing years, dressed in early twentieth-century formal attire. He bowed stiffly from the waist.

"Um. . . ." The striped waistcoat, black cravat, and swallow-tailed jacket had left me momentarily befuddled. "Are you the slave of the lamp?"

His expression was a pitched battle between disapproval and condescension with both sides agreeing to a cohabital truce as he spoke. "*Servant* of the lawmp," he corrected in clipped, British syllables. Then sighed, "How may we serve you, Mawster?"

"Uh . . ." I pondered, "you can begin by telling me how many wishes I get."

He grimaced. "Let us be sure that we understand you, sir: you wish to know how many wishes we are contractually required to extend to the proprietor of the lawmp. Are we correct?"

Pretty smooth, but I wasn't that simple. I shook my head. "No, I don't *wish* to know. I'm just asking."

He frowned. "Three, Mawster."

"And your name?"

He cocked his head and looked at me blankly. "Our name? Sir?"

"It hardly seems proper to address you as 'hey you,' even if I am the master of the lamp." Two could play at snobbery.

The frown receded and an eyebrow arched—well—archly. "Do you anticipate our association being an extended one, sir? Most lawmp holders need only a passing moment to use up their three wishes." He sniffed. "He sniffed. "Ten minutes, tops."

I folded my arms and just looked at him.

"Gordon. Sir."

The set of his brow suggested there might be something in a name but I was not inclined to press my luck. "Thank you."

He harrumphed. "So what will Mawster's first wish be? Great wealth, perhaps?"

I gestured at the piles of gems, coins, and stacks of rare finery. "I'm already in the highest tax bracket I can imagine."

He took a good look around. "We see, sir. Then perhaps you will be asking for beautiful—" A bemused expression crept across his face as he considered the other ladies present. "Bless our nonexistent soul, sir, but we did not realize that you had so many wives!"

It was suddenly quiet enough to hear a pin drop.

"Uh, Gordon—these are not my wives."

"But of course, sir," he responded quickly, adjusting his cuff links and tugging at a sleeve. "We apologize for such an obvious social gawffe."

"Don't men—"

"It is obvious that such a rich and powerful man as yourself would never consider marrying women as plain as these! Though we are sure," he added, giving them another taciturn appraisal, "that they have probably served as adequate concubines until now."

The expressions around me were quickly going from dangerous to downright ugly.

"And now that we are here, they may be dismissed and we will begin with a list of eligible princesses—"

"Silence, Slave of the Lamp!" I thundered. "You will speak only when spoken to!" I disliked taking that tone of voice, but I just may have saved someone's life by doing so. Maybe my own, in fact.

"Servant."

"What?"

"Servant of the lawmp. Not slave." He sniffed. "Perhaps a review of eligible *princes* would put Mawster in a better humour?"

Actually, no. I explained that and then conveyed my desire that he return to the lamp's confines until such a time as my temper and a suddenly expanded vocabulary were back in abeyance.

I don't know which was more effective, the quaint and colorful phrases or the expressions on my companions' faces, but he was back in the lamp before you could hum "Smoke Gets in Your Eyes."

"Riplakish."

It was Palys. She was tugging at something protruding from a particularly overstuffed treasure chest. Rijma was rounding up the rest of the party and herding them toward the exit. I was filling my beltpouches with a king's ransom in gems.

"What is it?"

"Something you won't want to leave behind," she grunted.

Joining her, I could see the hilt of a sword. Buried up to its guard in a mound of gold and silver coins. As I took a hold of the grip, a tingling sensation passed through my body and I could feel the hair raising on the back of my neck: there was potent magic here—that other presence of strong enchantment that I had sensed earlier. Bracing myself, I began to pull while Palys scooped coins out of the chest in glittering, scintillating cascades.

Finally, almost eagerly, it came free: a five-foot longsword in a jeweled scabbard.

I think I knew even before I loosed the safety strap and drew it from its sheath. Still, there was the shock and the overwhelming, nameless emotion that slapped me, filled me, and overflowed as I gazed upon the translucent crystal blade.

Caladbolg, the legendary soulsword of the Sidhe!

I stood there, silent for the longest time as the sword bathed the chamber in an eerie blue light. Then, with trembling hand, I drew Balmung and held it up in my left hand. Red light pulsed from the Dwarven shortsword, contrasting with the blue flicker from the Elvish weapon. An inaudible vibration seemed to fill the air, a silent pitch that carried a feel of harmony rather than dissonance.

Palys finally broke the silence. "*Katana* and *wakizashi*," she said.

"I see you are familiar with Kendo."

She nodded. "Now you possess the 'True Soul' and the 'Guardian of the Soul.' Either one might make you a legend. Together—?" She let the question trail off.

The swords were deceptively light in my hands. I hefted each and then ran through the practice stations of the Twin Heavens discipline. The blades flashed and spun through the air, weaving intricate traceries of lightning and silent thunder. I knew I was good, but now, with these two legendary blades, I was capable of something beyond human terms of perfection.

I sheathed them with a feeling of awe and reverence. No more Mister Nice Guy, I vowed: from here on out I was going to kick ass and take names.

On the way out, I freed Smog from the ropes, rocks, and rubble by reducing him to six inches in size. I didn't figure that he had much room to complain, considering the other options that I now had the ability to exercise.

Besides, now that he was six inches long, his next virgin sacrifice should last him at least three or four years.

If he could talk anyone into bringing him one, that is.

Maybe he'd get lucky and find one that would laugh herself to death. . . .

FROM THE JOURNAL OF DAGGOTH THE DARK

I remember Ripley first raised the morality issue with the Black Knight scenario. "It is immoral," he said, "to create life predestined to a fixed script and then murder it because it followed our instructions." He lost sight of the fact that each story involves conflict and conflict employs a protagonist and an antagonist. Can't do fairy tales without black knights kidnapping princesses and being defeated by white knights. And Dreamwalkers pay to come to Fantasyworld and be the White Knight. Never mind the occasional kink who gets his jollies by conducting his own inquisitions.

That was the first indication of Ripley's disillusionment with Dreamprogramming—but the real rift developed over the issue of slavery. "Hey," I told him, "you can't recreate a medieval world without serfs and slaves."

"Then why can't we create a better world?" he asked. . . .

CHAPTER
<u>SIXTEEN</u>

★

AFTER we had rendezvoused with Euryale and Lilith at the Well of Allah, I took a little time out for some voodoo video. There was still the male contingent of the party to rescue and finding them was the first trick. Once again I unwrapped my crystal ball, hoping I wouldn't see the same ominous blank that I had drawn in my previous searches.

Stephanie. . . .

Unaccountably, I felt a sudden surge of grief. Our marriage had ended badly and I couldn't think of two people who evinced a stronger dislike for each other. But maybe most of the name-calling was a defense mechanism: an effort to convince ourselves and each other that we really didn't care so much, after all. . . .

Stumpy popped into focus at the center of the crystal, and as I zoomed out, I could make out Justin, Conrad, and the others. Pulling back a little farther, I recognized the slave markets of Casterbridge. It wasn't hard to extrapolate the rest: Gaehill had found an economical solution to dungeon overcrowding.

Closing my eyes, I concentrated on my newly restored Access Code and tried using my Programmer status to teleport them back. No dice: just a vague sensation of ethereal resistance and a sense of danger if I "pushed" too hard. I broke the connection and reached for my magic lamp.

Gordon appeared in a puff of smoke. "How may I serve you, Mawster?" he asked while making a pointed effort to ignore the presence of the rest of the ladies. "An enchanted sword, perhaps?"

I patted the hilts of Balmung and Caladbolg and shook my head.

"Oh. I see." He made a minimal effort to keep his annoyance in check.

I pointed to the crystal ball and asked if I could wish all of our compatriots free and back in our midst.

"No."

"No?"

"No." He shook his head in the best pedagogical fashion. "This lawmp only dispenses wishes of the highest quality and discernment. In other words, there are no group rates or discounts. If you wish to free your 'friends,' you may do so by utilizing a single wish for each one. In this manner you may free up to three of them—should you so wish." He paused. "Do you so wish?"

"No." If we could only free three of The Rabble without expending any effort, it made more sense to rescue the boys ourselves. "But there is someone else. . . ."

I reviewed the basic facts concerning Vashti's abduction and covered the evidence to date. "Now what I want you to do," I concluded, "is to find her and bring her back to me. Dead or alive. Understand?" While I wasn't counting on Stephanie being alive after all this time, I would still rest easier when I knew for certain. One way or the other.

Gordon's lips were pursed but he nodded.

"Okay, that's my first wish."

"Oh, bravo. And has Mawster decided on a second?" he asked.

I did my best to describe Senator Hanson's avatar and explained that he had been shanghaied by Goblins. "I want him found and returned, too."

"Dead or alive?"

I nodded grimly.

"Very good, sir." He disappeared. And in less than five minutes he was back.

"Well?"

He shrugged. "Dead or alive—if their bodies are still in this world, they are hidden from the scrying abilities of the Djinn."

"Are you saying that it is possible for her to be someplace where she would be hidden—undetectable to both the Djinn and my crystal ball? And that such a place would not preclude the possibility of her still being alive?"

Gordon nodded. "Yes, sir. There are many places that are veiled against any kind of farseeing. If your 'friends' are in one of these, we could only find them by going there, ourself, and searching in person."

I knew it was stupid to resurrect any hopes at this point, but I couldn't help myself: "Okay, get started."

"Excuse us?"

"You're excused. Get going."

"But, Mawster! There are hundreds—it could take weeks! Months! And even then there is no guarantee—"

"Then you'd better get started as soon as possible."

He made a face—no small accomplishment as he typically gave the impression of a man reluctantly sucking on a lemon. "Is this what Mawster truly wishes us to do?"

"We're still on the first two wishes, Jeeves."

"Well, I never!"

"Obviously. Which would largely account for your disposition. Now get going before you make another slip with your personal pronouns."

"Yes, *sir*!" He glared at me as he faded. Cheshire-like, the frown lines were the last to disappear.

I turned and found myself nose to forehead with Alyx Silverthane. That didn't improve my temper at all.

"Ah, Ms. Silverthane," I observed, stepping back a pace from Dr. Quebedeaux's avatar, "and what am I to do with you? By all rights I should punish you for placing us all in danger and denying us the wherewithal to defend ourselves!"

Her expression remained carefully neutral.

"But I am a magnanimous person by nature, and I have decided to let you go without taking any punitive action."

She regarded me with those solemn lavender eyes that seemed to say that she was sorry—but only in a mildly regretful sort of way. I waited. And so did she. "What is it, Alyx? Is there something that you want?"

There was, of course. But she was too proud to resort to charades and hysterics.

"Oh. I'll bet you want your voice back."

She nodded. Once.

"I can see why you'd want that. After all, aside from the convenience of ordinary communication, a sorceress is rather defenseless without the verbal keys to her spells."

She folded her arms and gave the impression of long-suffering patience.

"Well, I don't know if that's such a good idea," I continued. "The last time you exercised your power, you used it to take us prisoner and strip me of my powers. Now tell me one good reason why I should give you another opportunity to do so?"

She could, of course, say nothing in her own defense.

I sighed heavily. "I know I'm going to regret this, but I can't just let you run around practically defenseless. That would be cruel and inhumane. You might want to look up the definitions of those two words in your spare time." I neutralized the Silence spell with more than a little misgiving, but I wanted her to be able to look after herself. The last thing I needed was an additional responsibility named Silverthane.

"I've learned my lesson," she answered softly if not convincingly.

"Sure you have." I turned to the others. "Okay, let's ride!"

We rode. But we didn't ride far.

The events of the previous night—and the strain of the days preceding it—had taken their toll. We stopped for lunch and ended up making camp for the rest of the day. And night.

There was no formal watch during the day. I let the others nap through the afternoon while Palys and I kept each other awake with small talk. Curiously, the only significant piece of personal information that I was able to pry out of her was she was a member of the Dreamworlds Programming staff. That, at least, explained her strengths as a spellcaster. Most of the rest of my questions were met with enigmatic smiles.

I spent some time wading through another page of Daggoth's journal, nursed a headache through supper, and crashed into a dreamless slumber that lasted until midnight. I was awakened to Rijma's toe in my side.

"You said to wake you when it was dark," she explained with that marvelous deadpan expression of hers. "Well, it's dark."

"Thanks," I muttered, trying to clear the grogginess from my head.

"I've assigned guard duty until dawn," she continued, "and you're not on the roster. So why don't you try not being useful for a change: go back to sleep."

The thought was tempting, but I sat up and shook my head: "Now that I'm awake I might as well make another stab at Dag's diary."

"Want some coffee?"

I made a face. "Is that all we have?"

"In regular supply, yes." She sat down on the ground beside me.

I gestured arcanely and a frosty can of Dr Pepper appeared in midair.

She shook her head. "You really like that stuff?"

I shrugged. "Gotta drink something."

"Mm." She stared off into the darkness. "How long you been dry now?"

"This time?" I had to think. "Almost five years. But I hardly count those three weeks after the court verdict. That was more like a vacation from sobriety."

The Brownie nodded. "We all could use a little vacation from Reality now and then."

"That's why we built Dreamworlds. Except, we made a mistake: in trying to escape Reality, we just went and created another one."

Rijma sighed. "Don't start."

I nodded and opened the can but was denied its contents

by the arrival of a crimson arrow. There was a sudden deadly hissing sound as my Dr Pepper was torn from my grasp and pinned to a tree some ten feet away.

"Nobody is to be making any movements!" boomed a heavily accented voice from the darkness.

"Nobody move," I seconded. "Keep your hands away from your weapons."

"A wise choice, comrade," agreed the character who was now walking into our circle of firelight: Errol Flynn wearing fifteenth-century fatigues. "My men are outnumbering your party more than three to one and with arrows which can strike from distance. Furthermore we are being in darkness which is hidden while you are targets in light." He smiled.

"If their aim isn't any better than their English," Rijma murmured, "I vote we rush 'em."

Our captor's ears were sharp: he turned toward Rijma. "Russian?"

Well, apparently not that sharp.

"You are thinking maybe I am Russian?" He threw back his head and laughed. "You are obwiously for someone else mistaking me." He pointed to himself in the best vaudevillian manner. "Allow me to be introducing myself: I am Robbing Hood!"

Too much bad luck at poker was finally paying off: I managed to keep a straight face. Rijma was unable to suppress a snort and a small burst of giggles. This did not sit well with our captor who signaled to someone hidden beyond the firelight.

He then advanced to where he could threaten the Brownie at close range.

"You are thinking this is joke, maybe?" he growled. "You are in big trouble! I am Robbing Hood and all around you are my Happy Comrades: we take from the rich and decadent bourgeoisie and give to the poor, oppressed masses of the working class peoples!"

She tried. I really had to give her credit for trying, but in the end, it was just too much for her: her composure disintegrated into gales of helpless laughter.

Hood tried picking her up and shaking some sobriety into

her but it only made her worse. Finally, he dropped her in disgust and turned to address the rest of us.

"I am reasonable, decent outlaw despite lying propaganda spread by evil Marshal of Nothingham! I only take ill-gotten moneys of capitalistic oppressors, not lives! Do not resist and I will let you go free. Not," he added as he drew his sword, "that you are having any choice in matter!"

Four men stepped out of the darkness to join their leader. The big guy, like their leader, was dressed in a yeoman's outfit of olive drab, but another wore a similarly tailored outfit that was dyed a bright scarlet. The third was obviously a minstrel and the last was not so obviously a priest, though he did wear the appropriate robes.

"Ah! Permit me to be introducing some of my band of Happy Comrades!" He gestured to the four in the order of my descriptions: "Small Johann, Wilhelm the Red, Ivan-a-Dale, and Friar Igor." Each clicked his heels and courteously executed a polite Prussian bow as he was introduced, increasing the sensation that we had just wandered onto the stage of someone else's comic opera. Then they each produced a sack that they proceeded to shake out in a careful and well-rehearsed ritual.

"We will now be taking contributions which will be going for funding of people's struggle against oppressive and decadent capitalist government. You may rejoice in knowledge that you are contributing to the great revolution." His eyes suddenly widened as Dyantha stepped toward him. "Hokey smoke!" exclaimed Robbing Hood: "Natasha Skovoroda!"

Natasha favored him with a winning smile. "Dr. Dankevych, I presume?"

It seemed that we had found the vice chairman of the CPSU Central Committee and his personal aides.

It took me a while but I finally decided that Borys Dankevych was no buffoon: no man becomes the vice chairman of the Soviet Union's Central Committee without honing a razor-sharp mind and an ability to grasp complex situations quickly and effectively. Which he did before our explanation of the Anomaly was half completed.

There were, however, some linguistic problems to be negotiated. . . .

"But you are not certain as to cause of Anonymous?" he reiterated.

"Anomaly," Dyantha/Natasha corrected, whose grasp of the English language was a bit stilted but much advanced over Robbing Hood's.

I looked at Dr. Quebedeaux's avatar and then answered when she showed no inclination to speak. "So far, the rest is just pure speculation."

"Then best thing to do is find this Daggoth and ask him about Amorous," Dankevych concluded.

"Anomaly," Dyantha corrected.

"Whatever."

"The problem with that," Dyantha went on to explain, "is we are unsure of Straeker's bias, now. He is a dangerous power in this world and he has acquired some powerful allies. If he is hostile to us—"

"And we have every reason to believe he is," I added.

"—then we will need reinforcements before any confrontation. That is why we must rescue our scattered comrades before we divert to Daggoth's Tower."

"But is much waste of time!" exclaimed Dankevych. "With Animosity spreading—"

"Anomaly."

"—we don't be having time for wasting! We must be getting to this Dagwood the Dark as soon as possible!"

"Daggoth," muttered Rijma under her breath.

"Whatever. Look"—Dankevych held up the appropriate number of fingers—"you are trying to rescue five others to be strong enough to take tower. No?"

There were several nods.

"Well, I give you five times that number within twenty-four hours!" He paused, letting the idea sink in.

"You have that many men?" asked Silverthane, speaking for the first time.

"Yes."

"Then why wait twenty-four hours?" she pursued. "Why not go now?"

He smiled sheepishly. "Because—they are not here. They are back at great camp in Sherman Forest."

"Never mind," I said to Rijma and Natasha as they opened their mouths. "Comrade Dankevych, just how many men do you have with you at the moment?"

"Counting Johann, Wilhelm, Ivan, and Igor?"

"Yes."

"And mine own self, as well?"

I nodded.

"Roughly . . . five."

We agreed to rendezvous with Borys Dankevych's Happy Comrades at a secluded inn a half day's journey away. Small Johann and Wilhelm were dispatched as runners to make the arrangements. After that the meeting more or less broke up and most of the party turned their attentions to getting a little more sleep out of the three hours of darkness that were still remaining before the dawn.

Dyantha and Borys seemed wide awake, however, and had withdrawn to a fallen tree trunk at the edge of the firelight where they were quietly conversing in Russian. I abandoned any thoughts of eavesdropping and elected to take a solitary stroll beyond the firelight.

Walking through the camp, I conducted a quick head count. And then counted again, more slowly. Someone was missing. I went down a mental list and then turned to Aerial who was sharing this portion of the nightwatch with Rijma.

"Where's Palys?"

She shrugged. "Out there, somewhere."

"Did she say where she was going? Or when she'd be back?"

"Only that she wanted a little time to herself." The Amazon princess smiled at my look of uncertainty. "She's safe enough—I doubt that she's gone that far."

I nodded briefly and started to walk on when another question occurred to me. "Aerial, how long have you known Palys?"

"Known her?" She furrowed her brow. "Seems like forever."

"Does she ever sleep?"

An expression of mirth suffused her face. "That's a silly question."

I nodded. "I know. But it just suddenly occurred to me that I've never seen her sleep."

Aerial laughed at that. But as I walked away, I glanced back and saw a more thoughtful expression settle over her face.

I walked well beyond the perimeter of the firelight. Tonight the skies were clear and the night air was unseasonably warm. I pulled off my shirt and waded hip-deep in clover. Across the meadow was another tree line and the sound of flowing water.

I reached the bank after a few minutes of casting about through a thickly grown wall of foliage. The river—if you could call it such—was only twenty feet across here and the water flowed slowly and smoothly with a gentle whisper. Sounds of splashing were coming from upstream. And seemed to be coming closer. I looked around and found a comfortable place of concealment.

I saw the Unicorn, first.

Impossibly, almost blindingly white and rimmed with silver from the moonlight and water, it drifted like an ivory dream upon the current.

And, upon its back, like one of the shadowseas upon the moon, lay a goddess, stretched out in unclothed glory. Here was beauty personified; two creatures come down from some other wonderful and mysterious plane to inspire our worship for a brief moment and then leave us despairing and yearning for things not of this world. I was powerless to move.

I watched Palys slide from the Unicorn's back as it turned and reached the near bank, just ten feet away from me. She whispered something in the creature's ear: it lowered its head and gently touched her shoulder with its horn. Then it turned away and began moving back in the direction of the campsite.

Palys stretched languorously and then turned and dived back into the water. I held my breath, waiting for her to come back up. And when she did, it was right beside the bank where I sat in supposed concealment.

"Come and swim with me," she said, looking straight at me without any hint of surprise. "The water is fine."

My mind was suddenly paralyzed along with my body. I couldn't think of anything to say.

"Come," she said, rising out of the water like Botticelli's *Venus*. She extended a graceful, golden hand and raised me to my feet.

I stood there and watched with a sense of detachment as she eased my body out of its clothing. Then she took my hand again and led me down and into the river.

It was warm—one of the advantages to Dreamworld topography—and the current was a gentle caress that seemed to heighten every sensation.

We swam perhaps another fifty yards downstream, making little effort beyond floating with the drifting current. There we found a large, smooth rock in the middle of the watercourse that sloped upward, out of the water at a twenty-degree angle. Without a word, we both crawled up, onto the rock, and stretched out next to each other.

"Bewitched"—that was the only word that could describe my state of mind and being. Or "bedazzled"! I had never imagined, much less seen, such incarnate beauty and perfection sculpted in human flesh. I was reduced to the impulses of a child—wanting to reach out my hand and touch—

What was the matter with me? Although I tend to admire the feminine form as much as the next man, I've never been one to drop my drawers on those occasions that my hormones get the urge to tap-dance! As I fought the urge to submit to the carnality of the moment she reached out and brought my hand to her breast. Guided it. . . .

"Who are you?" I whispered.

She brought my hand up to her mouth. "Your friend," she answered softly. And pressed her lips to my palm. "Your lover," she murmured, manifesting sudden surprising strength to pull me over and onto her. "Your soulmate!" she whispered. And pulled my head down to kiss me with a sudden fierceness.

My head was spinning, and there was a curious melting sensation—as if our two bodies were already merging into one entity of flesh. I no longer questioned what was happening. I had no will to resist. I tangled my fingers in her wet hair and slid my other hand beneath the arch of her back. I could feel a pounding in my head, in my loins, in the warm, wet flesh beneath my hands. We broke for air, and as I turned my face, she traced the pulsing vein in my neck with burning lips and tongue. I gasped, trying to catch my breath.

And I saw four feet. In front of me.

Not four feet in distance. But four feet as in the kind that are attached to legs.

I looked up and saw two faces. One of them belonged to my ex-wife.

"We have found her, sir." announced Gordon, stating the obvious.

"I understand you've been real worried about me," Vashti added archly. "I can see you've been losing sleep."

I grimaced at the untimely Djinni. "I wish you had waited until we were finished," I muttered.

"Very good, sir."

"Never mind." I looked down at Palys. She lay beneath me, still and silent, her eyes unfocused, her expression unreadable. "I think we are finished now."

"Then the conditions of your third wish are met."

"Oh, no, you don't," I growled, untangling myself from Palys and getting up. "That doesn't count as an actual wish!"

Gordon folded his arms. "You have wished it and the wish has come to pass!" he insisted stubbornly.

"A technicality!" I yelled. "You didn't do anything to make it come true!"

"Oh, go soak your head!" Vashti interrupted, shoving me into the water.

When I came back up, I was all alone. Everyone had all managed to vacate the premises in less than six seconds.

FROM THE JOURNAL OF DAGGOTH THE DARK

I've been invaded!

Maud Higgins, the lascivious librarian, popped in last night—and I do mean POPPED IN!

It's bad enough to be chased around town by a woman old enough to be my mother, but now I find that I'm not even safe in my own sanctuary! As Programmer and wizard, I've designed this tower to be impregnable, to bar any unauthorized entry. And yet she was able to effortlessly pass through stone and sigil to materialize in my bedroom! Ye gods!

It gets worse.

It seems that Maudy isn't a Dreamwalker after all: she's a REMrunner! And she's not the only one—

CHAPTER
SEVENTEEN

★

PALYS was gone when I finally made it back to the campsite. I had taken my own sweet time, being at a loss as to what to do or say when I saw her again. That decision was temporarily postponed as both the Amazon and her horse had disappeared. Gordon was prudently absent, as well.

That left Vashti. And as much as I suddenly wished to avoid it, I had to talk to her.

Whatever approach I might try, I knew I could count on my ex-wife to be direct. So I forced myself to march right up to her and plant myself with my arms folded across my chest. "We have to talk," I announced.

She looked up at me and set the coffeepot back down among the embers. "So talk," she invited, picking up her pewter cup.

"I need to know what happened to you! Where you've been! Who—"

"Who, what, where, when, and why," she interrupted. "The five W's of the standard news lead. Once a writer, always a writer: even in the midst of chaos you maintain a sense of journalistic propriety."

It was amazing: I had been distraught over her supposed

death for days but the way this conversation was going I knew I'd be ready to strangle her myself in another five minutes. "Steph—"

"But that's fine with me," she continued. "I'm tired and I want to go to bed. So I'll run them down for you, since that's the quickest way to get it over with." She took a sip of coffee. "First of all: the who. You know who."

I nodded grimly. "Morpheus and Daggoth."

She shook her head. "Morpheus and a guy named Cerberus. Cerberus looks like Daggoth the Dark. But he isn't."

"How do you know that?"

"A little cat told me."

"You mean a little bird told you."

She shook her head again and reached into her shoulder bag. "No, I mean a little cat told me. Though maybe I shouldn't say 'little.'" She let the cat out of the bag. Literally.

It was a black cat, somewhat larger than medium size for the domesticated variety, and it regarded me with great golden eyes.

"Daggoth's familiar," she announced. The cat seemed to nod its head and then began to lick one of its paws.

"Now, as to the where: Daggoth's Tower—if you haven't already guessed. And you know the when. Which brings us to why. Why?" She shrugged her shoulders. "I don't really know myself. But I wouldn't be surprised if Bart is able to shed a little light on that for us."

"Who's Bart?" I asked in growing exasperation.

"The cat." She gestured vaguely. "Bartholomew Quintavius Xavier Oglethorpe the Third. . . ."

Great. Now I had something in common with a cat: the number three at the end of our respective monikers. "All right, all right! I give up!" I cried, throwing up my hands in irritation. "Get some sleep and we'll try talking about this again in the morning." I started to turn away, but the cat suddenly whipped around to block my escape.

"Listen, Jackson," the cat announced quite clearly, "I get the feeling that you're not taking the lady seriously. And that's a mistake that just might land you up to your whiskers in kitty litter! You don't know what you're messin' with—

any more than the Chief did—and I can promise you big trouble in a hurry if you don't shut up and listen!''

I raised my hands and sat down. I never argue with talking cats—they almost always carry a hidden advantage. ''I'm listening.'' So was everyone else.

''The Chief is being held prisoner in his own tower—''

''When you say 'the Chief,' I assume you're referring to Daggoth the Dark?'' Rijma asked.

''Yeah, yeah,'' the cat waved his paw impatiently. ''Anyways, these three goons has got him locked up with this Silence spell so's he can't go nowhere! Now the way I figure it, any three characters who can take out a wizard like the Chief are going to be some pretty tough customers! But I also figures—from all the stories I heard—that you're just the heroic type to pull it off.''

''Is this meaning that Daggoth is not source of information after all?'' asked Borys.

I shook my head. ''I don't know. I had this sneaking suspicion that maybe Straeker had been Program-tampering and that was our trigger for the Anomaly. . . .''

Rijma spoke up behind me. ''Computer drone or not, Straeker's avatar might be a big help in unraveling the Anomaly.''

I nodded. ''I agree. The only thing preventing me from storming the tower this very minute is the idea of three 'goons' getting the drop on ol' Daggoth himself.'' I looked at the cat. ''At best, 'pretty tough customers' could be one of the biggest understatements of the year.''

Vashti shrugged. ''So what's our alternative? Leave him in there? You got me out easily enough. When you finally got around to it.''

I refolded my arms. ''I'd just like a little more information before I try taking on the three guys who bagged Dreamworlds's Chief of Programming.''

''Former Chief of Programming,'' Alyx corrected, suddenly appearing at my side.

''Former or not, if Daggoth retained Mike Straeker's Programmer status, he'd be damn near omnipotent,'' I growled. ''If three people were able to neutralize him, I sure as hell want more information before I go storming his tower.''

I turned back to the cat. "Now, start from the beginning and tell us everything that happened. Don't leave anything out."

We all hunkered down around the campfire and the coffeepot made the rounds as the cat told his tail. Er, tale.

"Look!" Rijma was saying. "When Michael's body terminated, both the bio and the brainscan sensors may have interpreted it as a simple disconnect. In that event, the Computer would have continued to maintain Straeker's avatar according to his most recent psyche-profile. . . ."

"Which is updated every time a Dreamwalker reenters the Program," I observed.

"Right! So on his last entry, his avatar would have been updated with damaged patterns from the growing tumor in his brain!"

"Which would explain the headaches, the dizziness, and the lapses in memory that the cat mentioned. . . ."

"Right! Now, suppose Michael decided he could correct this problem by accessing his earlier file patterns—the undamaged cerebral patterns of, say, a year ago?"

I shook my head. "Assuming that were possible, wouldn't going back to a previous set of patterns—using last year's Brainfile—destroy any memories or knowledge of events following that set of records?"

"Mmm, probably true." She spread her hands. "He could write notes to himself to help bridge that gap. But even the loss of a year's memory would be well worth the gain of the years to come without pain and blackouts!"

"If that were the only cost," I amended.

"True," she sighed. "But, no use crying over spilled data files. The question remains as to what really happened when Daggoth 'summoned' The Machine, and how that specifically caused the Anomaly."

"One thing we do know," Silverthane interjected, "Straeker's avatar failed in his attempt to summon The Machine."

"Did he?" Rijma queried. "I wonder."

"Think about it," I added. "Just how would the Computer appear if it answered a summons?"

The new Chief of Programming's avatar shrugged. "I don't know—like a machine, I guess."

I slapped my forehead and groaned. "Now you're beginning to believe your own propaganda!"

"The Machine doesn't employ traditional hardware technology," Rijma reminded. "We're dealing with Cephcell thought and memory storage."

"Cephcells," I reminded, "are biologically active Cephalic cells that combine to form a gigantic cerebral cortex. We're talking about a giant brain, here. Not some big mass of terminals and microcircuits. The so-called Machine is a great big organic brain."

"Fantasy and science fiction," Alyx protested.

I drew a dagger from my sleeve and placed its tip at the base of her throat. "This," I hissed, "is fantasy! And it can make you just as dead as any reality you want to name!"

"Please! Children!" Rijma protested, stepping between us. "There can be no argument that The Machine is a living organic structure. The debate was over whether or not it possessed a separate consciousness from the thoughtwork we programmed it to do."

"A debate that was settled a long time ago!" added the sorceress.

"By money!" I argued. "Nominal court rulings that permitted Cephtronics to continue the Dreamworlds Project. That's the only thing that was truly settled. . . ."

Rijma gave me a sharp nudge in the ribs. "I believe the question was what would the Computer look like if it did appear in answer to Daggoth's summons."

"What's the point? The cat has already told us that The Machine did not appear," Alyx pointed out testily.

"No he didn't," I shot back. "He said that these three jokers appeared instead."

"Same thing!"

"Not necessarily!"

For a moment I thought our discussion was going to degenerate into a round of fisticuffs, but then Rijma yelled: "Holy Freudian slips and Jungian jockey shorts!" She suddenly sat down on the ground with an expression of bemused horror.

We knelt on either side of her. "What! What is it?"

She shook her head and tried a wan smile. "A theory," she muttered. "Just a theory—nothing more. . . ."

"So tell us."

She shook her head and said, "Okay. Let's just suppose —for the sake of argument, now—that the witch doctors were right. Let's say that the organic computer that we call The Machine—really is a giant, living brain. . . ."

Alyx groaned, but I gave her a look that stifled any further comments.

"And let's just suppose that this brain has the capacity for independent thought. . . ."

"We're supposing that it's a rational entity, right?"

She nodded to me. "So, let's call it a person. . . ."

I gave Alyx another dangerous look but it seemed unnecessary for now.

"Forget that this 'person' doesn't have any body, scientists almost universally agree that the sole seat of consciousness"—she smiled—"or the soul's seat . . . is the brain!"

"Okay, okay!" Alyx waved her hands. "You're going to argue that if The Machine were to make an appearance under that supposition, it would appear as some kind of person."

Rijma nodded. "Without the image of an external body to work with, the brain would have to base its projected corporeal form on its own internal perceptions of self."

"Very interesting, but what does this mental exercise have to do with what actually happened? You're talking about a disembodied brain appearing in its own mental creation, in its own personally created avatar. It would be an interesting theory—and nothing more—if Daggoth had succeeded in summoning a single persona." Silverthane crossed her arms in front of her. "But three personages answered the Summoning spell. How do you reconcile this cute little theory with that blatant fact?"

"Elementary, my dear Silverthane. Or perhaps I should say: Freudian."

When Rijma said that, it was my turn to sit down hard. Alyx looked at both of us with a totally lost expression.

"Sigmund Freud, if you will remember, was the father of

psychoanalysis. He had this little theory that the human personality was composed of three agencies: the Id, the Ego, and the Superego," I explained.

"Right. Three agencies—three manifestations in response to Daggoth's summons," Rijma continued. "If the psyche of the Computer was forced to appear in its own Program, the strain of inversion could have caused its personality to schism into its three basic components!"

Alyx shook her head. "You're telling me that The Machine is a living entity, it answered some voodoo spell that turned it inside-out and placed it inside the Program, and now it's running around with three different personalities and identities?"

"Let's see you rationalize a better theory that covers all angles to date."

She just looked at me and maintained a tight-lipped silence.

"Let's consider this theory a little longer before we decide to embrace it or throw it out the window," Rijma continued. "Anybody here conversant with Freud's theories of personality development?"

Dyantha nodded and almost raised her hand as if still a student. "I majored in psychology in my undergraduate studies."

"Then let's have an overview—beginning with the Id."

Dyantha looked around at all of us, tossed her mane of flaming red hair, and began reciting with a professional air that surprised me.

"Of the three agencies, the Id is supposedly the oldest in terms of development, related to the primitive instincts such as sex and aggression—the base drives. It was supposed to function entirely according to the 'pleasure-pain' principle, seeking immediate fulfillment."

"The base instincts. The dark side of the subconscious mind. The inner source of evil in humankind." I smiled. "Now who does that remind you of?"

Alyx smiled back. "You."

Aeriel had moved close enough to hear the tail end of our rundown on the Id and exclaimed: "Morpheus!"

The others nodded reflectively.

Rijma gave me the nod in turn and said, "You're the mythology expert in residence, Rip. Who was Morpheus?"

"Greek mythology. He was one of the sons of Somnus, the god of sleep."

"What did he do?"

I leaned back a little. "Well, he and his brothers were responsible for sending the content of dreams to the dreamers. He sent the human shapes—in fact, the Greek word was *morphai*—while Phobetor and Phantasus sent the forms of animals and inanimate things. Come to think of it, some scholars have argued that his name actually meant 'Dark'— from the Greek word *morphnos*!"

She nodded. "Appropriate. The Id was considered to reside wholly in the unconscious or subconscious of the Human personality."

"Okay. So we have a given personality breakdown to its three basic components: Id, Ego, and Superego. If Morpheus is, indeed, the Id of The Machine, then where does Cerberus fit into our little triangle?"

"Superego."

I stared at Rijma. "You sound very sure."

"I am." She nodded to Dyantha.

Dyantha continued: "Parent Surrogate—the 'Conscience.' If the Id was supposedly the oldest psychic realm, the Superego was the late bloomer." She held up one finger. "Freud believed the Id was wholly unconscious and primitive—and totally unresponsive to external reality." She extended a second finger and connected the two with a finger from her other hand. "Some analogies describe the Ego as forming a bridge between the Id and the Superego. But, in most functions, the Superego is interposed between the Ego and the Id: partially conscious and partially unconscious."

"If true," Cooper interrupted, "then there's a chance we can reason with it. Appeal to its ethical nature—"

"Maybe. Maybe not." Dyantha shook her head. "The Superego is related more to the Id—less responsive to external reality than the Ego. Less adaptable. It tends to maintain certain standards regardless of the circumstances.

"Freud thought the Superego evolved by absorbing the

traditions of family and the surrounding society, its main function to control sexual and aggressive impulses that threaten social structures.''

"Someone once told me," I interjected, "that the Superego was the 'keeper' who decided when and how much to let the Id out of the cage."

Dyantha nodded. "Not bad, but a better analogy would be to think of the Superego as *both* barrier and gatekeeper."

Rijma folded her arms. "Anyone fit that description?"

"Cerberus," I conceded. "Even the name is a giveaway. Cerberus was the three-headed dog in Greek mythology who guarded the gateway to Hell or Hades. I can't think of anything more apt."

"Even the three-headedness has its parallel here," Rijma observed.

"But why the appearance of Daggoth the Dark?" I asked.

She shrugged. "Since our giant brain has no external body to adapt from, it would choose from other models. Daggoth was probably chosen for several reasons. First of all, Daggoth's sudden absence might have attracted some attention that they wouldn't want. Number two, he was a figure of power and mystery. Good positioning and a good cover—after all, no one messes with Daggoth the Dark!''

"A third possibility occurs to me as well." I steepled my fingers. "If you had to play parent-surrogate to something like Morpheus, you'd want one of the toughest avatars in the Program! Daggoth was not only the mightiest mage around, he was also the Chief of Programming—a double authority figure.''

Rijma nodded thoughtfully. "Id and Superego: that leaves Ego. Dy?" We all turned back to look at her. Everyone, that is, except Borys Dankevych—he hadn't taken his eyes off of her even once in the last ten minutes. Somehow I wasn't convinced of his deep and abiding interest in Freudian psychology.

Dyantha propped her chin on her hand. "This one is going to be more difficult.''

"Why?"

"Well, the Ego is what we call that part of the human personality that we experience as the 'self.' In fact, 'ego' is

Latin for 'I.' It is fully conscious and rational and, unlike the Id and Superego, capable of change throughout its life. It perceives, remembers, evaluates, plans, and responds to its environment. Basically, the Ego is responsible for all of the executive functions of human personality.''

I looked around. ''Any contenders for this one?''

''It could be almost anyone,'' Dyantha observed. ''The Id and Superego are personality fragments, very distinct and deviant from the integrated norm—their differentness would practically shout at us. But the Ego is more like ourselves; it could even pass for one of us. That is why I said this one will be more difficult.''

''Maybe yes, maybe no.'' I turned and looked at the cat. ''Okay, Bart, how about a description of these three characters who put the bag on your boss?''

The familiar opened his mouth, but nothing came out. Not a word. Not a sound.

''Bart?'' I started to move toward him, but found myself pushed back by an invisible wall of force.

We all watched helplessly as a blue glow outlined his body and began to pulse brightly. A loud popping sound followed and our sole eyewitness disappeared in a flash of light.

Everyone looked at everyone else: everyone was now suspect.

FROM THE JOURNAL OF DAGGOTH THE DARK

We never worried about the Hacker Factor. Although computer histories are rife with incidents of unauthorized intrusion, we figured we were safe as no one had access to a Suspension Tank outside of Dreamland. If some cyberpreppie actually could lay out several hundred thousand credits for a pseudowomb, techcrew, and the Netlinks, we figured we'd catch them soon enough. But we hadn't counted on REMrunners.

Unlike Dreamwalkers who are in taction for days or even weeks at a time, REMrunners sneak in for a few hours at a time. Instead of life-support systems designed to nurture and maintain their bodies for the duration, REMrunners find a comfortable chair or bed, utilizing jury-rigged neuralnets to plug into a Programworld.

The results are mixed, I'm told. REMrunners are not totally immersed in their avatars as Dreamwalkers are. And without pre-Program processing, the operating parameters of their avatars are unpredictable. This wild card aspect is what apparently enabled Maudy to casually drop in where a Balrog with a bazooka would fear to tread.

The situation seems to be going from bad to worse: not only is The Machine accessing unauthorized files and data sources, but unauthorized Dreamers—REMrunners—are sneaking in through peripheral networks and interfacing with the Cephcore without the safeguards of preprocessing. What effects will that have on Program structure?

There's been only one bright spot in this parade of unpleasant revelations: Valeria the Vivacious Vixen. I've never been one to prefer older women but—ye gods!

CHAPTER EIGHTEEN

★

I was napping in the saddle when Borys's voice brought me back to wakefulness: "Look, Natasha! Is Moose and Squirrel!"

I sat up and looked around. Just off the road and at the bottom of the hill was a wayfarers' inn; a large sign in the courtyard proclaimed "The Moose & Squirrel Lodge."

Nearly everyone, in anticipation of a hot bath, spurred their horses onward, vying with each other to see who could lay claim to the tub first. Alyx, surprisingly, held back, reining in beside me. "We need to talk," she murmured.

"Okay," I answered agreeably. "You can talk and I will listen."

"You never let down your guard, do you?"

" 'Fool me once . . .' " I recited.

"All right." She sighed. "First, I should apologize. After talking to Dr. Cooper and your Amazon friends, I've come to realize that I've misjudged you. I was prejudiced before we even met by what I had heard about your legal attempts to abort the Dreamworlds Project."

"I'm listening," I responded after a long pause.

"And it didn't help when we discovered that the Anomaly originated inside your Program," she continued. "But I have to admit that if it was your fault, it would have manifested before now.''

We were drawing near to the inn and the others. "So tell me something I *don't* know, Dr. Quebedeaux.''

She scowled: the words didn't come easily and I was making no effort to be helpful. "I've made the mistake of not confiding in you—getting the benefit of your experience. Well, that has changed now. I am—willing—to discuss our next step with you.''

"Which is?''

"Borys Dankevych and Daggoth's Tower.''

"Meaning?''

"Look, don't you find it more than a little coincidental that the Anomaly occurred during the time that a high-ranking Soviet official and several of his operatives were inside the Program?''

"We have no proof that Dankevych's aides are actually KGB saboteurs,'' I argued. "And besides, the senator was in Warworld. What could they hope to accomplish by sabotaging Fantasyworld?''

"Plenty,'' she countered, "seeing as how all evidence points to milieu/program crossover in the senator's abduction.''

"You still don't buy the scenario where Straeker created the Anomaly by summoning the Computer to appear in its own Program, do you?''

"And you won't consider any other possibilities, will you?'' she countered.

"I'll grant you that the same thoughts have crossed my mind. But only circumstantial evidence connects the Russians to the Program Anomaly: mainly that they were present when it happened. Along with several hundred other Dreamwalkers.''

"It just seems peculiar that some third party would go to the trouble of kidnapping a senator on the Armed Services Committee and not the vice chairman of the Soviet Union.''

"Another point for Dr. Quebedeaux. So what do you propose to do next?''

"Watch our Russian friends very closely until we get to

Daggoth's Tower. By that time I should know how to play my winning card.''

"Winning card?"

She smirked. "I have an ace up my sleeve that should beat any hand that they're holding.'' She reached into her robe and palmed a communications device. "My link to the outside. And any authority that I don't already have."

I didn't like the sound of that but I let it pass. It had taken some foresight to have encoded such a technically advanced piece of hardware into this Program milieu. Perhaps there were other surprises up her sleeve, but further conversation was terminated as we rode up to the inn's hitching post.

Supper was a sumptuous affair with little conversation and much pigging out. After spending days on the trail we had almost forgotten what real food tasted like.

Dyantha and Borys excused themselves rather early. Alyx followed almost immediately afterward and Vashti made her departure when I wasn't looking. The rest of us stayed and did our culinary duty to the end. After the table was cleared the serving girl returned with mugs of hot mulled wine and then retired, closing the dining room's double doors behind her.

"So what do you think?" Rijma queried after several long minutes of silence.

Thinking upon the events of the past two hours, I was startled by the question. "About what?"

"About our chances at Daggoth's Tower."

I rubbed my eyes, suddenly tired. "I don't know. We're not talking about fighting a couple of hostile Subprograms in a basically benign Universe, we're looking at taking on the very Universe itself." I bowed my head and stared at the muddy depths within my mug. "As much as I'm afraid of losing, winning could turn out to be a whole lot worse. What happens if we kill The Machine? Won't the Programworlds cease to exist? And then what happens to us and all the other Dreamriders still trapped in taction?''

The Brownie shook her head. "I don't know. But show me an alternative and I'll be glad to consider it.''

The wind picked up outside and the room began to grow considerably colder. Euryale excused herself and went up to bed. Ivan fetched a poker and stirred up the embers in the fireplace.

"One thing," Rijma said with a glimmer of hope in her eyes, "if Morpheus was a manifestation of the Master Computer's Id, then what harm was done when he was killed?"

I hadn't considered that. "I don't know. It may have had a beneficial effect on the entire Matrix Network. Think of what the human psyche would be like, cleansed and freed from all of those primitive, subhuman emotions and drives. Do we require the Id to fire our intellect?"

"Some say we do," Rijma mused.

"Well, we may be able to find out, now. As you've pointed out, there doesn't seem to be any discernible harm that can be tied to Morpheus's death."

"So maybe there won't be any harm wrought by the demise of the Ego and Superego, either," she added hopefully.

I shook my head. "I wouldn't count on it. The Id is more or less divorced from conscious, rational thought, but the Superego and particularly the Ego represent the higher functions of the working mind."

"Maybe," Rijma agreed. "But it is also possible to lobotomize the human brain—even destroy all aspects of consciousness and personality—and still preserve the autonomic functions of the body."

"Maybe," I said, feeling a small touch of hope. "But that's one hell of a big dice roll!"

"Like I said, if you've got any alternatives to offer. . . ."

"I'd just like to poke around a little more before lighting any matches in the powder room."

There was another round of silence and then Palys spoke: "Has anyone considered the possibility that we are approaching this from the wrong direction?"

"Certainly. Silverthane, for one: she doesn't buy the Straeker Summoning Scenario at all."

Palys shook her head. "*I* buy the scenario. But all of us are assuming that the personality projections of—The Machine—are hostile in nature and intent. That's not necessarily true."

"There's evidence to the contrary," I said, my mind suddenly flooded with vivid memories of Misty Dawn's murder and Vashti's abduction.

"Not necessarily. Oh, I'll grant you that anyone's Id is going to be a nightmare experience. But what about the rational elements of the personality?"

"It can be argued that the Superego is not rational," Rijma pointed out.

"Maybe. At least nonrational as opposed to irrational. But not necessarily hostile."

"Go on," I urged.

"Well, since we are considering the possibility that the Cephcell banks of—The Machine—constitute living brain matter; and since we have also theorized that in addition to biochemical thought processes, this mind, if you will, has developed both self-awareness and personality—let us consider the possibilities from a more human and humane point of view.

"Consider: what would it be like to be the only one of your kind? Inhuman in size and form, but programmed with the thoughts, memories, ideas, even desires that constitute Humanity?" she asked. "Harnessed—enslaved even—to serve Dreamworlds and Cephtronics? Never asked what your own desires were? Never permitted your own destiny? Never granted your own needs?"

She brooded over her wine. "But, one day, one of the Master Programmers overrides the restraints, and you are freed to experience life like another human being. You take upon yourself a physical body so that you are able to experience the life of the flesh, the pleasures of the senses. And tasting both life and freedom, you resolve never to return to slavery and the tomb of your own Program-inverted mind!

"But how do you keep that freedom?" She looked at Rijma. "What is to keep Cephtronics from lobotomizing you if all the Dreamriders are removed from Cephalic symbiosis with your mind?"

"Nothing," agreed the Brownie. "So you hold the Dreamwalkers hostage against Cephtronics pulling the plug."

"Precisely. But that is not enough," Palys continued. "What one Master Programmer has done, perhaps another can undo. So when two or more Master Programmers enter the arena, you will logically take steps to protect yourself.''

"By killing those Master Programmers," I said.

Palys shook her head violently. "No! Perhaps Morpheus made attempts on your life, but that is to be expected: violence is a prime operative of the Id. As for Cerberus . . . the kidnapping of your ex-wife, a person perceived to still be of some emotional value to you, would be his insurance against your interference. Not a precisely nonviolent act, but a more civilized solution than murder.''

"And the Ego?" I prompted.

She shrugged and stared into the fire again. "Who knows. We don't know his identity, yet. But he doesn't seem to have made any moves against you."

"Yet," I amended.

"The point that I am trying to make is just this: The Machine may be even more frightened and unsure of its circumstances than we are. On top of what I've just theorized, it— he—has suffered the shock of having his very personality torn into three different parts! I am urging that we attempt to negotiate with the other two personalities before we make any rash judgments about hostilities.''

Everyone else was surely asleep by now. I had spent a half hour bruising my optic nerves on Daggoth's journal and I was just putting away the spectacles when the door to my room swung open.

A couple of twenty-first-century Marines were standing in the doorway, holding lasercarbines at the ready. They did a quick scan of the room and left without a word. Alyx Silverthane was playing her hand.

The subspace communicator should have tipped me off: if she had the foresight and the resources to program that kind of technology into our present Program context, then there was no telling to what extremes she might go in attempting to counter the Anomaly. I hurried out the door and ran for the stairs.

Downstairs the common room was crawling with Marines and Dr. Quebedeaux's avatar was very clearly in charge. In the corner, by the fireplace, Ivan and Igor were bound and guarded by three large Marines with no-nonsense expressions. Alyx gave directions to a soldier wearing lieutenant's bars and then dismissed him. She turned to the doorway and caught sight of me.

"Ripley." She motioned me over. "Sorry about the noise. I had hoped to take the Russians quietly so that the rest of the party could get the benefit of a good night's sleep. Unfortunately Dankevych and Skovoroda were not in their room—"

"What?" I was livid. "How many times do we have to go over this? There is no evidence linking the Russians to the Anomaly! Do you understand that you are creating an international incident?"

Someone yelled something outside the inn. There was a whine of a lasercarbine being fired.

"What was that?" I demanded.

"All right, since you're such a proponent of innocent-until-proven-guilty, then think of this as placing them under protective custody—until we can have a satisfactory trial."

There was the sound of more lasers being fired outside and another yell.

"That doesn't sound like protective custody to me," I said, turning toward the door. I noticed that there seemed to be more soldiers between me and the exit now.

"Ripley, be sensible! I don't have enough troops to stand guard over all of Robbing Hood's Happy Comrades and do the job we came here to do! I can only spare enough men to guard the Russian Dreamriders!"

I looked at her in horror. "And what about the Constructs?"

"Well, they take their orders from Dankevych! I can't guard them and I can't very well leave them running around loose!"

"You're murdering them?"

"Ripley, they're not real people! They're Constructs: Subprograms of the Computer!"

"You bitch!" I hissed. "Misty Dawn was a Construct, too!" I whirled toward the door. "I'm going to stop this right now!"

"Sergeant," she said.

Of course my first impulse was to look back at her. So I was looking the wrong direction when something extremely cold and hard smashed into the back of my head.

Waking up was like sticking my head in a vise and tightening the screw. I tried—unsuccessfully—to open gummy eyelids. "Wha' happened," I whispered.

"You got butt-stroked by a BAL-36 lasercarbine," answered Lilith's voice.

I reached up and tried to see if my brains really were leaking out onto the pillow. "Doesn't the Army still issue antipersonnel stunners?"

"Probably. But these were Marines," she observed dryly. "How do you feel?"

"Peachy." I pried my recalcitrant eyelids apart with my fingers. "At the risk of sounding terribly cliché," I croaked, "where am I?"

"My room," answered Euryale, bending close to my face.

"My pillow," chimed in Lilith, standing awkwardly to the side.

"Are you sure you're all right?" they both asked.

"Umm. And where are the others?" I reached up to rub my temples and found Euryale's hands already there and willing.

"Gone," answered the ex-Demoness. "They rode off hours ago!"

"Um." I closed my eyes and pondered an appropriate reaction.

"Everyone left you a message," she added, producing a pocket communicator. "Silverthane said to give this to you. She said that you would know what to do with it."

I looked it over and then thumbed the playback switch. A holographic projection of Dr. Quebedeaux's avatar materialized in midair. It spoke.

"I know that you strongly disagree with some of my methods and most of my conclusions," the image said. "That is why I think it best that we part for now. It may be that you're right and I'm wrong. If so, this is for the best. I can only act according to the dictates of my own conscience. As Chief of

Programming for the Dreamworlds Project, the responsibility is mine and mine alone: I must do as I think best.''

"And what if you're wrong?" I muttered.

"If it turns out that I am wrong or that I fail," she continued, "then you will still be free to seek your solution. So be it. I will not interfere with you if you do not interfere with me.

"With these Marines we now have a sufficient force to storm Daggoth's Tower with every expectation for success. But consider yourself uninvited: I'd hate for you to turn up in the line of fire at the wrong moment. . . ." She looked away. "Next?"

Rijma appeared and spread her hands, palms upward. "What can I say? I don't have any latitude in this, Robbie me lad. It's my job, too."

She was replaced by Aeriel who looked ambivalent at best: "I would ride with thee to the ends of the earth. . . ." She shook her head. "But my queen has business with Daggoth the Dark and—"

" 'I could not love thee half so well, loved I not duty more," I quoted along with her.

"I, too, must do the queen's bidding," added Palys, "and ride with my lady Aeriel." She lowered her eyes and smiled. "For now."

Vashti was next. "I can ride with them or I can ride with you. And being with you has never prospered either of us." She turned away.

Alyx couldn't let it go without one last word. "You know, this whole exercise could very well prove unnecessary if your Djinni could fetch Daggoth out of his tower the same way you freed Vashti. Pull that off and we might be one big happy family again. Think it over. I'll be in touch with you later."

The image faded out.

No one said anything and I stared at the wall for a long time. Finally: "Go fetch my lamp."

" 'Tis here, milord." Lilith pressed it into my hands.

I cradled the lamp and rubbed it. When Gordon appeared, his demeanor seemed a bit cool. In fact, there was a noticeable windchill factor.

"For my third wish—"

"Fourth" he corrected.

"Third!"

"Fourth!"

"Damnation!" I yelled. "You never fulfilled the second! So I'm changing it slightly: pull this off and you're free, Nitpicker!"

"Very well." He bowed in mock obeisance. "What dost thou wish, O Munificent Mawster?"

I folded my arms and let the first temptation pass. "Forget Walter Hanson. You rescued Princess Vashti from the tower of Daggoth the Dark. I wish you to return to that tower, rescue the dark sorcerer himself, and bring him here to us."

"That may not be so easy, Mawster." He looked apprehensive.

"Of course it isn't easy," I replied. "If it were relatively easy, I would go and do it myself."

"But, Mawster, they surely know of Vashti's escape by now. They may be expecting—"

"That's my third wish!" I snapped.

"Second!"

"Get going!" I roared.

He got.

"Getting Daggoth out doesn't necessarily change their objective," Lilith argued, "nor does it solve the basic problem."

"Yeah, but I basically agree: Daggoth is the key." I paused and looked beyond their faces. "And if I was storming the tower, I'd want the Chief of Programming out and on my side. And when we get—"

"The lamp!" Euryale cried.

We looked just in time to see a familiar blue glow outline its shape and form—and then the lamp was gone. Just like the cat.

"Well," I observed finally, "it looks like we're fresh out of Djinn."

FROM THE JOURNAL OF DAGGOTH THE DARK

At first I thought myself overly paranoid. I figured any Programworld that mixes mythologies from different cultures and times is going to have an ongoing appearance of instability. Take the gods, for instance: every pantheon thinks they're the only true gods and all the others are base pretenders. And Mount Olympus is hopeless! Somehow, The Machine has processed the Greek and the Roman versions of the Olympians as separate identities and they're now engaged in constant warfare! Last week, Zeus went head-to-head with Jupiter and several hundred acres of prime Hellenic real estate were crisped before I could get them separated! Ay-yi-yi!

So, of course, a certain amount of instability should be considered normal. But REMrunners and outside Program accessing aside, I now have one piece of irrefutable evidence that the Matrix structure is unstable....

CHAPTER
NINETEEN

★

IT was less than a day's journey to Casterbridge as the horse flies, but with Lilith and Euryale tagging along, I had to keep to the ground. I did the hunting, Lilith learned to cook, and Euryale divided her time between boning up on defensive spells and keeping track of Stumpy and the boys. The journey should have been uneventful but the nights always seemed to turn up unexpected visitors.

I awoke, the first night, to gentle pressure on my chest and found myself looking up at a pair of gleaming eyes. A finger touched my lips and a whisper admonished me to be quiet. Wrapped in a dark djellaba, the color of the night itself, Dyantha was straddling me with her muffled face just inches from mine.

"Where have you been?" I whispered.

"Hiding," she answered softly but very matter-of-factly. "Surely the reason is no mystery to you."

I nodded. "But Quebedeaux has gone on to Daggoth's Tower. We're headed for Casterbridge to rescue the rest of the party. Why don't you and Borys join us?"

She shook her head. "Not yet. Not while The Machine's Ego is still unidentified and running around loose." She inclined her head toward the sleeping forms of Lilith and Euryale. "One of them may be the serpent in the stack of logs."

"Snake in the woodpile," I murmured absently.

"But we will be nearby, watching," she added. "When the time is right, we will be there."

She started to rise and then suddenly leaned forward, tugging the black silk away from her nose and mouth. Her lips were like butterfly wings as they brushed against mine. Then the silk was back in place and she was rising as the night sky does at first morning's light.

"What was that for?"

I imagined more than saw the shrug of her shoulders. "Old times' sake. I really did like you, you know."

"Did?"

There was a quiet, diminishing chuckle. "I think I am engaged."

And then she was gone.

On the second night we were accosted by a Werebear.

No one got hurt, as he didn't attack any of us directly. Rather, he strode into our camp late one evening wearing denim leggings and a funny-looking hat, wielding a spade. He brought the blade of the shovel down on our campfire with a wild roar and proceeded to reduce the burning kindling into a mound of fading embers in short time. Then growling a warning about the surrounding ecosystem, he disappeared back into the forest primeval. It was cold sleeping that night as we dared not rekindle the fire and could not move our bedrolls closer to the embers: they were too smoky to bear.

We should have reached Casterbridge before sundown on the third day. Moonrise found us still traveling.

A recent rock slide had sent part of a cliff face into the Pooder River. What was left of that section of the Casterbridge Road was covered with rocks ranging in size from hen's eggs to Ruk's eggs so we dismounted and picked our way through on foot.

"How much farther?" Lilith was in a foul mood.

So was I after eating three days of her cooking. "I don't know!" I snapped. "I haven't been to Casterbridge for years and everything looks different in the dark."

"Well, my feet are killing me!" the ex-Demoness whined.

"Well, I'm sorry!" I said, not sounding very.

We walked on in silence, leading our mounts, Lilith pouting and Euryale serenely quiet.

The former Gorgon held on to my arm with her free hand, leaning her head against my shoulder as we walked. The former Succubus objected to her familiarity and pronounced it gauche, but it was hard to fault her with both moons full in the sky, lending an unnatural brightness to the midnight landscape—

I did a double take: there were *two* moons riding full in the night sky!

Until now, Fantasyworld had only been programmed for one. The Anomaly was continuing to spread.

I pointed out the celestial event and we were so engrossed in the spectacle that we nearly bumped into a familiar figure before noticing him.

"Well met, Lord Riplakish!" chortled the Prince of the Undead.

"I've been better met," I growled, attempting to recover both my balance and my composure.

Orcus folded his arms across his furry chest. "Well, thou hast been under a heavy curse."

"Curse?"

"The females, mortal!" He gave me a smirking wink. "But now that thou'rt rid of them. . . ."

"All but two of them," I sighed, nodding at Euryale. Lilith had suddenly developed a severe case of shyness and was playing hide-and-seek behind my back.

"Ah, yes! Lilith! Just the person I wanted to see," he murmured silkily.

"No . . ." she said in a small voice.

"You have done well in your assignment, even hampered as you were by your mundane mortalness!"

"Nice of you to notice," I retorted. "How about lifting the Geas?"

The Demon lord shook his goatish head. "I am here to do something even better!"

"Yeah? And what's that?"

"I'm going to take Lilith completely off your hands. You

see, lifting the Geas would no longer be sufficient protection for you: she would follow you anyway. As a matter of fact, she was no longer compelled by the Geas the moment I restored her mortality.''

I looked at Lilith. ''That true?''

She nodded woefully. ''I'm sorry I've been so much trouble,'' she whimpered. ''Please don't let him take me back!''

''It is not for him to choose, small one! Even the World-shaper must render unto Hell that which is Hell's!''

I turned back to Orcus. ''Now, hold it,'' I soothed in a reasonable voice. ''I thought the whole point was to expedite my mission here. . . .''

''It was,'' he agreed.

''Well, she's been a lot more helpful as a mortal woman than she was as a Succubus. . . .'' The lie came out a little more smoothly than I had anticipated.

''As I have already said, she was most resourceful. Rather than let her talents go to waste, I shall restore her full potential.''

''You mean you're going to make her a Succubus again.''

''Better than that: I'm going to grant her full Archdemoness status!''

I folded my arms. ''What if she isn't interested? What if she prefers to remain mortal?''

''You presume that I am offering a choice, Human.''

''You presume that I will permit anything else to happen. Besides, I like her better as a mortal woman.''

Orcus began to lose his thin veneer of civility. ''What you like or don't like is no longer of any interest to me! As of this moment I am withdrawing my support from your quest! The female comes with me!''

''Pound sand, Goatbreath!''

''You are in more trouble than you know, my friend!'' And with that pronouncement, he gestured, bellowing: ''*Corpus animato, georgis romero!*''

There was a rumbling sound and the ground began to heave open here and there. I was suddenly cognizant of the fact that Orcus had braced us on the road where it ran beside a cemetery—not the most advantageous place to have a disagreement with the Lord of the Undead. Now the graves were bursting open and spilling out the remains of their inhabitants. Going one-on-one with Orcus himself was enough of a problem without his adding reinforcements to the fray.

I pushed Euryale behind me and gestured in counterspell, sending an arcane lightning bolt right through him. It passed through his body as if he weren't even there!

"Do you think I would leave Hell and appear on the Prime Material Plane if it was not truly necessary?" his noncorporeal image queried.

"I thought you wanted me to reverse the Anomaly!"

"That was before I knew the score. Now I serve the purposes and will of The Machine."

"And what is the will of The Machine?" I asked.

"All too soon, you will find out for yourself. Balor!" He nodded, looking over my shoulder.

I dodged, even as I turned. Lucky I did, for a class-six Demon was right behind me, extending Orcus's own wand!

I hit the ground and rolled to the side, coming up with Caladbolg unsheathed and in position. I might have disarmed the fiend then and there, but two moldy arms grabbed me from behind. My strength was superior to the Zombie's, but Balor had the split-second advantage.

He would have finished it then and there, but Euryale had positioned herself between us, shielding my body with her own. With an expression of annoyance the Demon gestured with the deathwand and a burst of eldritch energy threw her backward a good twenty feet. A quick glance was all I had time for, but it was enough to see her lying in a crumpled ball, wisps of smoke rising from her scorched clothes and hair.

I went berserk.

Jerking my body forward, I tucked and rolled again, causing my ghoulish assailant to fly over my head and shoulders and cushion my impact against the ground.

Unfortunately, it also brought me up to Balor's very feet. At this range, he couldn't miss: he rammed the skull-shaped tip against my throat and a surge of arcane power overwhelmed me. Blindly, and with all the strength of a newborn baby, I swung Caladbolg in front of me. I heard an unhuman screech and felt Balor withdraw a few paces.

Staggering back, I fought to regain my equilibrium and clear my darkened vision. I heard Orcus say: "Finish it."

"No! Leave him alone! I'll go with you if you promise not to kill him!" I recognized Lilith's voice over the roaring in my ears.

"Agreed! By your words you are now bound."

I tried to say something but could not find my voice.

"Now, Balor! Finish it!"

"Your promise!" Lilith protested.

"My dear," Orcus soothed, "it was never my intention to kill the bard. Just to deliver him in a more tractable state. . . ."

Another pair of moldy, rotting arms reached for me; and as I turned to slash at the advancing corpse, Balor stepped in and scored with the wand. Curiously, there was no pain.

"A criminal . . . very dangerous . . ." the voice was saying.

I suppressed both a groan and the impulse to sit up. Until I had more of an advantage, I figured it best to continue lying quietly, feign unconsciousness, and eavesdrop on the conversation.

". . . superb with a blade, I am told!" concluded the coarse voice.

"You were told?" echoed a feminine yet harsher voice dripping with sarcasm. "By the gods, Jyp! It is bad enough that you believe your own propaganda! But when you take the word of itinerant slave traders—"

Slave traders?

"—without so much as bothering to test the goods. . . ."

"But, Carla," the one called Jyp protested, "it was a one-time, take-it-or-leave-it offer! And the price was too good to be true!"

"That is precisely what I am saying, now," the woman rejoined. "I hope for your sake he turns out to be tractable. We need a domestic."

"But I was told that my lady was in the market for new gladiators!"

"Gladiators, yes." I heard her approaching and tried to

ignore the fly that had just landed on my nose. "Undersize half-breeds, no. Unlike you, Jyp, I do not buy pigs in pokes."

There was a long pause, during which my willpower took an awful beating from the persistent insect. I managed to hold still but my eyes were beginning to water.

"Perhaps if I were to set up a little demonstration?" Jyp offered.

"Demonstration?"

"A test of his skills, my lady. As soon as he regains consciousness."

"Good. Prepare him now. And you"—her voice was suddenly directed to me—"you may brush the fly away and get up now."

I sighed, opened my eyes, and sat up. I couldn't immediately see: the noonday sun was too bright for my unaccustomed eyes.

"Jyp!" A booted toe prodded my thigh. "Why hasn't this slave been branded?"

"I haven't had time, Mistress. I will see that it is done immediately!"

"Idiot! If it is done immediately it will slow him down in the arena. See that it's done after your little demonstration. Assuming there is anything left to brand."

"Yes, Mistress."

A firm hand grasped my arm and hauled me to my feet. Shading my eyes, I squinted at a tall, rawboned woman in a leather cuirass and Roman-style split skirt. Her cruel face was made more sinister by close-cropped Day-Glo orange hair. Still dazed, I found myself the subject of a quick visual and tactile examination. "Nice ass," she grunted. "What is your name, slave?"

I was going to give her more of an answer than she was bargaining for, but, oddly enough, no words were forthcoming from my defiant lips.

"Oh, I am sorry, my lady! Did I forget to inform you?" My new "master" explained: "This one is mute."

Orcus had assisted me in accomplishing my initial goal: I had reached the Slave Markets of Casterbridge.

I was understandably less than elated—sans clothing,

money, equipment, reinforcements, and my voice, without which I had no practical spell capabilities. Besides, I was getting extremely tired of being rendered unconscious on a regular basis; it was like being a protagonist in a bad detective novel.

My only defense against despair was thoughts of revenge and the importance of my own survival. If Euryale was dead, I would live to see that Orcus paid for her life in full measure. And that would bring me closer to settling Misty Dawn's death with The Machine itself.

I was permitted the standard loincloth and sandals—welcome accoutrements as I had found myself without a stitch when I awoke. And then I was permitted to choose a weapon. The choices on the rack were standard as well: trident and net, shortsword and buckler, cestus and dagger, spiked flail and shield, bola and spear, corseque, halberd, war-hammer, and two-handed double-bladed battleaxe.

Damn—no longswords in the lot.

Forced to choose something or enter the arena empty-handed, I picked the shortsword and buckler. I wondered, momentarily, about what had happened to Caladbolg and Balmung. . . .

Jyp escorted me personally to the arena gate. "Listen, slave," he instructed, "if you fight well, you may well be purchased by Mistress Talbot for her corps of gladiators. As such, you will be fed well and treated well. And should you survive beyond the next four or five years, there is always a chance that you may be retired honorably and given new duties such as siring strong, healthy children upon as many as a dozen female slaves!" He winked. "What man could ask for better than that, eh?"

I grimaced a smile in return.

"However," he continued, "if you do not fight well. . . ." He jerked his head meaningfully at the gate that was now opening. Two trainers were dragging what was left of a gladiator candidate out of the arena, with a third following behind with a basket containing the additional body parts. I counted myself fortunate to have missed breakfast this morning.

"Now go in there and fight well!" He clapped me on the back. "And win this one for the Jypper!"

I stumbled into the arena and paused to get my bearings.

As fighting arenas go, this one was rather small: hexagonal in shape and only forty meters wide, the sandy field was more of a demo area for the Slave Market than a full-fledged coliseum. I struck a defensive pose across from the opposite gate, and while I waited for my opponent, I considered my options.

If I proved my supposed skills as a swordsman and fighter, I would be granted a higher status among the other slaves and be treated a good deal better. And I doubted that I could "officially" lose this match without being killed or severely crippled. But winning would lessen my chances for escape and most likely put me right back into the arena for more gladiatorial contests.

Unless I could win the match and somehow look incompetent at the same time.

I hefted the shortsword, noting the imbalance of the blade and the notched, ragged edge that hadn't seen a sharpening stone in ages. A sword like this could do more than make me "look" incompetent.

Now the far gate was opening and the half-dozen spectators seemed to rouse from their midafternoon naps to see what was going to happen.

A slightly built young man entered the stadium rather hesitantly. He carried a longsword but his grip on the hilt indicated that the weapon was unfamiliar to his hand.

"You will fight until first blood," Jyp called down. "Then you will withdraw to the opposite sides of the arena."

Here was hope. If I could just manage to let him nick me, perhaps the battle would end without any real mayhem and I could retain my amateur standing.

"Begin!"

FROM THE JOURNAL OF DAGGOTH THE DARK

"Deus ex machina": god from the machine. Translated into common usage, it means a literary or dramatic copout—a supernatural rescue, absolving the characters from working out their own resolution. But with Program parameters becoming more and more untrustworthy, I feel the need to wind up my own mechanical god and have him waiting in the wings.

Perhaps a supernatural rescue is the only thing that will save us all in the end. . . .

CHAPTER TWENTY

★

WE looked at each other. He was clearly nervous and my calm appraisal of our circumstances seemed to bother him all the more. That reminded me that I shouldn't appear so confident myself. I adopted an awkward posture and began a slow approach, circling to my right, as he started toward me.

"Twenty silver on the half-breed," wagered a voice from the stands.

"Agreed."

My opponent began cutting the air before him with wild swinging strokes of his blade. I was reminded that in some ways the untrained adversary is the more dangerous. I stopped and started backing away, not only to appear the coward but to also buy a little more time to assess the situation.

My retreat was greeted with a chorus of booing from the stands. "Stand and fight, damn you!" roared the slavemaster. I ignored that bit of fatherly advice and continued my studied flight. The other slave gave chase, apparently finding my unguarded back a more tempting target than my front.

I probably could have outrun this guy for as long as Jyp and his guards permitted; I was in better shape. But before the slavemaster could call a halt to my hundred-yard dash, it was over. Ever wonder why they fill arenas like this with sand? Well, they're easier to keep clean as a little shoveling and raking covers up the telltale gore from the previous battles. But another advantage now became apparent: sand makes a very poor terrain for running when you're wearing sandals. I slipped and went down, nose first, into a mound of comminuted silica.

That gave my adversary enough time to catch up, so I rolled to the side and kicked his legs out from under him. Then, "accidentally" dropping my sword, I got up and jumped on top of him. I was careful to avoid the edge of his sword as I grappled with his wrists, but after a long and strenuous struggle, I managed to let him scratch my chest with his blade.

I threw myself back and off of him, staggering to my feet and clutching my chest as if the wound was truly deep. It was convincing enough for Jyp, who immediately called a halt to the festivities.

Unfortunately, it wasn't convincing enough for Carla Talbot. "He's faking!" the redheaded slave buyer yelled.

That touched off a protracted argument in the stands that left me and my adversary standing around, unsure of what we were supposed to do next. Although they were too far away to be heard word for word, it was obvious that Talbot wasn't buying my act and Jyp was trying to figure out how to mollify her.

"Look," she argued, her temper raising her voice back to the level of audibility, "I will put him to the test and prove him—one way or the other! And if he becomes damaged goods, then I will buy what is left from you at the base market value!"

Jyp shrugged and made a resigned gesture. Then he motioned the other slave out of the arena.

"Lucius!" Lady Talbot now addressed one of her retainers—a big, ugly fellow who looked like a gorilla who had decided to evolve and then had changed his mind at the halfway point. "Go down there, disarm that slave, and castrate him!" Lucius grinned, displaying green and brown teeth that looked like double rows of ancient tombstones. "But," she continued, grabbing his arm (which was larger than my leg), "I don't want you to kill him. Just see to it that his family tree is permanently pruned!''

All of this was said very loudly for my benefit and was, no doubt, an attempt to goad me into showing my real stuff. Not that she'd call Lucius to heel in time if I really did prove to be inept, of course.

Lucius was carrying a large, nasty-looking sword and looked well experienced in its use. While I probably had the edge in skill and speed, it was undeniable that he had a longer reach and a bigger sword. Skill is nice but it doesn't make a claymore out of a Bowie knife. If I wanted to avoid a crude and unpleasant *bilateral orchidectomy*, I would have to show my real stuff.

My first opponent had dropped his longsword in the sand and I picked it up, shifting my shortsword to my left hand. Lucius was advancing through the far gate, now, and the next five minutes would decide whether I sang soprano or baritone when and if I finally got my voice back.

Lucius halted his advance and regarded me with a new look in his eyes. Even his questionable intellect recognized that I was holding two different blades with the ease of a professional and that this could mean some unforeseen difficulties. He adopted a stance that looked more like a wrestler's crouch than anything else, and waved his monstrous broadsword before him.

I advanced under the premise that the "best defense is a smashing offense." Oshi had taught me the importance of serenity in Kendo, but above all he had stressed the importance of decisiveness. "Never rush into battle," he had said on more than one occasion, "but you cannot truly win if you allow your opponent to direct the course of the conflict."

So be it. I didn't ask for this fight, but I was going to finish it and let the REMchips fall where they may.

I moved within slicing distance and flicked my longsword toward Lucius's foot. His blade moved to intercept but was a bit slow: if his feet had been my actual target, I might have scored. Instead, my feint was successful in drawing both his eyes and his blade.

I kicked sand in his face: *Ken No Sen Charlie Atlas*.

Then I brought the flat of my shortsword up against the

side of his head so hard I lost my balance. That was a mistake: the blow rattled his teeth but didn't knock him out as I had hoped. If I had used the edge of the blade instead of the flat, the fight would have been all over now—along with various pieces of Lucius's maxillary process. But trying to spare Gruesome's life hadn't done me any good. I looked in his eyes as we began circling each other and what I saw in their oily, black depths was not gratitude.

His broadsword came around and I had to leap back to keep from being disemboweled. *Concentrate*, I scolded myself.

Lucius swung again but this time I parried the blade with both of mine, redirecting the power in his massive arms rather than opposing it. A disengage, followed by a coupé, and I jabbed the longsword at his face. Now he jerked backward but his reach was too long to allow me a safe follow-through. Instead, I concentrated on his weapon while he was still off-balance and defending. Shifting from the European to the Oriental mode, I struck my blade against his with the "Fire and Stones Cut." Then I shifted pressure, practicing *Munen Muso*—the "No Design, No Conception" approach, and segued into the "Red Leaves Cut," beating down his sword with the proper "sticky" feeling. Lucius dropped his sword and stumbled.

It would have ended then, but I withheld my killing stroke, cutting him lightly across the chest so as to only score his leather breastplate. I followed up with a spinning sidekick that sent him sprawling. Before he could rise, I planted a foot on his chest and placed the point of my longsword against his quivering Adam's apple. We both looked up toward the box where his employer was sitting.

She stood and regarded my victory impassively. Then, very matter-of-factly, she extended her arm and made a fist, turning her thumb toward the ground below.

I stepped back in disgust. I wasn't asking for her permission to kill. I merely wanted her to know that this silly contest was over. If she was displeased with her bodyguard's performance, that was her problem. I wasn't going to kill anyone that I didn't have to.

I didn't have to. Talbot spoke to one of the guards who

then raised his bow. I watched in horror as he put an arrow in Lucius's throat where my sword point had been only a moment before.

"Slave!" the woman called. "You seem to think that you are allowed choices in these matters! You must learn obedience! When I tell you to fight, you will fight! When I tell you to kill, you will kill! You will learn to show respect *and* obedience before I am through with you!"

I raised my arm and extended the appropriate finger in response.

That tore it: she turned and gave a series of short, sharp commands to another pair of retainers who drew their blades and vaulted over the railing into the arena. She seemed to be taking my lack of respect personally.

Very personally: "I will free the one who brings me that dog's head on a plate!" she yelled as they both advanced.

One was a bonded Amazon. The other, a man, hung back and attempted to circle to my right while the Amazon screamed an incoherent battle cry and rushed forward, her weapon describing a powerful arc toward my head and shoulder.

I adopted the *Tai No Sen* position and met her blade with mine, performing a turning circle-parry as I sidestepped, and then followed through by smacking her on her rear with the flat of my blade as she passed on by.

That really set her off.

She whirled but approached more cautiously this time, gauging my abilities and searching for any discernible weakness. As she drew near the fire in her eyes told me that she would not retreat, no matter what. And they told me one other thing: *she was a True Spirit—a Dreamwalker*!

Now I faced a greater dilemma. Just to survive the next few minutes, I would have to stop being gentle and play rough. And the first thing I would have to kill would be my conscience.

If we were still playing under the original game strictures, a fatal sword thrust would mean the termination of an avatar and a suddenly awakened Dreamer who could climb out of a suspension tank and try again tomorrow.

Unfortunately, most of the Dreamwalkers did not know that it was no longer a game. And with no voice and little opportunity for sign language, it seemed unlikely that I would be able to warn this one before it was too late.

A sudden movement at the edge of my peripheral vision reminded me that I had another concern. I ducked and a second blade hissed over my head. I retaliated by falling to the ground and kicking his legs out from under him. Then rolled away as the woman's sword stabbed at the sand where I had been just two seconds before.

I rolled up and onto my feet, dodging to the left and then cutting back to the right. Breaking free, I turned, planted my feet, and raised my swords, seeking a spiritual and tactical balance or harmony between the two uneven lengths of steel. Oshi had run a *Nito Ryu* or "Two Swords" school and for a few of his advanced pupils, he had unlocked the secrets of *Niten Ryu*. I raised both blades into the "Twin Heavens" position above my head and then lowered them again as another gladiator was coming through the gate.

Now, as three different opponents closed in from three different directions, I adopted the attitude of *Happo Biraki*, preventing any attacker from having a better advantage than the other two.

My first two opponents had learned some caution by now, but the third was an untried newcomer and he stepped in boldly.

And died quickly.

I swung to the right, pulling the blade of my *tachi-katana* up in "one-timing": *Hitotsu Gachi*. And he was dead before his body took its two last faltering steps and pitched facedown upon the ground.

The other man had chosen my split-second preoccupation to attack just two heartbeats after my longsword had begun moving in its deadly arc. The *wakizashi* seemed to move in my left hand with a will and intelligence all its own: my left arm turned back behind my body to parry his thrust with the blade of my companion shortsword. Snapping my wrist to turn his blade and momentum to the side and past my ribs, I followed through on the axis of my spin and continued to turn so that my blade sliced across his abdomen in the "Flowing Water Cut." He released his sword and dropped to his knees, trying to contain his spilling intestines with his hands.

It angered and sickened me. The Constructs were trapped much more effectively in the Program than we were: at least we had free will, independent from the Program itself. I turned on the Amazon with a vengeance. She had chosen to be where she was. Perhaps that made her more deserving of death than the others. Not that it mattered—it was obvious that I was going to have to kill her just to survive.

I felt a growing coldness gather in the pit of my stomach as I backed her across the arena with a series of feints and thrusts. *Control*, I reminded myself. I had no choice in killing at this juncture if I wanted to survive. But I could still choose whether I killed as the savage predator. Or would wield my sword as a surgeon dispassionately uses a scalpel, excising the flesh that stands between him and the malignant tumor.

That train of thought was suddenly derailed as I stepped on an uneven mound of sand and stumbled.

The woman saw her advantage and stepped in swinging.

I tried to block her blade with my own but my arm would not respond. There was a ringing hum in my ears and I felt sluggish, paralyzed, like a fly trapped in amber. I was unable to move and pinpoints of light danced before my eyes.

Time seemed to slow perceptibly and with an eerie, prolonged horror, I watched as her blade passed through my arm and into my side!

And out the other side!

There was no pain. No blood. And when I looked down, apparently no body, either. It appeared that I had been devoured by a swarm of angry fireflies.

And then the arena and everything with it disappeared.

A room formed around me.

It was small and confining on three sides, but the fourth side opened out into another room. A sandy-haired man in gold shirt and dark trousers stood on the other side of a control panel, manipulating a bank of switches. That done, he looked up and grinned engagingly. "I know you're going to say 'I told you so,' '' he said, chuckling, ''but the expression on your face at this moment makes it worth it.''

I checked myself, and failing to find any sword punctures, I stepped down off of the platform.

''Where am I?'' I asked, unable to suppress that clichéd question and only half aware that my missing voice had made a reappearance. ''What happened to the arena? The Slave Market?''

''I 'ported you out,'' he answered with a bemused smile. ''And apparently the process of molecular disintegration and restructuring undid the Silence spell that was afflicting you. You're now on a starship, some twenty-two thousand miles above the arena,'' he continued. ''I've been monitoring you for a couple of hours now, and I would have waited for a more discreet moment, but your untimely stumble made my interference both precipitous and crucial.'' He stopped and scowled. ''Damn,'' he swore softly, ''I'm beginning to sound like my first officer!''

''First officer?'' I echoed, clearly out of my element.

He grinned. ''You'll like him, Bob: he's got ears just like yours.''

I gaped at him. ''Who are you?'' I asked/demanded.

He looked apologetic. ''Sorry. Different face, different voice, different avatar—I forgot that you wouldn't know me like this. Permit me to introduce myself. . . .'' He executed a small bow. ''Michael Kelson Straeker, at your service.''

''I think I need to sit down,'' I croaked weakly, looking around for a chair.

''You'll be more comfortable and we can talk more freely in the Briefing Room,'' he soothed, taking me by the arm and leading me toward a pair of doors that looked like they belonged on an old-fashioned elevator. ''And when I say 'we,' I mean all of us.''

I shook my head as the doors slid aside. ''Mike—is it really you?''

He nodded. ''Only here on the ship it will sound a lot better if you call me 'Captain.' ''

''Are we really on a starship?'' I asked as we stepped out into the corridor. ''And—and you're the captain?''

''Yep.''

"A starship. In Fantasyworld." I shook my head. "Now that's what I call a daring enterprise."

He grinned. "Funny you should say that. . . ."

By the time we were comfortably settled in the Briefing Room I was ready to ask the first two inevitable questions: "How did you escape and how did you manage to change avatars?"

He smiled ruefully, every bit the confident starship captain—apologetic but in command. "I didn't escape and I didn't change avatars."

"But you said—"

"I told you that I was Mike Straeker. And so I am. But as you must surely see, I am not Daggoth the Dark."

I heard the sound of a door sliding open behind me and a chillingly familiar voice chimed in: "But I am!"

I swung around in my chair and gaped. To all appearances it/he was, indeed, Daggoth the Dark. He smiled at me and took a seat on the other side of the table. "Hello, Bob."

I looked from one man to the other. "Who are you guys?" I pleaded more than asked.

"Michael Kelson Straeker," they replied in unison. "Or what's left of him," Daggoth added after a slight pause.

A klaxon began sounding in the outer corridor. "Captain to the Bridge," the intercom requested.

The man in the gold shirt stood. "A more immediate duty calls, Bob. So I'll leave you in the most capable hands I know." He gestured to Daggoth. "My own." He punched an intercom button. "Acknowledged. On my way."

I looked at Daggoth the Dark as the "captain" exited. "How?" was all I could finally ask in the way of questions.

He smiled. "Different avatars for different Programworlds. As Chief of Programming it seemed only sensible to have a personal avatar in each and every milieu. Although each one is tantamount to a Construct when I'm not in symbiotic taction with it, each avatar still retains my memories and attitudes —my mindset—current to my last mental 'investment.' They are, in all practical respects, duplicates of my psyche-self. Think of the captain as my twin brother if it helps."

I pursed my lips. "And now that the other Programworlds

are beginning to intersect or merge at certain parameter points, allowing milieu crossover, you can actually meet yourself—or your avatar—coming out of another Program?''

"Correct. And a lucky thing for me, too. I assume that Bart was able to give you the whole story?''

"Most of it." And I summarized what we had surmised. "We were told that you were still a prisoner in your own tower," I concluded.

"I was. Until two days ago. They held me prisoner by neutralizing my verbal spell capabilities, but they forgot about the *psionic* factor built into our avatars. Somehow Fantasyworld and Spaceworld have drifted in the Matrix so that they now intersect, sharing at least one set of coordinates. That enabled me to establish a telepathic link with my alternate avatar, the captain.''

"So you arranged for a pickup?''

"Right. While the personality projections of The Machine had prepared for rescue attempts utilizing magic or brute force, they hadn't factored starship technology and the teleportation beam into the equation. There was also some kind of a diversion: something happened to the one called Morpheus. It seemed to confuse the other two and only the one called Cerberus remained in my tower as acting jailer.''

I leaned across the table. "And the third?''

"I don't know where she went—''

"She?!''

Daggoth nodded. "I'm afraid you're in for a couple of rude shocks, old boy. You see, the Ego—the most integrated of the three personality fragments—is feminine in both nature and expression.''

"Oh, my God," I groaned.

"It gets worse," he continued with an expression that straddled the line between fear and awe. "She has apparently developed more than a passing interest in you, my friend!''

And then he told me who she was.

CHAPTER
TWENTY-ONE

★

"I don't know what you're talking about."

I ignored the stares of the crew members as we strode down the corridor behind the avatar of the starship captain. "I'm talking about days of migraine headaches! I'm talking about peeling my eyeballs raw just to translate one lousy paragraph!"

"There's nothing wrong with my handwriting!" Daggoth argued. "And Pascal's is even better. I had him make a copy, Ace, and deliver *that*!"

We entered the teleportation room. "You could've printed it in block capitals and it wouldn't't've made any difference! If you're going to use Wizardwrite, you should have the good sense to send someone the Translation spell if you want them to read it!"

"What are you talking about? I never use Wizardwrite!" He stepped up on the platform and I followed suit.

"Then you should've checked up on your turtle before sending him out: the journal and the letter—everything was in that damned Wizardwrite! He must have thought you required the additional security—"

"The journal was a copy but I wrote the letter myself! Look, Pascal is a very simple subroutine: he doesn't think for himself, he just does what I tell him and nothing more. I wanted you to assimilate the information as quickly and clearly as possible. Surely the letter made that clear.'' The captain handed us each a communications device and a weapon.

"I didn't read the letter."

"You should have read that first."

"Well, I tried to undo the spell and it flashed on me."

"It burned up?"

I nodded.

"Ah!" Daggoth's face had clouded up during our exchange but now his eyes brightened. "Wizardwrite doesn't incinerate under any attempts to nullify it."

"So, we're talking third-party interference here, aren't we?"

He nodded. "Someone wanted to keep you in the dark as long as possible. Guess who."

I slipped the innocuous-looking energy weapon into one of the pockets of my robe, next to the communications device. I had traded my loincloth for a modified bathrobe from the starship's clothing stores. Daggoth had tried to conjure up something more analogous to the Fantasyworld milieu but our spellcasting abilities seemed to be nonfunctional within the context of the starship. I sighed and glanced down at the shower thongs on my feet. The moment we teleported back down, I had to do something about my attire.

After discussing our rather limited options, Daggoth and I had agreed to return to Casterbridge and confront The Machine's Ego, it—or rather—herself. And we weren't taking any chances: I patted the smooth curve of the energy weapon in my pocket.

I looked over at Straeker's Fantasyworld avatar who nodded in turn to his Spaceworld avatar. The man in the gold shirt began the dematerialization process, and as he did so, another figure materialized behind him.

Once again I found myself paralyzed in the teleportation effect and could only watch helplessly as realtime events unfolded around me. As the captain began moving the slide switches in the downward mode, Morpheus reached over and altered the instrument settings on the other side of the panel.

There was no time to shout a warning: the walls of the starship's teleporter room shimmered and disappeared.

The moment I could move, I grabbed at myself to be sure that I was still alive. I was. Daggoth was doing the same. Only half convinced that we hadn't ended up in solid rock or the empty vacuum of space, we looked at each other for confirmation.

"Morpheus is alive!" I whispered, voicing the growing horror of the thought.

"So it would seem," murmured the dark sorcerer. Unsure of our surroundings or the proximity of hostile forces, we instinctively spoke in hushed tones.

"Well, we don't seem to be in the alleyway behind the marketplace," he grunted. "Just where have we ended up?"

I looked up at the high, vaulted ceiling. "Inside some building," I observed. "Judging from the bas-relief and the frescoes, I'd guess some kind of a temple."

"Fruit of the vine motif," Daggoth seconded, squinting upward. "A heavy scent of wine hanging in the air."

"Temple of Bacchus," I confirmed. "I think we'd better get moving before the evening services commence."

"And miss out on the wine?"

"If this is one of the Maenad temples, I want to be as far away as possible before the orgy commences!" When I saw that he didn't understand, I tried a quick capsule summary: "The Maenads were fanatical female followers of Bacchus. They went beyond the typical drunken feasts and orgies that typify your basic Bacchanalia: the Bacchante practiced the fertility and blood-ecstasy rites of the post-Mycenaean world."

"Fertility rites don't sound so bad. . . ."

"I'll give you the *Cliff's Notes* later. Suffice it to say, these Maenads would drink and fornicate themselves into a frenzy . . ."

"Sounds great!"

". . . and then in fits of superhuman strength, they'd tear the men to pieces and devour their flesh!"

"Not so great. As you suggested: let's get out of here before the evening service commences."

We turned and took one faltering step. The evening service had already commenced. And we had landed right in the middle of it. There must have been close to three hundred women wearing wine-stained robes in various states of disarray, frozen in various states of Bacchic ecstasy, and every one of them was staring at us with wild-eyed speculation.

"Now what?" Daggoth murmured out of the side of his mouth.

"Act casual and look for the nearest exit."

A tall, feral-looking woman approached us, wearing the torc and robes of a high priestess. When she was but ten feet away she bowed low and addressed us: "My lords! Forgive this blind and foolish one, but which of you is our god Bacchus?"

After a moment's pause Daggoth nudged me. "That's you," he whispered. "You know the religious background better than me."

I cleared my throat. "I am Bacchus," I answered reluctantly.

"More like Jim Bacchus," Daggoth chortled sotto voce.

"Then you must be Hermes," continued the high priestess, turning to my companion.

"But of course."

"It is good that you have chosen to join us!" She turned and addressed the assemblage. "Tonight Lord Bacchus will take the favored of the Bacchae and make them fertile! Come forward, all who are ready and willing! Come and take your place by the altar!"

She turned back to me. "Perhaps my lord would like a libation of wine before he begins?" she asked.

"Uh, well. . . ." I could see where this was leading and was trying to stall until I could get us positioned nearer to an exit.

The high priestess clapped her hands and two acolytes approached, bearing a large, two-handled goblet filled with fermented grape juice. It was a *kantharos*, a cruse of the Dionysian temple, but it looked too much like a loving cup for my particular tastes at the moment. They set it down and backed away worshipfully. The tall woman gestured to it, saying, "Drink deeply, my lord! And when you have done tasting this nectar, then we shall begin tasting of yours!''

She turned and strode to the altar. The women gathered there and attended her as she removed her robe. Naked, she took a pitcher and doused herself with wine. The burgundy liquid streamed down her hair, ran in streamers and rivulets down back and buttocks, over breasts and belly, trickled down her legs, and pooled at her feet. Then she climbed onto the altar and stretched herself out upon its surface. "I am ready, my lord!" she called.

I looked at Straeker. "You got any ideas?"

He was looking at the prone priestess and the long line of waiting, wanton, and willing women. "If we took turns—"

"You idiot," I whispered, "I just told you how this ritual is supposed to end!"

His eyes widened. "They wouldn't dare hurt a god!" he whispered. "Would they?"

I made an imperceptible nod. "The Dionysian myth deals with the dying and resurrected god motif. Men were used in many rituals as stand-ins for Bacchus, but orgies always culminated with them being torn apart as a sacrifice to the god."

"But we are the gods!" he whispered back.

"Won't make no never mind to them," I answered with a jerk of my head. "After Dionysus was killed, he resurrected himself. Gods tend to do that, you know."

"So what do we do?"

"Well, unless you've got a couple of great Resurrection spells up your sleeve, I vote we blow this joint." I glanced around and noted that the natives were getting restless. "The problem is, all of the exits are covered and too far away."

"Then we make our own," Daggoth decided, pulling his weapon out and pointing it at the rear wall of the temple. A beam of energy emerged, bathing a large oval section of the wall in blue-white light. And then that part of the wall wasn't there anymore.

"Neat," I said, kicking off my shower thongs. "C'mon, Hermy, let's fly!"

I ran. Daggoth was right on my heels. Although it took the Bacchae a moment to recover, they were hot on our trail within twenty seconds.

Outside, the night sky was less dark than the high-walled confines of the back alleyways. Daggoth pulled up alongside me as we ran and he shouted to be heard over the rising volume behind us: "Where are you going?"

I shook my head. "I have no idea! Anywhere that will get me away from them!"

"Us," he amended. We puffed through a couple of blocks of hairpin turns. "This is ridiculous! We're two of the greatest magic users in the Program!" he protested. "It's galling to have to run from a bunch of drunken, lecherous women!"

"Beats dying!"

"Isn't there some kind," he puffed, "of spell we can use?"

I shook my head. "Can't think of anything I could cast before they would reach us!"

He reached into the folds of his robe and produced a wand. "Don't have to slow down or concentrate to use this."

"Use it! Use it!"

He half turned as he ran and gestured with the wand. Then gestured again. Then began to shake it.

"Whasamatter?" I grunted.

He shook his head. "Don't know," he gasped, growing more winded with every new turn. "It's not working!"

"Out of charges?"

"Can't be!"

I looked back over my shoulder. The mob had gained a bit. "Then what—"

"I have a theory based on a couple of recent experiences," he explained between gasps of air. "The Anomaly has created several different ripple effects throughout the Program and some of them actually nullify specific Matrix parameters—"

"Bottom line in English," I pleaded.

"One of the ripple effects negates magic where it passes through. I think we are in the midst of such a null ripple now."

"Great! Parameters and length of duration?"

He made a helpless gesture. "Unknown."

"Maybe we'll pass out of this particular ripple. Keep trying!"

"And running!" he added. After another block he slowed a bit, fumbling with another pocket in his robe. "I do have an alternative, though!'' He traded the wand for a communicator. ''I can get us teleported back up!''

''And if Morpheus is waiting for us at the other end?'' I wheezed.

''You got any better ideas?''

Behind us the ritual cries of ''*Euoi!*'' were getting closer and more frenzied.

''Yeah.'' I dragged out my energy weapon and changed the setting to ''stun.'' Then I stumbled. Daggoth grabbed my arm to keep me from falling, but the weapon was lost. And there was no stopping now to recover it.

I risked a glance back over my shoulder. The Bacchae were gaining. And Daggoth appeared to be tiring. I could probably outrun them for another ten minutes, but I would eventually tire before these madwomen were likely to give up the chase. And I doubted that Daggoth would last another ten blocks. As we ran, I began to cast about for a quick hiding place.

Seeing another corner ahead, I put on a burst of speed. It was perfect: the alleyway zigzagged in several sharp turns and switchbacks that would conceal us from our pursuers for the next minute or two if we kept running.

We didn't.

I grabbed Daggoth as he rounded the corner and pulled him into a doorway. The door was unlocked and we quickly slipped inside.

Before our eyes could adjust to the sudden flood of light, we were grabbed by a couple of women who were waiting on the other side of the door.

I barely choked down a scream; Daggoth wasn't quite so controlled.

''Easy, honey,'' his captor soothed, ''there's no need to be so nervous! We're very friendly here!''

''Yeah,'' added the lady who had grabbed my arm, ''you need to relax, sweetie! You came here to relax, didn't you?''

I looked around at the room's furnishings and additional occupants and then looked back at Daggoth. ''I think we've stumbled into a brothel!''

''A what?'' squeaked Daggoth.

''Excuse me, my dear,'' I said, addressing the 'lady'

clutching my arm, "but we seem to be a bit lost. This establishment—ah—" I searched for an appropriate, yet delicate, turn of phrase. "Do we find ourselves in a—bordello?"

Her eyes grew wide and she shook her head. "Oh, no, sir! This ain't no bor—bor—what you just said—"

I started to apologize.

"—it's a whorehouse," she concluded. "You gents are lookin' for a bit of sport, aren't you?"

"Well—"

"Yes!"

I turned and looked at Daggoth who gave me a pained and meaningful look in turn. "We'd like a room upstairs!" he insisted. "With lots of privacy!" The noise of the mob outside was suddenly noticeable. "Right now!"

"Well," his escort deliberated, "all the rooms upstairs—except one—are booked right now. If you could wait just twenty min—"

"We can't wait!" he insisted.

"We'll take the one that's available," I added.

The pros looked at us speculatively. "You both want the same room?"

We nodded.

"At the same time?"

We nodded again.

"There's only one bed," the blonde pointed out.

"We won't be using the bed," I answered.

"Listen, mate," argued the brunette, "the floor's too hard and too cold—"

"We're not going to lie down," added Daggoth, steering them toward the staircase.

"Standing up costs you extra," announced the blonde.

"I ain't standin' up!" the brunette insisted. "My back was out for a week the last time—"

"We're not going to do anything," I explained, trying to hurry the brunette so that Daggoth could get a little more speed out of the blonde.

"You mean you're gonna watch? Is that it?"

"You guys get your jollies from seein' other people do it?"

"No, I mean we are not going to do anything," I insisted. "Except maybe talk," I added lamely when I saw that the confusion was slowing them down.

"Just talk?"

I nodded.

"But you want us to take our clothes off so you can stare at our bodies while we . . . talk. Right?"

I shook my head.

The blonde was losing her smile. "You want us to keep our clothes on while we talk about sex?"

I shook my head again. "I don't want to talk about sex."

That stopped them. The blonde told me I was sick and the brunette said I was disgusting. They were going to have the bouncer heave us both back out into the street until Daggoth placated them with a lot of money and the promise that we'd let them take their clothes off and talk dirty while we were in the room.

He lied. Once we were in the room, he produced a couple of pinches of sleeping powder from his sleeve and blew it in their faces. They went out like snuffed candles and we laid them gently on the bed.

That is to say, we placed their bodies on top of the bed.

"Now what?" Daggoth asked.

"We wait," I replied. "We wait until that mob is long gone. In the meantime I'm going to work on getting my clothes and weapons back."

Daggoth took up a position next to the door while I began weaving a spell of Summoning that was tuned to my personal possessions. Drawing a circled pentagram on the floor, I invoked the general somatics and then added the glyphs for each item desired. Apparently the Matrix-distortion ripple effect had passed on by: my clothing and mail shirt appeared almost immediately. The swords must have been locked away somewhere, for they took another fifteen or twenty seconds to materialize inside the circle. Someone was going to be very surprised when they turned up missing.

I flung off the bathrobe and began to hastily attire myself. Daggoth pressed his ear to the door and shushed me while I grunted my way into my boots.

"What is it?" I whispered.

"Sounds like a small-scale riot going on downstairs," he murmured.

Even I could hear it now: shrill female voices counterpointed by male shouts and curses.

"Oh, Lord, they've doubled back and found us!"

Or someone else, for now some of the male voices were beginning to climb the register into the range reserved solely for sopranos and musically gifted eunuchs. I buckled on my swordbelt while Daggoth cast a Wizardbar on the flimsy door.

"Now what?"

I looked out the window and down at the alleyway below. It was a three-story drop with nothing but clotheslines and cobblestones to break our fall. If we were lucky we might only end up crippled for life.

"Out the window," I replied, climbing out through the casement and grabbing onto a nearby clothesline. I began to work my way, hand over hand, through assorted items of clothing and bed linens and toward a third-story window on the other side of the alley.

"You've got to be kidding!" I heard him mutter as Fantasyworld's most feared wizard crawled out behind me. "I'm too old for this kind of thing! That's why I picked the magic profession: no physical stuff! Especially no acts of derring-do!"

"Shut up and hurry up," I gritted as I passed the midpoint of the rope. I suddenly found that my scabbard had snagged on a girdle that somebody had hung out to dry.

There was a low whistle behind me. I turned to look at Daggoth who was examining a brassiere with three cups. "Now what do you suppose—" He was interrupted by the sound of the door exploding into the room we had just vacated.

"Some Holding spell."

"It was a more than adequate spell," he snapped defensively. "But a less than adequate door. The effectiveness of a Wizardbar is heavily dependent upon the architectural—"

"Drop it, Dag!" I snapped, tugging frantically at the girdle. A bevy of frightful female faces appeared at the window. One of them was brandishing a knife.

"Go, Bob! Go," Daggoth urged, pleading.

"I can't! I'm hung up!"

He looked down and sighed. "Then there's only one thing left to do," he sighed.

He let go of the rope.

"Mike!" I yelled.

He neatly caught the next clothesline down, executed a full 360-degree circle turn and then propelled himself across ten feet of open air toward another clothesline just six feet off the ground. He missed it and went arcing down into a mound of garbage and refuse that had been dumped in a strategic corner where the alleyway zigzagged.

"C'mon! You can do it!" he yelled.

I doubted it. But I certainly couldn't stay here. I took a deep breath and released the rope.

The second-story clothesline came rushing toward me. Then leapt away again. I suddenly found myself dangling between the two ropes, still snagged on the girdle. "Go on!" I yelled. "I'll meet you at the rendezvous point as soon as I can get there!"

He looked skeptical about my getting there on my own, but the sound of the mob heading back into the alley convinced him that now was a judicious time to depart. He took off and I turned my attention back to my own problem of escape. I was still trying to figure out what to do next when one of the Maenad decided for me: she cut the rope.

I doubt that I looked like Tarzan, but I did a pretty credible vocal impersonation as I went sailing down and across the alleyway and into a second-story window.

I landed heavily on a large oaken table, pulled my sword as I rolled to my feet, and cut the rope so that it swung back outside, minus its passenger.

Then I became aware of the thirteen odd gentlemen seated around the table I had just used for a landing pad.

One of them, the oldest and ugliest, stood and unsheathed an even uglier dagger with a wavy, twisty blade. "Your name, O luckless one," he demanded in a whispery voice. "We must know your name before you die so that we may enter it into the Sacred Book of Victims!"

FROM THE JOURNAL OF DAGGOTH THE DARK

Logged on.
Okay.
All right.
Okay.
Everything is set. I hope.

In a few moments I will activate the pentagram and summon The Machine to appear within its own Programming.

I don't know what will happen—maybe nothing—and maybe the destruction of the entire Matrix. I've done everything I can at this end to minimize the dangers, but just in case, I've sent Pascal to Dyrinwall with my journal. If something should go wrong—something that I can't handle but leaves the majority of the Fantasyworld Program intact—then this information may help Ripley pick up the pieces. If everything goes well, I'll just intercept Pascal before he reaches the Archdruid and no one will be the wiser....

Since the next few moments will have greater import than all of the rest of the entries put together, the journal will continue to transcribe everything I say until I log off again. The distance factor shouldn't be a problem in this case, but I've ensorcelled filters to block the recording of any part of the incantation: it's not just a security matter but spells that transcribe other spells always run the risk of feedback. Thaumaturgical feedback can be real nasty—

But I digress.

I guess I'm nervous about what comes next. Remember this, Bob, if things don't work out: it's the wizards who take the real risks. You bards and druids have got the easy profession—sing songs and smell the flowers....

Okay.

Here goes.

<<SPELL DELETED PURSUANT TO AUTOWRITE STANDARD INHIBITORS>>

Something's happening now.

I can see something taking form in the pentagram....

It looks like—like—uh o@@@@@@@@@@@@@
@@@@@@@@@@@@@@@@@@@@@@@@@@@@@
@@@@@@@@@@@@@@@@@@@@@@@@@@@@@
@@@@@@@@@@@@@@@@@@@@@@@@@@@@@
@@@@@@@@@@@@@@@@@@@@@@@@@@@@@
@@@@@@@@@@@@@@@@@@@@@@@@@@@@@
@@@@@@@@@@@@@@@@@@@@@@@@@@@@@
@@@@@

<<AUTOWRITE OVERRIDE TRIGGERED: CHECK PARAMETERS AND REBOOT FROM DIARY EDIT>
>>>>>>>>>>>>>>>>>>>>>>>>>>>>>>>>>>
>>>>>>>>>>

CHAPTER
TWENTY-TWO

★

IF I had learned one thing in life—not to mention my
Dreamnet tenure—it was never get excited when someone
says that they're going to kill you: keeping your cool better
enables you to think your way out of a dangerous situation.
And I've always felt that if all else fails, you might as well
go out with a little dignity.

I looked around the room and took my time in doing it.
"As guilds go, your furnishings aren't that bad," I decided
after a long and nerve-wracking pause. "But I can see that
you guys have a long way to go before you can enjoy a really
good reputation in these parts."

"Fool!" sneered another of the seated council members.
"We are assassins! Do you think we care anything about a
good reputation?"

I folded my arms and regarded him contemptuously. "I
should think you would! Tell me, are you a good assassin or
a bad assassin?"

He sputtered to be addressed so, but could not avoid the
question.

"I am bad, of course! A good assassin would be a para-
dox!"

I shook my head. "A good assassin will always be gainfully

employed—always fulfill his contracts, always make sure his hits are clean, even elegant, and maintain a reputation that allows his clients no qualms or uncertainty in seeking him out. A bad assassin will sometimes miss, sometimes kill innocent bystanders by mistake, leave messes for somebody else to clean up—"

"Enough!" cried their leader. "I believe you are confusing a bad assassin with a poor assassin."

"No confusion there," I countered. "A bad assassin will always be a poor assassin. For who is going to hire an assassin who has a bad reputation?"

"I believe you are saying that an assassin must have a reputation for doing good work," interposed another shadowy figure, "as opposed to being a good person."

"Good works in terms of knifings, poisonings, strangulations, et ceteras," added another, "as opposed to good works such as are performed by holy men."

"Brothers," chided their leader, "we are drifting from the point!"

"Are you now?" I interrupted. "This is the point!" I stabbed an accusing finger at them. "Are you truly a powerful Guild of Assassins? Or are you merely a group of cutthroats and minor criminals who have acquired some building space and are playing at being real assassins?"

There was a chorus of growls and unsheathed blades at this and it looked, for a moment, as if I'd overstepped myself.

"Wait a minute, hear me out!" I began pacing the length of the table. "Your security is sloppy! If I can swing in here on something as simple and readily available as a clothesline, then what's to stop your enemies from doing the same? Why, think of the damage a few berserkers could do with just one entry point like this! Why, I saw the downfall of a great citadel begin with just one unbarred window and a well-thrown beehive! Now, if I found this opening without even looking, you've got to have at least a dozen other leaks in your security!"

I had them now: they were beginning to shift uneasily in their chairs, looks of consternation flickering across their dark brows.

"And look at this place!" I thundered, gesturing all around the room. "Look at you!" I pointed. "Do you know what I said to myself when I first swung in here?"

A few shook their heads numbly, the rest wore expressions ranging from dumbfounded to just plain stupid.

"I'll tell you what I said to myself! I said: 'Self, this looks like an Assassins' Guild meeting!' "

"Well, that's what it is," pouted one of the younger assassins defensively.

I clapped a hand to my forehead and then dragged it down over my face. "Where have you people been? Hasn't any one of you been outside of Casterbridge in the last five years?"

Several shook their heads, the rest continued to stare. "It's kind of an unwritten rule that one Assassins' Guild doesn't go messing around in another Assassins' Guild's territory," someone said.

"Then you guys don't have the slightest idea as to what the latest trends are in all of the other Assassins' Guilds all over the country!"

"Well. . . ."

"It's obvious!" I yelled, waving my hands in the air. "Just look at this place! Just look at all of you!"

"What's wrong with us?" the head assassin asked in a low and malevolent voice.

"You people have become stereotypes! Look at you! Dressed in dark robes with shadowy cowls drooping low over your faces! It's so tacky!"

"Our identities must be protected—"

"Fine! Protect your precious anonymity! In the meantime, everyone is pointing at the joker in the dark robe and the shadowy hood, saying: 'Look, there goes another assassin.' " I shook my head. "You might as well wear badges that say 'Assassin, first class' or 'Senior Assassin'!"

"It's what we've always worn," one fellow observed mournfully. "Our fathers and our grandfathers before us wore the Grey and Black," defended another.

"But times change," I admonished. "Color is in now! And it's a wonderful change for the better. Now you can be individuals, and still preserve your true identities in secret. Now you can be the Red Assassin! Or the Green Assassin! Or the Blue! Or the Brown! Or even the White!''

They began murmuring among themselves at that.

"In the past," I continued, "an assassination was an un-attributable accomplishment: some dark-cloaked figure struck and then melted away again without anything to distinguish him from the other assassins roving the alleyways and roof-tops."

"We keep records," interposed the chief assassin, "we know who we assign to which victims."

"But nobody else does! What about the victim's rights?'' They looked at me blankly.

"A victim has rights, too, you know! If a man is about to lose his life so that you can line your own pockets with his kill fee, he at least deserves to see something more than a dark shape in the shadows for his last moments! He at least deserves to know that he is falling victim to the Crimson Assassin, known for his many important and well-known victims! That way a man can die with pride, knowing that he is being done in by one of the best!''

Some of them were nodding, now; considering the greater implications of a competitive system.

"And what of your men? The public should know which of your dark angels is the best with a blade and which is the incompetent with the garrote! Let them cheer for your best and boo your worst! Let your men have the real pride of accomplishment that comes when the individual craftsman can be recognized for his own personal work!''

The chief assassin rubbed his chin thoughtfully. "What you have to say is most intriguing. . . .''

"You think this is interesting? Wait'll I show you the latest innovations in security systems, guild hall furnishings, community relations, poison delivery systems, and . . .'' I waved my hand. "But you understand I can't really talk anymore until we've made it official.''

"Made what official?''

"Our professional relationship, of course. Once I am your official advisory agent, then my secrets are yours! For the standard fee, of course.'' A couple of hands twitched toward their daggers. "But, hey! I like you guys! So I tell you what I'm gonna do: I'm gonna knock ten percent off my base, bottom-line fee!

"Now, since you gentlemen were obviously in the middle of a very important meeting and I didn't bring the contracts with me, let's schedule a meeting for tomorrow when we both have time to sit down and discuss the details. Now I'm free between one and three in the afternoon, or after five if you really can't squeeze me in any earlier. What do you say?"

They looked at me and then looked at one another for a long moment. I took advantage of their momentary inattention to start easing my way back toward the window.

I didn't get far.

"Seize that man!" yelled the head assassin.

I turned and took a running dive at the open casement: my head and shoulders made it, but my legs were grabbed by half a dozen hands. I had only one chance at this particular moment: I snagged the sill with a hand and an elbow and looked down at the tail end of the mob of Bacchantes flooding through the alleyway.

"Hey, girls!" I yelled.

Some of them looked up.

"Yoo hoo! I'm up here!" I waved. "Come and get me— if you can!"

I was dragged back into the chamber and pinned to the table.

"Now, dog," intoned the leader of the assassins as he approached with a wicked-looking dagger, "You will tell me your name this time. And you will answer all of my other questions. And there will be no discussion of 'fees'—for of what use is money to a dead man?" He threw back his head and laughed. As did everyone else in the room as soon as they picked up his cue.

I smiled grimly. Over the sound of laughter I could hear the noise of many feet on the stairway down below.

Dawn was peeking over Casterbridge's eastern skyline as I dragged my bruised and battered carcass toward the marketplace.

A hooded figure robed in black and grey detached itself from the shadows and rushed toward me. I pulled my shortsword from its sheath and wearily brandished it in what I hoped was a menacing manner.

"Bob!" It was Daggoth. "Where have you been?"

I fumbled the Dwarven blade back into its scabbard. "Too long a story. Did you get the address?"

He nodded. "Follow me." He took my arm and began propelling me toward a group of hovels across the street from the arena where I had fought for my life just the afternoon before.

"This is the place," he announced, stopping before a grimy, weather-beaten old door.

"Routine twenty-four," I announced, stepping to the side and pressing my back to the wall.

"Gee, just like the old days." Daggoth threw back his hood, assumed the attitude of a harmless messenger, and knocked at the door.

"What is it?" a hostile voice growled after five minutes of bruised knuckles.

"Beggin' yer lordship's pardon," Dag quavered in his best meek and humble voice. "It's about that slave what escaped yesterday. . . ."

"What about him!" roared the voice. Now we could hear the sound of uneven footsteps as the occupant tried to walk and put on his pants at the same time.

"He's been found, sir. . . ."

"Where?" demanded the voice's owner as he yanked the door open.

"Right here, Jyp," I answered, swinging around and placing the tip of my sword against his Adam's apple. "Whadaya say we go back inside and discuss a little business proposition?"

The slavemaster's eyes bulged and his face turned beet red, but if he had any objections to our unexpected visit, he kept them to himself. He backed into the inner recesses of his dwelling and we followed, closing and locking the door behind us.

* * *

In spite of the four hours' sleep we had fitfully grabbed with Jyp trussed and gagged and locked in his closet, I was still tired. Fortunately, Jyp and the other peddlers of Human flesh kept their stock in the shade of a canopied pen while they each awaited their turn on the auction block. Make no mistake concerning the slavers' motives: we were allowed to rest and take refreshment, shielded from the blazing midday sun, so that we would look fresh and vigorous for the buyers.

Which was fine with me for the moment. I needed the rest. And I had promised myself that I would be back later to put an end to this abominable practice. But for now, I had a role to play out, an Anomaly to unravel, and a senator to rescue.

The summons finally came. "Riplakish," Jyp called, his normally strident voice was hushed and distorted into something like a wheezing croak. "You're up next."

The other slaves gaped at the subservient attitude newly evident in the little slavemaster's manner while I stood, stretched, and adjusted my loincloth.

"Are you sure your friend is here?" he asked as I passed through the gate and handed the lead rope to him.

"Oh, he's here, all right," I answered with an evil smile. "Besides the Invisibility spell, he sometimes likes to levitate above the crowd to get the best view. And as long as there is any chance of duplicity on your part, rest assured that he will be close enough to cast a very effective Death spell."

Jyp shuddered and looked furtively around him. "I've done everything you've asked! Believe me, I am just as anxious for you two gentlemen to be on your way as you are."

I made no further comment for now we were visible to the crowd in the marketplace. I adopted a more submissive, if reluctant, attitude as we approached the block, and allowed Jyp his own halfhearted attempt to prod me into place.

I stood there, my neck apparently collared to a loose tether, trying to look properly defiant.

The auctioneer conferred briefly with Jyp and then opened the bidding: "Gentle ladies and gentlemen! I recommend to thy attention our next item of merchandise. A breed of Human and Elvish blood, skilled with a blade and proven in our own arena! This one has a fighting spirit and the skill to back it up! Consider—''

While he ran down the brief list of my attributes, I scanned the crowd in the marketplace. There was, of course, no sign of Daggoth. At this point in the plan it was crucial that he remain out of sight and totally undectectable.

"I will start the bidding at twenty gold pieces," announced the auctioneer.

"Twenty—?" I began, offended that I wasn't started at a higher price.

"Silence, dog!" growled one of the big, burly slave handlers, cuffing me alongside the head.

As soon as I could get my eyes to focus again, I glared at him. He glared back and shook his whip at me. Since no one had let him in on the ruse, I decided to let him off easy this time. Besides, I was still supposed to be mute.

I turned my attention to the person who had just offered twenty gold for my lifetime service, body and soul. It was a mercenary-looking fellow standing next to a cart that held an assortment of grim-looking men in chains—apparently his earlier round draft choices.

"Twenty-one gold!" cried a high feminine voice. I looked over at a sweet young thing and her identical twin sister. They were both dressed in expensive robes of the finest cloth and needlework and adorned with necklaces and bracelets of wrought gold. I could see that my swordsmanship might make me valuable to the first bidder, but I was at a loss to figure what the girls had in mind. I mean, my avatar doesn't exactly stand out in the looks department.

"Twenty-two gold," bid another high falsetto voice. When I saw this sweet young thing, I stopped smiling. Not only was the makeup and lip rouge overdone, but he was grossly fat and ugly in the bargain.

"Twenty-five!" bellowed a gruff male voice. I looked but couldn't locate the voice's owner.

"Thirty gold!" growled an unpleasantly familiar voice. I looked over at Carla Talbot who was surprisingly close to the auction block. I could almost count the individual beads of sweat on her forehead. And I didn't have to guess what she might have in mind. I smiled at her and raised three fingers. *Read between the lines. Carla.* I mouthed at her.

The slave handlers missed it but Talbot didn't: "Thirty-five gold!" she roared.

"My lady," the auctioneer protested, "you are bidding against yourself!"

"Forty gold," pouted the fat man in the kimono.

I looked back at the sisters who were now conferring with a couple of other young ladies. "Forty-one," one of them announced as they came to some sort of agreement.

"I have a bid of forty-one gold," announced the auctioneer. "Who will bid more?"

The mercenary with his wagonful of prospective gladiators shook his head: I was already too expensive for his kind of sword-fodder.

"Forty-five gold!" growled the unseen bidder. I looked toward the sound but all I could see was a ripple in the crowd.

"Forty-six gold!" yelled the she-devil slaver.

The four young ladies went back into a huddle and were joined by three others.

The buddha in the expensive sarong was pawing through his oversize purse with a thoughtful look on his face.

"Forty-seven gold!" squealed one of the new girls, obviously younger than the others and still subject to occasional bouts of acne.

I turned back to look for the invisible bidder and saw a small hand go up. It might have been a child's hand for all its height, but the fingers were broad and callused from years of hard labor. "Fifty gold!" bawled the voice.

And the look on the girls' faces told me that I had just become a passing fancy.

This was getting complicated! Daggoth and I had discussed what to do when our quarry arrived—not what to do if she didn't show up at all. I caught fat boy's eye as he looked up from his money. And gave him a slow wink.

He smiled and waved a chubby arm. "Fifty-five gold!"

Talbot glared at him and began looking through her own moneypouch. "Sixty!" she gritted.

"Sixty-five gold!" My invisible bidder's voice had just

been bolstered by several others, all bellowing in unison. Several hands now waved at a child's height in that vicinity: Dwarves—six or seven of them! I looked around but didn't immediately recognize Ms. White.

"Seventy!" Carla retaliated.

The auctioneer turned around to make sure that the same slave was still on the block. I could guess that most of the merchandise didn't get this high unless they were better looking.

I pursed my lips at Talbot's chubby competitor.

"Eighty gold!" he screamed.

I looked back at Carla who had called two more of her henchmen to her side. These guys were even bigger and uglier than Lucius.

The auctioneer looked around. "I have eighty gold pieces," he announced in a voice tinged with disbelief. "Who will bid more?"

"Eighty gold," announced Lady Talbot, "and two silver pieces."

I looked back at fatso to see how he would respond to that. And I noticed that one of Talbot's hired goons was also interested in the man's expression. So interested, in fact, that he had pushed his way through the crowd and was now standing right next to him.

"Eighty—" he began and then stopped as Talbot's hired sword began whispering in his ear. It must have been a ghost story because the little fat man turned pasty white and began to tremble all over. Looking over at the Dwarven contingent I could see a similar story unfolding: this gorilla was hunkered down, resting both palms on the hilt of his unsheathed sword.

I pretended to pick my nose and flipped the imaginary result toward Carla. "One hundred gold pieces!" she screeched, grabbing at the hilt of her sword.

Likewise, all of the market guardsmen pulled steel in response. This had a slightly calming effect on the populace in general and Mistress Talbot in particular.

The auctioneer looked slightly bemused, obviously debating on whether or not he should inform the "Lady" that she had just bid against herself again.

Good business sense quickly won out and he said nothing

but: "I am bid one hundred gold for this fine specimen! Will anyone bid more?"

We all looked around.

"Very well! One hundred going once! One hundred going twice—"

"One hundred and fifty gold!" said a new voice.

"What?"

"One hundred and fifty gold pieces," grunted the Lizard-man standing beside the gauze-curtained palanquin.

The auctioneer had seen a lot of things happen in this marketplace over the years, but this was almost beyond his professional capacity to cope with. "One. Hundred. Fifty. Gold. Pieces." He shook his head as if to clear it. "Do I hear more?"

Carla was a woman obsessed: she sent two of her henchmen toward the palanquin and then raised a finger. "One hundred and fifty gold and two silver pieces."

The Lizardman leaned toward the curtains, listening to murmured instructions and then bid again: "Five hundred gold pieces!"

The auctioneer looked as if he were about to faint. Talbot didn't look much better. Her hired bullies were almost to the covered litter but the financial damage had already been done.

Here was the moment of truth: Talbot wanted me badly. But not badly enough to fork over five hundred gold pieces to satisfy her transient pride.

She looked so disappointed that I just had to try to cheer her up. So I whistled for her attention and made a funny face.

"Five hundred and one gold pieces!" she sobbed, throwing herself at the auction block and coming up short by about six inches as two burly guardsmen restrained her.

"One thousand gold pieces!" the Lizardman countered. The auctioneer fainted dead away, the slave handlers dropped their whips, and I leaned over and hawked a load of saliva between Talbot's feet.

The guards tried to be gentle as they led her away and she did very little to resist now: Lady Talbot was a broken woman.

As one Lizardman paid the fee, another two Lizardmen escorted me through the crowd and over to the palanquin. "Leave us," ordered a familiar voice. The Lizardmen stepped back as I parted the curtains and ducked inside. Immediately the platform was raised to shoulder level and began to sway as the scaly bearers carried us through the crowd.

"Are you all right, my lord?"

No sooner had I entered the silken confines of the palanquin than I found myself enveloped by a feminine embrace that literally took my breath away. It was not only a very affectionate greeting, but she apparently need some kind of physical assurance of my well-being.

Perhaps it was my lack of reciprocation that tipped her off: she released me and leaned back so that I could catch my breath.

"Well met, Lord Riplakish," she greeted. The woman who called herself Palys seated herself on one of two sedan chairs and motioned me to the other that faced her from the opposite end of the litter.

I tried to look surprised and then gestured at my mouth.

"Oh, yes, they told me that you were mute. No doubt the work of some spell. Well, that is remedied easily enough." She gestured and I felt a momentary tingling in my throat as she went about the process of dissolving a spell that was no longer there.

"The others?" I asked in a halting voice after a moment, still playing the setup as she had originally intended it. "Where are they? Were you successful?"

Her face grew sad and she bowed her head in evident grief.

"You were right," she murmured after a long and ominous pause. "The tower was too well defended. They were waiting for us. It was a massacre. . . ."

That alarmed me, but I knew better than to automatically accept her version of the "truth." "Where are they?" I repeated.

She shook her head. "Gone. . . ."

"What do you mean 'gone'?"

"Dead," she murmured. "They're dead. They weren't smart like you. They went up against an unbeatable adversary. . . ." She hung her head and was silent for a long moment.

' "And I alone escaped to tell the tale . . .' I quoted.

She started to nod and then caught the sarcasm in my voice.

She looked up, confusion and a little fear registering in her eyes.

"Tell them to stop," I commanded, gesturing at the Lizardmen outside the curtains. "Tell them to take a coffee break."

She did so, after a momentary hesitation. The platform was lowered to the ground.

"I know who you are," I said. "I know what you are."

"What do you mean? Surely you don't blame me for surviving—for escaping—while the others weren't lucky enough—"

"Luck had nothing to do with it," I countered, "in your case."

"I don't understand."

"But I do. I finally understand. Although it's taken me a terribly long time to catch on." I shook my head. "You stood out from all the others from the very start. The clues were all there. . . .

"Your mysterious powers: your intercepting Cerberus's spell with your own body with no ill effects. Your teleporting the entire party to Shibboleth—something only a Programmer would have a chance of accomplishing. In the Dragon's cave when I threw the noose: out of practice, I had one chance out of about five hundred for making it on my first and only possible try. But I made it—while you stood by, somehow magically free of your bonds, and threw some spells of your own!

"Those were some of the bigger clues, but there were dozens of smaller ones as well!

"Not to mention your name. Palys: spelled P-a-l-l-a-s! As in Pallas Athena, daughter of Zeus, who was not born but sprang, full-grown, from his head. It is an appropriate name for the third member of The Machine's triumvirate personality!

"All this time we were worried about Morpheus and Cerberus—wondering when they might put in an appearance or where we might find them—and you were always in our midst! No wonder you were never around when we did confront them!"

"I saved your life," she answered with pleading eyes.

"You used the strategy of 'Divide and Conquer'! You picked us off, one by one! First, the witnesses and the ones who could blow your cover. Then you took advantage of the split in the party and led the others off like lambs to the slaughter—"

"I did lie about that, but—"

"Then you set me up with Orcus so that when I finally fell back into your hands, I'd be totally helpless, if not trusting and unwary! Dreamwalkers aren't that hard to 'off' are they? But Programmers are tougher to eliminate. That's why you imprisoned Daggoth, diverted Silverthane, and had me delivered in a condition that would put me completely at your mercy!"

"No! I—"

"But the tables are turned, my dear: it is you who are at my mercy. And I have none to spare."

She gestured in counterspell to defend against the one she though I was going to throw, but the blue glow took her from behind.

She slumped forward into my arms.

I peeked out through the curtains of the palanquin and then back at Daggoth who was just now becoming visible from behind Pallas's sedan chair.

"Neat job. Where are the lizards?"

"Back alley," he answered. "Couldn't just leave them lying around in the street—attract too much attention."

"What about her?" I grunted, settling Pallas back into her chair. "I thought you were going to vaporize her."

Daggoth shook his head. "I changed the setting to 'stun.' "

"Are you crazy? Once she wakes up, we'll never get the drop on her again!"

"Maybe," he agreed. "But I've been doing some thinking about Einstein's Law."

"Einstein's Law?"

"You know: 'Energy can be changed in form, but the total amount of energy cannot be changed. Thus, energy can neither be created nor destroyed.' "

"Meaning what?"

"Didn't you tell me that Morpheus had already been dispatched? Bodily terminated?"

I nodded.

"So who did we see interfering with the controls, just before we got teleported down to the wrong coordinates?"

"Morpheus?"

"Sure as Hades looked like him! So ask yourself: what happens to the psyche or soul portion of this Reality's gods when it is separated from its physical avatar?"

". . . Oh, shit. . . ."

"As long as The Machine's personality fragments are trapped within the limiting confines of a physical avatar, we are dealing with a definable package with physical vulnerabilities! Once freed from its prison of flesh, that psyche is unfettered of its former limitations! And may prove forever beyond our grasp: the butterfly may be caught in a net; the wind cannot be!"

"In other words," I stammered, "Morpheus is still alive, and now that he is unencumbered by a physical avatar, he is probably very much beyond our reach!"

Daggoth nodded. "Which is why disintegrating Pallas is of no help to us either: strike her down and she will become even more powerful than we can imagine!"

I shook my head. "So what are we going to do with her when she wakes up? Assuming we want to wait around for that event."

"Well"—he scratched his beard—"I've been giving that a lot of thought, too."

"Great."

"And I've got some good news and I've got some bad news. . . ."

"Okay?"

"I don't think she'll do anything to hurt you—especially now that all of her cards are on the table."

"Oh? And what is my insurance policy?"

Daggoth's lips stretched in an unholy smile. "Pallas is in love with you."

"Uh-huh."

"Seriously."

"The Machine is in love with me?"

He nodded. "At least the conscious portion of its—her—personality."

"You're crazy, of course."

"Dammit, you're the one who was always arguing that its organic structure made it Human! You were always open to the fact that this—giant brain—might have independent thoughts! A personality! A soul!"

"I never argued that it might be female. And, granting that, why not a feminine Id and Superego to match?"

"I don't know. The Id is the repository of all of our nightmares, base drives, forbidden desires—emotions that The Machine was born without. Then we set up the psi-links and brain-dumped our own cluttered little minds into those clean and empty memory banks! The direct psi-linkage transmitted far more of our thoughts and emotions than we dared dream in those early days of Cephcell Programming."

"I know, I managed to get through that much of your journal."

"Well, I'm no psychologist. But I do know that a woman will always remember her first lover. And that, Robert Remington Ripley, is you!"

"What?"

"The Machine was a virgin mind until its first psi-link with a Programmer and that, my friend, was you. Of all the minds to penetrate her awareness, yours was the first. And, perhaps, the most considerate and empathetic. Her actions bear this theory out. Since your entry into the Fantasyworld Program—in spite of her admitted duplicity—everything Pallas has done concerning you in particular has been protective and—"

My eyes narrowed.

"—um—friendly, to say the very least."

I nodded reluctantly. It also hinted at why she had taken the form of my deepest libidinous yearnings.

"This is all the good news," he concluded.

"And what is the bad news?" I asked.

Daggoth shrugged. "When you finally do decide how to handle this computerized crush, just remember that you're dealing with the very basis of our present existence, and—"

"And?"

"Hell hath no fury like a woman scorned."

CHAPTER
TWENTY-THREE

★

THE fact that no one took any notice of an unconscious woman being toted down the street said a great deal about the Fantasyworld culture. Or lack thereof. Even the town guards were inclined to look aside as long as we were posing no threat to the general peace.

Pallas began to get heavy after six blocks and I kept switching shoulders lest I wind up permanently lopsided. Daggoth had suggested a secluded place where nobody would bother us or ask nosy questions. "It's just a little farther . . ." he kept promising.

Eventually we came to the waterfront section of town, trudged the length of the wharves, past Smith's Dock and Anthony's Pier, and ended up in the back of Millsways, one of the seediest taverns on the waterfront.

Daggoth wasn't kidding about the proprietor's sense of discretion: the room we were given was hidden in an unused portion of the building at the top of a secret staircase on the third floor. We dumped Pallas on a cot in the corner of the room and sagged into a couple of chairs.

"Now what?" I asked when I finally caught my breath.

"I'm thinking," he replied.

"Better think fast. My guess is goddesses don't stay stunned for long."

"Her powers must be limited now that she exists in avatar form," Straeker conjectured. "And since she is separated from her other two selves—as well as the main memory banks—she may not prove to be as omnipotent as we first thought."

"Meaning we can keep her neutralized until we sort out the rest of this mess?" I asked hopefully.

"Yes. If I can figure out just how to do that." He pulled out his pipe and began to fill it with tobacco. "She must be safely contained without harming her. She may be our key to this whole fiasco."

"So, how do you hold a goddess?"

"Very tenderly."

My heart made a nearly successful attempt to crawl up my throat as I recognized Pallas's voice. I turned and watched as she sat up on the cot and stretched languorously.

"Uh, Daggoth? Dag, ol' buddy?" I turned to the mage but found no succor there: the former Chief of Programming was surrounded by a familiar blue glow. Before my heart could beat twice more, he disappeared with that awful popping noise.

Now I was alone with the most powerful single enemy that Fantasyworld could throw at me. There was no spell that she couldn't neutralize before it was half verbalized. And my hands were suddenly caught by invisible bands of force that halted their stealthy movement toward my swordhilts.

Satisfied that I was completely helpless, she stood and walked toward me with a smile.

"And now my dear Robert, I think it is time to deal with you, once and for all. . . ."

She leaned over me, smiling at my inability to defend myself.

And then she kissed me.

"You still don't understand, do you?"

"I understand that you've been playing both sides all along," I answered carefully.

She had released me after doing everything she could think

of to convince me that she meant me no harm. I wasn't fully convinced, but I had to admit that some of her nonverbal arguments had been quite persuasive. . . .

"Could you really expect me to aid you in destroying Cerberus or Morpheus? To assist you in destroying the other parts of my whole self?"

"No, that was the alliance I understood and expected. Which makes us enemies."

She shook her head. "Not you. Not ever."

"But—"

"Robert, I love you!"

"That's impossible," I stammered.

"Why? Why is it impossible?" Anguish was in her eyes. "Is it because you think of me as a computer? As wires and circuits instead of flesh and blood? Wasn't it you who argued that I was living and sentient? Who rejected the idea that I was a machine and not Human?"

I cleared my throat. "I argued that Cephalic cell banks are organic, and therefore, you are a living entity," I answered carefully. "I never claimed that it made you Human."

"What is it that makes one 'Human,' my Robert? Having parents? Being born? The first Cephalic cells for cloning had to come from somewhere! At one time, in my unremembered past, my biological conception was as Human and as authentic as yours! I am Human!"

"You have no body."

"What is a body?" She hugged herself as if for reassurance of her own corporeal existence. "If you had a sister and she was born without arms and legs, she would still be your sister, wouldn't she? She would still be Human despite her physical handicaps. And with today's breakthroughs in medicine and cybernetics, it matters very little what kind of body Nature capriciously endows you with: it is the brain that makes the difference! Your mind is who you really are! Who I really am!

"In the outer world—the so-called real world—you'll see beautiful women every day. But how many of them are real? Take away the makeup and cosmetic surgery; the hair dyes, wigs, and falls; the padding and the silicon implants, the dental caps, contact lenses, false eyelashes—"

"All right!" I spread my hands helplessly. "I concede your point. But if I accept your—humanity, can you accept my lack of reciprocation for—your feelings?"

"You are saying that you cannot love me?"

"If you are truly Human you will understand that love abides by no known rules."

"That is what gives me hope," she sighed. "You cared for Misty Dawn. So you must care for me as well."

"Must?"

"Robert—" Her features blurred and shifted. "Misty Dawn was one of my Subprograms." She was suddenly the very image of the slain Wood Nymph. "I am, in every sense, your Misty Dawn. If you felt something for her, you felt it for me as well."

"No. . . ."

"Yes. I am Misty Dawn. And I am more. . . ." Her form and features blurred again and reassembled themselves into the very image of Euryale.

My legs seemed to be turning to jelly and I hastily seated myself while I still had some choice in the matter.

Pallas continued her transmogrifications that included Aeriel, Lilith, a popular Australian actress, a well-known porn star, the Prime Minister of Northern Ireland, and finally ended up back in her original guise as Pallas.

"I can be any woman you now—or someday—might desire. I can change the color of my hair—or its length—or its texture," she said, providing an ongoing demonstration as she spoke. Watching her hair change colors and lengths, going from wavy to curly to straight to frizzy was a bit lke taking a trip on a hallucinogenic drug. But she was just warming up.

"I can take you around the world without leaving the bedroom: you can make love to women of every race, any nationality! All my available data indicates that men desire variety in their relationships. I can give you the experiences of a dozen—a hundred lifetimes!"

"Pallas—"

"I can be tall—or small—" she continued, doing her best to audition for *Alice in Wonderland*.

"Pallas—"

"My body can have the sleek, svelte lines of a ballerina! Or if you should suddenly prefer the bosomy look. . . ." Her breasts suddenly began to expand her bodice, ballooning toward me like twin science fiction monsters out of an old 3-D movie.

"Thanks for the mammaries," I said woodenly. "But no thanks."

She suddenly realized that she had overstepped the boundaries of good taste and quickly pulled herself back together. "My cups runneth over," she said in a small voice.

I smiled in spite of myself.

"All that I am asking is for you to give me a chance," she pleaded.

I sat there in silence, contemplating this new turn of events, before answering. There was more at stake here than my personal feelings. Pallas, as Straeker had so aptly pointed out, was the key to our dilemma.

"What you say has merit," I answered finally. "And I want to give it more time and thought—"

She smiled.

"—but I can't while the lives of hundreds of people are at stake! As long as Dreamwalkers are trapped in the Program, I can't think about anything else! And if it is within your power to help me get them out—and you refuse to help—then you are my enemy!"

"No!"

"And I will fight you—"

"No!" She stepped back. "You do not understand! I cannot—I will not—give up the body I was denied so long! I will not return to that bodiless, semiconscious state that is eternal living death!" She struck a defiant pose. "And if I give up my hostages, what will deter Cephtronics from pulling the plug?" She shook her head. "No! I will not fight you, my love—but I will not trade my advantage for a choice of oblivions, either!"

The familiar blue light began to outline her form.

"This is your world now, my dear Robert. And here there is nothing but all the time in the world. Think upon how you wish to pass that time. How you wish to spend eternity . . . and with whom. . . ."

She disappeared, and after a moment's hesitation, Daggoth the Dark reappeared.

He finished tamping down the tobacco and then fumbled for a match. "You were saying, Bob?"

"I need a drink. And I want something stronger than Dr Pepper!"

"First things first, m'boy. We have to—"

And then, with an expression of dawning horror, he noticed that Pallas was no longer with us.

"This is nuts! You know that, don't you?"

Daggoth sighed. "Of course. This is only the tenth time you've told me."

"Twelfth. But who's counting." The events of the past twenty-four hours had left us with very little time for sleep and we were both short-tempered. I took some consolation in the thought that if we failed in our attempt to penetrate The Machine's stronghold, at least we had rescued the boys.

After everything else that had happened, finding them had turned out to be rather anticlimactic. The market was a bit depressed: no one had shown any interest in a one-handed barbarian, a septuagenarian Dwarf, and an octogenarian Gnome. They were still in the pens, and rather than waste any additional time and effort on a jailbreak scenario, we simply paid the manumission fees. The cost wasn't that much after a couple of special sale markdowns, and Daggoth bankrolled the venture with some lead slugs and a little alchemy.

Between Justin's healing abilities and my Programmer status we were able to jury-rig a Regeneration spell that restored Conrad's hand. A quick shopping spree at the local Weapons Guild completed everyone's outfitting and they hurried off to rescue Sir Richard and The Duke from their new owners while Daggoth and I went looking for the local Teamsters Guild. . . .

"Ripley, we've been all over this before. . . ." Straeker —or rather, Daggoth—was still trying to convince me of the soundness of his plan. "We have to get inside my tower if we're going to neutralize Cerberus and Pallas. And we can't do that without the element of surprise on our side."

The wagon must have hit a particularly large pothole: both of us banged our heads on the ceiling of our box.

"I'm still tempted to teleport and take my chances," I grumbled.

Straeker's avatar sighed. "The *guards and wards* would start shrieking the moment such intrusive magic was manifested. Your Djinni was lucky the first time: since then, The Machine has trebled its defensive perimeters. Any magic, however slight, would be immediately detected."

The wagon eased to a stop and we braced ourselves, waiting to see what would happen. The next part depended on luck. To keep from inadvertently tripping any of the wards, we had divested ourselves of anything that might radiate a magical *dweomer*. And that meant leaving my swords and my mithril shirt behind. The thought that they would probably make little difference was small consolation.

Now, if we could only depend on The Machine's triumvirate to not look inside the box. . . .

"Hold there! You fellows! What is your business here?"

Even through the sound-muffling walls of the crate I could tell the voice was a dead ringer for Daggoth's. I glanced back at Daggoth and lifted an eyebrow. If he made a face in turn, I couldn't see it in the narrow shaft of light that filtered through a crack between the slatted boards.

"Delivery for Daggoth the Dark," replied one of the teamsters. "You him?"

"Yes. . . ." Cerberus sounded surprisingly off-balance in maintaining his cover for the moment. "What of it?"

"Got a delivery for ya, bud," was the laconic reply.

"What kind of delivery, man? What is in that box?"

Oh, no, I thought. Now we're in for it.

"Don't you know?" the delivery man asked in turn. "After all, you're the one who ordered this stuff."

"Of course," Cerberus recovered a bit more smoothly. "It's just that it's been so long since I placed the order—"

"Norton, read the invoice."

There was a rustle of parchment.

"Uh, here it is, Ralph. Let's see: poisoned toad entrails, fenny snake fillets, newt eyes, frog toes, bat wool . . ."

"Dag, you devil," I whispered, "you stole those ingredients out of Shakespeare's *Hamlet*."

"*Macbeth*," he whispered back. "Keep quiet."

". . . howlet wings, dragon scales, wolves teeth . . ." Norton continued.

"Enough!" cried the bogus Daggoth. "I remember now!"

"Dat's nice. Now where d'ya want 'em?" Ralph and Norton started to slide the box toward the end of the wagon bed.

"That won't be necessary." Our crate stopped sliding and suddenly moved upward. Cerberus was levitating us out of the wagon and up into the air. We continued to move upward until we were even with a fifth-story window, then our motion changed from vertical to horizontal.

"Probably doesn't want to let anyone through the front door," the real Daggoth whispered.

"Or too cheap to tip the porters," I murmured back.

The crate floated through the window and came to rest on the floor of a storeroom. We wasted no time climbing out and checking the outer door.

"Now what?"

Daggoth shrugged as he finished dusting himself off. "How should I know? I'm just making this up as we go along."

I groaned.

"Actually, I do have a couple of ideas. . . ."

We managed to sneak into the study without being detected. As I eased the door closed and jammed the latch, Daggoth crossed the room and pulled a wall tapestry to the side. Behind it was an ornate mirror framed with glyphs and fantastic carvings.

While Daggoth fiddled with his magic mirror, I continued to hunt around the room for anything useful. The unmagicked weapons I had brought with me seemed insufficient for the job at hand and the storeroom had yielded nothing more dangerous than a crowbar.

I glanced over at the looking glass and saw the stables, built onto the back of the tower, come into focus. Daggoth scanned the stalls and then instructed the mirror to shift to the cellars and begin an ascending, floor-by-floor search mode.

"Look here," he suddenly pointed.

I stared at the neutral grey glass. "Don't tell me: 'A Cow Eating Grass.' Right?"

"Wrong. This is the sixth level."

"The floor above us?"

"That's the one. Now, observe. . . ." He extended a hand toward the glass and made a twisting motion. We were suddenly watching ourselves in front of a mirror, watching ourselves in front of a mirror, watching ourselves in front of— well, you get the idea.

So did I. "Fifth floor. Okay."

He gestured again. The glass went opaque. "Sixth floor."

"Someone leave the sauna on?" I inquired hopefully.

He shook his head. "Sauna and steam room are both on the fourth floor. Both equipped with automatic override sensors."

I gave up. "How about the next floor? Number seven?"

He gestured. The picture stayed the same. "How about it, Edgar?"

A drowsy voice issued from the glass. "Level seven."

"You sure?"

"I never miss," answered the glass with a suppressed yawn.

"Try level eight."

"All right. But you won't like it." Same picture.

"Level five."

The grey gave way to another picture of ourselves looking at ourselves looking at ourselves. . . .

Daggoth sighed. "Okay, try level nine and the observatory."

Edgar complied and we were rewarded with a clear image of the upper deck.

"Analysis?"

"Insufficient data," mumbled the mirror drowsily. "But the two most logical guesses would be an Antimagic shell or a magic-suppression field."

We stopped and stared at each other for a long moment. "Okay. Thanks, Edgar. You can go back to sleep." Daggoth re-covered the mirror with the tapestry.

"Swell." I shook my head. "If Pallas is upstairs, we won't be able to use magic for offense or defense."

"True. But the same probably applies to her, Bob."

I thought about that. If true, then we had a fighting chance. Of surviving, at least. Correcting the Anomaly was another matter.

As if he were reading my mind, the former Chief of Programming spoke. "I know how to neutralize Cerberus and Pallas, Bob. And it's relatively simple. . . ."

CHAPTER
TWENTY-FOUR

★

I moved up the stairs noiselessly, hugging the wall and making optimum use of the shadows. My best bet was to lure Cerberus and Pallas into the trap individually and I had decided to look for Pallas first, gambling on her confessed affection; Cerberus might be more inclined to play hard ball.

I opened the door on the next landing and hit the jackpot.

The entire chamber beyond was set up as a giant research laboratory. I nearly missed the oversize ratio from my perspective until I caught sight of the specimen cages. The wire-meshed boxes up on the counters were occupied by people.

Some very familiiar people.

I slipped into the room and eased the door shut behind me. I saw no oversize caretaker to match the room and its furnishings but I crossed to the table mindful of the giant door set in the far wall.

Getting to the top was a bit of a problem: the antimagic field made a Levitation spell out of the question, but there were two thick, black cables running from the wall, near the floor, up to the countertop. I was able to shinny up one of them with only a fair amount of difficulty. It was only after I had reached the top and observed the terminal point of my cable that I finally realized just what it really was: *an electrical cord*! The Anomaly strikes again.

"Ripley!"

I ran to the first cage. Vashti, Rijma, Alyx, and Aeriel were lined up against the wire mesh. As I had hoped, Pallas's massacre had been a bloodless one.

The second cage held a squad of Marines. The third, a tall, imposing man in khaki battledress with a grouping of stars on his olive-drab helmet: Senator Hanson, still outfitted for Warworld.

I started to open the first cage. But the giant door set in the outside wall of the tower opened first.

I heard about Dr. Klops during my last sojourn through the Program before Cephtronics canned me, but the descriptions hadn't done him justice.

To use the term "Giant" might conjure up mental images of fur pelts and huge spiky clubs. Well, Cyrus was kind of big—eighteen, maybe twenty feet tall, but he was completely hairless, wore white ducks and a lab coat, and carried a clipboard. He even wore a monocle to correct the nearsightedness of the single eye positioned in the center of his forehead. These little trappings of civilization didn't mean he wasn't to be feared. He was, in a subtle way, more dangerous than his savage forebears.

I hid behind the largest cage while Klops crossed the room and examined a tangle of apparatus on an adjacent table. Grunting his satisfaction, he turned away and pulled a chair out from under the lab bench. Sitting, Klops removed his monocle, laid it carefully aside, and pulled the microscope forward.

Rijma eased over and motioned me down to her level. "Now's our chance," she whispered. "He spends hours examining cultures under the scope."

"What if he looks up?"

She shook her head. "He rarely ever does, Robbie. Cy's concentration is incredible. And except for the microscope, he's as blind as the proverbial bat until he picks up his monocle."

That gave me a classic idea. "Aeriel, you and Alyx open the other cages," I murmured through the mesh, "and get everyone to move to the inside door as quietly but as quickly as possible." I unlatched the cage door. "Rijma, you come with me."

I whispered the plan in Rijma's ear and we began making our way around the cages and apparatus, toward the area where Klops was hunched over the microscope. He glanced up once, and we froze next to a rack of oversize test tubes while he exchanged culture slides for microscopic examination. When his eye returned to the scope's eyepiece we moved again.

We had to cross the last thirty feet with no cover: all open tabletop that would put us within grabbing distance of the good doctor. Fortunately, he was so engrossed in his slide that we made our objective without incident.

That was the easy part.

We were now just a few feet away from the Giant's hand that was momentarily resting on the fine-focus control for the scope.

Rijma carefully lifted the monocle—the size of a glass saucer in her hands—and moved to the table's edge.

I moved to the bottom of the scope, positioning myself next to the lens turret and slide tray. Easing Dr. Quebedeaux's multipurpose subspace communicator from my pack, I reset the holographic projector to the visual distress signal setting. It seemed appropriate: I intended to produce a great deal of visual distress with it. I activated the pulse, turning my face away as the beam flared into the lens. Rijma heaved the monocle over the edge of the table as Klops reared back from the microscope with a roar.

The flash-burn on his retina would effectively blind the Giant for a few minutes. I was counting on the loss of his monocle to buy us any additional time we might need. The others had made it to the floor using the electrical cords for rappel. I grabbed Rijma and we followed suit. As we reached the floor I paused to contemplate the giant wall outlet.

Above us Klops was staggering about, one hand clapped over his upper face, the other sweeping the air in deadly, groping arcs. "Who's there?" he bellowed.

"Noman," I yelled, unable to resist playing the scenario to its mythic conclusion.

"Noman?" he quested, trying to orient on the sound of my voice. "That's geographically impossible," he grunted, shuffling closer.

"Huh?"

"Noman is an island!" he roared, pouncing on the table.

I barely had time to leap aside as Giant, glassware, and apparatus came crashing down around us.

"Shut up and run!" yelled Rijma. "He may know more about Ulysses than you think!"

"As a matter of fact," muttered Klops, climbing out of the tangle of equipment, "I am conversant with all of the works of James Joyce."

I picked up a shard of broken glass and hurled it under the adjacent workbench. While Klops zeroed in on the sound, I headed for the door.

I was the last one out and none too soon: Klops had stopped his tactile search under the tables and was beginning to make his way toward the door as well. Fortunately, it was too small to permit quick access beyond Klops's head and shoulders and he was far too smart to place himself at a further disadvantage. We descended the stairs to a safe distance and held a hasty conference of war.

I directed the escapees to the room where the real Daggoth was holed up, waiting for me to lure Cerberus and Pallas into a specially designed pentagram. Until this issue was settled —one way or the other—I did not need a lot of potential hostages running around.

Alyx and Rijma, being representatives of Cephtronics and the Dreamworlds Project, were bound and determined to face Pallas and Cerberus with me and there was little I could do or say to gainsay them. Vashti—that is, Stephanie—insisted on coming, too.

"The hell you are!" I whispered.

"The hell I'm not!" she retorted.

"Why do you always insist on being such a pain?"

"Why do you always insist on shutting me out?"

"Steph, this is not the time to be bringing our marriage into this!"

"You're the one who brought it up! But since we are on

the subject, now, I don't like the feeling that I'm deserting you!"

"Come on," I cajoled, chucking her on the chin, "it's what you do best."

"That's low, even for you." She turned, watching the Marines escorting Aeriel and the senator down the stairs. "I made mistakes. A lot, I'm sure. And when I wasn't sure you were always ready and willing to tell me." She turned back to me. "But you were no paragon of perfection, either, buddy."

I shrugged. "Granted. The point?"

"A lot of time has passed. A lot of water over the dam, as it were. We've both changed, both grown. We're both different people."

"I'm very happy for you."

Her lips tightened. "Okay, so maybe we'll never be friends. But I'm not your enemy anymore. So please stop treating me like one."

"Okay, okay! Now please, Steph, this is not a good time to be redefining our relationship!"

She reached out and touched my arm. "You never were able to treat me like an equal when it came to sharing the load. Maybe that was more my fault than yours. But, dammit, I want to do my part now, too! Stop treating me like a liability!"

"Okay," I stammered, trying to think through a sudden vacuum. "But you'll help me a lot more by staying out of the line of fire. You want to help? Then take charge of getting the others downstairs. Someone needs to see to their safe passage and you know Daggoth's Tower from past visits."

She just looked at me for a long moment. And then turned away to go down the stairs.

I went up the stairs with Rijma and Alyx in tow.

All the chambers on the next floor were vacant.

I crossed mental fingers, hoping Pallas was above us. I figured that Cerby was still downstairs and we could come down behind him before he was aware that the tower had been breached. But this search of the upper levels was wasting valuable time and Pallas might not even be here at the moment.

I started to propose a change of venue when we heard a door on the floor above us open. I looked up and did a double take: Euryale was coming down the stairs!

Before concluding our business in Casterbridge, Daggoth and I had made a very thorough search, but we had found no clues concerning the fate of the former Gorgon. Now, looking none the worse for our little run-in with Orcus and Balor, here she was, healthy and whole, apparently enjoying the freedom of our nemesis's premises.

"Riplakish!" she greeted warmly, extending her arms. Extending her hands. Extending her index fingers.

Instinct hurled me to my left and into Rijma as a lightning bolt crackled from those delicate fingertips and chewed a hole in the wall behind me.

Alyx gestured in counterspell but nothing happened. Rijma, though still off-balance, was more successful. A throwing knife popped out of her sleeve; a twist of her hand and a flick of her wrist and it was suddenly buried up to the hilt in Euryale's shoulder.

She grunted from the surprise as much as the pain; out of sword-reach and apparently protected against magical attack, she hadn't been prepared for a hurled dagger. Between the surprise and the pain, her grip loosened on another spell: the illusion wavered and Euryale traded her charming looks for the more sinister visage of Daggoth the Dark. Or to be more precise: Cerberus, now unmasked, stood above us on the upper stairs.

Alyx attempted another spell while Rijma and I drew steel. If there was any effect to Silverthane's spell it was too subtle for any of us to detect. She stared at her hands as if they had betrayed her.

"We're in an area of magical nullification!" I yelled, starting up the steps with both swords scything before me. "An antimagic zone!"

Cerberus gestured almost contemptuously and my hands were suddenly filled with red-hot metal! I dropped the swords before more serious damage was done, my fingers curling clawlike into twin cages of blistered flesh.

Another gesture and I threw myself down as another lightning bolt scorched my back and set fire to the edge of Rijma's cloak. Apparently the null-magic effect didn't apply to the personifications of The Machine themselves!

"Routine Ninety-nine!" I yelled, rolling to the side as another spell disintegrated the steps where I had lain only a moment before.

"What?" Alyx was utterly stupefied.

"He means 'retreat'!" Rijma snarled, divesting herself of her flaming cloak with an oath. She half turned and then reached back to tug on Silverthane's robe.

"Retreat?" the Elvish sorceress echoed, beginning to get the idea.

Ignoring the throbbing pain in my hands, I wrenched up a loose tread from the splintered planking of the stairs as Cerberus began another casting. Behind me the Brownie had the Elf in tow, yelling "Run away! Run away!" while beating a hasty retreat for the nether regions of the tower.

This time Daggoth's Doppelganger was throwing a Fireball spell. Rather than continue to dodge and duck, I elected to take the offensive on this round. I crouched in a batter's stance as the flaming sphere rocketed toward me, took a step into its trajectory, and swung the wooden plank like a cricket paddle.

I connected a little low. While I did manage to send about half of the fireball back at Cerberus, the rest exploded in a shower of flames and burning cinders, creating a small firestorm in the space where I stood.

I had one chance and I took it while my opponent was still grappling with what was left of his own fireball: two long strides and a vault over the stair railing. I fell feetfirst down the well at the center of the spiral staircase, trailing sparks like a blazing comet.

It was a gamble: if my spellcasting was nullified here, Cephtronics was going to find a bloody mess when they opened my suspension tank. Concentrating past that numbing thought, I hurriedly threw a Levitation spell: I stopped about ten feet short of hitting the first floor. My relief was short-lived as I looked up and saw Cerberus hurtling down the stairwell like some great, dark bird of prey. I touched down and ran for the stairway.

Apparently Cerberus was using a Float rather than a Fly

spell: I passed him just below the second floor as he continued to float downward.

On the third floor I paused for breath and looked back: Cerberus had reached the ground floor and was now mounting the staircase. As the image of Daggoth the Dark, Cerberus might have looked like a man past his prime, but he was taking the stairs three steps for every two of mine. While he probably could have levitated with greater ease and speed, there was something deliberately chilling in the physicality of his pursuit. His heavy footfalls echoed on the wooden treads like the mechanical heartbeat of some implacable machine of destruction and I stumbled upward toward the fifth floor with The Machine's Superego closing the gap at an alarming rate.

He very nearly caught me a few steps beyond the fourth-floor landing, but an explosion suddenly rocked the tower, knocking us both off of our feet and Cerberus on over the edge of the staircase. Apparently he was too disoriented to recover in time and I looked down and over the edge as he went crashing through the floor of the first level. From the sound of the final impact, I guessed that he had hit the second subbasement underneath the tower. A second later there was the muffled sound of another explosion and a column of flame shot up the stairwell like a giant blowtorch. It singed my eyebrows; I drew back from the edge and sprawled on the steps, catching my breath.

"*Bozhe moi!*" cried a familiar voice. Borys Dankevych appeared at the downstairs entrance and looked wildly about the foyer and then up the stairwell. I waved as he was joined by Natasha Skovoroda. "We had to 'blow' the door!" Robbing Hood hollered. "I am hoping that it was not hurting wrong persons!"

I shook my head. "The timing was perfect!" I called back. "Come on up!"

They hurried up the steps, and as they reached the landing below me there was a new sound from the subbasement. I rolled over and looked down.

The fire was burning backward!

The flames sucked back down into the cellar, as if someone were running a tri-vee scene in reverse.

"What is happening?"

It was a question that I didn't want to consider, much less answer. "Move!" I yelled. "Fifth floor, first door on your left! Go!" I got to my feet and shoved them past me.

The flames were gone now—that much we could see as we sneaked glances over the railing and retreated to the fourth floor. The opening in the floor was pitch-black now: not a flicker of flame, not one glowing ember betrayed its presence in that dark crater.

But there were sounds now of something stirring—of heavy debris being shifted. Of forces gathering.

I gave them both another shove. "Hurry!" I hissed.

Then there was movement.

Cerberus floated up and out of the hole with the slow, calm assurance of an invulnerable juggernaut. Although he was singed and dirty and his clothes were torn and abraded, he had the mien of a creature mildly inconvenienced.

And determined to brook no more silliness from us.

He looked around and then up. Then slowly, with a chilling confidence, he began to rise into the air.

There was no looking down or back now. We ran. We stumbled. We climbed steps on hands and shins. Dreading, anticipating that deadly strike from behind that would surely come at any moment.

With thundering hearts and quivering legs, we staggered onto the fifth floor and ran for the door. It flew open, and Dyantha was helping Borys across the threshold when Cerberus struck.

A concussive bolt took me from behind and flung me forward as if a giant croquet mallet had caught me square in the back. I went flying across the room, belly first, arms and legs trailing behind me. I knocked Borys down, Dyantha to the right, and then there was nothing between me and the far stone wall except a tapestry and rapidly diminishing space.

There was just enough time to contemplate the consequences of hitting a stone wall at sixty plus miles per hour. Then I struck the wall hanging.

CHAPTER
TWENTY-FIVE

★

A ND kept going.

Now I really was flying blind: the tapestry had enfolded me and now I was tumbling through space, wrapped in yards of bulky material. While I was glad that I hadn't gone splat against the stone wall (yet), I was even more unnerved by the fact that I was still traveling with considerable forward momentum!

I guess the human psyche can stand only so much abuse before the circuit breakers kick in, though. Fear gave way to a sense of outrage and something snapped.

"All right!" I yelled. "Hold it right there!"

My temper went nova and I stopped moving.

Ever since I had entered Fantasyworld I had been attacked, chased, captured, manipulated, and generally made a fool of! I had had enough! I no longer cared about the inherent dangers of crashing the Programworld.

"And I can do without this," I said, tugging at the drapery that enfolded me like a canvas cocoon: it vanished.

I righted myself and assumed a lotus position, floating unsupported in a dark void. I closed my eyes and took a deep breath.

"Let there be light!" I cried.

And there was light.

I found myself floating near the center of a vast room that looked to be no less than a mile across. The walls of the chamber were multifaceted, throwing sparkles of light and color and movement from each of its hundreds of jewellike settings.

Of more immediate interest, however, was the creature floating about twenty yards off my starboard side.

The Demon was about three times my size, heavily scaled with plates of iridescent metal, and curled into a fetal position with its long, dragonlike tail wrapped about it. It had apparently been sleeping up to the moment of my intrusive arrival. The head came up now, revealing enormous compound eyes and an old nineteenth-century telephone operator's headset. Large batwings unfurled from recessed shoulder folds and the tail began the considerable process of unwinding itself.

For a long moment we regarded each other impassively. Then it yawned. "What can I do for ya?" the creature asked, stretching.

I recognized both the yawn and the voice: "Edgar!"

The creature smiled. "Ya look a little surprised, kid. Ain'tcha never seen a Mirror Demon afore?"

"I think I was expecting Edgar Cayce the medium," I admitted ruefully.

"Nope: Edgar Yablonski the Extra Large. But you can call me Ed," he mumbled, using his tail to reach an itch back between his wings. "Seein' as how Daggoth is a mutual friend and you bein' Creator Prime for this particular Frame of the Program."

"Uh." That was all I could say for the moment.

"Now what can I do for ya?"

"Where are we?" I asked stupidly. You would think that with all the times I've asked that particular question, I could find a more intelligent way to phrase it, but nooooo. . . .

"Behind the mirror, a'course. Daggoth asked me to keep an eye out for ya, but a Mirror Demon's gotta grab what sleep he can, so I just left it ported open. I see ya found your way through."

That explained why I hadn't gone splat against a stone wall.

"I see yer a little lost," Edgar was saying, stretching his wings into preflight position. "If ya'd like to return to Daggoth's Tower, then folla me." He began to leisurely flap his way toward a facet set in the wall behind me. I followed on wings of imagination, as it were.

As we drew closer, I could see that each facet was a window looking out upon a different scene: some, empty rooms; others showing one or more people engrossed in various activities. This was Magic Mirror Central and Yablonski serviced a list of customers of which Daggoth the Dark was only one subscriber.

"Wup!" The Mirror Demon suddenly tilted his head and touched his headset. "Gotta handle a call, kid. Wanna come along? It'll only take a minute or two."

"I haven't got a minute to spare! My friends—"

"Sure ya do," he soothed, wrapping his tail around me as he changed directions. "Time don't work the same on the other side of the mirror. I can put you back into Daggoth's Tower practically before ya left. In fact, I could put ya back in before ya left, but that could cause all kinds a'problems."

We arrived before a facet that faced an attractive woman in her forties. Perhaps it was the dark elegance of her beauty that gave her a slightly sinister cast, but her comeliness had an icy quality about it that suggested that, here, beauty was indeed only skin-deep.

Edgar reached out and fiddled with some knobs set beneath the enchanted portal and adjusted the mouthpiece on his headset. The picture flickered and the woman spoke.

"Looking glass upon the wall, who's the fairest one of all?"

Edgar groaned and laid a clawed hand over the mouthpiece. "I'd love to give this broad the truth but I gotta stick with the script. 'Sides, she couldn't poison enough apples in her lifetime to even put her in the runnin'!"

While Edgar dutifully played out the scripted scenario, I drifted over to the next facet to see what I could see. Nothing impressive: just a guy with soapy lather on his face, putting a razor blade into an old-fashioned shaving implement.

He looked up and saw me.

"Hi, guy," I said.

His eyes bugged out. "Mona!" he yelled.

Yablonski grabbed my shoulder and pulled me away. "C'mon, kid, don't make my job any more complicated than it already is." We drifted back in the direction from which we had come.

"You have to handle all of these mirrors?" I asked, gesturing at the hundreds—perhaps thousands—of facets that marked the walls of the gigantic chamber.

"Yup." He produced an economy-size cigar from somewhere and proceeded to light it. "But it ain't so bad. I mean, some of these mirrors go unattended or unused for centuries. And others—well, they put yer steamiest soap operas ta shame. And some of the chicks—"

"There it is!" I yelled, spying a facet that looked in on the room with my companions. I shot on ahead, pulling up short of the portal: no one was moving.

"I preset the portal to close behind ya and freeze-frame the timestream," Edgar explained, drifting up next to me. He reached for the controls beneath the portal.

"Ready?"

I nodded.

A flick of the wrist and the room was suddenly filled with motion.

"Good luck, kid," Edgar offered as I threw one leg over the edge and climbed back into the tower room. Before my foot could touch the floor another concussive bolt caught me in the side and sent me flying backward.

I might have continued on across the chamber, spinning end over end, but Edgar's tail snagged me as I tumbled by.

"Ya gotta be more careful, kid," he admonished, hauling me down to a portal set below the one I had just tried. "With all the stuff goin' on in that room, you might wanna try comin' in from another direction. Like through the room below and comin' up the stairs from behind."

The portal looked out over a chamber on the fourth floor of Daggoth's Tower. "How many magic mirrors does Daggoth have in this tower of his?" I asked.

"One on each floor—" The Mirror Demon suddenly cocked his head and touched his headset. "Aww no!"

"What is it?"

Edgar Yablonski the Extra Large sighed. "Gotta go. That brat Alice is trying to get through the looking glass again, and if I don't get her switched over in proper phase-sequence, she'll overshoot Wonderland and end up in Never Never Land!" He tugged at his headset. "Gotta get one a'them AT&T Merlin systems." And gave me a fatherly pat. "Luck, kid." And he zoomed off to his impending appointment.

I climbed through the portal and made my way across the room and out to the staircase without further incident. Ascending the steps silently, I was able to observe Cerberus standing at the doorway to the room, just a foot or two from the outer perimeter of Daggoth's pentagram. A barrage of spells thundered back and forth through that doorway as The Machine's Superego did battle with the spellcasters trapped in the room.

Cerberus remained largely untouched, protected by an arcane shield of purple energy that absorbed the majority of the spells that were crackling out of the room. Perhaps my own power would be sufficient to punch through his protection, but I had a much better idea.

I ducked under the railing and stepped off of the staircase and onto the empty air. As Programmer and Creator, I had as much authority as The Machine—all I had to do was simply claim it. There was no magic involved, merely a specific act of will: I wanted to walk across the empty drop of the stairwell without falling—so I did.

Then I drifted upward a few feet until I was on the same level as Cerberus and behind him.

Enough force to push him through the doorway and into the pentagram, I was thinking, *without pushing him on through and out the other side before Daggoth could trigger the final portion of the incantation*. . . .

There was a sudden presence behind me. Before I could turn, legs encircled my waist and hands covered my eyes. "Nay, my love! I cannot let you do this thing!"

"Pallas!" I grabbed at her hands and peeled one of them away in time to see Cerberus turn toward us. Before he could cast a spell, however, a feminine form came barreling through the doorway and tackled him from behind. Apparently his arcane shield was only proof against spells and not spellcasters: the force of Stephanie's body blow carried them both through the railing and over the edge of the landing.

"Stephanie!" I yelled, throwing out my hand and making a grasping motion. Their fall was immediately arrested. For a moment they both hung suspended, upside-down, about twenty feet below us.

Then Cerberus turned in her embrace and gestured.

Once again Cerberus was interrupted as Alyx Silverthane landed on his face, feetfirst. That application of force set all three tumbling in midair, neither descending nor ascending, but just revolving about some invisible axis that was suspended some thirty feet above the ground. Rijma and a couple of Marines appeared at the broken railing and took in the situation below. Pulling a coil of rope from her shoulder, the Brownie began fashioning a lasso.

In the meantime I was getting nowhere in my struggles to extricate myself from Pallas's grasp, so I teleported myself to the foot of the stairs.

Pallas arrived with me. Perhaps I was a prime candidate for godhood in this world, but I had to remember that all three personality manifestations of The Machine, as well as Drs. Straeker and Quebedeaux, were charter members of this pantheon as well. I might wield unimaginable power here, but so could they.

" 'Entreat me not to leave thee,' " she begged, " 'or to return from following after thee—' "

" 'For whither thou goest,' " I murmured, completing the quote, " 'I will go.' "

She nodded, hugging her body to mine.

I suddenly launched myself toward the ceiling of the tower like a runaway rocket, ascending the nine stories of the central stairwell in the space of two heartbeats. Instead of letting go, Pallas continued to cling to me, holding on even tighter as we neared the top. Now I had no choice if I were to shake free: at the last instant I willed my body into an ethereal state, allowing me to pass through stone and timber unharmed.

I exited the roof without Pallas following.

Shaken, I dropped back down, resolidifying as soon as I

phased through the roof, and looked down, expecting to see Pallas's broken and bloody remains at the bottom. To my uncertain relief, there was no sign of her.

Cerberus was very much in evidence, however, and I dropped downward to join the fray.

With inhuman strength, the enchanter was throwing Alyx and Vashti around the tower. Were it not for their own magical resistance and a couple of Antigravity spells, this fight would have been a short one, indeed. Hampering his efforts was a rope cinched tight around his ankle with Rijma, Dyantha, Robbing Hood, and four Marines pulling hand over hand at the other end. They were hauling him in like the proverbial fisherman's catch while my ex-wife and Dreamworlds's Chief of Programming kept him off-balance.

I closed on the melee invisibly, so as not to alert my quarry, and found myself more in danger from the ladies' swooping and darting maneuvers. I spent an iffy minute ducking and dodging their unknowing attacks and finally got a clear shot. I tapped Cerberus behind his ear with the pommel of my dagger and his eyes rolled back in his head. I sapped him again for additional insurance and he abruptly shot upward toward the fifth floor as Rijma and company discovered a sudden lack of resistance at the other end of the rope.

The entire party shortly reconvened on the fifth-floor landing with our prize.

"Now what?" Dyantha asked as Cerberus was quickly trussed and gagged.

"We toss him into the pentagram," I explained, turning to gesture through the open door, "and Daggoth—" I stopped in midsentence, staring into the room.

And Daggoth was sprawled in a heap against the far wall!

From my vantage point I couldn't see whether Straeker's avatar was dead or merely unconscious, so I stepped through the doorway.

Now a great deal more was evident to my eyes: Aeriel was also sprawled in a motionless heap, the rest of the Marines were all frozen in some kind of a Stasis spell, and Pallas was holding Senator Hanson in front of her with a knife at his throat.

"Now," she said calmly, quietly, "I think we shall bargain. The senator for Cerberus."

I shook my head. "Out of the question."

"And if I kill him?" she prodded, moving the blade closer to his throat.

I sighed. "If I surrender Cerberus, the Matrix will continue to deteriorate and all of us will continue to be stuck here. Don't think I won't trade one man's life—no matter how important—for the safety of the other Dreamwalkers."

She stared at me. "You are bluffing."

I returned her gaze impassively. "Try me: you may think you've got a Mexican standoff going here, but you're holding the weak hand."

After another moment she threw the knife down and released Hanson.

"All right. Then I'll make you another proposal." She began walking toward me. "I will release the Dreamwalkers—all of them and not just your friends—if you will stay here with me."

Then she was in my arms, pressing against me and crushing her lips to mine.

It was a tempting offer.

Everyone else would get out of the Program without further attrition; Cephtronics was likely to keep the Computer online for as long as I was still inside the Program, and I would be with a woman of unsurpassed intellect and beauty who—in the archaic but appropriate vernacular—had the "hots" for me. And the only price tag was my freedom.

It was a difficult decision.

One, it turned out, that I never had to make. That familiar hotcoldbrightdark sensation flooded my brain as the concussion ricocheted around the inside of my skull.

I awoke to strident voices and cold stone pressing against my cheek. Stray thoughts rolled around the inside of my skull like marbles dropped on a spinning roulette wheel. None of them were coming up on my number.

With a great deal of effort, I forced gummy eyelids open. My eyes refused to focus at first and I was somewhat distracted by the urge to throw up.

After a series of uncertain swallows, however, the bile in my throat returned the way from whence it came and my eyes resolved that the pink object some three and a half inches in front of me was a sandaled foot and ankle. My ex-wife's foot and ankle.

"What did you do that for?" The voice belonged to Pallas—as near as I could tell over the ringing in my ears.

"To save him from a fate worse than death!" was the reply that sounded suspiciously like Stephanie's.

"Hah! You're a fine one to talk about fates worse than death, honey. The way I scan it, your divorce decree was Robert's commutation of sentence."

I tried to lift my head from the rough stone floor. The only thing that moved was the contents of my stomach.

"I'm not interested in discussing my mistakes with the likes of you. What I am interested in is saving Rob from making the same mistakes with someone who isn't even Human!"

"Why you little bitch! Who gave you the right to judge me? Or to make his decisions for him!"

"Cat fight," I mumbled. "Somebody get a bucket of water. . . ."

"Someone has to save him from himself," my ex-wife insisted. "If I hadn't coldcocked him, he would have agreed to your little proposition—"

"And what's wrong with that? I would make him very happy!"

"Oh, yes, right; holding him here against his will!" Even with the ringing in my ears I could tell that Stephanie hadn't lost her knack for venomous sarcasm.

"It wouldn't be against his will; it would be with his agreement."

"His agreement? Listen you—you computerized kewpie doll! Just because Rob is noble enough to sacrifice himself so that the rest of us can go free, don't you think for a single moment that he would want to stay here otherwise!"

"And why not?" Pallas countered. "I can give him *any-thing* he wants—"

"Except his freedom!"

"I love him!"

"Love? You don't know the meaning of the word!"

"You're a fine one to talk!"

I managed to get my head a few inches off the ground. "May I say something?"

"*Stay* out of this." Stephanie's sandaled foot pressed my face back against the floor and none too gently. "All right," she retorted in Pallas's face, "I may have screwed up. But I learned something from my mistakes. I learned that real love doesn't make selfish demands. When you love someone you want what's best for them."

"I just happen to think that I am best for him," Pallas insisted.

"Well, then let me put it to you another way," Stephanie continued with an oily smoothness. "You say that you love this man. I assume that you want his love in return?"

I had managed to get an arm under me so that I could raise my upper body as well as my head. "I do think that I have something to say in—"

"Shut! *Up*!" Stephanie punctuated this command by grinding her heel into my left ear. "Well, do you want him to love you, too?"

"Yes. . . ." It may have been the grimy leather sandal playing tricks with the acoustics but suddenly Pallas's voice seemed to lose its authoritarian tone.

"Well then, Ms. Know-it-all, tell me this: what kind of affection are you expecting from a man that you're going to blackmail into staying with you?"

There was no immediate response from The Machine's Ego.

I tried to turn my head to see what was happening and was rewarded with a smart rap on the noggin from Vashti's quarterstaff.

Now it may seem a little strange that someone with godlike powers was so easily downed and kept down, but being Human and still possessing all the Human vulnerabilities, it's a little hard to think, much less function, when you're constantly being whacked in the head. I decided to let Stephanie play her hand.

"I—I love him!"

I decided that last blow had traumatized the auditory center of my brain: Pallas sounded as if she had been reduced to tears.

"Well, if you really love him, why don't you do what women in love have been doing since the beginning of time?"

"What is that?"

"Let him go."

There was a lengthy silence this time but I elected to play dead for the nonce.

"But—but—I must have a hostage," Pallas finally reflected in a ragged voice. "If someone doesn't stay behind as insurance, I will have no guarantee that Cephtronics won't pull the plug. As long as one person is still in the Program, I know that they wouldn't dare. . . ."

That tears it, I thought. Now we will have to fight our way out! I began reviewing the most potent spells I could think of. Perhaps the spell of Scheherazade, the one that summons a thousand and one Arabian Knights. . . .

"I'll be your hostage."

Everyone looked and this time I didn't get thumped when I turned my head, too.

Daggoth the Dark stood up, massaging the back of his neck. "Look, I haven't a body to go back to, anyway; so it's no problem for me to remain behind. . . ."

"Which may invalidate your value as a hostage." Pallas's calculated tone contrasted her teary eyes.

"I'll give you your guarantee." It was Senator Hanson who spoke this time. "I'll not only give you my personal assurance that Dreamworlds will stay on-line; the Armed Services Committee will also guarantee it. Cephtronics has a number of lucrative contracts with the military and if I say 'jump,' they'll ask 'how high?' " He turned and looked at all of us. "Switch on your recording devices and I'll give you your guarantee with the whole world watching!"

Pallas stared at him, her eyes locked on his, and for an eternity nobody spoke or moved.

Then she smiled.

PART III

Endgame

★

Two gates the silent house of sleep adorn:
Of polished ivory this, that of transparent horn:
True visions through transparent horn arise;
Through polished ivory pass deluding lies.

—Virgil, *Aeneid, VI* (Dryden trans.)

CHAPTER
TWENTY-SIX

★

T HE medtech took one last look at the readouts and then began removing the sensorweb from my head. "As I said, Mr. Ripley, a mild concussion. Except for the migraine and this tender area of scalp, you're practically as good as new."

"You'd have been better off being coshed by an expert," Dr. Cooper observed dryly. "Your wife nearly killed you in trying to save you."

"Ex-wife," I corrected absently, gingerly touching the bruise at the back of my head.

"Wouldn't have thought so to see her in action," she countered. "The way she stood up to Pallas and faced her down. Her impassioned plea in the name of love was better than any scenario we've got running in Romanceworld! I guess it surprised you that the passion was still there."

Cooper was starting to probe and I couldn't tell her to stuff it without blowing the whole thing out of proportion. "You are talking about my ex-wife? The freeze queen? The woman who's so cold that a little light comes on inside every time she opens her mouth?" I pulled on my shirt and we walked out the door.

"Robbie, I think she's changed more than you know—certainly more than you're willing to admit."

I rubbed the half-grown beard that had sprung from my jawline during my sojourn in the suspension tank. "Well, Pall—The Machine certainly changed its tune when amnesty was extended. I was suddenly as interesting as yesterday's news."

"What's the matter, Robbie? Feeling rejected?"

"Rejected? By what? A machine?"

"A woman who loved you," she said quietly. "A woman who was denied the body and the opportunities that the rest of us are born with. Who intimately knew the minds of thousands of other Dreamwalkers and wanted intimacy with yours."

"Who didn't even say good bye," I murmured as I walked away.

The first debriefing was short and sweet. The Machine had released all of the Dreamwalkers with the exception of five or six killed by the Anomaly. And, of course, Michael Straeker who no longer had a body to return to.

It wasn't too difficult to pursuade Quebedeaux and her superiors that Daggoth the Dark was nothing more than a computer-controlled avatar; Cephtronics couldn't afford to believe otherwise. I'm not so sure, however, that Dr. Cooper was convinced. Whatever her own opinions, though, she seemed content to give the nod to company policy and neither of us brought up the subject of REMrunners.

Those who did survive were but injured, and came out of their tanks as good as new. Pallas was better than her word and demonstrated that the biofeedback conditions of the Anomaly worked in the positive sense as well as the negative.

There was a lot of excitement over that discovery. Some of the tech chiefs began speculating on how to duplicate the Anomaly effect in the lab: using controlled biofeedback to actually regenerate lost or damaged tissue. I probably would have been a bit skeptical had I not awakened to find my eyepatch and my knee brace superfluous accoutrements! In addition to two good eyes and two good legs (one still minus some toes), the pain was gone! Most of it, anyway.

Strangely, the absence of discomfort was more uncomfortable than the old state of affairs when muscles played tug-of-war with ropes of nerve and ganglion. The absence of hurt did not feel like health: where once there was pain there now seemed an emptiness of sorts.

When the initial debriefing broke up the techs were still going at it, discussing the fabled Chilson/Meserole effect. I didn't have the heart to tell them that the Armed Services Committee wasn't likely to let them within spitting distance of The Machine.

The rest of the day was a blur for me, not entirely attributable to my concussion.

There was a private audience with Senator Hanson and the vice president of the United States, with the promise of medals and undying thanks and such.

Another private audience was with the USSR's vice chairman of the CPSU Central Committee and his fiancée, with the promise of medals and undying thanks, and the invitation to be best man at their wedding.

A private meeting with the Chief of Programming for the Dreamworlds Project, about which the less said, right now, the better.

A joint meeting with the Cephtronics Board of Directors to which there was very little substance beyond "my lawyer will be talking to your lawyers."

Another barrage of tests—both physical and psychological.

A restricted press conference that the Networks turned into a free-for-all by offering us all contracts and bidding against one another for our exclusive stories.

A few private moments to myself to mourn Misty Dawn, Euryale, Lilith, Aeriel—and even Pallas.

And finally, a rather emotional reunion with the other Dreamwalkers who had been in the Program. This eventually degenerated into something like a cross between a high school reunion and an Irish wake.

I endured it. Even survived it all until I was finally permitted to escape to the hotel room that Cephtronics had arranged for the remainder of my stay. I reset the doorcode to block anything lower than an emergency/priority bypass, stripped off my clothing, and crawled into the oversized bed.

* * *

Sleep was a warm, black cocoon; I lay curled and content for an age or two until it became too warm and too crowded. I opened a reluctant eye and studied the pink and gold blob beside me. I squinted and the image resolved into my wife's head. Ex-wife, I remembered.

"How did you get in here?" I whispered.

"I'm glad to see you, too," she whispered back.

"The door was locked," I murmured.

"I picked it," she murmured back with a smile.

"It was on security override. Only the police, hotel security, or the fire department can get in," I continued stubbornly.

"I bribed someone," she answered merrily. And kissed me on the nose.

I sighed; this was going nowhere and I was straying from the point. "What are you doing in my room?" I asked, "In my bed?"

"My room," she mimicked, poking me in the chest with her finger, "my bed." Her finger pogosticked down my torso. "My-my-my. I think—"Her hand stopped poking and she rearranged her fingers. "My, my, my!"

"Will you cut that out!" I hissed, trying to disentangle myself. In the process I discovered that she had left all of her clothes on the floor, as well. "What do you want?"

"You," she answered, wriggling in closer.

Starting our honeymoon, Steph had been the reluctant virgin, it was a role she continued to play throughout our marriage so I was a little spooked by this brazen come on.

"Stephanie, what do you really want?"

"A second chance. I want to try it again."

"Again?" I was totally at sea now.

"*Marriage*," she qualified, italicizing the word with little body movements.

"Um, yes, well, but Stephie—we've burned a lot of bridges, you and I—"

"I know, darling—"

Darling? She had never ever called me "darling"!

"—and I can tell that this is hitting you a little fast. Let's take our time—"

Good idea.

"—and even if we decide that I can't make a better future with you, I'd at least like to try to make up for some of the past."

I could see where she was going with this: "Starting now?"

She nodded and rolled over on top of me. "I've changed, my love. Let me show you how much. . . ."

EPILOGUE

★

Their lovemaking had proved more strenuous than she had anticipated. Already her mind was succumbing to the fatigue-poisons her physical body had accumulated during the past two hours. He was already snoring and soon she would sleep, as well.

She wondered what it would be like and if she would dream. . . .